# HELIUS
# LEGACY

## S. ALEXANDER O'KEEFE

LIVE OAK
BOOK COMPANY

Published by Live Oak Book Company
Austin, TX
www.liveoakbookcompany.com

Distributed by Live Oak Book Company

For ordering information or special discounts for bulk purchases, please contact Live Oak Book Company at PO Box 91869, Austin, TX 78709, 512.891.6100.

Design and composition by Greenleaf Book Group LLC
Cover design by Greenleaf Book Group LLC

Publisher's Cataloging-In-Publication Data
(Prepared by The Donohue Group, Inc.)
O'Keefe, S. Alexander.
  Helius legacy / S. Alexander O'Keefe. — 1st ed.
  p. ; cm.
  ISBN: 978-1-936909-21-6
  1. Land titles—United States—Fiction. 2. Inheritance and succession—United States—Fiction. 3. Billionaires—United States—Fiction. 4. Petroleum industry and trade—United States—Fiction. 5. Conspiracy—Fiction. I. Title.

PS3615.K44 H45 2012
813/.6                                        2011912298

  Print ISBN: 978-1-936909-21-6
  eBook ISBN: 978-1-936909-22-3

First Edition

# ACKNOWLEDGMENTS

To my beloved family and to the many good friends who encouraged and supported this endeavor, I owe a debt of gratitude that can never be paid. To the talented technical experts and editors who advised, guided, and assisted me in so many critical respects, I am honored by, and deeply appreciative of, your invaluable assistance.

# CHAPTER
# ONE

*Austin, Texas*
*December 3, 1999 / Friday / 5:30 p.m.*

The limousine was about five miles outside the city of Austin when the phone in the leather console chimed quietly. Carter T. Mason, chief executive officer and chairman of the board of directors of Helius Energy, looked at the number on the small screen. It was Charlie Gatwick from NewMark Capital, the lead agent on the bond deal. Mason waited for the phone to ring again before he picked it up.

"Mason."

"Hello, Carter, Charlie Gatwick."

"Charlie, I hope you're back in Oyster Bay enjoying the evening."

"I wish. I'm still in Manhattan."

Mason knew Gatwick was in Manhattan, and he also knew why he was calling, but he feigned ignorance.

"We had the final underwriting meeting tonight," Gatwick said.

"Excellent. I hope all is well."

"It is. The deal's a go. Some of the banks wanted to do more diligence on the financials, but we convinced them it wasn't necessary."

1

"Exceptional. This deal is going to be good for both of us."

"I couldn't agree more. Carter, I'm sorry, I have to run or I'll miss the next train."

"Go, enjoy your weekend. You deserve it."

"Thanks. You, too."

A rare smile came to Mason's face as he placed the phone back in the cradle. The leveraged buyout he'd put together five years ago was about to pay off. The proceeds from the bonds would enable Helius to cash out the expensive financing used to buy out the old stockholders. The lower interest rate on the new debt would dramatically improve Helius's bottom line. After three solid quarters of earnings, Mason intended to take the company public again. *I should make seven hundred million after capital gains, and still retain voting control.*

Mason's reverie was interrupted by another call. It was his wife, Michelle. Mason ignored it. He knew why Michelle was calling. She wanted to make sure he remembered the dinner party at their French provincial mansion on the outskirts of Austin. Mason typically refused to attend family gatherings except on holidays. After twenty-four years of marriage, Michelle was used to apologizing for his absence.

The guest of honor was Michelle's father, William Carmody. The old man was dying of cancer, and Mason suspected he was making his final round of good-byes. When Carmody had called Michelle from Dallas last week, he'd asked to see the entire family on this visit. Mason found the demand surprising. Carmody hated him. It had taken the old boy about five years to figure out that Mason had only married his daughter to gain access to Carmody's political connections, and secondarily, to bear the family heir.

Being a political power broker, Carmody might have been able to choke down Mason's ruthless opportunism if he'd kept it to himself, but Mason had done no such thing. Once his son, James Mason, was born, Mason had disabused Michelle of her fairy-tale view of their marriage. Ten years of alcohol and drug addiction had followed. Although Michelle had eventually recovered, after years of expensive help, she was a shell of the vivacious young woman who'd left the Carmody home two decades earlier.

Mason had initially refused to attend the dinner, despite Michelle's tears, but he'd reconsidered. His paranoia about the bond deal had tipped the scales. Carmody couldn't stop the offering, but he might be able to persuade some of his cronies at the Department of Corporations to issue a temporary hold on sales in the state of Texas. The hold would only have a minor effect on the deal, but Mason wasn't willing to take any chances. If listening to the old fool for an hour would eliminate a possible threat to the bond deal, he'd do it.

When the phone on the console chimed a third time, Mason looked over in irritation, but he smiled when he recognized the number.

"Good timing, Mac. I'm about to put another ten million in your pocket. I know you don't—"

"Carter—"

"—need it, but then—"

"Carter, God damn it, listen to me. *We've got a problem.*"

No one spoke to Mason that way—no one except James McNamara. Mac had been the Mason family's lawyer for almost fifty years. He brought to the table an encyclopedic knowledge of corporate law and a level of ruthlessness that the Mason patriarchs, and in particular, Carter Mason, fully exploited.

"What's the problem?"

"Where are you?"

"In the car."

"Anyone with you?"

"No, not now."

"The problem . . . the problem is the deed."

For a moment, Mason was confused; then the dark history of the long-buried conveyance document came back to him—a history that could pull down both Helius and the Mason family if it became public.

Mason forced himself to wait for Mac to continue. He could hear the old man drawing on the worn pipe that rarely left his mouth and then slowly exhaling the smoke into the air. After a quiet cough, Mac continued.

"I just got a call from Jonas over at county records. It seems a certain Richard Steinman, a reporter from the *Statesman*, has been investigating Helius's land records."

Mason exploded. "What! For thirty years we've been paying that—"

Mac's gravelly voice cut off Mason's tirade. "It was a fluke, Carter. This Steinman showed up when Jonas was in the hospital for two days. Some kind of heart problem. A temporary clerk gave him access."

Mason mentally raced through the possibilities.

"Mac . . . the archives . . . they're huge, and we had the deed misfiled eighty years ago. Even if this Steinman knew what he was looking for, he couldn't have found it in two days. It would take weeks."

"No. The files were cleaned up last year. A special audit team went through the place from top to bottom as part of the imaging project. The log shows he pulled the chain of title on BlackJack, and if he went back far enough . . . "

Mason hunched forward in his seat, pressing the phone against his ear until it hurt.

"He wouldn't have gone back more than a century. No one does that today. Do we know—"

"No, we don't know, but we know he had access to the box where the deed's filed, and we . . . we *must* assume the worst," Mac said, his voice hardening into a command.

Mason closed his eyes, trying to shut out the nightmarish sequence that would be ignited if the deed was made public. *How can this be happening?* Then he remembered something his grandfather said when they'd talked about the deed over a decade ago. He didn't say it explicitly, but the message had been clear. *There's no one left to cause a problem. They're all dead.*

"Wait, we don't have a problem, Mac. This . . . it's not an issue anymore."

"I know what you're thinking, boy. And maybe you're right. Maybe there's no one left to make a claim. On the other hand, your great granddaddy just might have missed someone. Either way, it doesn't matter. Not even those Wall Street folks are stupid enough to underwrite a two-billion-dollar bond deal when one of the company's most valuable assets could get yanked off the balance sheet by some Johnny-come-lately looking to collect his billion-dollar inheritance. And we can't tell them, 'Don't worry, folks, Granddad killed all potential takers a long time ago.'"

Mac was right. The numbers behind the bond offering were thin, and the BlackJack field—the field subject to the deed—was a key asset: a safe, domestic oil field with massive proven reserves that generated a huge stream of cash. If the syndicate underwriting the deal suspected the field had a material title problem, the offering would be frozen until the problem was fully investigated and insured. That couldn't happen.

"Mac, this doesn't make any sense. Why would a reporter look at title records going back to 1885?"

"Can't say for sure, but I can make a pretty good guess. Do you remember that sunset law we spent a whole lot of lobbying dollars getting passed about ten years ago?"

"Vaguely."

"Well, let me refresh your memory. Ten years ago, a land-use group that Helius controls persuaded the legislature to pass a law voiding any power of termination incorporated into a deed recorded more than a hundred years ago, if the power wasn't exercised by December 31, 1999. That's about four weeks from today. So the way I figure it, this smart-ass reporter decided to try to find one of these damn things for an article, and hell, why not start with the most valuable piece of dirt owned by the biggest dog in town?"

Mason shook his head. The threat had always seemed so distant, even unreal.

"This can't happen, Mac."

"You're damn right, boy. This is one of those times when you're going to have to go way off the reservation. You and your friend Mr. Paquin are gonna to have to do whatever it takes to bury this thing. Do you hear me, Carter? Whatever it takes."

"I got it."

Mason hung up and dialed Paquin's direct line. A female voice answered.

"Hello, sir, how may I help you?"

"I need Paquin. I need him now."

"Sir, Mr. Paquin is in Cameroon. He's not scheduled to call in for two hours, and we can't reach him by cell phone at his current location."

For a moment, rage seized Mason, and then he remembered the problem he'd sent Paquin to solve, or, more appropriately, eliminate. It was a hundred-million-dollar issue. Mason had never worked with Paquin's second-in-command before, but he couldn't wait for Paquin. Steinman had to be stopped tonight.

"I need to speak with Paquin's number two . . . Severino. Get him, now."

# CHAPTER
# TWO

Austin, Texas
*December 3, 1999 / Friday / 7:30 p.m.*

Richard Steinman didn't notice when the bartender placed a fourth round of beer on the bar. He was staring at the mahogany surface in front of him, underscoring lines of imaginary text with his index finger. Richie had memorized every word, comma, and period. His finger slowed as it passed under the restrictive covenant, and he softly read the words aloud, nodded, and then erased the memory with a napkin.

Richie looked up for a moment and noticed the beer, but his eyes returned to the lacquered surface in front of him. His finger traced the branches of the genealogical tree, which had taken weeks of research to construct, recalling each name from memory. At the top of the tree was Thomas O'Neill, the original grantor in the century-old deed. A series of branches sprang from this source, but each withered away, leaving only one. This branch led to a man named John Caine, Thomas O'Neill's sole surviving descendant.

Mr. Caine was a lucky man. He was about to become one of the richest men in the world, and he was still alive. Every other member of the O'Neill clan had died in a series of "accidents" between 1910 and 1918, with the exception of Caine's grandfather. Richie suspected the deaths weren't accidental. He also suspected that Caine's ancestor had only survived because his birth record didn't appear in the official county records. The genealogist had found the record in the archives of a small church in East Texas. The discovery had led Richie to John Caine, the last O'Neill heir.

Richie wiped the bar with the napkin again, tiring of what had become an obsessive ritual. He looked up and stared at his reflection in the mirror behind the bar. A thirtyish-looking man, with thinning dark hair, an overly round face, and a modest nose looked back at him. The large-framed glasses he was wearing magnified the dark circles under his eyes, and the twenty pounds he'd added to his five-eight frame during the past two months made his gray suit look uncomfortable. Richie closed his eyes and tried to forget the story for a moment, but it was impossible. *I have to get this thing published on Monday.*

The story would draw a nationwide audience. Intrigue, mystery, and death were not an everyday affair at the top of the Fortune 500, and the old deed would give the story an exotic twist, drawing readers from across the spectrum. The story would also pull down Helius Energy and one of the most powerful families in Texas—the Masons. But only if the story was published, and that's where the game would get complicated.

Richie had only been with the *Statesman* for a year. His law degree had earned him a spot writing stories on legal matters, but they were limited to local interest stories. Anything of national significance was transferred to the paper's big-name investigative guns, Crowley or Williams. Richie knew the same thing would happen once the paper realized what Richie had discovered. If he was lucky, his name would be mentioned at the tail end of the first article. After that, he'd receive a small bonus and a ticket back to the trenches. Richie wasn't willing to let that happen.

Richie planned to give Marc Friedman, the assistant editor he reported to, just a taste of what he'd found. Once Friedman was hooked, he'd insist upon a meeting with the *Statesman*'s entire editorial board.

Then it would be a game of chicken. Richie would give the board a choice: agree to publish the story under his name, or he'd e-mail the monster to the *Dallas Morning News*. It was a big play, but he had to take his shot. In the meantime, he'd kept the story to himself.

The steady vibration of the phone in his pocket interrupted Richie's thoughts after the third ring.

"Hello."

"Richie?"

"Yeah. Who's this?"

"Celine . . . from the County Recorder's Office."

It took Richie a moment to put a face to the name—Celine, the clerk in the Travis County Clerk's Office who'd let him look at the title documents a week ago.

"Oh, hi, Celine. What's up?"

"Mr. Jonas called me down to his office today."

Richie remembered Jonas—the clerk in charge of the archives. When Richie had asked for access to the original deeds, the old putz had shoved a bunch of forms at him, without even looking up from his computer. When Richie returned the next day with the completed documents, Celine was sitting at Jonas's desk. The gregarious twenty-something had been sent over from another department to fill in for Jonas for the day. Richie had taken full advantage of Celine's good nature and ignorance. The combination of his press card and a few white lies had been enough to get him access to the original files on the BlackJack field.

"Oh. So . . . how's my friend Jonas doing?"

"Not good. He had the access log from the day you came into the office. He wanted to know exactly what boxes you looked at and why."

"Uhh . . . okay, so what—"

"Richie, when I came back and gave him the list of boxes, he . . . well, I thought the old guy was havin' a heart attack. His face turned all white and his hands started shaking. When I asked him if he was okay, he tried to cover it up and then kind of pushed me out the door. Do you know what's going on? I thought you said this was routine stuff for the paper?"

"Yeah...that's right. Look, don't worry about it, Celine. I'm sure it's just a missing form. That guy's big on—"

"I sure hope so. I don't want to get in trouble over this."

"You won't. Did . . . did Jonas say anything else?"

"No . . . but I felt so bad I waited outside his office for a minute, hoping I could tell him that I was sorry for whatever was wrong. But I left when I heard him on the phone. Man, was he upset."

"Upset? Did you hear him say anything?"

"No, not really. Well, I remember one thing, because he said it twice, and he said it kinda loud."

"What's that?"

"He said, 'I know there's only four damn weeks left.'"

"He said that? Are you sure?"

"Real sure. He said it twice."

Richie's throat tightened, and he had to force out the words. "Thanks . . . thanks, Celine."

Richie flipped the phone closed before Celine answered, shoved it back in his pocket, and reflexively pushed his heavy-rimmed glasses back to the bridge of his nose. When he put his hand back on the bar, it was trembling. *The right of termination expired at year end—in four weeks. Jonas must have known about the covenant. Whoever was on the phone . . . it . . . they had to be with Helius. They knew what he had.*

"Sir, would you like another beer?"

Richie looked over at the tall blond woman behind the bar, momentarily forgetting where he was.

"Beer?"

"Yes. That would be your fifth," the bartender answered, as she turned to another customer.

"No . . . no," Richie said, as he stood up from the barstool and pulled on his overcoat. He glanced up at the clock on the far wall as he crossed the room, slowed, and then reached for his phone. *I gotta get to Caine . . . he . . . .* Richie took another step and then stopped again. *I need a backup on this . . . Andrea. Shit! I should have sent her that package yesterday.* The mariachi band in the restaurant part of the bar began to play as he dialed the first number.

# CHAPTER
# THREE

*Hesperia, California*
*December 3, 1999 / Friday / 5:30 p.m. Pacific time*

John Caine's arm rose and fell to a steady rhythm, pounding the blackened hammer into the glowing length of metal resting on the anvil. A persistent sound outside the converted barn interrupted Caine's concentration, and he stepped back from the forge. It was Sam, his golden retriever. Caine glanced at the clock on the other side of the room. It was an hour past the dog's mealtime.

"I'm coming, Sam," Caine yelled, a smile in his voice, quieting the irate retriever.

Caine looked down at the Norman broadsword he was forging for a doctor in Philadelphia. The customer, like most of Caine's clientele, was willing to pay a premium for authenticity. That was Caine's specialty. The materials and methods that he used to forge his weapons were the same as those used by the original blacksmiths a thousand years earlier, right down to the laborious process of shaping the metal.

Caine removed the protective glasses from his face, revealing striking gray eyes and a nose that remained straight despite the fact that it had been broken twice. A bead of sweat dripped from his light-brown hair and flowed past a graying sideburn and then over a small white scar on the right side of his strong jaw. A second scar, above Caine's left eye, gave his handsome face a lived-in look.

After closing the hood over the forge and resting the hammer on a nearby ledge, Caine walked across the room to an old wooden table and picked up a copper pitcher. He took a long drink of water and then pressed the pitcher against his forehead, closing his eyes. Caine was no stranger to intense heat. He'd served with the French Foreign Legion for more than a decade, and a good part of that time had been in Africa. Despite the experience, the forge room had seemed like an inferno during the past week.

Temperatures in Hesperia, California, were typically in the low fifties to the mid sixties during December, but the nearby Mojave Desert had flexed its muscles in the past week, driving the temperature into the high eighties. The unseasonable heat wave, a broken air conditioner, and the intense fire required to forge the heavy sword had tested Caine's endurance. He was looking forward to a couple of days of rest and ice-cool air at his cabin in the nearby San Bernardino Mountains.

After finishing the water, Caine walked to a large sink against the wall and pulled the heavy fireproof shirt over his head, revealing powerful shoulders and arms, and a set of visible abdominal muscles. Caine splashed water on his face and chest and wiped himself down with a coarse towel. When the towel brushed a dark furrow in the upper part of his right arm, he unconsciously reduced the pressure, remembering the searing pain from the AK-47 round as if it were yesterday. He'd been running at a full sprint when he was tagged. The pain and shock from the wound had caused him to stumble, but he'd quickly recovered and continued running at the same brutal pace. The people chasing him that day weren't in the business of taking prisoners.

For a moment, Caine stared in the mirror, reliving the memory, and then he heard Sam barking again.

"I'm coming!"

Caine noticed the red message light on the phone near the door as he walked out of the forge room, but he ignored it. He would pick up his messages later.

# CHAPTER
# FOUR

*Austin, Texas*
*December 3, 1999 / Friday / 7:30 p.m.*

Andrea Marenna hung up the phone and looked at her watch in frustration. The conference call had lasted an hour and a half, and this was the fifth multi-hour session with opposing counsel. At this rate, it would take a month to document the settlement.

Andrea scanned the desk for her time sheet, which she knew was buried somewhere under the stacks of paper arranged in rows on her desk. She started to move a partially complete trial brief and two stacks of evidence to one side, and then reconsidered. If she lost her place, it would take time to find it again. She wrote the time entry down on a sticky-note and stuck it on the side of her computer, alongside five others.

Andrea started to reach for her overflowing inbox when Julie Trent, her assistant, opened the door and walked in.

"Your exalted senior partner is on the phone. He wants to talk with you about a new client—now. Also, you had five calls while you were on the phone. I e-mailed you the list."

Andrea looked over at the petite blond who'd been her assistant and friend for the last five years.

"Thanks, but not really. Anything urgent?"

"One. Richard Steinman said he has to talk to you today, but wouldn't explain. I think he was calling from a bar."

Andrea closed her eyes for a moment. *God, I need some rest.*

"Are you okay?" Trent asked, concern in her voice.

"Nothing that a week of sleep wouldn't cure, but that's not going to happen. Please put Kelly through."

Trent put another stack of paper in Andrea's inbox and placed a birthday card on top of the stack. The card had a big "34" on the front.

"Happy thirty-fourth," Julie whispered with a mischievous smile as she turned for the door.

Andrea smiled. "Thank you so very much for reminding me."

"Relax, you look great."

"Thanks, but I suspect I look like a zombie. I know I feel like one."

"No comment. By the way, do you still need me?"

"No, and thanks so much for staying late."

"No problem. See you Monday, and get some sleep."

"Thanks, I'll try."

# CHAPTER
# FIVE

*Austin, Texas*
*December 3, 1999 / Friday / 7:30 p.m.*

The two men sitting in the dark gray Cadillac STS outside Selena's Restaurant & Bar were a study in contrast. The driver, Simon Vargas, was a dark-skinned Latino, about five-eight, with the powerful physique of a dedicated body builder. His face and head were clean-shaven, and he wore a small ring of gold in his right ear. The man in the passenger seat, Julian Anders, was a six-and-a-half-foot-tall Nordic giant, who carried two hundred and fifty lean pounds on his rangy frame. Anders's unkempt mane of reddish hair was tied back in a crude ponytail, and he had a day's growth of beard on his face. Both men, however, shared a common characteristic. They were hired killers.

"Okay, cowboy, listen up. His car is that green piece of shit over there. When he comes out of the restaurant, you work your way over to him. I want you to cross his path just before he reaches his car, right there," Vargas said, pointing to the shadowed area Steinman would pass through on the way to his car.

"When you get close enough, *quietly* persuade him to get in the back seat when I pull up—no blood, no shooting, no bullshit. You got that?"

Vargas spoke in a monotone, never taking his eyes off the front door of the restaurant.

Anders didn't look up from the sports page he was reading when he answered. "Don't sweat it. I'll be right friendly to Mr. Steinman."

Vargas glanced over at Anders. He was all too aware of the big man's reputation. Anders had started with Helius as a roustabout working high-risk well sites in the Gulf of Mexico. When one of his periodic barroom rampages had put him in a Mexican jail, Paquin had posted bail and offered him a job as part of Helius's private security force. Vargas, who was number three in Paquin's internal hierarchy, believed this was a mistake, but Paquin hadn't asked for his opinion.

When Tony Severino had pulled Anders into the operation, Vargas had told him that Anders was the wrong guy for this kind of job. Severino had told him they had no choice. For some reason, this Steinman guy was a high-priority target, and Anders was the only other asset available.

Vargas sat up straighter in his seat when a man fitting Steinman's description walked out of the Mexican restaurant. He glanced down at the picture taped to the dash. It was the target. Vargas turned to Anders, but he was already looking at Steinman.

"I got him," Anders said.

Anders dropped the newspaper on the floor and eased out of the car, pulling a dark blue pea coat with him. Vargas waited until Anders was about fifty yards away from the target before he started circling around the lot to the location of the snatch. He paced his speed to coordinate with Anders's progress.

Vargas scanned the lot and the nearby street for potential problems. He'd worked for a special army unit in Columbia when he was in his early twenties. On three occasions, they'd snatched drug kingpins off the street in Caracas. Public reaction to a snatch hadn't been an issue there. Witnesses got out of the way and kept their mouths shut. The reaction in Austin, Texas, would be different. This op had to be quick and quiet. Vargas had made that clear to Anders, but Anders liked playing outside the lines.

As he drove past the front of the restaurant, Vargas could see a problem in his rearview mirror. A man and woman in their early thirties walked out of the restaurant and began to follow Steinman down the walkway across the lot. Steinman was about twenty yards ahead of them, but he'd stopped to search for something in his pocket. The couple was now too close for the snatch to work.

*Let it go, Anders. We'll grab him up someplace else.* Vargas's grip on the wheel tightened, as he watched Anders continue to walk toward Steinman. If Anders grabbed the reporter now, they'd have to take out the couple behind him. Anders might not have a problem with that, but Vargas did. Severino's instructions were explicit: the snatch was to be quick and quiet.

Vargas lowered the window and held out his arm with a closed fist, signaling an abort. Anders had a clear view of Vargas across the lot, but continued walking toward Steinman. *Stop, you asshole!* In frustration, Vargas punched the gas, drawing a squeal from the tires, and held his arm up again. Steinman turned quickly and looked over at the Cadillac. Vargas tried to pull his arm back down before Steinman saw him, but he wasn't quick enough. *Shit!*

Vargas looked straight ahead and continued to drive down the lane. When he looked across the lot again, Steinman was walking rapidly toward his car. Anders had changed his direction. His new angle would take him behind Steinman and the couple. Vargas could see the smile on Anders's face.

"Screw you, too, redneck," Vargas said aloud, as he watched Anders change direction.

*Austin, Texas*
*December 3, 1999 / Friday / 7:35 p.m.*

Richie walked from the entrance of the bar to the pedestrian walkway that divided the parking lot. His car was parked on the far side of the lot. When he was about thirty yards from the restaurant, he reached into his pants pocket to find his car keys, but they weren't there.

After checking the other pocket and his overcoat, Richie stopped and reached inside his suit jacket and found the keys.

When Richie looked up, he noticed a man walking in his direction from the left side of the lot. The man was wearing a dark blue coat and jeans. His hair was tied back in a ponytail. Richie looked directly at the man for a moment, but the man didn't look in his direction. It was almost as if he were avoiding eye contact.

A sharp squeal on his right drew Richie's attention. A dark Cadillac was driving slowly down the lane that ran along the outside of the parking lot. The car was parallel to him. The bald Latino man driving the car was just pulling his arm inside the driver's side window. The man turned away when Richie looked at him.

Richie watched the Cadillac ease its way down the lane between the cars for a moment. Then he turned and looked over at the man in the dark coat and jeans again. The man had slowed his pace and changed direction. He would pass somewhere behind Richie instead of in front of him. Richie heard a woman laugh behind him and he looked over his shoulder. A man and a woman were walking about fifteen yards behind him. Richie looked over at the red-haired man again. There was a slight smile on his face.

Richie started walking toward his car again. His pace increased. *This is insane. There's no way Helius would come after me.* When he reached the twelve-year-old Buick, Richie unlocked the door, slid behind the wheel, and pressed the lock button. Richie looked in the mirror for the Cadillac as he backed out of the space, but the view in that direction was blocked by a minivan pulling out of its space.

When he reached the end of the lot, Richie looked in the mirror again. The minivan was pulling away in the opposite direction. Its headlights played over a car facing in his direction. It was the Cadillac. The bald Latino man was behind the wheel. The man in the dark coat with the ponytail was just climbing into the front seat. Both men were looking at the Buick. Richie's unease turned to fear.

Richie forced himself to ease the Buick into the flow of traffic when he pulled onto the city street. His eyes alternated between the rearview mirror and the traffic in front of him. The glare from the headlights behind him made it difficult to see if the Cadillac was following him. Two intersections later, Richie spotted the Cadillac. It was three cars back.

Richie accelerated and began to pass the cars around him. He stared in the rearview mirror, trying to pick up the Cadillac again. When his eyes returned to the front, he was less than three feet from the bumper of the car ahead. Richie jammed on the brakes. The car behind him, a Toyota, slammed on its brakes to avoid a collision, and then raced past Richie on the left. When the car passed him, Richie had a clear view of the Cadillac. The two men in the car were looking directly at him. There was no question. They were following him, and now they knew that he was aware of it.

*I need to find a cop . . . Shit, I can't. I'm at least two drinks over the limit.* Richie leaned back in the seat in frustration, and glanced in the mirror. The Cadillac was right behind him. The two men were no longer making any effort to be inconspicuous. *I'm safe as long as I stay on the main streets. I'll head back to the* Statesman. Richie picked up the phone to call his office, but then he hesitated, and dialed information.

"Austin, Texas. I need Kelly & White. It's a law firm."

The information operator found the number and connected him.

"Kelly & White."

"Hello."

Richie looked in the mirror at the Cadillac. Then he looked ahead at the meandering traffic in front of him.

"May I help you, sir?"

The impatience in the receptionist's voice drew Richie's attention back to the phone.

"Andrea Marenna."

"I'm sorry, sir, but the office is closed for the day. Would you like voice mail?"

*That's right. It's after seven on Friday night.*

"Shit!"

"Excuse me, sir?"

"I'm sorry, voice mail."

Richie glanced in the mirror. The Cadillac was still behind the Buick. Richie looked ahead and saw a side street on the other side of the road. He punched the gas and yanked the wheel hard to the left, hoping to lose the Cadillac. The Buick raced through a narrow gap in the oncoming traffic flow, drawing a cacophony of angry horns.

The old car came into the turn with too much speed and skidded across to the far right side of the street. Richie had to pull the wheel back to the left with both hands to avoid sideswiping a parked car. The cell phone in his right hand was jammed against the steering wheel. As he struggled to get control, Richie heard Andrea's recorded voice direct him to leave a message after the beep. A moment later, he heard the tone.

"Andrea, it's Richie. I need help . . . with a story. I know this isn't fair, but I'm really in a bad spot."

Richie floored the accelerator once he regained control, and the Buick roared down the narrow street.

"I need you to call a guy. His name is John Caine. He lives . . . he lives in Hesperia, California. Look, I know this sounds crazy, but I think this guy owns—"

A dispassionate voice cut him off. "Your message has been received. If you would like to send this message as recorded, press one. If you would like to add to this message, press two. If you would like to cancel—"

Richie looked down at the phone, struggled to find the number in the dark for a moment, and then he pushed the number two. When he looked up again, a pickup truck was pulling out of a gas station in front of him. There was no time to hit the brakes. Richie threw the wheel to the left, putting the Buick into the oncoming traffic lane. The move caused him to drop the cell phone. It bounced on the seat and then dropped to the floor in front of the passenger seat.

Richie looked up again. A yellow panel truck was about forty yards away from him, coming in the opposite direction. He floored the accelerator to get past the pickup truck on his right, and then pulled the wheel hard to the right. The Buick missed the front bumper of the pickup truck with only inches to spare. When he looked in the rearview mirror, Richie could see the Cadillac behind the pickup truck.

Realizing that he only had seconds left on Andrea's voice mail system, Richie began to yell over the roar of the engine.

"Andrea . . . shit . . . Please call this guy. Helius may want to kill him to prevent him from getting his . . . shit! Don't pull out, you frigging idiot! Andrea, he may be the last one. I don't know the guy, but I need him to call me. I'm going to try to send you a package . . . Amelia Teatro. She has the—"

As he raced through the next intersection, ignoring the yield sign, Richie heard the recorded message on the cell phone cut off his message.

"Thank you," the voice said, and the call ended.

# CHAPTER
# SIX

*Austin, Texas*
*December 3, 1999 / Friday / 8:05 p.m.*

"Okay, Mex, he made us. What's your next move?" Anders drawled, a smile on his face. Vargas's face tightened, but he ignored the intended insult. He had bigger problems. The reporter had picked up on the setup too quickly. Now the asshole was trying to outrun them in that piece of junk. Vargas's instructions were to grab Steinman, work him for information, and then kill him. But Severino had made it clear: if they couldn't make the grab, take him out.

"Okay, cowboy, in another mile we'll be in the warehouse district. It should be almost empty now. I'll pull up behind him and you take out one of the rear tires. Just the tire, Anders. That's all."

Vargas glanced over at the Glock 23 pistol sitting in Anders's lap. The six-inch suppressor attached to the barrel would make the shots undetectable over the engine noise. One of two things would happen: they'd grab Steinman out of the wreck, or Steinman would be dead and it would look like an accident. Either way worked for Vargas.

"When the car stops, I'll pull in front of the Buick. If Stein-man's alive, throw him in the trunk. I'll go through the car—sixty seconds from start to finish. Got it?" Vargas said, glancing over at Anders.

Anders just smiled as he slid a magazine into the Glock, chambered a round, and flipped off the safety.

When Vargas looked back at the road, the Buick was taking a hard right down a narrow alley between two warehouses.

"Shit! What the fuck is he doing now?" Vargas growled.

*Austin, Texas*
*December 3, 1999/ Friday / 8:06 p.m.*

The left side of the car began to lift off the ground as the Buick sloughed through the turn into the alley. For a terrifying moment, Richie thought the car was going to roll, but then it stabilized and he jammed the accelerator to the floor. The Buick raced down the dark alley between the two industrial buildings, bouncing up and down on the uneven road.

Richie reached over and grabbed the FedEx envelope sitting on the passenger seat, which he'd addressed to Andrea yesterday, quickly glanced ahead, and then pulled a stack of documents out from under his seat. He tried to stuff the documents into the floppy envelope, but the opening closed each time he pushed them together. In frustration, Richie jammed one of his knees against the lower part of the steering wheel to hold it in place, grabbed the documents in one hand and the envelope in the other, and shoved them together. As the documents slid into the envelope, the car drifted against the concrete wall of a warehouse that bordered the alley on the right, throwing a stream of sparks over the hood of the car. Richie dropped the package and pulled the wheel hard to the left, and then pulled it back to the right again to avoid slamming into a loading dock on the other side of the alley. After guiding the car back into the center of the alley and locking the steering wheel in place with his knees again, Richie grabbed the envelope, closed the flap, and dropped the package on the passenger seat.

At the end of the alley, Richie slowed and took a hard left onto a darkened street and then jammed the accelerator to the floor. Seconds later, he heard the screech of tires and the roar of another engine to his rear. He guessed that he had a sixty-yard lead on the Cadillac, but that wouldn't last. The other car was faster and more maneuverable than the old Buick.

Richie looked up and down the street, praying for a FedEx drop, but it wasn't there. He looked through a gap between two warehouses on the right side of the street and saw a bright yellow DHL truck parked one street over. DHL was a FedEx competitor, but if the driver found the package, there was a good chance he'd drop it in a FedEx box. It might take an extra day to get to Andrea, but he had to take the risk.

Richie saw an alley ahead. He prayed that it went all the way through to the next street and pulled the wheel hard to the right. The front of the Buick made the turn, but the rear end fishtailed into the building on his left. The impact smashed Richie's head against the driver's side window. Pain exploded in his head, blinding him for a second. Rage came with the pain, and he jammed the accelerator to the floor.

The alley between the two streets went all the way through to the next street. The Buick barreled out of the alley and slid sideways across the wide street to the curb on the far side like a giant ship. Richie could feel the blood dripping down the side of his face, but he focused on the open rear bay of the DHL truck ahead of him. He lowered the driver's window, which was now cracked and stained with blood, and threw the package into the open bay as he passed the truck.

Richie looked in the mirror as he raced by the truck. The Cadillac was just racing out of the alley. *They didn't see the package!* Richie floored the gas pedal and held it there. Within seconds, the car was doing ninety miles an hour down the empty street. For a minute, the Buick started to pull away from the Cadillac, but the other driver compensated, and the Cadillac began to close the gap. *I need to find a busy street.* Richie glanced repeatedly to the right and left, hoping to see lights indicating a more populated area. As he passed a low-rise building on his left, he saw what looked to be a small shopping center several blocks over.

A fraction of a second before the Buick started into a left turn, two nine-millimeter shells ripped into the right rear tire. A third shell missed the tire, ricocheted off the street and ripped a hole in the Buick's gas tank. As the car slid into the turn, the punctured tire collapsed, putting the Buick into an unstoppable roll. The car flipped over and slid across the street on the roof. The driver's side door slammed into the fire hydrant on the far side of the street, killing Richard Steinman instantly.

*Austin, Texas*
*December 3, 1999 / Friday / 8:08 p.m.*

Vargas jumped out of the car the instant the Cadillac skidded to a stop, and raced over to the overturned car. He tried to get a clear look at the driver through the shattered windshield, but the checkered glass made it impossible. He walked around to the driver's side and looked through a hole in the window at the broken body of Richard Stein-man. Blood was all over the place. The reporter had to be dead.

"He's dead," Vargas said, without emotion.

"No shit. Check the car and let's move," Anders drawled from behind him, a grin on his face.

As he ran around the rear of the car to get to the passenger side, Vargas caught the smell of gas. He glanced downward. The area under the rear bumper was covered with a spreading black stain.

Vargas slowly eased open the upside down door on the passenger side of the car, praying that it wouldn't generate a spark. The reporter was hanging upside down, held in place by the seat belt. The side of his head was a bloody mass.

Vargas leaned into the car and checked the reporter's pockets, ignoring the blood spotting the arm of his sport coat. His search yielded a worn brown wallet, a black comb, and a few pieces of paper. As he started to back out of the car, Vargas noticed the outline of a flat square object in Steinman's shirt pocket. He reached in the pocket and pulled out a black computer diskette.

Vargas scanned the rest of the car again and spotted a cell phone and a piece of paper resting on the roof of the upside-down car. He grabbed the phone and the paper and shoved them in his pocket. Then he heard a quiet "whoosh" outside and threw himself out the door. The rear of the car was in flames.

Vargas wanted to check the trunk, but was dissuaded by the flames licking out from under the car. A pall of black smoke was beginning to form over the burning wreck. He glanced up and down the street. It was still empty, but that would change in minutes. They had to get out of there. He threw his sport coat in the back seat of the Cadillac and slid into the driver's seat. Anders looked over at him, a grin on his face.

"Not a bad day's work, Mex."

# CHAPTER
# SEVEN

San Bernardino County, California
December 3, 1999 / Friday / 7:30 p.m.

Caine pulled the Jeep Cherokee into the covered space beside the cabin and looked out on the mountain landscape. The cabin was located about six miles outside the resort town of Snow Valley, California, on five acres of land. A snow-covered alpine forest surrounded the cabin on four sides, with only the incoming dirt road breaking the virgin landscape.

Caine's nearest neighbor was about three miles to the south, on the road back to town. Although the surrounding area would eventually be developed, it would take at least another five years. The utility infrastructure would have to be extended before new homes could be built. The lack of utilities wasn't a problem for Caine. The former owner of the cabin had installed two independent power systems. A large solar panel covered the roof, and a propane generator, which easily could have supplied power to another two homes, was housed in a concrete block-house located next to the cabin.

The cabin itself was about two thousand square feet. The first floor had a dining room, a master bedroom, and a central living room with a fireplace. The second floor had two large bunk rooms.

The house was built on a slope. The architect who'd designed the structure had enclosed a part of the rear slope, creating an above-ground basement. The rear door to the basement had been designed to allow the former owner to drive his Arctic Cat directly into the sloped back-yard. The door rolled up from the floor to the ceiling overhead.

Caine had never owned a snowmobile until he'd bought the cabin, but since the Arctic Cat had come with the house, he'd kept it. Although he preferred cross-country skiing, Caine took the big machine for a spin around the adjacent valley several times a season.

After putting away his supplies, Caine changed into cross-country ski gear and opened the door to the backyard in the basement. A concrete ramp ran from the door to the backyard. The ramp was covered with snow, allowing Caine to glide into the backyard and then make his way toward the valley beyond. The door behind him was on a timer. It would close after a sixty-second delay.

As Caine skied across the yard, Sam, his golden retriever, raced past him, running easily in the four inches of powder. Caine started out slow and then settled into a fluid rhythm that was fast, but sustainable. As he glided through the giant firs, his mind wandered to another alpine forest seven thousand miles away.

In December of 1987, an Ariane rocket launched by the European Space Agency had crash landed in the Dinaric Alps region of Yugoslavia. The transport rocket had been carrying a NATO spy satellite—an American-designed wonder that incorporated the most sophisticated surveillance technology in the world.

In 1987, Yugoslavia was a communist country. Although it was officially "nonaligned," this status only meant the country didn't move in complete lock-step with Moscow, like East Germany and the other members of the Warsaw Pact. None of the NATO leaders working on the crisis had any illusions about what would happen if a diplomatic contest developed between NATO and the Soviets over the possession of the downed satellite: the technology would end up in the hands of the Kremlin, erasing a ten-year technological lead.

The Pentagon had proposed a surgical air strike on the crash site, but this option was vociferously opposed by NATO's European members. They argued that an overt military action would severely damage the West's relations with the Soviets and their Warsaw Pact allies. They also pointed out that there was no guarantee an air strike would destroy the satellite's most critical components.

The insertion of a covert team with the capability of destroying the sensitive parts of the satellite was the only other alternative. Since the Soviets would be looking for the downed rocket as well, this option was extremely time-sensitive. Fortunately for NATO, a covert-operations unit within the French Foreign Legion was training in the Italian Alps, across the Adriatic Sea from the crash site. John Caine had been a member of that unit.

Five hours after the Ariane rocket went down, a military cargo jet strayed into Yugoslav airspace. The five paratroopers on the jet made an HAHO jump at thirty-five thousand feet and glided twenty-five miles inland to the location of the crash site. Caine remembered, as if it were yesterday, floating downward through the frigid Yugoslav air to the snow-covered slopes half a world away.

When they arrived at the site, one member of the team, Jacques Maltier, established a radio link with a U.S. Navy frigate. The Perry class ship was racing up the Adriatic in order to get close enough to launch one of its two SH-60 helicopters for the planned extraction.

The leader of the team, Colonel Etienne Ricard, and Sergeant Danny MacBain were tasked with inserting the four explosive devices into the satellite. The fifth member of the team, Joe Vlasky, a squat, muscular Pole, was in charge of cutting the necessary holes for the explosives. Caine was ordered to serve as a lookout on a ridge about a quarter-mile distant from the crash sight.

The explosives employed by the team were designed to generate a high level of heat, but minimal blast. If they were placed in accordance with the diagram provided by the Pentagon, the explosives would melt the most sensitive parts of the satellite. The process of inserting the explosives should have taken less than thirty minutes, but they were forced to burn another hour digging a trench under the rocket in order to place the last explosive. The delay put them outside their window of safety.

While the rest of the unit was working on the downed rocket, Caine scanned the horizon with a pair of binoculars for incoming aircraft. On his last scan over the northwest sector of his search pattern, he'd spotted an approaching aircraft—a Soviet Mi-28 Hind. The giant, well-armed helicopter was used by the Soviet military to provide both quick transport and devastating attack power.

The unit had been warned that the Soviets would rush one of their own Spetsnaz teams to the site, from one of their bases in Eastern Europe, once they identified the location. These highly trained commandos formed the tip of the Soviet military spear.

As Caine watched, a squad of ten men wearing white-and-gray camouflage suits and carrying AK-74U 5.45mm assault rifles, rappelled to the ground about seven hundred feet below Caine's position. The helicopter, undoubtedly at the end of its fuel capacity, headed off the way it had come, as soon as the soldiers were on the ground.

As Caine watched, the Soviets established communications and then started to climb up the slope toward Caine's position. The move was understandable. The knoll was the highest point in the immediate area. The Spetsnaz team would be able to scan the surrounding area for half a mile in every direction from the pinnacle, giving them a clear view of the downed rocket and the Legion unit struggling to destroy it.

When Caine radioed the information to Ricard, he directed Caine to move to the north side of the slope and draw the enemy toward that position with nonlethal fire. The distraction would give the rest of the team the time they needed to complete the demolition. As he skied through the California forest more than a decade later, Caine remembered racing to the second position and laying down harassing fire on the advancing soldiers. The Soviet team had taken the bait.

Thirty minutes later, the Soviets realized their mistake when the explosives inserted into the core of the satellite exploded south of their position. Having been denied their prize by Caine's ruse, the Spetznaz unit was not inclined to let the Legionnaire who'd led them astray escape their grasp. Caine's race to reach the extraction point had been a close-run thing.

The sound of Sam's barking shocked Caine out of the grip of the memory. It took him a moment to realize that he was racing across the snow at a brutal pace. The dog, sensing his agitation, had started barking. Caine slowed to a stop and the dog raced over.

"Take it easy there, buddy. Everything's okay. Nobody's after us tonight."

# CHAPTER
# EIGHT

*Austin, Texas*
*December 3, 1999 / Friday / 9:45 p.m.*

Andrea finished the trial brief and left it on the table beside Julie's desk. The birthday card on the edge of the desk caught her attention when she walked back to her office. She stared at the big red "34" for a moment. *God, where has the time gone?*

When she started at the firm seven years earlier, Andrea had known what she was buying into: years of long hours, stress, and hard work for a shot at partnership and the big paycheck that came with it. Now that she was reaping the proverbial fruits of her labors, she wasn't sure the price was fair, particularly since hard work and stress were still her constant companions.

Andrea turned her chair around and looked through the wall of glass at Austin's cityscape. *So what? I'm thirty-four. I'm not sliding into middle age tomorrow. And what should I be doing right now that I'm not? Sure, Mr. Right hasn't come along, but . . .*

Most men found her attractive. She worked out regularly, and at five-seven, one hundred forty pounds, she weighed only ten pounds more than she weighed in high school. Her social life was limited because she spent twelve to fourteen hours a day in the office, six days a week. That kind of involuntary servitude made it difficult to meet anyone other than her male colleagues, and after the last two disasters, she didn't intend to date another lawyer any time soon.

Andrea looked across at the picture of the big Italian man sitting in the center of her credenza. He was holding a steel lunch bucket and wearing a yellow construction hat. There was a big smile on his face. Andrea had the same big brown eyes and light olive skin as her father, but at this point in her life, she wasn't sure she could manage a smile like that.

Andrea gently lifted the picture frame. *I wish you were around to tell me what I'm doing wrong, Dad. I could use some advice.* A small smile came to her face. She remembered running to meet her dad at the door when she was a little girl. Although he was always tired and covered with dust from the construction site, her dad had never complained about being an ironworker. He'd always seemed happy to go to work in the morning. *Or maybe he just didn't want me to know . . . and maybe I should spend less time analyzing everything.* Andrea put the picture back on the credenza and looked at the pile of paper on her desk. *That's it. I'm done for the day.*

# CHAPTER
# NINE

Helius Energy was named after the ancient Greek god who raced across the sky each morning in a celestial chariot, bringing light to the world. The palatial lobby of the company's world headquarters fully exploited its namesake. The wall facing the main entrance was covered in jet-black marble impregnated with thousands of semiprecious stones, giving it the appearance of the night sky. In the midst of this black expanse, a golden statue of Helius, astride a black chariot drawn by four silver steeds, was bursting through the wall into the lobby. The sculpture was more than twenty feet tall, and the array of lights playing across the Olympian vision gave it a kinetic magnificence.

Mason's office was on the fiftieth floor, which was the executive suite. In contrast to the ostentatious décor below, the executive floor had a more solemn tone. The elevators opened to a broad lobby with twelve-foot ceilings that were lit by two large chandeliers. The walls were a striking black marble, trimmed with rosewood baseboards, moldings, and cornices. The floor was covered with a plush Persian

34

rug. The wall behind the large rosewood desk where the receptionist sat was dominated by a four-by-six-foot portrait of William T. Mason, the founder of Mason Oil, later renamed Helius Energy.

Mason's eight-hundred-foot office occupied the southwestern corner of the executive floor. A massive mahogany desk was centered in the far corner of the office. The glass wall behind the desk offered spectacular views of Austin's skyline. A black granite conference table, with six chairs that matched the style of the desk, was situated in the corner, to the right of the desk. In another corner, a dark leather couch faced a coffee table and two matching leather Queen Anne chairs.

One of the two interior walls was decorated with marble bookshelves that held rare books and works of art from throughout the world. Another interior wall was covered by a map of the world, which identified every known major oil or gas reserve. A series of large red and black pins dotted the display. The black pins identified those areas where Helius already held drilling rights; the red pins identified the areas where Helius was in the process of acquiring rights.

Mason was sitting at his desk looking over the documents that Severino's team had recovered from the computer disk found on the reporter's body. One document was a rough outline of a newspaper article. The second was a PDF copy of a deed dated May 1, 1885. The third was a set of notes detailing the backup data supporting the facts in the draft of the article. Mason had read and reread every line, comment, and footnote in the reporter's documents. The point-by-point indictment against Helius and the Mason family was devastating.

Mason's father, William, had died of a heart attack when Mason was in college. Richard Mason, his grandfather and the chairman of Helius's board of directors, had brought him into the company and groomed him for the position of chief executive officer. His grandfather had told him about the "deed problem" the day he'd been appointed chief operating officer of Helius, fifteen years earlier.

Although Mason had listened to his grandfather's description of the "problem," the threat had seemed unreal, ridiculous even. Mac had brought the magnitude of the threat home to him a week later, after he'd scoffed at the "Old Man's" bogeyman.

"Boy, you've got to listen to me real good on this one. Real property is a sacred commodity in this country, and that's particularly true here in Texas. If a man says in a deed you can only use this land as a park, or it reverts to his heirs, and a hundred years later you use that land for a grocery store, then under the law of Texas, the heirs of the original grantor can come and take that land away from you. End of story."

"Okay, I got it. But if the thing is such a problem, why don't we get rid of the deed, or . . . substitute a forgery for the original? Hell, we should have the resources to get that done."

"Carter, land fraud is a very old game, and systems have been developed so that kind of bullshit can't happen. Authenticated copies of every deed in this state are maintained in both paper and electronic form in a number of secure locations. We cannot, I repeat, cannot destroy the originals, or substitute a forgery. What's there is there."

"Mac, come on, what's the worst case? Some idiot takes the property. We remove the wells and take the hit. Sure, the field's a big cash engine, but we'd survive. We'd have to downsize, but we'd survive."

"It's a little bit more complicated than that."

"Why?"

"Well, let me see, Helius has pumped about eight hundred million barrels of oil out of that field. Even if we assume a five-dollar-per-barrel profit, that's over four billion dollars that Helius has taken out of the property. If I was one of old O'Neill's heirs and found out about that little old deed, I'd say Helius owes me about four billion, plus about fifty years' worth of interest. Run those numbers on that fancy calculator of yours and then dump that liability onto Helius's balance sheet."

"What? There has to be a statute of limitations on this thing."

"We're working on that, but it's not a guaranteed fix."

"Why?"

"That's complicated," Mac said, making it clear that he was not going to elaborate.

"Mac, there's no way—"

"Yes, Carter, there is. Make no mistake, if that door gets opened, the demon that comes out could take down Helius and the Mason family."

During the lunch Mac had related the whole story. BlackJack had originally been a part of a ranch owned by an old Irishman named Thomas O'Neill. O'Neill was the youngest of five brothers who'd left Ireland during the potato famine and went to work in the bowels of a Scottish coal mine. The four older boys had saved a part of their meager wages each month and used the money to send Thomas O'Neill, the youngest, to America, just after the Civil War.

O'Neill had worked his way west with the Union Pacific Railroad, saved his wages, and used the money to buy a small patch of land in East Texas. Each year O'Neill had saved enough money to rescue one of his brothers from their hellish existence, but in the end it had been too late. The mine had done its work. One of the four brothers died on the ship coming over, and the other three died of lung disease within five years after they arrived.

By the time of his own death, at the ripe old age of eighty, O'Neill had increased his land holdings to ten thousand acres. Since O'Neill didn't have any sons, and his two daughters wanted no part of the cattle business, O'Neill had reluctantly consented to sell the land upon his death to Jackson T. Mason. Jackson owned a smaller ranch on the western edge of the O'Neill property.

Title to the land passed in 1885. The use restriction in the deed stated that if Jackson Mason or any subsequent owner extracted minerals, or any other substance from beneath the surface of the land, for a profit, then title would "revert to the heirs of Thomas O'Neill." The restriction was the old man's way of getting even with the mine owners he held responsible for the deaths of his brothers.

In 1885, Jackson Mason had considered the reversion clause to be a piece of nonsense put there by a half-crazy Irishman. He had no intention of digging up the land. He was a rancher. In 1885, Mason's view of the world was understandable. It would be another decade before the first oil well was drilled in the Lone Star State, and the man who wasted the time and money to drill that hole was considered a fool by his contemporaries. Within fifteen years, the world had changed. Oil had become liquid gold, and Texas was prime oil country.

Unlike his father, William T. Mason, Jackson Mason's only son, fully understood the value of oil. In 1910, William hired a drilling firm to sink four exploratory wells on the land. Although William Mason knew about the deed restriction, O'Neill's two daughters had married and moved away from the area twenty years earlier. As far as he was concerned, the restriction had died with Thomas O'Neill.

The first two wells that William Mason drilled brought up nothing but water, but the third well struck a giant oil reserve. The oil strike changed William Mason from a small cattle baron to an incredibly wealthy oilman. Being an avid gambler, Mason named the oil field "BlackJack."

The surviving O'Neills never asserted their termination right under the deed because they weren't aware that it existed. The secret, however, did not remain buried. In 1914, Jedediah Dickson, a lawyer representing a competitor of the newly incorporated Mason Oil Company, found the clause while researching Mason's land holdings for his employer.

Fortunately for the Mason family, Dickson was both smart and unscrupulous. Instead of putting his client's rival out of business by disclosing the reversion to the surviving members of the O'Neill family, Dickson elected to pursue a more profitable course. He blackmailed William Mason for four long years. Knowing Mason's reputation for ruthlessness, Dickson had sent him a partial copy of a letter that Dickson had left with an undisclosed third party. The letter instructed the holder to open and publish the enclosed material in the event of his death.

Although Dickson was a careful man, he underestimated William Mason's intellect and determination. Mason incrementally pieced together Dickson's personal universe with the help of some very capable former Pinkerton operatives, and he ultimately found the human repository of Dickson's secret threat. The Louisiana lawyer holding the dead man's letter had died a slow and painful death, and Dickson's own death had been even more painful.

Several weeks after his lunch with Mac, Mason had suggested to his grandfather that the company should develop a database on O'Neill's heirs.

"Doesn't it make sense for Helius to track these people down and keep tabs on them?"

His grandfather's response had shocked Mason. "That's not necessary, Carter."

"Why not?"

"Because . . . because your great-grandfather already did that."

"A smart man. We should do the same thing."

"Carter, my father did more than track them down."

"What do you mean?"

"You know what I mean. Now leave it be."

Mason's grandfather had not been explicit, but the implication was clear. William T. Mason had helped the surviving heirs of Thomas O'Neill into the grave in order to make sure they could never make a claim. Unfortunately, William's extermination effort had not been completely successful. According to Richard Steinman's notes, at least one of O'Neill's heirs survived his great grandfather's genetic rundown—a man named John Caine.

The good news was Steinman hadn't revealed his story to anyone at the *Statesman.* Mason suspected that Steinman had kept the story secret in order to make sure that no one else stole his thunder prior to its publication. If that was the case, Steinman's paranoia was an incredible stroke of luck. It gave Mason a chance to put the cork back in the bottle, at least until year end. After that, the sunset law would eliminate the termination right.

Mason stood up and looked out over the city lights through his wall-to-wall window. He wished Paquin were here. He needed the former STASI agent's intelligence, skill, experience, and, most importantly, utter ruthlessness. Mason had never worked with Severino, Paquin's second-in-command, before, and he didn't trust his background. Both Paquin and Severino were killers, but Paquin understood how important it was to keep the company's black-ops handiwork secret. He didn't know if Severino, who'd been a mob enforcer before he joined the Helius security team, had the same skill set. Unfortunately, he couldn't wait for Paquin to get back from Cameroon. Steinman could already have alerted John Caine about the existence of the reversion. They had to eliminate the last heir. *It's time, Mr. Caine, for you to join your ancestors.*

# CHAPTER
# TEN

*Douala Airport, Cameroon*
*December 3, 1999 / 9:50 p.m.*

The two men standing on the observation deck overlooking the tarmac were almost invisible in the darkness. They were alone. No one else was inclined to endure the unseasonable heat and humidity.

The men were watching the line of people waiting to board the Air Brussels jet parked about a hundred yards from the terminal. They'd arrived forty-five minutes before boarding time and intended to wait until the plane departed. The younger of the two men, Pieter Boutreau, was dressed in a short-sleeve linen shirt and a pair of jeans. The older man was dressed in a khaki suit and a white shirt.

Boutreau, a Belgian national, had spent most of his life in West Africa, and he'd taken the Air Brussels flight a number of times. The 10:00 p.m. flight generally left on time. At 9:50 p.m., Boutreau broke the silence.

"It seems the Irish priest doesn't plan on coming."

Nicholas Paquin, the second man, drew on his cigarette and exhaled slowly before answering.

"He still has time."

"I'm told he's a stubborn man. My bet is he'll stay and try to clear his name."

"Maybe. Is there any chance the bishop rescinded the expulsion order?"

Boutreau shook his head and pulled a thin cigar from his shirt pocket.

"No. The old man is suspicious of European priests generally, and he hates homosexuals."

"What about the two boys?"

"They said exactly what their mothers told them to say. By now, they've probably forgotten the whole thing."

"And the women?"

"I paid them two grand each in francs. I could have got it done for less, but you told me to be generous."

"What about the photos of the spill?" Paquin said.

Boutreau smiled as he lit the cigar.

"The rolls of film in his bag are blank. We destroyed the originals. The overnight package with the only copy is in my car. The clerk at his hotel was a good capitalist."

Paquin nodded.

The two men watched the line of passengers board the jet. When the line was almost gone, Boutreau spoke again. His voice was quieter. "If he stays, I can do it. His hotel is in a bad area. A fatal mugging won't generate too much interest, even if he's European."

Paquin waited until the last two passengers climbed up the steel ramp and disappeared into the plane before he answered.

"No. It has to be quiet, without violence and away from Douala. If he stays, we'll let him start south to the village. When the bus stops at Kribi, we'll do it. It will look like a snakebite. The news will take two or three days to get back here and another day or two to get to his friends in Europe. By then, most people will be thinking about the holiday."

Boutreau nodded as he watched the two men pull the stair ramp away from the door of the plane. Paquin shook his head. It appeared that Boutreau was right. The priest was determined to receive his last rites in the continent of Africa. The ramp was halfway back to the terminal when two men emerged from the lower level of the building, and walked in the direction of the waiting jet.

One of the men, an older African man, was dressed in the tradi-tional black habit of a Catholic priest. The second man was younger, white, and casually dressed in jeans and a short-sleeve polo shirt.

Boutreau nodded toward the two men.

"The black is the bishop's aide. Father Rourke, you know."

The younger man had a shoulder-length mane of black hair and handsome features. The older priest was carrying a backpack in one hand. His other hand was gripping the younger man's arm, half guid-ing, half pulling him toward the waiting Airbus 330.

The young priest angrily gestured with his free hand as he walked. The older man nodded sympathetically, but continued to guide him toward the plane. At the foot of the stair ramp, which had been restored to its position against the door of the plane, the older priest held up a hand with quiet authority, stemming the tide of protests. Then he lowered the backpack to the ground and spoke earnestly to the younger man, as the flight attendant waited impatiently at the top of the ramp. When the older man finished, the young priest hesitated for a long moment. Then he gave the other man a quick embrace and walked up the stairs carrying his backpack.

Paquin waited until the jet was taxiing down the runway before he turned to leave. The ruin of the priest's reputation and his expulsion from the country by the local bishop was the lesser of two evils. Helius couldn't allow the priest to continue to badger the local authorities about the spills fouling the waters near the small village where his missionary effort was located. Either he had to stop, which the young priest would never do voluntarily, or he had to die. Eliminating the spills wasn't an option. The government of Cameroon had seen to that.

Four months after Helius had secured the offshore oil lease from Cameroon, the interior minister had informed the company that all five offshore wells had to be in place within seven months, or the lease was forfeit. A French oil company was behind the demand. The French company had offered the minister a huge bribe and a larger profit split, if the minister could find a way to transfer the drilling rights. To meet the new deadline, Helius had been forced to cut corners, which meant spills were going to happen.

When the problem had surfaced, Menard Onwuallu, Helius's "fixer" on the African continent, had cryptically notified Mason that he would solve the problem. When Paquin had demanded specifics, Onwuallu advised him that he intended to kill both the priest and the local French oil executive behind the scheme. The two killings would be intentionally brutal in order to convey the "right" message to the French company and the troublesome minister.

Paquin had rejected Onwuallu's proposal and taken over the operation himself. Onwuallu's typical brutality could backfire in this situation. If the murders were traced to Helius, the environmental movement would turn the priest into a martyr, focusing even more attention on the spills. The bad press would give the new oil minister the excuse he was looking for to terminate the lease.

Paquin's plan was more discreet, less risky, but just as effective. Destroying the priest's reputation ensured his expulsion by the local bishop. It also made him a poor spokesman for the environmental cause. A priest accused of molesting two African boys was not a sympathetic figure, no matter how just his cause.

Paquin left Boutreau at the airport and took a cab to a private airfield outside the city, where a private jet was waiting to take him back to Austin. The drive through the dark and dusty streets of Douala brought back old memories. Africa had been his first overseas assignment as a STASI officer twenty years earlier. He'd been assigned to work with a KGB unit in Ethiopia, after the Soviet Union had persuaded Fidel Castro to dispatch fifteen thousand Cuban troops to assist the Ethiopians with their little war against neighboring Somalia.

After the fall of the Berlin Wall in late 1989, he'd left the doomed STASI and moved into corporate security work. The rules of the new game were somewhat different, but he'd adapted. Problems had to be solved, and he knew how to do it. People were willing to pay for that skill. Sometimes threats or bribes were sufficient. Other times, more drastic measures were required.

## *Douala Airport, Cameroon*
### *December 4, 1999 / 10:20 p.m.*

The small African man sitting in the back of the airport waited until the two white men had left before walking to a nearby pay phone. A man with a deep baritone answered on the first ring.

"Onwuallu."

"The priest got on the plane."

"That's too bad. Well, we must be patient. Destroying Mr. Paquin is a prize worth the waiting for. Thank you, Mr. Porter."

"You're welcome, sir."

# CHAPTER
# ELEVEN

San Bernardino County, California
December 4, 1999 / Saturday / 11:30 p.m.

As the Learjet began its final approach, Severino looked out the window at the lights below. He tried to ignore his tension headache and the uneasy feeling in his stomach, but he knew that wasn't going to happen until the target was put down. Severino didn't have a problem with Mason's kill order. He just didn't like planning the operation and making it happen in one day when the target was on the top of a mountain over a thousand miles away. That kind of logistical nightmare was out of his league. He could also do without Mason's "there's no room for error" bullshit.

Paquin planned the difficult ops, and on a high priority deal like this he would typically run the execution from start to finish. Severino's job was to follow orders, and he was comfortable in that role. That wasn't going to happen on this one. Paquin's jet was still on the way back from Africa. Worse, they couldn't reach him by phone because of a storm over the Gulf. Whether Severino liked it or not, this op was his baby from start to finish.

The good news was the hit should be a piece of cake. The target was a nobody, and he didn't know they were coming after him. *With the muscle and firepower that I'm bringing to this party, it should be a real easy job, unless . . . unless someone on the team does something stupid.*

Severino glanced over at the two lean, hard-looking Latino men sitting across the aisle from him. He only knew them as Juan and Miguel. The two men usually worked with Simon Vargas on jobs in South and Central America. They just happened to be in town for a meeting with Vargas when Mason ordered the hit. After listening to Mason's threats, Severino had pulled them into the operation. He wasn't taking any chances.

The two men had been part of a paramilitary unit in Nicaragua, before they moved on to private security work. Vargas said they knew their business and followed orders, which was good enough for Severino. He would have felt better if Vargas was a part of the team, but that was against protocol. When Paquin was out of town, one of them had to be on call back at the command center in Austin.

It was the third member of the team, Julian Anders, who spooked Severino. Severino had considered leaving him off the team, but had reconsidered the decision at the last minute. Anders knew how to use a gun, and he had no problem with killing. Anders's problem was that he didn't follow orders. Two months earlier, Severino had sent Anders and two local thugs to persuade a labor organizer in Caracas, Venezuela, that Helius crews were off limits. Severino's orders had been clear. The beating was intended to be a message, no more. It was not to be fatal.

Anders had put his own spin on the order. He'd beaten the head organizer half to death and then stamped on the man's spine after he was out cold, paralyzing him for life. Even the local thugs working the job with Anders had been taken aback by his brutality. The incident had blown over without trouble, but Severino knew they'd been lucky. If the foreign press had gotten wind of Anders's rampage and traced it back to Helius, it could have been a disaster for the company. Severino intended to keep Anders on a short leash this time.

The Learjet landed at what formerly had been Norton Air Force Base in San Bernardino County, California. In 1995, the Pentagon had closed the sprawling facility and turned over control to the county. A part of the facility was being leased by the county to a private aviation firm, while the state and local officials argued about an overall reuse plan. The base was located at the foot of the San Bernardino Mountains, where the target's cabin was located, making it an ideal staging area for the op.

Severino smiled wryly to himself as he mentally walked through the plan again. After five years of working with Paquin, the military jargon that Paquin used as a matter of course had now become a fixture in his own descriptions. Unlike a lot of the people who worked for Paquin, Severino wasn't ex-military. He'd worked as an enforcer for the Garellis, one of the second-tier crime families in New York, for ten years. In 1995, that life had come to an end, when a rival family had won a turf war. As a part of the settlement with the rival family, the Garellis had offered up Severino, who'd killed a number of the other family's top people. Severino had gotten wind of the deal and staged his own death in order to get out from under the sanction. His "accidental death" was caused by a meth lab explosion. The police found an unidentifiable body in an abandoned warehouse along with Anthony Severino's burned wallet and a half-melted class ring. In the overworked world of NYPD Homicide, the evidence was sufficient for the positive identification of one dead mobster. No one missed the intoxicated homeless man that Severino drafted to serve as the corpse.

After quietly leaving New York, Severino had drifted from job to job in the South, making enough to survive, but no more. He'd ended up working as a short-haul trucker for a subsidiary of Helius in Morgan City, Louisiana. Somehow, Paquin had learned about his background. When Paquin sat down at his table in the local bar, without an invitation, Severino was convinced he'd been sent from New York to punch his ticket. Paquin had allayed his concerns, explaining that he was in the business of solving problems for their mutual employer. He told Severino that he knew about his New York background, but it wasn't a problem.

Paquin had told him that he might be able to use Severino's help on special jobs that paid well, but declined to provide any specifics. A week later, Paquin asked him to transport several boxes from an older part of the port area to a private airport outside of town. Severino had shown up on time, completed the job, and picked up five hundred bucks for a night's work. Over the next three years, the jobs had gotten bigger, along with the money. Eventually, Severino had become one of Paquin's trusted lieutenants, performing "services" throughout the world for his consulting firm. All of the work, directly or indirectly, involved Helius, and most of the work wasn't all that different from what he used to do for the Garellis.

The pilot of the Learjet, Ed Wilson, taxied the jet up to the ancient hangar at the far end of the airfield, and the sliding steel doors slowly opened. A middle-aged man with gray hair tied back in a ponytail drove out of the hangar in a squat vehicle, hooked up a cable to the front of the jet, and towed it into the hangar. *Good. Cochrane's here.*

When Severino climbed out of the jet, followed by the rest of the team, Cochrane was waiting at the foot of the stairs. Severino was surprised by the size of the old building. Cochrane noticed the look on his face.

"Big, isn't she? This monster was built for B-52s. Those old birds were big bastards. Yessiree."

Cochrane's Alabama drawl grated on Severino. When Ed Wilson walked down the stairs of the jet, Cochrane walked past Severino and gave Wilson a friendly slap on the shoulder.

"You looked a little shaky on your approach, old man. I just might have to give you a few pointers. Can't have you bumpin' into my chopper."

"Piss off, hillbilly," Wilson responded with a smile.

Both men were in their late fifties and had served a tour in Vietnam during the last years of the war. Wilson had flown a series of fixed-wing aircraft in South Vietnam and Laos, as a pilot with Air America, an airline formed and run by the CIA. Cochrane had served in the United States Army as a warrant officer in the First Air Cavalry Division. Although both men were good pilots, their "cowboy" attitudes hadn't played well in the buttoned-down civilian air transport industry. After the war, they'd moved from job to job, inevitably becoming less and less employable. By the time Paquin hired them, the two men were hauling freight for small-time smugglers.

Severino looked skeptically across the hangar at the ugly gray-brown Vietnam-era "Huey" (UH-1) parked next to the Lear. As far as Severino was concerned, it looked liked a big piece of shit, and that scared the hell out of him. The chopper was their transport up the mountain.

"How's the chopper?"

"Don't you worry about that old girl, chief. She may look a bit worn, but she's almost new where it counts. Oh yeah, and since you told me this was such a big deal op, I brought a little something special along just in case us peaceful folks were to find ourselves in need."

Cochrane had a big smile on his jowly face as he walked over to the chopper's big sliding door and pulled it open. Severino stared at the ugly black machine gun lying on a tarp, just inside the side door of the chopper.

"What's this shit?"

Cochrane smiled, missing the anger in Severino's incredulous voice.

"What we have here is an M60D machine gun. I only got a hundred rounds, but—"

Severino cut him off. "We don't need it, Cochrane. This is going to be a nice quiet operation."

"Fine with me, boss, but you can never tell. Sheeit, I dropped enough of those Rangers and Greenie Beanies into what was supposed to be some real quiet LZs, but the hell if we didn't take some heavy goddamned fire comin' and goin'. Guess those VCs didn't know they weren't supposed to be there," Cochrane said, patting the M60 affectionately.

Wilson, who'd walked over to admire the big M60, smiled at Cochrane's comment, and joined the conversation.

"Roger that. Y'all never know when you're gonna find yourself knee-deep in shit."

The aging chopper, the big gun, and the talk of a possible firefight struck a nerve in Severino. He'd killed a number of people as an enforcer for the Garellis, but he'd only been in one situation that could be called a gun battle. A pimp who'd refused to pay protection had opened up on Severino with a .44 Magnum just as he was getting out of his car with two muscle heads. The incoming rounds blew the Lincoln's front windshield all over Queens Boulevard. Severino remembered lying by the curb struggling to get his Beretta out, as round after round ripped into the car above him. The three of them had managed to put down the pimp and get away from the scene, but he'd been scared shitless during the entire fight.

Cochrane's talk of a possible firefight brought the memory streaming back, and with it, the fear. The feeling enraged Severino and exacerbated the pain pounding in his temples.

"Let's get this straight, Cochrane. This is a quiet in-and-out deal against a soft target. The schmuck will probably be asleep when we show up. So forget about your LZs, VCs, or any other kind of Vietnam bullshit. We get in and out, real quiet. Are we totally fucking clear on that?"

Cochrane and Wilson looked over at him with surprise.

"Yeah, no problem, boss, in and out real quiet," Cochrane repeated with a tight smile.

As Severino walked around the other side of the chopper toward the office, Anders glanced up from the M16 that he was checking over. Severino could see the grin on his face out of the corner of his eye. *Screw you.*

# CHAPTER
# TWELVE

*San Bernardino County, California,*
*December 5, 1999 / Sunday / 2:30 a.m.*

Caine had been asleep for about an hour when he heard the sound of the low-flying chopper. A surge of adrenaline raced through him, and he sat up in the bed. For a moment, he struggled to identify his surroundings, and then he remembered. Sam was growling quietly, more in reaction to Caine's tension than to the noise from the chopper. Caine reached over and stroked the dog's head.

Caine tried to get back to sleep, but gave up the effort twenty minutes later. He pulled on his jeans and shirt and walked into the dark kitchen. Sam followed him. He stopped in the middle of the room and looked out the window. The night sky was cloudy, but there was enough of a moon for him to see the snow-covered driveway and the dark tree line beyond. He reached for the light switch on the wall to his left, but stopped before he touched it. *There was movement in the trees.*

Although the kitchen was dark, Caine instinctively stepped out of the limited ambient light coming in the window, to the darkest part of the room. He stared intently at the stand of trees just beyond the

Jeep. It took Caine a moment to pick up the movement again and to identify what he was looking at. Four figures were just inside the tree line. As he watched, they stopped and separated into two groups. Two of them started around the house to the right. The other two began to circle to the left, toward the rear of the house.

The dog standing beside him emitted a low growl.

"Shhh, buddy. Let's see what we have here," Caine whispered reassuringly and opened the utility drawer on his left. He pulled out a small pair of binoculars and focused on the two figures moving toward the rear of the house. Both men were armed. From the outline of the weapons, he guessed they were carrying mini Uzis or Skorpion submachine guns. The guns had elongated barrels—*suppressors.*

Caine turned his attention to the two men who were circling around to the right of the cabin. They were carrying similar weapons, but the larger of the two men had a gun sticking out of his backpack. It looked like a shotgun.

Caine lowered the binoculars, questions screaming through his mind. *Who the hell are these guys, and why am I suddenly a target after all these years?* Caine decided to leave the questions for another time and focus on staying alive. He had to get out of the cabin before the assault began. Caine dropped into a crouch and walked over to the coat closet in the hall. He pulled a sweater over his head and grabbed a dark blue ski-jacket. Then he dropped to one knee and pulled out the black backpack resting against the rear wall of the closet.

The retriever, sensing his intent to leave, put one of his front paws on Caine's knee. Caine scratched the dog around the collar area. For a moment he considered staying with the dog and making a fight of it in the cabin, but then rejected the thought. The cabin was a trap. Staying put would just get them both killed. His best course was to get out fast and leave Sam behind. The opposition would be forced to follow him, leaving the dog safe in the house. He'd have his neighbor down the road pick up Sam up later.

Caine spoke to the dog quietly.

"Sam, you have to stay here. Once I go, they'll have no reason to come in."

Caine grabbed the backpack and crawled rapidly toward the cellar stairway. He eased down the stairs silently, with the dog following in his wake. There was a storage room in the rear of the basement where Caine kept supplies and the dog's food. The room had no exterior windows. He turned on the overhead light, drew a bucket of water from the sink for the dog to drink and ripped open a bag of dog food. To distract the dog, Caine placed one of the large rawhide bones that he kept on the shelf beside the bowl of water. Sam lay down and started in on the bone. Caine reluctantly closed the door behind him, praying that Sam would keep quiet and be safe.

The black Arctic Cat was parked in front of the door that led to the backyard. Caine checked the gas gauge. It was about three-quarters full. That should be enough fuel to get him to the town. He opened the backpack and pulled out a Sig Sauer P226 pistol, three magazines, and a black nylon shoulder holster. He slid one of the magazines into the Sig and chambered the first round. Then he put the gun back in the shoulder holster and pulled it on. He put the other two magazines in his front pocket.

Caine knew that he would be most vulnerable in the ten to fifteen seconds that it would take to cross the thirty yards of open space before the tree line. Unless he could create some kind of diversion, it could be a very short ride. Caine opened one of the pockets on the inside of the backpack and pulled out a flare pistol, along with three long cartridges. He selected the bright orange cartridge from among the three and loaded it into the pistol. He put the other two cartridges away and closed the pack.

Caine glanced at his watch as he pulled on his hiking boots. It was 2:58 a.m. No more than eight minutes had passed since he'd spotted the men in the forest. He considered going back upstairs and trying to pin down their position before he made his run, but decided against it. He had to rely upon speed and surprise to get him out of a kill zone. The Cat would give him the speed, and if the flare performed its magic, he should have all the surprise he needed.

Caine pressed the button that activated the door to the yard. When the door was three feet off the ground, he rolled into the open space, closed his eyes, and fired the flare into the night sky. Then he rolled back into the basement and climbed on the Arctic Cat, counting to himself. When he reached the count of five, he closed his eyes tightly and turned his face away from the now open door.

The flare exploded in a single stunning flash of white on the count of seven. Two seconds later, the flare went dark, and Caine roared down the ramp into the snow-covered yard. The flare was a specialty load. It was designed to draw the attention of the enemy in a night fight and then explode with a blast of intense white light. Anyone looking at the flare when it exploded would be blinded for thirty seconds and suffer impaired vision for several minutes.

Caine heard confused yells to his right as he raced across the yard. When he was about halfway to the tree line, Caine heard automatic weapons fire coming from a gun equipped with a suppressor. The shooter traced a line across the yard just behind the Cat. Caine pressed himself flat against the machine, expecting the shooter to correct his line of fire, but then it was too late. The Cat rocketed through the trees and roared into the dark forest beyond.

# CHAPTER
# THIRTEEN

San Bernardino County, California
December 5, 2000 / Sunday / 2:45 a.m.

Severino and Juan, one of the two Nicaraguan soldiers, were approaching the west side of the backyard when Caine fired the flare. Both men dropped to their knees and watched in confusion as the flare raced upward into the night sky.

"What's this shit?" Severino said as he watched the flare's trajectory. Seconds later, there was an explosion and a flash of brilliant white. Severino closed his eyes. When he opened them again, a white after-image clouded his vision. He was temporarily blind.

As he struggled to blink away the after-image, Severino heard the roar of a high-pitched engine coming from the rear of the cabin. He pointed the Uzi in the direction of the sound and squeezed off a burst, but then he stopped. Anders and Miguel were on the east side of the cabin. If he fired blind, they could be hit.

Severino stood up and stumbled into the backyard, the Uzi held in front of him. His eyes were watering, but his vision was coming back. The engine noise that he'd heard was rapidly fading to the south.

Severino fired a long burst in that direction. *It was a snowmobile. The bastard has a snowmobile and he's getting away.*

Juan ran into the yard, holding his hand over his eyes as if to shade them from the sun and raised his Uzi to fire. Severino's harsh rebuke stopped him.

"Stop, you idiot. Can't you see the son of a bitch is gone!"

Severino called out to Anders over his face mic.

"Anders, where are you? Anders!"

"Here, goddamn it."

"Where? I can't see you."

"How the fuck do I know? I can't see anything but white," Anders growled back, giving Severino a moment of satisfaction. Severino squinted hard at the eastern edge of the yard and saw Anders trudge out of the tree line, followed by Miguel. Anders was holding his shotgun in one hand and rubbing his eyes with the other.

Severino yanked out his cell phone and dialed Cochrane.

"Hey y'all, what the hell—"

"Can it, Cochrane, I need that chopper here now! The bastard's getting away on a goddamn snowmobile! You hear me, Cochrane? Now!"

"Roger that."

Severino's frustration grew as he listened to the whine of the snowmobile fade in the distance. Five minutes later, the big chopper appeared over the yard and slowly descended into the open space. Severino ran to the passenger side door and pulled it open.

"A map. I need a map," Severino yelled to Cochrane over the deafening noise of the rotors.

Cochrane pulled out an aerial map from between the two seats and handed it to Severino. Cochrane pointed to a small structure on the map that was circled in red. "That's the cabin. Due west is the town of Snow Valley on Route 18. My guess is our boy will head for the town. There's a five- . . . maybe six-mile stretch of forest between the cabin and the outskirts of the town. No one lives there. We've got to stop him within the first three or four miles, or it's over."

Severino looked over his shoulder into the rear of the chopper. Anders, Miguel, and Juan were inside.

"Go," said Severino, grudgingly impressed by Cochrane's analysis.

The chopper rapidly gained altitude and began a controlled slide to the west. Severino struggled to understand what had just happened. The flare unnerved him. *Who would have something like that? Who is this guy, some kind of wacko survivalist?* A loud string of curses coming from the rear of the chopper drew his attention.

"I'm gonna blow the shit out that goddamn son of a bitch," Anders yelled as he pulled the tarp off the big machine gun. Cochrane noticed what he was doing in the mirror and yelled back to him.

"Y'all know how to use that M60?"

"Shit yeah, I can use any goddamned gun," Anders yelled back.

*San Bernardino Forest*
*December 5, 1999 / Sunday / 3:09 a.m.*

Caine stopped the Arctic Cat about a half mile west of the cabin on the far side of a steep ridge. He put the machine in neutral and listened. The noise was unmistakable: a chopper was landing near the cabin. He suspected it was the same chopper that had woken him up thirty minutes before the hit team showed up. One of two things would happen. Either his pursuers would make a quick exit and consider the mission a failure, or they'd continue the hunt in the chopper. Caine listened quietly until he was sure of their choice. The chopper was coming his way.

Caine considered trying to escape through the forest on the Arctic Cat, but rejected the option. The forest was patchy, and his trail would be easily visible in the snow. Once they spotted it, the chopper would run him down in seconds. If he wanted to get out of the forest alive, he had to change the game.

Based on the approaching sound, Caine estimated that he had three or four minutes before the chopper found his trail and caught up with him. He scanned the area around him. There was an open space on the far side of the hill. He drove the Arctic Cat down the hill until he was near the bottom of the slope. Then he parked the machine and pushed it over onto its side. He took off his ski jacket, laid it on the ground next to the Cat and stuffed it with snow. If he was lucky, the chopper would descend and investigate.

When he finished, Caine ran to the nearby tree line and pulled a Franchi SPAS-12 shotgun from his pack and began loading the magazine tube. The close-quarters combat weapon had a pistol grip, and offered the shooter the option of selecting a semiautomatic or a pump-action mode. Caine finished loading the last of the eight rounds into the magazine tube as the chopper came over the hill.

The chopper passed overhead and circled around. When it approached the second time, automatic weapons fire was pouring out of the open side door. Puffs of snow were flying into the air all around the Arctic Cat. When the machine settled into a hover, Caine heard a loud guttural roar over the sound of the engine, and heavier projectiles pounded into the slope around the Cat. The noise stopped and then started up again. Caine was confused for a moment, and then he recognized the heavier weapon. *They have an M60 on that chopper.* Caine watched the fire pattern. Whoever was firing the M60 was an amateur. Not one of the bursts hit the Cat.

Caine watched the chopper slowly descend. The sliding door on the left side of the chopper was closed, which made that side blind and defenseless. If the chopper came down another fifty feet, he might have a chance.

### San Bernardino Forest
### December 5, 1999 / Sunday / 3:45 a.m.

"Lower, Cochrane, lower, I can't see shit," Severino yelled over the roar of the engine.

"I am. I am. Do you want to end up in the goddamn trees?" Cochrane answered as he struggled to keep the big machine in the center of the open space.

Severino was holding the passenger-side door open with his right foot. The Uzi in his hands was pointed out the door. Anders was standing at one end of the doorway in the rear, holding his shotgun at the ready. The Nicaraguans were at the other end.

Severino smiled. They'd caught up with the bastard in nothing flat. *Where are you, asshole? Just stick your head out and I'll blow your ass away.*

Three blasts split the air and the chopper suddenly yawed to the right, throwing him back in his seat.

"What the—"

Cochrane's yell cut him off. "Shit! He's on the left. He's blowing the shit out of us!"

Severino glanced past Cochrane out the window on the left and saw a figure rhythmically pumping round after round into the chopper from a short black shotgun. For a moment, he was mesmerized by the sight, and then the chopper whirled past the man's position. Rage flowed through him.

"Turn this piece of shit around now! I want that bastard dead!" Severino yelled, looking wildly from left to right, trying to find the shooter again in the dark. Cochrane slowly wheeled the big machine around, trying to bring the target back into their field of fire again. Severino tightened his seat belt and braced his foot against the door frame.

Anders and the two Nicaraguans began laying down a hail of fire even before the target came into view. Without thinking, Severino responded to this uncontrolled firing by firing a burst from his own weapon out the door. As the machine wheeled around, the speed of the turn increased, giving Severino only seconds over the area where the target was a moment ago. Severino turned toward Cochrane, enraged.

"What the fuck are you doing?"

"I'm trying to get—"

The windshield on Cochrane's left exploded, cutting him off. Cochrane instinctively raised his left hand up to cover his eyes. Severino heard Anders yelling over the rapid series of booms coming from outside the chopper.

"He's behind the tree! Get down!"

The shock of the attack paralyzed Severino. The chopper whirled around, again putting the shooter on the blind side of the chopper. Severino turned to yell at Cochrane, but stopped when he saw his face. Blood was pouring down from a gash on his forehead into his eyes. The pilot was struggling to keep the blood out of his eyes, without losing control of the chopper. As Severino watched, the chopper started to slide downward and to the left. He looked out the front window and involuntarily started to stand up when he realized how close they now were to the giant fir trees on the far side of the slope.

"Shit! We're going down!"

Anders looked into the cockpit when he heard Severino's yell. His eyes were drawn instantly to the front windshield. As they watched in horror, the hovering machine slued in slow motion into a stand of snow-covered firs. For a second, the big machine seemed to rest on the nearest tree. Then the rear rotor shattered against the heavy boughs and the chopper began to plunge downward.

### San Bernardino Forest
### December 5, 1999 / Sunday / 4:05 a.m.

As soon as the chopper hit the trees, Caine ran down the slope to the far side of the Arctic Cat and pushed it upright. A few of the gauges were shattered and he could smell gas, but the engine came to life when he punched the ignition. As Caine raced up the next hill, he glanced over his shoulder. The chopper was plunging into a dense stand of trees.

Caine stopped a half mile away from the downed chopper and checked the compass on the dash. The needle pointed due west. If he stayed on this heading, he should be able to see the lights of Snow Valley within twenty minutes. When he put the Cat in gear again, Caine realized that he'd left his winter coat back at the ambush site in his rush to escape. Now that the adrenaline in his system was beginning to recede, he could feel the intense cold. If he didn't find shelter soon, hypothermia would begin to take hold.

As he drove through the dark forest, Caine tried to ignore the cold and focus on what he would do when he reached the town. Snow

Valley was a small town, with only three or four small inns. Whoever was after him could pull up a list of these places on the Internet, or just stop by the local coffee shop and ask about nearby accommodations. With that information in hand, finding out whether a guest had arrived within the last hour or two would just require a phone call.

Caine wasn't prepared to take that risk. He had to find a place to stay where they couldn't find him. Like most of the resort towns in the area, Snow Valley had a number of weekend cabins. At this time in the morning, he should be able to break into one of these homes without drawing attention, and find food and water. More important, he should be able to find a coat. Once the sun came up, he could work on getting transportation off the mountain.

# CHAPTER
# FOURTEEN

*Austin, Texas*
*December 5, 1999 / Sunday / 4:15 a.m.*

Paquin was advised of Mason's attempts to contact him as the Learjet passed over the West Coast of Florida. He dialed Mason's private line.

"Mason here."

"It's Paquin."

"Where . . . never mind that. We have a problem."

The strain and impatience in Mason's voice surprised Paquin. Mason was typically calm, even cold, in their conversations.

"This problem must be eliminated quickly and quietly," Mason said. Paquin didn't respond and Mason continued.

"A reporter from the *Statesman* discovered something . . . information that could severely damage the company. The reporter is dead, but we have—"

"Were there any complications?" Paquin interrupted.

"No. Vargas will fill you in," Mason said. "We have two other problems. The reporter sent a package containing the damaging information to a lawyer here in Austin. Your people have the shipping receipt, so we know the package will arrive on Monday, by FedEx. You have to get that package, before anyone opens it. I don't care how—"

"We'll get the package," Paquin said quietly.

He considered the information. What could the reporter have discovered that was so damaging? All of Helius's black ops were under his supervision. Tying one of those operations back to Helius would be extremely difficult. All of his people worked for corporate blinds in countries that took their secrecy laws seriously, and he would have been alerted if anyone had started to investigate.

"Very well. Our second problem is more complex. There's another individual who's a threat. In fact, he's an even greater threat than the reporter. *Your* lieutenant, Severino, assured me that this problem would be eliminated last night, but it's after 4:00 a.m. and I've heard nothing. I need answers, Mr. Paquin, and I need them now," Mason said, cold anger in his voice.

Paquin had a number of questions for Mason, but this was not the time, and the red call-waiting button on the Airfone was blinking. After what Mason had just told him, he wanted to take the call. It had to be from either Vargas or Severino.

"I'll deal with the problem."

"Do that," Mason said and hung up.

Paquin picked up the other line.

"Paquin."

"It's Vargas. Severino and his team are in deep . . . a critical situation. He needs to talk with you. You can reach him on his cell."

"I see," Paquin said.

He dialed Severino's cell phone.

"Severino here."

"This is Paquin. What's the status of your mission?"

There was a distinct hesitation, and then Severino spoke in a tightly controlled voice. His description of the mission plan struck Paquin as overkill, but he didn't make any comment. Severino typically favored muscle over stealth, and the pressure from Mason would only have exacerbated the tendency. Severino's description of the events became louder and harsher as he continued.

"An hour ago, we landed about a mile from the target's cabin. Four of us approached the site. We were setting up a perimeter when the target fired some kind of flare into the sky. The fucking thing exploded and blinded us. That shit—"

"Go on," Paquin interrupted.

"The target used the flare as a diversion and took off into the forest on a snowmobile. We followed his tracks in the chopper. The bastard, he set up an ambush. He waited until the chopper dropped down to investigate what looked like a crash, and then he took out the chopper with a shotgun. That fuck—"

"Mr. Severino, I need to know your situation, no more. Are we clear?"

Paquin's interruption choked off Severino's tirade.

"Clear. The crash site is several miles from the cabin. It's deep in the forest, so it should remain out of sight for a while. We suffered minor injuries, but everyone can walk out of here. The target escaped in the direction of the town on the snowmobile. We need to get rid of this wreck, we need directions out of here, and . . . shit, we'll need transport."

Paquin was stunned by the scope of the disaster. They would have to move quickly to get the situation under control.

"Give me the GPS coordinates for the crash site," Paquin said.

Severino had anticipated the request and relayed the coordinates to Paquin from his handheld GPS device. Paquin instructed Severino to hold.

Four minutes later, Paquin came back on the line.

"Walk due south of your position for a mile and you'll hit a dirt road. Follow that road southwest for a half mile to a paved road. Go west on that road for another three miles. That will put you in the town of Snow Valley. You'll be contacted within twenty minutes with more information."

Paquin leaned back in the leather seat after the call and considered his options. He needed to deal with the crash site immediately. The chopper would have to come out in pieces to avoid discovery.

Paquin picked up the phone and dialed Simon Vargas.

"Vargas, it's Paquin."

"Did you reach Severino?" Vargas said.

"Yes. We need to get rid of that chopper . . . in pieces, quickly and quietly. I don't want to use locals we can't control unless we have no other choice," Paquin said, thinking his way through the problem as he spoke.

Vargas hesitated before responding.

"There's a way. Helius has an oil field services outfit in Long Beach. They repair the offshore rigs, so they should have top-of-the-line cutting and welding equipment there. If you can get me access to that equipment and another chopper, I can put it together."

"Where are you going to get the labor?" Paquin said.

"Tijuana is two hours south. It's full of chop shops. I have a contact there. He should be able to line up five or six cutters real quick, for a price. If everything works out, we can have that bird cut up and trucked out of there in twelve hours, max," Vargas said.

Paquin nodded to himself. It could work.

"Set it up. I'll get you what you need. One other thing, have someone arrange transport for Severino and his team. They need to track down the target," Paquin said.

"Done," Vargas said and hung up.

Paquin reviewed the situation after his call with Vargas. He'd done as much damage control as possible. Now he had to focus on reacquiring the target. He also had to advise Mason that his "problem" was still out there.

# CHAPTER
# FIFTEEN

*San Bernardino County, California.*
*December 5, 1999 / Sunday / 5:00 a.m.*

The house that Caine broke into was a three-bedroom modified cottage. It was all but hidden from the neighboring homes and the street by the trees surrounding the property. Caine entered the house through a rear window by forcing a partially unhooked window lock.

After cleaning up and drinking three glasses of water, Caine laid down on the carpet in the living room, with a cushion from the couch underneath his head. That position put him beneath the windows and it gave him quick access to the rear door in case the owner showed up.

Caine pulled the cell phone out of his pocket and dialed his answering service. Although he routinely called in for messages when he was away from the business, his motivation for calling this time was different. He suspected the attack on the cabin was related to his past service with the Legion's black ops unit. Nothing else made sense. If his guess was correct, he might have received a message from another member of the unit, the Legion itself, or from France's external security and counterintelligence service, the Direction Générale de la Sécurité Extérieure.

Caine had five voicemail messages. He skipped past the first three, after listening to the first second or two from each recording. They were all business related. When Caine hit the fourth message, the caller's voice was initially difficult to hear over the mariachi band and the loud voices in the background, but then the background sound faded.

"Hello, Mr. Caine, my name is Richard Steinman. I work for the *American-Statesman*, a newspaper here in Austin. I've been working on a story. You own . . . or should own a very valuable piece of property here, in Texas. The story is . . . complicated. It's critical that I talk with you. This is a big deal. I'm trying to get the story into Monday's edition. Look, the people that own the property, or think they own the property, they're not going to be happy about this. You need to be careful. I know this sounds crazy, but it's for real. I'll call you later tonight. If for any reason I don't get back to you, call me. If you can't get to me, call . . . call Andrea Marenna. She's a lawyer here in Austin—a friend." The caller left his own cell number and a number for the other contact, Andrea Marenna.

The message didn't make sense to Caine. Under normal circumstances, he would have just deleted it, as an off-the-wall sales pitch, but tonight's attack made him hesitate. The call and the attempted hit seemed too close to be coincidental. For a moment he considered the possibility that the caller might be part of the team that tried to take him out, but it didn't add up. The message was left at 5:45 p.m. Pacific Standard Time, on Friday night. That would make it about 7:45 p.m. in Austin. If he'd picked up the message before the attack, he might have taken precautions, or stayed away from the cabin altogether.

Caine decided to check on Steinman's background before he called him directly. He dialed information and asked for the number of the *Statesman*. Then he dialed the number. A message informed him that the *Statesman* was closed, but it referred him to an extension for emergency news tips. He pressed the extension and a receptionist picked up.

"Night desk. How can I help you?"

"Richard Steinman, please."

There was a moment's hesitation. "Mr. Steinman is not available."

"Can you page him? This is urgent. It relates to a story he's working on."

The receptionist hesitated again and said, "One moment, please."

There was a pause and another person came on the line.

"Hello, this is Susan Bell. I'm the night manager. May I ask who's calling?"

"John Caine. Mr. Steinman left me a message yesterday. He asked me to track him down right away. I just picked up the message, so here I am."

There was a silence then the woman continued.

"Mr. Caine, I'm very sorry. Mr. Steinman was involved in a traffic accident Friday night. He . . . he didn't survive. If you call back on Monday, I'm sure that we can find someone who can help you."

"I see. Thank you. I'll do that."

Caine hung up. His mind was racing. The sequence of events bothered him. The reporter had left the message at 7:45 p.m. on a Friday night. Later that night, he ends up dead. Twenty-four hours later, a well-organized hit team tries to kill him. *It doesn't make sense. I don't own any property in Texas, and why would I be in danger if I did?*

Caine was born and raised in Waco, Texas, but he'd left twenty years ago to join the army and he'd never returned. Back then, everything he owned fit in a duffel bag. Steinman must have made a mistake, but that might not make any difference if the people who were after him believed he was the real McCoy. On the other hand, the attack might have nothing to do with Steinman's call. It could be just a coincidence.

Caine ran a hand through his hair and yawned. He had a lot of questions, but very few answers. To find the answers, he had to get out of Snow Valley, alive. Caine looked at his watch. It was 5:30 a.m. A wave of fatigue washed over him, but he forced himself to focus. He had to put together a plan of action.

Calling the police and asking for protection wouldn't work. The situation was way outside the boxes they lived in. They'd assume he was a wacko, on drugs, or a criminal who was being hunted by his own people. Best case, he'd end up parked in a station house for several hours, or longer, while they checked him out. When they didn't find anything, they'd push him out the door, making him an easy target for whoever was after him.

Educating the police about his background with the Legion unit was not an option. Caine was bound by various French secrecy statutes, and although those laws might not carry much weight in the United States, they meant something to him. He wasn't inclined to break his word to the Legion, or more importantly, to the other members of his unit. If the disclosures hit the press, and they would, every member of the unit would be placed at risk. Until he had more information, the police were not an option.

The bottom line was he had to deal with this on his own. That meant getting out of Snow Valley and down the mountain. The problem was the area was a natural trap: There was one road in and one road out, and his transportation options were limited. There were no car rental places in the town, and although the county probably ran a bus up and down from the City of San Bernardino once a day, that was a real risky option. It was too obvious and too slow. If the other side was even halfway organized, they'd have the bus stop staked out hours before it arrived.

As he considered and rejected each option, Caine remembered something that might offer a way out. There was an old gas station about a quarter of a mile to the south of the cottage. The owner stored five or six old cars behind the station. If any of the cars ran, Caine might be able to rent or buy one from the station owner. The opposition wouldn't be expecting that.

Caine looked at his watch again. It was unlikely the station would open before 7:30 a.m. He set his watch alarm for 7:00 a.m. and closed his eyes, hoping for an hour of desperately needed sleep.

The alarm on Caine's watch woke him at 7:00 a.m. For a second, he was disoriented, but then he remembered where he was and why he was there. He turned off the alarm and walked to the bathroom. After splashing water on his face and running a comb through his hair, Caine started to look for a coat.

Caine found a closet in the hallway adjoining the kitchen, but the only coat hanging in the closet was an old brown windbreaker. It wasn't much, but anything would be an improvement over the sweater. Caine glanced at the shelf in the closet and saw nothing of interest, but then he spotted a worn black Stetson on the floor. He picked up the hat and worked it back into shape. Anything that changed his appearance was an asset.

After wiping down the surfaces in the cabin that he might have touched, Caine moved to the kitchen and looked out the window overlooking the backyard for several minutes. When he didn't see any movement, he slipped out the back door and jogged to the stand of trees bordering the next street. It was empty. Caine walked along the side of the street in the direction of the town, moving at an unhurried pace. It was cold, but the jacket kept in more heat than the sweater, making it bearable, and he knew the temperature would rise by mid-morning.

As he drew closer to the main street, Route 18, the housing became denser, and there was some early morning activity. A car pulled out from a driveway; a woman jogged past him in sweats, wearing earphones; and a man came out of a house, talking on a cell phone. The phone reminded Caine of something that Steinman had said in his message—*the attorney in Texas, Andrea Marenna.*

Caine checked his watch. It was 7:40 a.m., which made it two hours later in Texas. It might be a little early for a Sunday morning, but Caine didn't have time to be polite. He dialed the number he'd stored on his cell phone after listening to Steinman's message. The phone rang four times, and a woman's voice with a mild Texas accent answered. It was a recording. Caine pressed the pound sign to cut off the greeting and left a short message.

"Ms. Marenna, my name is John Caine. I'm a friend of Richard Steinman. He asked me to give you a call. Can you please call me back? It's somewhat urgent." Caine left his cell number and hung up.

## San Bernardino County, California
### December 5, 1999 / Sunday / 7:00 a.m.

The five men sitting around the table in the rear of the Snow Valley Café were nursing their steaming coffee mugs in silence. They'd already ordered breakfast from the middle-aged waitress. When she returned with their order, Severino waited until she had put down the plates before he spoke to her.

"Excuse me, my car died and we need to get to a meeting in San Bernardino today. Is there a bus station, or better still a car rental place in town?"

The waitress was refilling the five coffee cups on the table and she answered without looking up from her task.

"There's no bus station, but a bus does stop at the strip center two lights down in front of the Texaco station. It comes at 11:00 a.m. every day. Now as for rental cars, I think you folks would have to go to Big Bear City for that. It's up the road about five. But I couldn't tell you who rents, and I can't imagine anyone will be there at this time in the morning. Your best bet is probably the bus, honey."

Severino didn't need transport. It was already on the way. He wanted to find out what was available to the target, John Caine. He waited until the waitress had walked back to the counter. Then he spoke to the group.

"Center has been monitoring the local police bands. There hasn't been a peep about this fucking nightmare. That means our boy hasn't contacted the cops. My guess is the guy is either hiding out, or he's going to try to find a way off the mountain on his own. If he tries to escape, that works for us. There's only one road out and the lady says transport is real limited."

"Whoa," Cochrane said. "Something doesn't make sense here. Why wouldn't the guy just drop a dime to the cops and get a free ride down the hill?"

Severino had been thinking about that ever since Center called him on the way into town.

"I figure it only one way. The guy's dirty, so he wants to stay away from the police as much as we do. Bottom line, it doesn't matter. Whoever he is, we need to get him," Severino said.

Cochrane just nodded.

"Our transport should be here in five, so eat quick. Anders, you and Juan take one truck. Drive north about a mile, maybe a mile and a half. Cochrane and Miguel, you're with me. We'll cover the south side in the other truck. If you see anything, contact me. Don't take any action. Clear?"

Severino looked around at the four other men. Cochrane, Juan, and Miguel nodded. Anders, who was shoveling eggs into his mouth, didn't answer.

"I'll take that as a yes, Anders," Severino said.

# CHAPTER
# SIXTEEN

*Austin, Texas*
*December 5, 1999 / Sunday / 9:40 a.m.*

The musical tones of the phone slowly drew Andrea Marenna out of a fitful sleep. She rolled onto her back and wondered how she could still feel this tired after a full night's sleep. She fumbled for the phone on the nightstand beside her bed and knocked the receiver to the floor. She groaned in frustration, threw off the covers, and walked over to where the phone had fallen between the wall and the nightstand.

The message program had picked up by the time Andrea reached the phone, and she was too tired to remember the override code. When the call ended, she pulled up the number on the incoming call menu. She didn't recognize the number or even the area code, which was surprising. Her number was unlisted and she only gave it out to a few friends and to work. She pressed the code and listened to the message.

"Ms. Marenna, my name is John Caine. I'm a friend of Richard Steinman. He asked me to give you a call. Can you please call me back? It's somewhat urgent."

Andrea didn't recognize the caller. She dropped the phone on the bed and walked into the bathroom. *Richie Steinman! I didn't call him back yesterday.* As she reached for a towel, Andrea noticed that her jewelry box was neatly pushed up against the mirror beside her hair brush. She stared at the box for a minute, confused. She remembered taking off her earrings and putting them in the box yesterday afternoon before she went out for a run. *I know I left that open.*

The box was also in the wrong place. She never pushed her makeup and jewelry boxes against the mirror. The counter was wide and she knew from experience that leaning over it in the morning left water stains on her clothes. She reached over and pulled the box back to the center of the counter, shaking her head. *I must be losing my mind.*

When she came out of the bathroom, Andrea sat on the rumpled bed and pressed the redial button. The phone rang twice before it was answered.

"Hello, Caine here."

"Hello, Mr. Caine, this is Andrea Marenna. I'm returning your call."

"Thanks for getting back to me. Richard Steinman asked me to call you."

"Is this about legal advice?"

"No. Steinman left me a voice mail. He asked me to call you, if I couldn't reach him."

"Richie works for the *Statesman*. I suggest you—"

"I did call them. They said Steinman died Friday night in a car accident. So you're—"

"Wait. Did you say that Richie was dead?"

"Yes, that's what they said. I'm sorry to upset you. Unfortunately, I'm in a somewhat difficult situation here, and I believe it has something to do with Mr. Steinman. Do you have any idea why he would have referred me to you?"

Andrea was stunned by the news of Richie's death. How could it have happened?

Suddenly she realized that the man on the phone, John Caine, was asking her something.

"Ms. Marenna, I've never spoken to Mr. Steinman before. Do you have any idea why he would be calling me?"

"No, I'm sorry, I don't."

"Do you have any idea why he referred me to you?"

"No. Well, we're friends, but no, I don't know."

"Is it possible . . . could Mr. Steinman have stumbled into something that got him killed?"

It took Andrea a second to process what Caine was asking. *Kill Richie? What is he talking about? This is crazy.* When she answered the question, Andrea knew she was overreacting, but she couldn't help herself.

"Mr. Caine, Richie was a great guy and no, nobody would want to kill him. The idea is ridiculous. Now, if you don't mind, I have to go."

*San Bernardino County, California*
*December 5, 1999 / Sunday / 8:00 a.m.*

Caine made a wry face when he heard the dial tone and put the phone back in his jacket pocket. He looked up and down the main street from his concealed location on the side street. Tourism was Snow Valley's biggest industry. The main drag had the usual collection of small retail outlets and restaurants. Jake's Mobil station was at the very end of town, directly across the street from where Caine was standing. Jake's was an old-fashioned "service" station, with two large repair bays and the obligatory row of old cars and trucks parked out back. There was no sign of activity at the station, but a new black pickup truck was parked out front. If Caine was lucky, Jake was an early riser with a new black pickup.

Caine had to leave his limited cover and walk across the main street in plain view to get to the gas station. He'd considered scouting the surrounding area before he crossed the street, but rejected the idea. If the opposition was already looking for him in the town, they would see him cross the street one way or another.

Most of the original gas stations in the area were now owned and operated by large chains that offered self-serve gas, cigarettes, candy, and drinks. Basic repair work was not part of the mix. Jake's was a holdout. The gas pumps were there, but repair work was the main event, and by the look of the cars parked around the station, Jake's target market was late-model used cars and trucks.

The building itself was a fifties-era structure. It had the standard two repair bays and a small attached annex that served as an office. As Caine walked by the closed repair bays on the way to the office, he glanced in the garage windows. The cars in the bay had seen better days. Stacks of tires were piled against the walls, and rows of shelves were loaded with new and used parts. The floor was a patchwork of oil stains.

In spite of the circumstances, Caine smiled to himself. When he was seventeen years old, he'd spent weekends, summers, and holidays working at a garage not unlike this one. He'd started out washing parts and doing cleanup work, but had quickly graduated to oil changes and then to tune-ups. By the time he joined the army, there was nothing under the hood he couldn't fix. He remembered one of his high school girlfriends accusing him of being "a damn motor head," when he told her that he had to skip their Saturday night date to replace the carburetor on his car.

The door to the office was partially open. Caine knocked lightly, pushed the door open, and walked into a small waiting room. A yellow vinyl couch and a Formica table occupied one side of the room, and a rack of motor oil cans occupied the other. The top half of the Dutch door at the other end of the room was open, allowing Caine to see into the back office area.

He walked up to the door and looked into the next room. An old desk and several filing cabinets, with stacks of papers on top, filled up most of the narrow room. The walls were decorated with yellowed NASCAR posters. In the midst of this clutter, a man in a worn green mechanic's uniform was leaning back in a wooden swivel chair, reading the newspaper. A steaming cup of coffee was parked on the edge of the old desk.

Caine knocked on the wall and said, "Good morning." The paper lowered several inches, revealing a full head of white hair and pair of blue eyes.

"I know I'm a little early, but I'm in a bit of fix," Caine said, with a wry grin.

The blue eyes just looked at him for a second longer and then the paper lowered another six inches, revealing a pleasantly lined and worn face, with a white mustache.

"How can I help you?" the man said in a voice that wasn't quite friendly, but wasn't unfriendly either. Caine had thought about his response to this question before he entered the garage. He had two choices: He could tell the truth about the last eight hours, or he could lie. Caine lied.

"Well, this is somewhat embarrassing, but the short version is my girlfriend and I had . . . a disagreement this morning, and she took off with my car. That's bad, but it gets worse. I need to catch a flight out of John Wayne Airport at 11:30 a.m., and it's not something I can miss. Unfortunately, the car rental place in Big Bear doesn't have anything available, and the bus down to San Bernardino doesn't show up for another couple of hours. That's too late, I'll miss my flight."

The old man lowered the paper and shook his head regretfully. "I'd like to help you out, but we fix cars here. We don't rent them."

Caine nodded his head. "I guessed that was probably the case. On the other hand, you've got a whole parking lot of old clunkers in the back. As long as one of those cars will run long enough to get me down the hill, I'd be willing to buy one for a reasonable price."

The old man considered this option for a good twenty seconds, and then he smiled, "Hell, boy, those cars out back aren't old clunkers. Those are bona fide classics."

# CHAPTER
# SEVENTEEN

After hanging up the phone, Andrea walked into the kitchen and made a cup of coffee. She tried not to think about the call until she had her first couple of sips. Maybe this guy Caine was just a nut, or maybe he had the wrong guy and Richie was perfectly fine. She had to know. She picked up the phone again, dialed information, and asked for the *Statesman*.

"*Austin American-Statesman.*"

"Richard Steinman, please."

"May I ask who's calling?"

"Yes, Andrea Marenna. I'm a friend of Mr. Steinman."

"One minute, please."

There was a short delay, and then another voice came on the line.

"Hello, this is Stan Mitchell. Ms. Marenna, what is your relationship to Mr. Steinman?"

"I'm a friend. Is there a problem?"

There was brief hesitation. "Ms. Marenna, Mr. Steinman was in an automobile accident Friday night. He was pronounced dead at the scene. We were only recently able to contact his family, and I was concerned that you might be a family member who had not yet received word."

Although Andrea had braced herself for this, the confirmation of Richie's death shocked her. "I understand. Thank you."

She started to hang up, but then she remembered something that the caller, John Caine, had said.

"Wait, can you tell what happened?"

"Our information is that the accident occurred at about 9:00 p.m. Friday night, and that Mr. Steinman was killed instantly. The police are still investigating the incident."

"The police? Does that mean that it wasn't an accident? Who was driving the other car?"

"I don't know. The police are still investigating. Mr. Steinman's car apparently rolled over, and he was killed."

# CHAPTER
# EIGHTEEN

*San Bernardino County, California*
*December 5, 1999 / Sunday / 9:00 a.m.*

Caine looked over his new "classic" car, a 1968 Pontiac GTO. This trophy had cost him $1,200, which was about $900 too much. The lower body of the car had gaping rust holes and the maroon leather in the rear seat looked as if it had been in an extended cat fight. Although the GTO's big engine started up without a problem, it ran rough, and the roar from under the car suggested there wasn't much left of the muffler. Still, Caine couldn't help smiling when he looked at the old machine. It brought back a lot of memories.

The '68 Pontiac GTO, or "Goat" to the muscle car crowd, had been a hot car in its day, with its muscular styling, big eight-cylinder engine, and explosive performance. If he'd been sixteen, and about to take a spin through downtown Waco in his three-year-old GTO, life would have been good, but he wasn't sixteen, and he wasn't taking a joyride. He was forty-four, and he was attempting to escape a team of killers in a thirty-year-old car that looked and sounded like it wouldn't get him more than five miles. Jake smiled as he looked over at him from the front of the open repair bay and said, "Don't worry, she'll get you there."

Caine waved to the old man, climbed into the car, and turned the ignition key. He was impressed when the big eight-cylinder roared to life on the first turn. After letting the car idle for several minutes, he slowly pressed the gas pedal down and eased the clutch into first gear. Despite his care, the engine gave off a muted roar that would have been more at home at the Indy 500. The engine noise bothered Caine more than anything else about the car. The sound was loud enough to draw a look from both the good guys, as in the local cops, and the bad guys.

The danger zone was the next five-mile stretch. Although Jake had let him keep the old license plates, the vehicle wasn't registered. If the cops were feeling energetic this morning, they might pull him over on the basis of the car's condition, and demand his license and registration. If that happened, his little escape plan was out the window.

Even if he avoided the police, things would get real exciting if his pursuers spotted him during the next couple of miles. Once he hit Route 330, the winding road that led down the mountain, his odds would improve. There was no room to set up an ambush, and the endless switchbacks would make it difficult for them to take him from behind.

The cell phone in the windbreaker rang as he pulled onto Route 18, but Caine ignored it. He needed to keep his mind on the road. He tried to minimize the engine noise from the GTO by staying light on the gas pedal as he eased the car into the still sparse, but growing, morning traffic. Although his effort muted the engine's throaty growl, the sound was still loud enough to be an attention magnet.

About a mile and a half from the station, Caine passed a side street on his right, and saw a dark-colored SUV parked by the side of the road. He thought he saw two men in the front seat, but the reflection of the morning sun off the GTO's dirty windshield prevented him from confirming the sighting without drawing attention. When he turned his eyes back to the road ahead, a group of teenagers in a car coming in the opposite direction cut in front of the Honda immediately ahead of him, in order to get to a McDonald's on the opposite side of the road. The driver of the Honda overreacted, jamming on his brakes.

Caine hit the GTO's brakes to avoid hitting the Honda in the rear, but the response was sluggish. There was no way the GTO was going to stop in time. Caine glanced to the left and saw an opening in the oncoming traffic flow. He swerved across the center line, just missing the rear of the Honda, downshifted into second gear, and hit the gas. The GTO shot past the Honda and Caine pulled back over to the right. The GTO's acceleration surprised Caine. Unfortunately, the roar from the engine had been equally impressive.

Caine slowed to a more sedate pace and moved to the right lane, but when he glanced in the mirror, it looked like the damage was already done. The black SUV from the side street he'd passed a block earlier was pulling into the flow of traffic behind him.

Caine avoided staring into the rearview mirror, but he monitored the SUV as he drove along with the flow of traffic. A male Hispanic in the front passenger seat made a call on a cell phone, never taking his eyes off the GTO. Caine's adrenaline level started to climb. The men in the SUV might just be on their way to the ski slopes, but Caine somehow knew that wasn't the case. If his suspicions were right, the passenger in the SUV had just called ahead to alert another car further down the road to his approach.

Caine knew he had to prevent the two cars from forcing him into a box. Once his mobility was limited, they could take him out with a well-placed shot. In a worst-case scenario, they could force a crash and take him out in a firefight. It would be messy, but after last night's failed assault, Caine had an idea that these folks wouldn't have a problem with that.

Caine knew the roads in the area, but he'd still taken another look at the map before he left the gas station. There was only one road down the mountain within the next ten miles. That was Route 330. The road he was traveling on, State Route 18, was the only road that intersected Route 330 from this direction. That didn't leave him with a lot of options, but there might be one that would give a better chance of escape. A smaller access road ran parallel to Route 18 for about four miles and then merged back into the main road, just before the intersection with Route 330.

Caine looked to the right and could see the access road in the distance. The next side street was two hundred yards ahead. It ran all the way out to the other road. If he timed it right and the GTO held together, he might be able to escape the box and beat the lead car to Route 330.

Caine started to accelerate, but slowed when a second SUV pulled out of a parking lot and cut in front of the Toyota Camry two cars ahead. Instead of speeding up to stay with the flow of traffic, the SUV began to slow down. The frustrated driver of the Toyota passed the SUV on the left. The SUV in front of him was now separated from Caine by a red pickup truck. There were three men in the SUV ahead of him. It had to be the lead car. The game had begun.

Caine glanced in the rearview mirror. The rear SUV was now directly behind him. The side street was now about eighty yards distant. The driver of the SUV in front moved to the extreme left side of the lane and turned his left blinker on, as if he intended to execute a left turn across the opposite traffic lane. The Chevy pickup truck took advantage of the opening and moved to pass on the inside right. The move gave Caine three choices. He could try to shoot through the gap after the pickup. He could allow himself to be boxed in and hope that his pursuers didn't take any action before he reached the side street. Or he could try to pass the lead SUV on the left, assuming he could find an opening in the oncoming traffic flow, and then cut back over in time to turn down the side street, on his right.

Caine weighed the options and reached a decision. If he tried to pass on the right, the bigger vehicle would have no problem forcing him into the curb. Once he was stationary, they could put two bullets in his head and drive away. Caine didn't like the second option any better. Whoever was in the SUV would know the side street represented an escape route. There was a good chance they'd make their move before he reached it. His best option was to feint to the right and then try to make the pass on the left, but to do that he needed to find a break in the oncoming traffic flow.

Caine looked down the road to the left as he began to feint to the right and follow the pickup truck that was moving to pass the lead

SUV on the inside. Ahead he saw a forty-yard gap in the opposite traffic flow. Unwilling to wait for another chance, Caine punched the accelerator and raced toward the gap to the right of the lead SUV. Both SUV drivers reacted as he anticipated. The driver of the lead SUV gunned his engine and turned sharply to the right in order to cut off the gap. The driver of the rear vehicle punched the accelerator and raced after Caine.

Caine shot for the gap on the right just long enough to make sure that the two big SUVs committed themselves, and then he made his move. He popped the clutch, downshifted into second gear, and jammed the gas pedal to the floor. Simultaneously he whipped the steering wheel to the left into the oncoming flow of traffic. The GTO left two strips of black rubber and a pall of blue smoke in the road as it roared over the center line and rocketed by the lead SUV on the left. The driver of the lead SUV tried to swerve back to the left, but the move was too late. Caine was already past the lead car, and the move almost wiped out the second SUV that was right on his tail. Both drivers saw the danger at the same instant and slammed on their brakes, giving Caine an additional lead. When Caine looked in the mirror, the driver of the lead SUV was frantically waving the trailing car ahead.

Caine held the car in second gear as long as possible to get the maximum acceleration from the old machine. The GTO raced past the red pickup truck and cut across its path, making a hard right down the side street. The GTO crossed in front of the pickup so fast that the car was down the side street before the other driver hit the brakes and blew his horn.

The black SUV on Caine's tail tried to repeat Caine's maneuver. Although the SUV made it past the red pickup truck, at the last second the driver realized that he was going way too fast to make the turn. He skidded past the entrance to the street into an empty parking lot. Once he had the vehicle under control, the driver did a U-turn and raced back to the side street. The SUV bounced over the curb, fishtailed, and then roared down the road after the GTO. The trailing SUV continued to race down Route 18.

Caine could see the alternate road in the distance and kept the accelerator buried to get the most out of the straightaway. The SUV in the rear was about two hundred yards back. Based on the GTO's performance, Caine believed the car could easily beat the two big SUVs in an acceleration contest. A top speed contest would be a different matter. The GTO had more power, but the front wheels were so far out of alignment that the vibration from the wheels would pound the car to pieces at high speed.

As he approached the intersection with the access road, Caine downshifted and tapped the brakes in anticipation of the turn. The wheels howled in protest and Caine had to use up the entire road to make the turn. As soon as the car straightened out, Caine punched the accelerator, and the old machine raced down the road.

Caine glanced to his rear as the speedometer ratcheted to the right. Only one of the SUVs was on his trail. The other car was almost certainly trying to beat him to the point where the road merged back into Route 18. Caine did not intend to let that happen. He reached over and pulled the Sig Sauer out of the black backpack that was sitting on the front passenger seat, flipped off the safety, and chambered a round. Then he laid it on the seat. The standard magazine for a P226 held ten nine-millimeter rounds. Caine's gun was a special law enforcement model that held fifteen rounds.

The access road reconnected with Route 18 about three miles ahead. Caine was hoping that the morning traffic on Route 18 would slow the lead SUV's progress enough to give him the edge in the race. With a little luck, he would intersect the road well ahead of the second SUV and still have a decent lead on the car in his rear. That would get him to the relative safety of Route 330.

Caine glanced at the speedometer. The GTO was closing in on 115 miles per hour. He could see the convergence of the two roads in the distance. Caine looked in the rear mirror. The SUV in the rear was visibly gaining on him. This was going to be tight. Caine looked over to the left in order to get a fix on the location of the second SUV coming down on Route 18. For a second, the forest line between the two roads was too dense for him to see anything, but then it started to thin out and he saw the other chase car. The second SUV was parallel to his position on the interstate and there was only one car in front of it. After that, the road was clear all the way to the intersection point.

Caine took the only course open to him and pushed the gas pedal down even further. The speedometer needle climbed to 125 miles per hour. As he suspected, the GTO's wheels couldn't take the higher speed. The front-end started to vibrate like a machine gun. The pounding shattered the glass pane covering the speedometer and popped the glove compartment door open. Caine looked over at the SUV on Route 18. The driver was racing past the car in front of him in order to beat Caine to the point where the roads merged. Caine had a slight lead on the SUV, but the other vehicle had a shorter distance to cover and more speed. It would be close, but the GTO would arrive in second place.

The SUV behind him was now within forty yards. The SUV racing parallel to him on Route 18 was about the same distance away. Caine decided that he'd played the passive quarry long enough. He reached over with his left hand, grabbed the P226, and extended his arm out the window. He fired five rounds at the SUV across from him on Route 18. Then he pulled the wheel sharply to the right, giving him a clear view of the SUV to the rear, and fired six rounds at the front of the vehicle, leaving four rounds remaining in the magazine.

# CHAPTER
# NINETEEN

San Bernardino County, California
December 5, 1999 / Sunday / 9:30 a.m.

Cochrane had been working his way past the line of cars in front of him to the open space he could see on the road up ahead. Some of the drivers in front had pulled over to the right when he'd all but climbed up on their rear bumper, but others had just ignored him, forcing him to dodge into the opposite lane to pass them. Now he had a problem. The SUV was behind a tractor trailer truck, and a series of curves in the road was making it difficult to find a clear space to pass the truck. The truck driver wasn't making his job any easier. He seemed to be intentionally riding the edge of the centerline in order to thwart Cochrane's effort to pass. Severino's rage was reaching the point of explosion.

Cochrane swerved out once again in an effort to pass the truck, but was forced back into his lane by the oncoming traffic.

"Get that fucking piece of shit out of the way, or I'm going to blow your goddamn trucker ass away," Severino growled in frustration.

As soon as they passed through the curve, Cochrane went back to riding the centerline, trying to catch the next piece of clear road.

"Bingo! We have daylight after the next car," Cochrane crowed as they passed through a curve in the road. Cochrane waited impatiently for the car at the front end of the gap to pass him, but the car slowed as it approached, making a run around the truck in front more risky with each passing second. The instant the approaching car passed the SUV, Cochrane jammed the gas pedal to the floor and swerved into the opposite lane. The SUV hurtled toward another oncoming car. Cochrane cut sharply in front of the tractor trailer, fifty feet ahead of the approaching car. The driver of the tractor trailer blew his air horn in anger.

Now that the road ahead was finally clear, Cochrane was determined to make up lost time. He pushed the SUV's speed to 120 miles per hour. Cochrane saw the sign warning of an approaching curve and he backed off on his speed, but he still came into the curve too fast. Cochrane pulled his foot off the accelerator when he realized his mistake, but the big SUV continued to wallow across the road. It crossed the centerline and slid inexorably toward the guardrail on the left side of the road. Cochrane could hear Miguel praying in Spanish in the rear seat.

The SUV was less than five feet from the guardrail when the curve eased and then straightened out. If another car had been coming in the opposite direction, they would have suffered a head-on collision, but the road was clear for another fifty yards. Cochrane let out the breath that he had been holding and pulled the car back into the right lane.

Severino hadn't slept in the last thirty hours. During that time frame, he'd been forced to plan a mission that was outside his pay grade, his chopper had been shot out of the air by a supposedly vanilla target, and now he was in a high-speed chase. Cochrane's near fatal miscalculation pushed him over the edge. He seized the Uzi and jammed it into Cochrane's ribs.

"You stupid shit, you almost dumped us over the goddamn cliff! I should—"

Severino's tirade was interrupted by the cell phone on his belt. He ignored the first ring, but then he picked up the phone. The call would be from Paquin. He'd arrived at the local airport an hour ago and taken control of the operation.

"Severino."

"What's your road marker?" Paquin asked, in a clipped voice.

"It's . . . SB 158," Severino said.

There was a short hesitation.

"I just spoke to Anders. He's right behind the target. You should see him converging on your right," Paquin said.

Severino looked to the right, but his view was still blocked by a stand of trees. When they passed the trees, he could see the old car racing down the other road on a parallel path. Blue smoke was pouring out the car's tail pipe. Anders and Juan were about fifty yards behind the target, steadily closing the gap.

"Yeah, we got him," Severino said.

Cochrane had pulled up behind a white BMW. He looked over at the GTO roaring down the road to his right and then looked ahead. The two roads had to intersect less than a half mile ahead. Although the GTO had a slight lead, Cochrane knew he could eliminate the gap if he could get past the BMW. He floored the accelerator, and pulled into the opposite lane, passing the BMW. Severino, still shaken by the near-crash, glanced over at the speedometer. They were doing about ninety miles an hour and the speedometer was rapidly climbing.

"Get it done," Paquin said and ended the call.

Severino glanced back and forth between the two cars and the rapidly approaching intersection point. The SUV was continuing to accelerate. They were closing the gap. Severino checked the magazine in the mini Uzi. Once they pulled in front of the target, he was going to empty the entire twenty-five-round magazine into the GTO's windshield. At this speed, the target would lose control and almost certainly be killed in the resulting crash. Severino hated the target for making him work this hard. A high-speed wipeout worked for him.

The gap between the two roads had narrowed to the point where Severino could see the face of the figure in the other car. As he watched, the driver's side window on the old Pontiac opened, and a man looked directly across at him. There was no fear in that face, just cold deter-mination. A fraction of a second later, the driver's left hand extended out the window in one smooth motion. There was a black automatic in his hand. Severino heard the distant reports from the gun and then the window behind him exploded.

"Fuck! Get down!" Severino choked out, as he dropped his head below the window line. His own window exploded a second later, letting in a blast of cold air and the roar of the engine. Cochrane reacted to the exploding glass and Severino's scream by pulling the wheel to the left. The blast of the horn from an oncoming car caused him to overreact, and he yanked the wheel hard to the right, causing the SUV's left rear tire to come off the ground. In a desperate effort to regain control, Cochrane took his foot completely off the gas.

After recovering from the shock, Severino cautiously lifted his head enough to glance across at the target. The other car was just reaching the intersection point ahead of them. In a rage, Severino whipped the Uzi out the window, intending to empty the entire magazine into the rear of the other car, but Cochrane's yell stopped him.

"Stop! You're gonna hit Anders!"

Severino froze, realizing Cochrane was right. The other SUV had just pulled onto Route 18. It was racing after the GTO. Severino noted with satisfaction that Anders was blasting away at the target with his own Uzi from the passenger-side window. Anders's ability to do any damage was cut off when the GTO roared down the turnoff for Route 330 on the right.

Juan, the Nicaraguan who was driving Anders's SUV, raced into the turn after the GTO, making the same mistake that Cochrane had made minutes earlier. He failed to realize that the GTO, despite its age, could carry more speed through the curve than the big Suburban. Anders, a former truck driver, saw the mistake as soon as he leaned back into the SUV to reload.

"Whoa, whoa, whoa!" he yelled as the SUV raced into the curve, slamming his hands against the dash for emphasis. Juan reacted by taking his foot off the gas and pumping the brake pedal. Since the SUV had already started into the curve, Juan's action exacerbated the leftward rolling action. Anders, feeling the SUV going into a terminal roll, yelled, "No fucking brake!"

Then he grabbed the wheel and pushed it to the left, away from the inside of the curve.

Anders's move stopped the roll, but it put the SUV across the centerline into the path of an oncoming tow truck. Realizing that if he yanked the wheel back to the right, the SUV would roll for sure, Anders steered for the breakdown lane on the opposite side of the road. The driver of the tow truck in the opposite lane was so surprised by the move that he failed to react by steering to the right at the same time, avoiding a head-on collision. By the time the other driver did react, the SUV was already out of his way, but it wasn't out of danger.

The SUV slid into the guardrail on the far left. On the other side of the rail, the slope dropped seven hundred feet to the next plateau. The county had reinforced the guardrails in the past five years after several fatal crashes had occurred on this stretch of road. But for this, the SUV would have blown through the barrier and plummeted down the slope. The left side of the big vehicle scraped along the edge of the barrier for thirty yards until Anders pulled the wheel slowly back to the right. Then he growled "Brake now" to the terrified Nicaraguan.

When the SUV came to a dead stop, Anders and Juan looked over the guardrail at the sheer drop down the side of the mountain.

Cochrane slowed as he passed the other SUV, which was now on the wrong side of the road. Anders was climbing out of the front passenger-side door. He waved Cochrane on in disgust. As Cochrane passed the second SUV, he saw Juan get out of the driver's side and start to walk around the rear of the SUV. Cochrane smiled to himself. Anders wasn't going to risk another cliffhanger like that one. He would be doing the driving from now on, even if that prevented him from blasting away at the target.

Cochrane hit the gas again as soon as the SUV came out of the hairpin turn, but the GTO had already disappeared around the next turn. Although Cochrane had never been down this road before, he knew from the map that it made a series of hairpin turns over the next five miles, as it traveled down the mountain. As a hardcore car enthusiast, he knew the GTO would steadily pull away from them over this stretch, unless the driver made a mistake, and from what he'd seen so far that wasn't likely. Cochrane thought about telling Severino that catching the GTO was a lost cause, but one look at his face convinced him to let the matter ride. He'd figure it out soon enough.

As the SUV started into the next curve, Severino's cell phone rang again.

"We're about four miles out of Snow Valley. We're still after the target, but—"

"I need the next road marker." There was a sharp urgency in Paquin's voice.

Severino looked out the window at the road marker they were passing.

"We just passed marker 163."

"Hold on," Paquin said. He came back on the line five seconds later.

"You will turn left on the dirt road that should be coming up within a quarter of a mile. The road is between markers 164 and 165. This will take you back to Route 18. You will take Route 18 south."

"Wait. That will take us away from the target. We can still get this bastard."

Paquin cut off Severino's argument, his voice hard and impatient. "You have your instructions. Follow them. Your current route is no longer viable."

Paquin's message cut through Severino's frustration. Paquin's communication people were monitoring the police channel. The local police must be waiting for them down the road.

### San Bernardino County, California
### December 5, 1999 / Sunday / 9:45 a.m.

Caine looked in the mirror again. This was the third switchback he had passed through without seeing either of the SUVs in the mirror. Although he continued to work the road, holding on to as much speed as possible through the turns and accelerating on the straightaways, he eased up a little. Unless the old car gave out on him, he was safe for the moment.

When he came around the next corner, his adrenaline level shot back up again. A California Highway Patrol car was parked in a turnout on the other side of the road, and the officer was placing a series of orange cones in the road. *He's setting up a road block. Someone must have called in the chase on Route 18.* The Snow Valley police were probably setting up the other end of the roadblock up on Route 18. Although Caine had been pushing the GTO, he was just coming out of a curve when he saw the CHP officer, and his speed was within the limit. Caine gave the officer a friendly wave as he passed and continued on his way.

Caine looked in the mirror as he was disappearing around the next curve. The CHP officer had pulled his car across one lane of the road. Caine increased his speed once he was out of sight, but not to a level that would draw attention. Although it was possible that another team was racing to cut him off at the bottom of the mountain, he considered it unlikely. He was more worried about getting pulled over by the police.

Caine took the first major road south when he reached the bottom of the mountain, and then took as many turns as possible for the next ten minutes, heading generally westward. He continually checked the mirror, but there was no pursuit. When he reached the city of Riverside, he pulled into a crowded shopping center and parked the GTO in between a minivan and a pickup. After waiting another five minutes and scanning the lot for possible signs of pursuit, Caine felt satisfied that he'd escaped the trap.

As he leaned back in the seat and tried to relax, Caine realized he was thirsty and hungry. He hadn't eaten anything in the last ten hours. He looked around the shopping center and saw a Rite Aid pharmacy. When he opened the car door to get out, he noticed his cell phone on the floor of the car. The message light was blinking.

After buying two bottles of water and a couple of energy bars, Caine sat down at one of the tables outside the store and drank half a bottle of water as he pulled up the message menu on his cell phone.

The number on the screen had an Austin area code. It was the attorney in Texas, Andrea Marenna. She had called him back.

Caine made a call to a neighbor down the road from his cabin, who was a friend, and asked her to pick up Sam and take care of him for a couple of days. Then he called Andrea Marenna back. She picked up the phone on the first ring, a good sign.

# CHAPTER
# TWENTY

Andrea tried to read the morning newspaper and relax with a second cup of coffee after leaving the message on John Caine's cell phone, but it didn't work. After ten minutes, she put down the paper and stood up. *Why doesn't he return the call?* Andrea decided to take a shower and get dressed. She brought the phone into the bathroom.

After showering and putting on a pair of jeans and a pullover sweater, Andrea turned on the morning news. She could only catch one or two words from the talking heads over the noise of the hair dryer, but she could tell by the pictures that nothing earthshaking had happened in the last twelve hours. The phone rang just as she turned off the hair dryer.

"Hello."

"Hello yourself."

"Oh, hi, Mary."

"What am I, a second-class citizen now?"

"I'm sorry. I just was expecting someone else. It's kind of . . . "

"Complicated? Sounds like another work-related problem, Marenna. I just wanted to let you know there's a 5K run along the Town Lake Loop next Saturday. Tom Engel will be there."

"Mary, I'd love to get there, but I'm attending a seminar."

"As in a work-related seminar."

"Mary—"

"Remember what I told you?"

"Change your life, or it will change you. I got it, coach."

"Good. I'm going to be checking up on you, girl. Oh, one other thing. Next week I'm out of town. So you'll have to run on your own Wednesday."

"Okay. And thanks, Mary."

"See you later."

Andrea and Mary had gone to high school together, and they'd both run middle distance races for the track team. Mary had gone on to run for SMU. After college, she'd started a sports rehabilitation clinic with an orthopedic surgeon, who later became her husband. They had two great kids.

Six months ago, Mary had decided that she needed to get her wayward friend on the right track. Mary's mantra was simple: Change your priorities. Spend more time on Andrea and less time at work. Andrea liked the advice; it was the implementation that was proving difficult.

Mary had also decided to try to "fix" Andrea's social life. Her less-than-subtle attempt to persuade Andrea to give Tom Engel a second chance was not going to work. Tom was a vascular surgeon who played tennis with her husband. He was a nice guy, but Andrea knew they had no future together after their first date. The good doctor had spent the first five minutes of their dinner date grilling the waiter about the ingredients in each dish and another five on the cooking methods. The phone interrupted the unpleasant memory.

"Hello, this is Andrea."

"Hello, Ms. Marenna, this is John Caine. I want to apologize for earlier today."

"I'm the one who owes the apology."

"No apology necessary, Ms. Marenna. I—"

"Please, call me Andrea. And I really am sorry, no excuses. With Richie's death and . . . other things, I guess I'm just a little out of sorts."

There was a hesitation on the phone.

"Mr. Caine—"

"John."

"John, I have to ask you this. Why did you ask me if . . . if someone would have any reason to harm Richie?"

"Let's just say that my life has changed since I received Mr. Steinman's message," Caine said.

"What are you talking about?" Andrea said.

"Last night some people broke into my cabin in Snow Valley, and this morning those same people were still looking for me."

"Why . . . what makes you think that has anything to do with Richie? Did you call—"

"Andrea, can you hold on a minute? I'll be right back."

"Sure."

Andrea walked over to a small window and idly stared out at the street three floors below. A man was walking down the sidewalk holding two cups of coffee. He was wearing a baseball cap, an oversized blue sweatshirt, and a pair of worn jeans. Andrea watched the man without interest, until he looked up. *I know you.* Andrea recognized the thick glasses and the odd sideburns that ran down the length of the man's jawline. She had passed him on the stairs yesterday when she was coming back from her run. He'd been wearing some kind of a uniform and carrying a tool case.

The man walked across the street toward a white van that was parked across the street from the building. A large V-shaped antenna was built into the roof. Before he reached the van, someone opened the rear door and waved to him. The man in the baseball cap handed one of the coffee cups to whoever was inside the van, looked up in the direction of Andrea's corner unit, and then climbed into the van. *Who is this guy?*

Caine came back on the line.

"I'm sorry. I had to move my car. Andrea?"

"Yes, yes, I'm here," Andrea said, in a distracted voice.

"Is everything okay?"

"It's nothing. I think you're starting to make me paranoid."

"Humor me."

Andrea didn't like the insistence in his voice, but she let it go. "It's no big deal. A man that I saw in the building yesterday just walked across the street and climbed into a van with a cup of coffee. Like I—"

"Does the man live in your building?"

"No. I think he was here to fix something."

"Andrea, do you have a cell phone?"

"Yes."

"Can you call me back using your cell? Do you have my number?"

"Yes, but why—"

"Please, just hang up and do it."

Andrea heard the dial tone and stared at the phone. For a moment, she wasn't going to call him back, but Richie's death made the difference. She walked over to the kitchen counter, picked up her cell, and dialed Caine's number.

"Hello, and thanks, Andrea."

"Mr. Caine, I just called back to say that I can't help you. I don't know anything—"

"Yes, you do, or at least someone thinks you do."

"What are you talking about?" Andrea said.

"If I'm right, there's a transmitter in your landline and that's a wire truck out front. That's why I asked you to call me on your cell. If they're already set up to pick up your cell transmission, it won't help, but if we're lucky, the transition may take them a little while."

"What? This is crazy. No one has done anything to my phone, and that van is just . . . a van."

"Andrea, staying on this line is not a good idea. I know you think I'm a nut, but think about this. Steinman's message said I could be in danger, and he was right. Those men who broke into my cabin last night were trying to kill me. Steinman died after he made that call, the day before. You need to get out of that place, *now.*"

"Why? Why would I do that? This has nothing to do with—"

"Andrea, if I'm right, the people in that truck outside are either cops of one kind or another, or they're very bad people. If you think they're the cops, then walk out and offer them a donut. If you don't think it's the cops, then you need to get out of there. So grab your car keys and walk out the back door. Go visit some friends and call me from their place."

For a second time, Andrea heard a dial tone.

### Big Bear City, California
### December 5, 1999 / Sunday / 1:30 p.m.

Paquin leaned back in the leather chair and looked out the window at the snow-covered mountains. The unmarked Gulfstream G200 was parked at the far edge of the Big Bear City Airport. Paquin had spent fifteen years hunting spies, criminals, and "subversives" for East Germany's feared secret police, the Ministerium für Staatssicherheit, commonly known as the STASI in the West. People in trouble tended to seek refuge in familiar places, with familiar people: family, friends, and coworkers. That common thread generally made finding them a matter of persistence, resources, and time. Paquin had all three at his disposal.

One part of his team was running Caine's name through a series of private information services that collected data for marketing purposes. Another, more select part of his team was working with rogue employees at the major credit card companies that sold information about cardholders under the table. If Caine had a credit card with one of these companies, they would know his location within hours, if he used the card.

A third group was pursuing a less high-tech route. They were contacting Caine's neighbors seeking information using various false pretenses ranging from the need to advise Mr. Caine of the imminent death of a sick relative, to an inquiry by a concerned employer about their missing employee. Paquin knew from experience that the system worked. If Mr. Caine followed the typical pattern, they should be able to find him within twenty-four hours.

The problem was that Caine had proven to be anything but typical. He didn't just escape from Severino's team. He'd planned and executed two almost lethal counterattacks. This suggested professional training, either as a soldier, or as part of a law enforcement agency. Although it was possible that Caine was some kind of neo-survivalist who'd educated and trained himself, Paquin discounted the possibility based on Severino's debrief.

Caine's failure to contact the police was another atypical factor that concerned Paquin. If Caine was avoiding the police because he had a criminal background, that would be a stroke of luck. Most criminals were undisciplined, followed habitual behavior patterns, and returned to familiar places. On the other hand, if Caine had avoided the police for another reason, the situation could be more difficult. He might be operating under a different set of rules, making it harder to predict his movements. The bottom line was Paquin needed more information to anticipate Caine's next move.

Paquin picked up his cell phone and dialed a number in Washington, D.C. A male voice with a southern accent answered the phone.

"Colonel James."

"Hello, Don, Dick Williams." There was a brief hesitation. Then Colonel Donald R. James, U.S. Army Intelligence, responded with feigned enthusiasm.

"Dick! Good to hear from you. It's been a while. How are Cathy and the kids?"

"Great, Don, it's good to hear your voice. Don, I hate to bother you on a weekend, but I need some information about an individual. His name is John Caine. He's in his early forties and lives in California. I think he may be ex-military, but I can't tell you what service he was with, or even if he was with an American outfit. So this is going to have to be a broad search. I need any information on this guy that you can find, and time is critical."

"A round of golf next week sounds great. Let me see if I can schedule a time at the club. I'll call you back in an hour, two at the most."

"Thanks, Don," Paquin said and ended the call.

Paquin's arrangement with Colonel James was simple. The colonel was paid five thousand dollars cash for each search of the military's extensive database. If the information was useful, the ante went up another two grand. Although the good colonel knew he was misusing a governmental resource, his conscience wasn't overly troubled. James had been advised that Paquin's employer, a large American multinational corporation, was using the requested information to assist the company in vetting employees, or getting a leg up on its foreign competition. What could be more American than that? The Commerce Department did that kind of thing full-time, on the taxpayer's nickel.

The colonel called back within the hour.

"Hello?"

"Dick? Don James. You were right. Your friend does have an army jacket. He joined up in 1974, served with a Ranger Regiment, and received an honorable discharge in the summer of 1979. He didn't see any action, but the file says he was a good soldier—hardworking, disciplined, and all that."

"Anything else?" Paquin asked.

"Not much."

"I see," Paquin said.

So Caine had been a good soldier twenty years ago, who'd never been in combat. That wasn't much help. It didn't explain the exotic flare, or why Caine had failed to contact the police. Paquin sensed from the silence on the other side of the line that James was not telling him something.

"Colonel, is there anything else in the file that you . . . as a professional soldier, might consider important?" Paquin hoped his appeal to the soldier's professional pride would induce James to disclose whatever he was withholding.

The colonel hesitated, and then spoke quietly. "There's nothing more in the jacket, but there are some interesting . . . codes at the bottom of the file. The codes are just a bunch of numbers, letters, and slashes, but over time I've figured out what they mean. Each code refers to a different agency. There are three sets of codes on this file. They refer to the DIA, NSA, and CIA."

"What does that mean?"

"Well, it could simply mean the file went to all three places and came back. Or the guy might have been vetted for an op that required special clearance. For all I know, he could be working for these folks. I just don't have access to that kind of info here."

Paquin could tell from James's tone that the links to the intelligence services made him nervous. He suspected that if he pushed the colonel to dig further, James would do nothing and report back that his efforts were unsuccessful. If he wanted any more information, he needed to pique the colonel's curiosity and then leave him alone for a while.

"Thanks, Don. That was very helpful. If you find anything else, we would really appreciate the information. The company is considering hiring this guy for a critical security detail, and we just want to make sure that we aren't making a mistake."

"I'll do that. Hey, you have a great weekend there."

"Thanks. You, too."

# CHAPTER
# TWENTY-ONE

*Austin, Texas*
*December 5, 1999 / Sunday / 1:00 p.m.*

A ndrea looked at the blank screen on the cell phone. She dropped the phone on the couch in frustration and walked over to the window. The van was still there. *I need to talk to someone about this, someone who knows about this kind of thing.* She picked up the cell phone and found Michael Bosmasian's name on the speed dial menu. She hesitated momentarily and then pressed the dial button.

"Hello, this is Mike."

"Mike, it's Andrea."

"Andrea. What a very pleasant surprise. What can I do for most stunning female lawyer in Austin?"

"Michael."

"I know, now we're just friends, but that doesn't mean I have to stop telling the truth."

"Mike."

"Okay, what can I do for *nicest* lawyer in Austin?"

"Better, but totally false."

"Now, Andrea, a Bosmasian never lies except to his own family."

Andrea could hear Michael's mother in the background yelling something at him in Armenian. She smiled in spite of the tension roiling her stomach. She remembered that Michael's mother came over on Sunday mornings and cooked him breakfast.

"Michael, I have kind of an odd situation that I want run by you. If you think I'm losing my mind, let me know."

"Love to, especially the last part."

Andrea summarized the two phone calls with John Caine and the call to the *Statesman*, and she gave him a description of the van parked in her lot. Michael listened without interrupting and then was quiet.

"Michael?"

"You're still working only civil cases, right? No criminal stuff?"

"That's right."

"And no flashy clients who might be walking on the edge?"

"None that I know of. We're a pretty conservative firm. General business lit and transactional work for local businesses."

"Well then, I wouldn't worry about it. What did you say this guy's name was?"

"John Caine."

Although Michael's response brought a wave of relief, when he asked for Caine's name she realized that he was holding something back.

"Mike, what is it you're not telling me?"

"It's nothing."

"Michael."

"Well, the guy was right about changing phones. If someone was—"

"So the van outside could be someone other than the cable or phone guy?"

"Look, Andrea, monitoring phone calls is a law enforcement tool, and we're both in agreement that there is no reason for either the police or the feds to take an interest in you. But just to make sure, I'll have someone from Austin P.D. stop by and take a look at the phones and check out the van."

"No, that's okay, Michael. I shouldn't have wasted your time."

"Andrea, relax, it's no big deal. I'll call over and see who's available and call you back with a time."

Andrea was about to agree, but then she reconsidered. If a uniformed cop paid her a visit, her neighbors would be knocking on the door within minutes wanting to know what happened. *What am I going to tell them—I thought someone bugged my phone? No way.*

"Thanks, Mike, but that won't work. I'm leaving for the next couple of days to get some rest. Maybe they can just check out the van."

Andrea could hear Michael's mother in the background telling him brunch was ready.

"Okay, the van it is. By the way, where are you going?"

"Just someplace local, for a change of scene."

"Do you want—"

"No, but thanks."

Andrea heard Michael's mother calling him again in the background.

"Good-bye, Mike."

"Take care, Andrea."

She felt foolish after he hung up. *What am I doing?*

# CHAPTER
# TWENTY-TWO

*San Bernardino County, California*
*December 5, 1999 / Sunday / 1:00 p.m.*

Caine sat in the parking lot listening to the local news on the car radio. The helicopter crash wasn't mentioned. That surprised him, but it was only a matter of time before the Huey was found. It was too big hide. The shootout on Route 18 wasn't mentioned either, but that was understandable. There were very few cars around when the actual shooting occurred, and all of the guns had been equipped with suppressors, except his P226. Although the P226 was loud, he'd fired his shots when GTO was still on the old access road and the only other cars in sight were the two SUVs.

Caine turned off the radio and mentally shifted gears. He had to put together some kind of plan. Whoever was after him obviously didn't intend to call off the manhunt until he was dead, which meant that they were out there trying to find him right now. If he wanted to stay alive, he had stay outside their net, until he figured out who was after him.

Although Caine knew how to play the part of a fugitive, he also knew it would make his life a lot more difficult. The ranch and the cabin were now off limits, which meant he would need to find a place to stay, get another car, and buy clothes and other necessities. He would also have to try to make as little electronic noise as possible, until he figured out what he was up against. Cell phones, credit cards, Internet accounts, and ATM cards all generated traceable digital signatures. If his pursuers had access to this commercial data, through an illegal source, they could pinpoint his location every time he accessed one of these networks.

The problem was he needed these resources to live. His cash needs alone would force him to use his ATM card at least once or twice a week, and avoiding the use of credit cards would be difficult if he was living out of hotels and driving rental cars. As he struggled to come up with a solution to the problem, Caine realized that he might already have what he needed in his wallet.

More than half of his business involved overseas customers. Servicing this clientele required letters of credit and bills of lading arrangements. Rather than spend the time and money setting up these arrangements every time he shipped one of his projects, Caine employed the services of a Cayman Island firm called Briggs, Ltd., as an intermediary. For a percentage of each transaction, Briggs painlessly set up and executed the international payment arrangements, assuring payment and delivery for both sides of the transaction.

As a part of his contractual relationship with Briggs, Caine had been required to form a Cayman Island corporation and to post a cash deposit to secure any liability arising from a failed shipment. As a perk, Briggs issued a Visa card to the Cayman corporation, with Caine listed as an authorized signatory. The identifying number on the Visa card application was the Cayman Island corporation's tax identification number, not Caine's social security number. Although there was no guarantee, it was unlikely that a typical name/social security search would turn up this credit relationship.

The cell phone in his jacket pocket rang, interrupting his thoughts. He looked at the phone number displayed on the screen. It was Andrea Marenna. Caine didn't mention his name when he answered, because she could still be in range of the surveillance team.

"Hello."

"Hello? John?"

The reception was bad, but Caine heard a turning signal in the background. She was in her car, which was good.

"Hello. Is everything okay?"

"Yes. I . . . I called a friend of mine, Michael Bosmasian. He's a prosecutor for the City of Austin. He's going to have the police look into this situation . . . informally."

"Okay."

"Mr. Caine, why do I get the sense that you're less than enthusiastic about Michael's help?"

Caine could hear the undercurrent of frustration and anger in the question. He didn't want to say anything that would provoke an argument, but he also didn't want to lie.

"Look, I hope Mr. Bosmasian can help. Believe me, I do. I just don't think he's going to find anything."

"And why is that?"

"When we changed phones, the surveillance team would assume the worst. If they are even halfway competent, the bug was removed ten minutes after you left the house."

"What? Look . . . I think you're way off base. Like I told you before, I'm a business lawyer who works at a small firm in Austin. *No one* would have any reason to tap my phones, to watch my house, or to do anything else like that."

Caine hadn't slept in twenty-four hours and he was getting tired of this conversation. *Why couldn't she see the obvious?*

"Andrea, all I am suggesting is that you should be careful until this is all sorted out."

There was a brief silence. When she spoke again, her voice was apologetic.

"I didn't mean to snap at you. I just have to get some help on this and the police are my only option. Look, I'm about to drive into a dead zone, so my phone is going to go out. I'll let you know what Michael has to say."

Caine saw through the evasion. She was spooked. Worse, she suspected that he was a crackpot who was making it up as he went along.

He couldn't blame her. He was a stranger. She had no reason to believe anything he said. Until she was confronted with irrefutable proof, he was wasting his breath.

"That sounds good. You have my number. Call me anytime, day or night."

"Thanks."

Just before the call ended, he heard a voice in the background say, "Welcome to the Portman Lodge."

*San Bernardino, California*
*December 5, 1999 / Sunday / 1:30 p.m.*

Caine put the phone down on the seat and stared at the shattered pane of glass covering the GTO's speedometer. He'd been lucky this time. The next time the probability curve might not be so kind. To turn this thing around, he had to start hunting the hunters. That meant he had to go to Austin. Steinman and the girl were his only leads.

Caine considered getting a night's sleep before he flew to Austin, but decided that he couldn't risk the delay. If Andrea Marenna wasn't careful, she could end up dead. In fact, she could end up dead even if she was careful.

Ontario International Airport was about thirty minutes away from the shopping center. If he was lucky, he could catch a flight to Austin later that afternoon. Caine called several airlines on the way to the airport and booked a seat on a 3:30 p.m. flight. He could wash up and buy some clothes, a carry-on bag, and other necessities at one of the malls near the airport.

That would still leave him without one critical item—a gun. He couldn't bring the Sig Sauer with him, and it would be difficult to walk into another city and buy a gun off the shelf, with a couple of boxes of ammunition. Caine knew someone who could probably get him what he needed when he landed in Austin, despite the short notice, but it would come with a price. Jaq Maltier would want to join the hunting party.

Jaq was the only other member of the old Legion unit who lived in the United States. He owned a Caribbean-themed restaurant in Houston, Texas, but the restaurant was only a sideline. Jaq's primary employment was in the international arms trade. Jaq's company provided technical support and training to customers of the arms industry all over the world. Although Jaq denied it, Caine suspected that Jaq's outfit provided more than tech support.

Caine dialed Jaq's restaurant and a male baritone answered the phone. "River Grill."

"Hello, is Jaq there?"

"Who wants to know?"

"Just say an old Legionnaire."

There was a silence, and then the unmistakably cultured voice of Jacques Augustus Maltier came on the line.

"Hello, this is Jacques Maltier."

Caine couldn't help but smile when he heard the voice. "Jaq, it's John."

"Johnny boy? Praise the Almighty. The lost and prodigal son has returned to papa."

"It hasn't been that long, Jaq. I called you last Christmas."

"No, *mon ami*, you *wrote* me last Christmas, and as I recall it was a one-liner. However, I did enjoy the dagger you made for me. That was an exceptional piece of work, so I will not call you to account for your ill manners."

"Jaq, as I recall the great State of Texas has its share of phones."

"*Oui*, but I outrank you."

"What? When did you get another stripe?"

"Last year. I gave it to myself. I decided that I deserved it after putting up with you for all those years."

Both men laughed.

"Jaq, I am going to be visiting Austin tomorrow. I have some personal business there."

"Exceptional. When you're done with your business, hop a plane down to Houston. I'll lay out the red carpet. We can do some fishing in the Gulf."

"I can't, Jaq. I have a full schedule, but I promise to make it on the next trip. By the way, have you heard any news about anyone taking an interest in the other members of the unit?"

Jaq's tone changed. "No. What's going on, soldier?"

Caine knew that Jaq would insist on getting involved if he gave him the whole story, and he didn't want that. This thing was his problem.

"I think someone may be after me, but I'm not sure who or why. I'm flying into Austin to meet with someone who may be able to help me find out what's going on. When I get there, I would feel a whole lot safer if I had a decent piece of hardware, like a forty-five, or a nine millimeter."

"I have a better idea. I'll meet you in Austin, and I'll make sure we *both* have enough hardware to deal with the problem."

"Look, Jaq, I appreciate the offer, but I have to jump on the plane. Believe me, if it gets crazy, I'll come running to you for help. But right now, I just need to do a little research on my own. Don't worry, I won't take any chances. Trust me on this."

Jaq answered after a noticeable hesitation. "I'll get you the hardware, but I want the whole story when you land in Austin. No bullshit, which is what I'm hearing now. Are we clear?"

"Crystal, Jaq."

"Call me when you get in," Jaq said, and gave him his cell number. "That will get you through to me, day or night."

"Done."

Caine ended the call to cut off any further demands for information from Jaq. He smiled to himself, picturing the frustration on the Haitian's roguishly handsome face. Jaq could taste the possibility of a fight and he wanted in.

Jaq Maltier's affinity for violence was not something he grew up with. He was born into one of the wealthiest families in Haiti, and this wealth had enabled Jaq to receive the finest education money could buy, including an economics degree from Oxford.

When Jaq returned to Haiti from Oxford in 1980, he met a girl who was part of a small underground democracy movement that was seeking to undermine the dictatorship of Haiti's president-for-life,

"Baby Doc" Duvalier. Caine suspected that Jaq had been drawn to the group by the danger factor, not the politics. Late one night, the group's meeting place had been raided by Duvalier's trained killers, the feared Tonton Macoutes. Three of the six members of the group had been killed during the initial assault, including Jaq's female friend. A fourth had been fatally wounded. The odds had changed when Jaq, who'd shot competitively since he was twelve years old, wrestled a pistol away from one of the attackers. Three of the attackers had gone down, permanently, with head shots. A fourth crawled out of the building with a chest wound that would later prove fatal. This stunning reversal of fortune convinced the rest of the assault team to wait for backup, giving Jaq and the survivors a chance to escape from the house.

Although his escape bought Jaq a temporary reprieve, the attacker that he'd wounded had recognized him, putting the young Haitian squarely in the formidable crosshairs of the Duvalier government. Unless he could find a way off the island, it was only a matter of time before they found him. The solution to his problem had been offered by an old friend from Oxford, who worked in the French embassy.

An officer of the French Foreign Legion was visiting the embassy from Paris, looking for local recruits. The friend suggested that it was unlikely the Legion would turn down an Oxford-educated shooting champion, who was in excellent physical shape and who spoke fluent French. His friend had been right. Although the Legion officer had made Jaq pay four times the going rate for a civilian flight out, as a donation, he'd arranged to get him on a military flight out of the country the next day.

Caine had met Jaq in the Legion's basic training program. Despite their cultural and educational differences, the two men had become friends. As an ex-Ranger, Caine helped Jaq to become an elite soldier, and Jaq had helped Caine learn French. After two years in the Legion, the two men had been assigned to an elite parachute regiment. A year later, the two men had been invited to join a newly formed special ops unit under the control of Colonel Etienne Ricard, one of the Legion's most decorated soldiers. Both men had accepted the invitation.

# CHAPTER
# TWENTY-THREE

*Ontario Airport, California*
*December 5, 1999 / Sunday / 3:30 p.m.*

The flight to Austin was only about three-quarters full, and thankfully the seat next to Caine was empty. He passed on the drinks offered by the flight attendant, eased back in the seat, and closed his eyes. Talking to Jaq had brought back memories of the other three members of the original unit, Colonel Etienne Ricard, Corporal Joe Vlasky, and Sergeant Danny MacBain. Ricard and Vlasky were still alive, but MacBain, the smiling Scot, had been killed in Africa, in a fight that John Caine had started and couldn't forget.

He could almost feel the painful memory easing free of its restraints and flowing, unwanted, into his tired subconscious. The village had been located on a bend in the Congo River, near the Tanzanian border. The locals called the place Shabundo, but the name didn't appear on any map. Caine had the high position that day. The hill that he was on overlooked the village and gave him a clear view of the eastern approach, which was where the trouble would come from, if it did come.

The African sun was three hours from the western horizon, but the stifling heat showed no sign of receding. Caine could still remember the feel of the sweat-soaked cammos against his back and the sharp grass pricking his bare forearms as he lay prone on the hilltop above the village. He remembered scanning the jungle on the eastern edge of the village through the scope of his FR-F2 sniper rifle and looking over the silent village. An old man was resting in the shade of a grass-and-mud hut, smoking a cigarette. A dog was lying on the ground beside him.

One of the local warlords had decided to assert control over the ancestral lands of two other neighboring tribes. When the other tribes resisted, the warlord had exterminated the residents of two villages within a three-days' march and started to move toward a third, more distant village—Shabundo. Neither the Congolese nor the Tanzanian governments had paid much attention to the threat until it was discovered that a small French missionary group was working in the village. This had changed the politics.

The Legion unit had been advised that their mission was to evacuate the French nationals. The warlord and the village were the responsibility of a company-strength Congolese force that should have been on site when the Legion unit arrived. When the Legionnaires parachuted into the area the night before, they'd discovered that the French missionaries, oblivious to the approaching threat, had traveled down river to another village the day before. The Congolese force was nowhere to be found. When this information had been communicated back to the commander of the Legion force in Oran, Ricard had been told to await further instructions.

Later in the afternoon, Caine had spotted movement on a hill to the east through his binoculars. As he watched the distant figures approach the village, the fatigue that had been trying to put him to sleep for the last two hours disappeared. He called in the movement over the radio. Each of the positions had been assigned the name of an American state to celebrate Caine's birthday that week. Caine's location was designated Texas, his home state.

"Texas here. We have movement on the hill due east of my position. There are at least five irregulars in sight and more are coming. They're armed with guns and machetes."

Jaq, who was north of Caine's position, closer to the village, responded first.

"Florida here, I see them. It's the warlord and his band of merry men. I can tell by the markings. They'll hit the village in about ten minutes."

Vlasky, who was to the south of Caine's position, followed up.

"This is New York. I got 'em, too. They're going to march right by my flank. What's the call, Washington?"

The question was for Ricard. He and Sergeant MacBain were located at the eastern edge of the village, behind a stand of trees. They were closest to the oncoming force, but couldn't see them, because they were lower down the hill.

There was a short hesitation, and then Ricard's voice came back.

"Hold. I'll put a call into command."

As Caine listened to the exchange, he watched the women from the village harvesting cassava in a small field notched into the side of the hill. The younger children were with the women. They were unaware of the approaching nightmare. Most of the men were tending animals, or hunting or fishing outside the village.

Caine watched the rebel scouts scan the village from their cover and then, seeing no threat, wave the balance of the force forward. Within minutes, twenty men were coming out of the jungle and heading toward the crest of the hill. About half of the men were armed with a disparate collection of guns. The rest were carrying machetes. The attackers would reach the women first.

Caine put down the binoculars, flipped the safety off the FR-F2, and zeroed in on the lead scout. The enemy was about five hundred meters away. The FR-F2 could fire a 7.62x51 millimeter slug seven hundred meters with accuracy in the hands of a skilled sniper. Caine, like every member of the team, was more than skilled.

Caine forced the memory back into its cage and opened his eyes. He needed to get some rest, not relive a past nightmare. He'd had enough of those for one day.

*Austin, Texas*
*December 5, 1999 / Sunday / 9:10 p.m.*

Caine needed to rent a car when he arrived at the airport in Austin. He wanted to avoid using one of the national rental chains if possible, and he also wanted to rent a used car. The cab driver that picked him up outside the airport directed him to a rental outfit about two miles away. The signs on the lot indicated that the owner was primarily in the business of selling cars, but rentals were apparently a part of the mix as well.

The sixtyish man sitting behind the service counter gave him a friendly nod when he walked in.

"How can I help you this evening?"

"I need a rental for three or four days, possibly as long as a week. Something used would be fine. I'd like a midsize or bigger if you have it."

"Sure do. Why don't we take a walk outside and you can pick one out yourself? Everything over on the left side of the lot is available."

Caine looked over at the two rows of cars and was going to select a midsize Chevy sedan in the first row, when he saw three pickup trucks parked in the back row. The vehicle would give him a measure of anonymity, the protection of additional mass, and, in a worst-case scenario, a place to sleep. He pointed to a black Ford F-150 with a cover over the flatbed.

"Is that one available?"

The man nodded his approval. "Sure is."

Caine paid for the car with the Briggs, Ltd. credit card and left the rental place with a full tank of gas and a map of Austin and the surrounding area. Caine pulled into the parking lot of a family restaurant about a mile from the car rental place. It was a good two hours past the prime dinner hour and the restaurant was only about a quarter full. Caine took a booth in the rear and ordered a light dinner, a pot of coffee, and a glass of ice water. While he was waiting for the order, he dialed Jaq's cell phone. The nearest occupied table was at least twenty feet away and the two women seated there were too engrossed in their own conversation to take any interest in him.

"Jaq."

"It's Caine. I'm back home in Texas."

"Good for you. You should come home more often. You're not getting any younger."

"If I'm getting old, buddy, then you must be bloody ancient."

"No way. We Haitians age slower than you white folks. Now, tell me what's going on and no bullshit this time."

"Okay, Jaq, but here's the deal. It's my problem right now. You have to let me deal with it my way."

"Of course, man, why would I want to get involved in your problems? I have plenty of my own to keep me busy. Now tell me what's going on."

Caine gave Jaq an edited version of what had happened during the last twenty-four hours. He intentionally downplayed the two attacks, hoping to minimize Jaq's reaction, but the Haitian saw through the effort.

"What are you doing, man, trying to get yourself killed? You've got to get your ass—"

The waitress had showed up with his order.

"Jaq, wait a minute."

Caine pushed the cell phone facedown in the leather bench seat and thanked the waitress. When he picked up the cell phone again, Jaq was still berating him.

"You need more firepower than what I put in that locker, and you need someone to watch your back. This is complete bull—"

Caine glanced at his watch. He had to eat and get moving, or he would have to wait until tomorrow morning to try to find Andrea Marenna.

"Jaq, buddy, I gotta go here. Where do I pick up your present?"

"You get right back to me. Do you hear me, soldier? We're going to do this thing together."

"I got it, Jaq."

Jaq growled, but answered his question.

"Go to the Amtrak station downtown. Your pickup is in locker 27B. The combination is 4, 4, 4, 4 until twelve tonight. Then it expires. Pick up the package, then call me. I want to know what the plan is."

"Right, and thanks, Jaq."

The train station was about four miles from the restaurant. Since it was a Sunday night, the station was almost empty. Caine walked over to the lockers against the far wall, and discreetly looked around for police or security before he opened up the locker. The only guard was on the other side of the station and he was engrossed in a conversation with the girl behind the ticket counter.

Caine typed the lock's combination into the keypad, and the door opened with a quiet click. A brown shopping bag was the only thing inside the locker. Caine pulled out the bag, closed the locker, and left the station. He opened the bag when he was back in the truck. The gun, a spare magazine, and a box of shells were wrapped in an old towel at the bottom of the bag. Caine flipped open the glove compartment for a moment, allowing the interior light to shine on the weapon. Then he closed it.

The gun was a Browning Hi-Power Mark III. The Mark III and its predecessor, the Mark II, were standard issue for hundreds of military and law enforcement organizations around the world. Caine had practiced with the Mark II when he was in the Legion.

The Mark III had a thirteen-round magazine, with a nine-millimeter load. Caine filled both magazines from the box of fifty cartridges. He put one magazine back in the gun and the spare in his coat pocket. Now it was time to pay Ms. Andrea Marenna a visit at the Portman Lodge. With a little luck, she was still alive.

# CHAPTER
# TWENTY-FOUR

*Travis County, Texas*
*December 5, 1999 / Sunday / 11:00 p.m.*

A ndrea had a moment of confusion when she awoke. Then she remembered that she was staying in one of the cabins at the Portman Lodge, a small family-owned resort located on the edge of Granger Lake outside Austin. The modest facility was comprised of a main lodge and thirty cabins located about a quarter of a mile from the lake on a steep slope. The rows of cabins were unevenly dispersed across three level areas carved into the slope at descending elevation levels. The last row was situated about fifty yards from the lake. During the spring and summer, the Lodge's guests had access to a small beach and the use of a boathouse along the lake shore.

The resort, which had a log cabin motif, was over fifty years old. The entire facility had been renovated about five years ago, leaving a rustic but comfortable haven, with all of the modern amenities.

Andrea had spent a week at the lodge with her dad when she was eight years old. The year her mother died. They'd returned for a week every summer after that until her father had passed away when she was in college. In recent years, Andrea had used the place as a weekend refuge. The peaceful surroundings and the happy memories helped her to wind down and regain her mental equilibrium when the stress from work became unendurable.

Since it was the off-season, only a limited number of cabins were open for rental, but half of them were empty when she arrived. Not many people wanted to visit the lake when it was forty-five degrees in the sunshine. Andrea's cabin was located two levels down from the main lodge, on a point. She had a view of the lake through the picture window in the front of the cabin.

Andrea had lain down to rest after she arrived, intending to read for a while, but had fallen asleep. She looked over at the red numerals on the digital clock on the table beside the bed. It was 11:00 p.m. She stood up and stretched and walked slowly across the bedroom to the short hallway that separated the bedroom from the bathroom, wary of tripping over her suitcase in the dark.

When she stepped into the hallway, she looked into the main room. The light from one of the lamps in front of the cabin was shining into the dark room, through a narrow break in the curtains. An unbroken stream of white ran from the window across the wooden floor. Andrea started to cross the hall to the bathroom, when she noticed that the stream of light disappeared for a moment and then came back. Then it went dark again and stayed that way.

She stopped in the middle of the hall, confused, but then she realized that someone outside the cabin must be blocking the incoming light. The undercurrent of unease that she'd kept under tight control throughout the day started to resurface. She ignored the feeling and walked into the front room, intending to pull the curtain on the front window aside to look out on the walkway. A slight noise to her left stayed her hand. She looked over and watched, mesmerized, as the knob on the front door slowly turned back and forth. For a moment, a wave of fear froze her in place. Then she took two quick steps to the right, giving her an oblique view of the walkway leading to the cabin, through the small opening in the curtain.

A man with a black ski mask over his face was down on one knee in front of the door to her cabin. He was inserting something into the lock. She stared at the man, incapable of accepting what she was seeing. Then a movement at the foot of the stairs drew her attention and eliminated any doubt about the terrifying reality in front of her. A second figure in a ski mask was crouched at the bottom stairs, scanning the surrounding area.

Andrea's breath caught in her throat, and her heart rate went into overdrive. *I have to get out of here.* The cabin had a back door, and there was a winding stairway at the edge of the yard that led up the slope to the parking lot. If she could slip out the door unnoticed and reach the parking lot, she could run to the main lodge.

Andrea let go of the breath trapped in her chest and slowly exhaled. The sound seemed impossibly loud. She eased back from the curtain and walked along the wall on her right until she was outside the view through the front window. Then she walked quickly to the back door, praying that she didn't trip on anything in the dark. The door in the back of the cabin was shrouded in darkness, and she fumbled for the doorknob. *Where is it!* In frustration, she began to pat the right side of the door furiously. Suddenly she found the knob. She turned it quickly and began to pull the door open, but it stopped with a sudden jerk, making a loud bang. *The chain latch!*

She glanced frantically backward into the cabin and saw the front door opening. She slammed the back door shut, yanked the chain off and then pulled open the door. Before she had taken a full step across the cabin's small back porch, a figure to the right seized her neck in a viselike grip. Her forward momentum carried her legs another step forward, but the iron-hard muscles forming the crook of the massive arm around her neck brutally tightened, stopping the forward movement of her upper body.

Andrea struggled to retain her balance, while at the same time grappling with the arm around her throat. The man with the arm locked around her ignored her efforts and began to drag her back into the cabin. Once she realized that she couldn't escape from the man's grip, she drew in a breath to scream. The figure behind felt the intake of breath and tightened his grip around her neck even further, putting crushing pressure on her throat. The vise cut off her scream and her ability to breathe. She began to struggle wildly as she fought to get a breath. Her assailant lowered his head to her face and growled a warning into her ear.

"You move, you die, bitch. You scream, you die. Relax and maybe you'll be okay for a while."

Although she felt as if she was being choked to death, Andrea forced herself to stop struggling. A long moment later, the monster loosened his grip around her neck slightly, allowing her to draw small gasping breaths into her lungs. A voice from inside the cabin said, "The bedroom's over here. Bring her in."

The word *rape* screamed in her mind and she started to struggle again. Again, her captor anticipated her effort and tightened his grip, yanking her body hard against his chest, all but cutting off her air supply. The man chuckled to himself and dragged her across the room.

"Relax, bitch. You can't do nuthin'."

Andrea was facing the back door as the man dragged her down the short hall. As she struggled futilely to get free, a second figure stepped through the rear door of the cabin. She assumed that the man was coming to help the other man drag her into the room. The man took three quick strides and stepped past her, placing himself between her body and the wall, and directly behind her captor, who was facing the interior of the cabin. The man dragging her belatedly realized that someone was behind him and turned his head to look back down the hall.

"Who the—" He never finished the question.

### Travis County, Texas
### December 5, 1999 / Sunday / 10:50 p.m.

Caine pulled into the parking lot of the Portman Lodge, avoiding the driveway that circled up to the front of the main lodge. He parked in the row closest to the road. On his way to the Lodge, Caine had called and explained to the clerk at the front desk that he would be dropping off a package of closing documents in the morning that required Ms. Andrea Marenna's signature. The young clerk obligingly confirmed that Ms. Marenna was staying in cabin thirty-two, but suggested that he might want to come to the front desk when he arrived and have someone bring him down to the cabin in a golf cart.

Caine walked over to a map of the facility located in a glass-covered marquee near the front of the parking lot. Cabin thirty-two was two levels down the slope from the main lodge, on a point over-looking the lake. A paved walkway provided direct access to the cabin from the lodge, but the map also showed a secondary stairway. The stairway ran down the steep slope behind the parking lot to the lake, passing directly behind the cabin.

Caine walked over the edge of the parking lot and found the stair-way. The Lodge apparently wanted to discourage the use of the stairs. The area wasn't lighted and a sign beside the stairs directed patrons to use the main walkway after sunset. Caine walked down the darkened stairs to the first landing and stopped for a moment, allowing his eyes to adjust to the dark. Then he continued, walking past the row of cabins on the first level.

About halfway down to the next level, Caine stopped and looked over the railing at the three cabins below him. He was able to distin-guish cabin thirty-two from the others by its forward location on the bluff. Caine was about to start down the next flight of stairs when a movement in the rear of the cabin stopped him. He eased into a crouch and stared at the outline of the figure that appeared to be wait-ing on the back porch of the cabin. Caine could tell by the outline that the figure was a man.

Caine looked to his left and noticed that a small trail ran along the left side of the stairway. He stepped under the railing and eased down the path, stopping behind a large tree surrounded by bushes. The man on the porch was standing against the wall beside the rear door, about twenty yards away. Caine knew from the figure's movements that he wasn't there for a friendly visit.

Caine started to reach for the Browning in his jacket, but remem-bered it was in the truck. He'd decided that meeting Andrea Marenna for the first time with a gun in his jacket might not be his best move, particularly after their last phone call. That perspective seemed incred-ibly stupid at the moment.

Caine worked his way around to the left side of the cabin using the trees and bushes as cover. He stepped on a fist-sized rock as he came around a bush. He picked up the rock and put it in his jacket pocket. It wasn't much, but it might give him an edge.

A sound from the rear of the cabin drew his attention and he stopped moving. A woman with shoulder-length hair, wearing dark jeans, a loose sweater, and tennis shoes opened the rear door of the cabin and started to run across the back porch. It had to be Andrea. The man against the wall was expecting this move. He seized the woman around the neck as she ran by him, and the woman began to struggle frantically.

Caine started forward, intending to cover the fifteen yards to the porch as fast as possible to prevent the man from killing her. As he moved out from behind the bush, the man with the arm lock around the woman's neck jerked her against his chest and said something in a harsh voice. Whatever he said had the intended effect, because Andrea stopped struggling. Satisfied, the man began dragging her back into the cabin.

As soon as the man passed through the open door, Caine sprinted across the yard, stepped across the porch and looked inside the cabin. A light shining from an open door further inside the dark cabin gave him a view of what was happening. The man dragging Andrea down the hall was facing away from Caine. He was at least six five and easily topped two hundred and sixty pounds. His bulging arm dwarfed her neck.

Caine took three quick strides and stepped past Andrea, putting himself within striking distance of her captor. Andrea must have reacted to his movement, because the man turned his head back toward Caine, exposing his open throat above her head. Caine's strike, a blade hand to the man's throat, was already whipping across his chest, when the man started to react to his presence. The man opened his mouth to yell, just as the blade of Caine's hand smashed into his throat with brutal force, cutting off any sound, and, temporarily, his ability to breathe. Caine's second blow landed a fraction of a second later, smashing into the gagging man's temple. The impact rocked the big man backward and he loosened his lock on Andrea's throat. Caine seized the opening, grabbing the man's wrist with one hand and his elbow with the other. He shoved the man's elbow upward and pulled his wrist downward in single fluid movement. The man wheeled around, with a grunt of pain. When the back of the other man's head was exposed, Caine released the man's arm and smashed the heel of his palm into the back of the man's head, in a quick piston-like movement. The strike had its intended effect. The man's body went limp and slid to the floor.

Caine glanced down the hall. The other men were still inside the room on the right. Caine turned, pulled Andrea to her feet, and pushed her toward the rear door of the cabin. As they went out the door, Caine heard movement behind him, followed by an enraged voice.

"Hey! What the fuck is going on!"

Caine moved to the right, out the doorway, and pulled Andrea beside him. The men inside were almost certainly armed. To get away, they would need a distraction—something that would buy them some time. Caine reached into his jacket and pulled out the rock that he'd picked up earlier. He threw it downward through the door of the cabin and yelled, "Grenade!" The rock skittered down the hallway into the main room, drawing yells and frantic movement within.

Caine turned and spoke in curt whisper, "Andrea, we have to get to the parking lot. Stay with me." Caine could barely see Andrea's face in the dark, but she nodded and followed him across the porch. When they reached the yard, Caine started to run. Andrea raced after him.

# CHAPTER
# TWENTY-FIVE

*Travis County, Texas*
*December 5, 1999 / Sunday / 11:15 p.m.*

About halfway up the stairs, Andrea slipped, and the man running beside her turned quickly and grabbed her hand, steadying her. Then he turned, still holding her hand, and continued to race up the stairway. When they reached the dimly lit parking lot at the top of the stairway, Andrea slowed, trying to catch her breath, and looked at the man ahead of her. He was about six feet tall, lean, and heavily muscled in the chest and arms. His hair, which was worn longer than she was used to seeing in the corporate world, was light brown with a tinge of gray on the sides. When he glanced back toward the stairway, she saw the outline of a strong jaw and a hard but handsome face in the semidarkness. He noticed she was looking at him, and his deep-set eyes looked directly into her own.

"Andrea, it's me, John Caine."

Then he continued to run down the length of the parking lot, pulling her along with him. Andrea was in excellent physical condition, but the desperate sprint up the steep stairs had winded her. She wanted to stop and catch her breath. She also wanted to find out what John Caine was doing here.

He turned back to her again and pointed to a black pickup truck parked at the end of the lot.

"There's my truck. We have to get away from here, now. We only have a few seconds."

As he started to turn away, Andrea resisted his pull. When he felt the resistance, Caine stopped and turned to face her, glancing quickly over her shoulder at the edge of the slope behind her. Andrea held up her hands in front of her, and tried to speak, while at the same time gasping for breath. Caine looked at her closely for a moment. The attractive woman who stared back at him didn't fit the image he'd attributed to the skeptical voice from earlier in the day.

"Wait . . . wait a minute. How did you get here? You . . . you said you were in California. And how did—"

"I flew in two hours ago," Caine interrupted her. "I knew you were here, because I overheard the bellman on our last phone call. Look, Andrea, you don't know me and have no reason to trust me, but if I wanted to do anything other than help you, I wouldn't be doing this little rescue mission. We have to get away from here, now. Those men will kill both of us if we stay here, and that eighteen-year-old kid behind the desk in the lodge is not going to stop them. So you have to make a choice. Either trust me, or not, but either way you have to decide now."

Andrea wanted more time to figure out what was going on. She had so many questions. A second later, the decision was made for her.

"Time's up," Caine said. "The bad guys are here. We have to go *now*."

Andrea glanced behind her and saw four figures racing up the stairway toward the parking lot. A rush of fear and adrenaline swept over her.

"Okay, okay, let's go." Then she ran after Caine as he sprinted over to the driver's side of the truck.

As soon as she climbed into the passenger seat, Caine drove over the curb in front of the truck onto the lawn that separated the lot from the state highway. As the truck accelerated across the lawn, he glanced in the mirror and yelled, "Get your head down!"

A second later, the rear window above her head exploded, sprinkling her with glass. Andrea put her head down even lower and glanced over her shoulder. The bottom left quarter of the rear window was now a crazy quiltwork of lines with a hole in the center. A part of her mind wondered where the bullet went. Then she looked up at the front dashboard. A furrow was ripped through the black leather padding to her left.

Andrea felt the truck bounce off the grass onto the shoulder of the road and race onto the state highway. The truck weaved wildly for a second on the rain-slick road. Then it straightened out and rapidly accelerated away from the lodge. After glancing in the mirror, Caine looked over at her.

"It's okay. We're out of effective range."

Andrea just stared at him. He glanced in the mirror again and turned back to the road ahead. She followed his gaze. The road ahead was empty and dark except for the light from the truck's headlamps. A mist began to cloud the windshield. Caine fumbled for the windshield wiper switch in the dark. After a second, he found it and switched on the wipers, clearing the view. Then he looked over at her.

"Andrea, I need your help. I need to know where this road goes, where the next town is, and whether there are any side roads that might help us stay away from these people."

Despite the pounding in her chest and the shock of the last five minutes, she surprised herself by giving him a ready answer.

"We . . . we're heading away from Austin, along the lake. The next town of any size is Clayton. It's about nine miles ahead. There may be side roads, but most of those on the right will dead-end at the lake. The roads on the left will head off into the foothills, but . . . some of them stop in dead-ends as well. We . . . we have to stay on this road for a while before we can get to another road that really goes anywhere."

Caine looked in the mirror again and then glanced over at the woman beside him in the darkened cab. She was looking over at him. For a second he caught her eyes, which were large and attractive, and then he turned back to the road ahead.

"Are you okay?"

Andrea just nodded and continued to look at him for a minute. This was the first time that she'd taken the time to look closely at his face, which was just visible in the dim glow of light from the instrument panel. It was more distinguished than handsome, if on the hard side, with a strong, chiseled jaw, gray eyes, straight nose, and a deep tan. Caine belatedly realized he was being scrutinized, and looked over at her.

"So what's the verdict?" Caine asked with a smile.

Andrea was surprised by his smile and a little embarrassed, but she responded with one of her own. "You'll do."

Caine glanced in the mirror again and his smile disappeared. She noticed the change and looked in the sideview mirror. She saw a pair of headlights in the distance. As she watched the lights, it was obvious the other car was gaining on them. When she turned back to Caine, he just nodded.

"Yeah, it's them, and they're really moving."

Andrea glanced over at the speedometer on the truck. It was touching ninety-five miles per hour, which shocked her. Then she noticed the roar of the engine and was surprised that she had hadn't realized how loud it was before. Caine looked in the mirror again and then looked over at her.

"They're gaining on us. I can't see the car, but it's a fair bet that whatever they're driving is a lot faster than this truck, so we can't out-run them."

Andrea looked over at him and waited. When he didn't say any-thing, she said, "So what are—"

"We have other options" Caine said, without taking his eyes off the road.

She looked at his face for a second, assuming that he was just put-ting up a front, but his demeanor didn't change. *What options?*

Without taking his eyes off the road, Caine said, "Can you check the map? It's under the seat beneath you. I need to know what the road looks like ahead. What I'm looking for is a sharp curve, or some-thing like it."

Andrea pulled out the map and started to reach for the overhead light over the console, but reconsidered after looking back at the shattered rear window. Instead, she flipped open the glovebox and used the dim light from within to illuminate the map. The road they were on was at the far edge of the map.

"It looks like we'll hit a series of bends in the road in about two miles. Then the road continues to meander around the perimeter of the lake, without any real turns."

Caine's eyes did a quick circuit from the rearview mirror to the front. Then he looked over at her and spoke with quiet certainty. "Andrea, this is how it is. We can't outrun them. So we have to take them out."

Caine looked back to the front and then looked over at her again and held her eyes for a moment.

"We have to work together to do this."

Andrea stared at him without comprehension. Caine looked over and continued, "About a hundred yards past the bend up ahead, I'm going to do a U-turn and park the truck on the other side of the road, facing back toward Austin. As soon as the truck comes to a stop, I'm going to run up the road and get in position."

"What are you talking about?" Andrea started with frustration, but Caine interrupted her.

"Listen to me, Andrea, I know this business. Trust me. We have to do this to survive."

Then he glanced in the mirror again and continued. "When I get out of the truck, slide over into the driver's seat and wait. If the ambush works, pick me up after I stop shooting. If it doesn't work, turn the truck around and get the hell out of here. Don't wait for me and don't stop for any reason."

It took her a second to process what he was saying.

"Shooting? With what? This is insane."

Caine didn't answer. He came down heavy on the brakes and the pickup rapidly slowed. Then he made a hard U-turn and parked the truck on the shoulder of the opposite side of the road, facing back toward Austin.

The instant the truck stopped, Caine jumped out and grabbed something from under the front seat and stuck it in his jacket pocket.

When he finished, he glanced up the road and then looked back over at her. The intensity on his face shocked her.

"There's no other way out, Andrea. If we don't get away from them, we're both dead. Okay?"

Andrea found herself nodding, not because she agreed with him, but because she simply didn't know what else to do. She slid over into the driver's seat and watched Caine sprint about forty yards back up the road. Once he hit the midpoint in the sharp curve, he ran up the embankment, dropped into a kneeling position, and pulled out a gun.

*Travis County, Texas*
*December 5, 1999 / Sunday / 11:45 p.m.*

Caine wiped the rain from his forehead and leaned forward as far as possible in order to get a view of the oncoming car. He could tell from the shape and the lights that the car was a big Mercedes-Benz sedan. The driver saw the curve in the road when he was about one hundred yards out, and started to reduce his speed. Just before the car started into the curve, the driver eased the car over the center line. This classic driving maneuver gave the driver more room to slide outward as the car raced through the curve. Caine had counted on it. It put the car closer to his position.

Caine's plan was to hit the front windshield first and then work the driver's side windows as the car passed him. If he could shatter the windshield or the window on the driver's side while the driver and the car were under maximum stress, there was a good chance the driver would lose control. At the speed the Benz was traveling, even a small error would cause a crash.

Caine waited until the car had started into the curve before he opened up with the Browning, firing as rapidly as possible at the windshield. The glass on the driver's side exploded after the third bullet, turning the windshield into an opaque spider web. The driver reacted to the unexpected explosion in front of his face by pulling the wheel away from the source of the incoming fire. This gave Caine a clear shot at the side window as the car raced past his position. He pumped four more shots into the car.

When the driver of the Benz recovered from his initial shock, the car was headed toward the edge of the road and the steep slope beyond. Seeing this new threat, the driver pulled the wheel back toward the center of the road and pumped the brakes. This combination was too much and too soon on the rain-slick road. The Benz wheeled around in a complete circle and was starting into a second rotation when it hit the shoulder of the road and disappeared over the far edge.

# CHAPTER
# TWENTY-SIX

*Travis County, Texas*
*December 5, 1999 / Sunday / 11:45 p.m.*

Andrea watched, mesmerized, as Caine fired round after round into the car racing around the curve. For an instant, she could see the white blur of the driver's face through the windshield, and then the glass shattered. The Mercedes weaved away from Caine, and then it spun out of control, finally disappearing off the shoulder into the forest below.

Andrea stared out at the silent, empty road and struggled to release the breath caught in her throat. When the involuntary constriction let go, she drew in a series of frantic breaths. A voice outside the truck drew her attention. She looked over to the right. Caine was running down the road toward the truck. She shifted the truck into drive and raced toward Caine, skidding to a stop a car-length past him.

As soon as Caine climbed in the truck, Andrea floored the gas pedal. The tires squealed in protest and spun for a second on the slick road, before gaining traction. Caine looked at her quickly and then turned to look out the rear window of the truck. When they were several hundred yards past the crash site, Caine turned back to front.

Andrea stared at the road ahead. Her hands were gripping the top of the steering wheel so tightly that she could feel the strain in the back of her hands and the tension in her neck and shoulders. She didn't look over at Caine, but she could feel his eyes on her. He leaned over slightly and looked at the speedometer.

"Andrea, you can slow it down. We're okay now."

A dam broke inside her.

"Okay? Okay? Are you out of your mind! You just shot a car off the road! We're *not* okay. You can be charged with assault with a deadly weapon, possibly attempted murder, and I can be charged with aiding and abetting. Don't you realize how serious this is?"

Caine looked out the rear window again, and then turned all the way around. He looked over at her for a moment, but she refused to look at him. Her eyes were glued on the road ahead.

"Andrea, being dead is pretty serious, too. If someone wants to prosecute me for trying to stay alive, I'll take that over the alternative any day."

Andrea's head whipped around, and their eyes met. A torrent of anger that she didn't understand was raging inside her. Caine saw the look and held up his hands in a conciliatory gesture.

"Look, Andrea—"

"No, *you* look. I want to know what's going on and I want to know *now*."

"Okay. I'll tell you what I know, but it's not all that much. Just . . . ease off on the speed a little. Please?"

For a moment Andrea wanted to scream at him, but she didn't know exactly why, or what she wanted to say. She took a breath and slowly exhaled, trying to slow down her racing heart and get control of her anger. The background roar of the engine suddenly registered and she looked down at the speedometer. The needle was bouncing in the high nineties. She eased her foot off the accelerator and looked over at Caine when the speed had slowed into the seventies. He was looking out the rear window again. She looked up in the rearview mirror. The road behind them was dark and empty.

"Where do you want me to start?" Caine said.

"Let's start with the basics. Where do you live and what do you do for a living?"

Andrea realized that the she was treating Caine like a witness in a deposition. She knew it wasn't fair, but she couldn't help herself.

"I live on a five-acre ranch outside the City of Hesperia, in California. Two nights ago—"

Andrea interrupted him.

"You skipped one. I want to know what you do for a living."

Caine hesitated for a moment and then answered.

"I forge medieval swords, daggers, spears, and occasionally a shield, for collectors."

Andrea looked over at him, the skepticism was plain on her face.

"Mr. Caine—"

"I know. It sounds odd, but it's true."

Andrea didn't say anything, but the expression on her face didn't change.

"Let me give you an example of how it works. Right now I'm working on a sword for a doctor here in the United States. One of his ancestors was a knight who served Henry II of England."

Caine hesitated long enough to glance out the rear window again and then continued.

"The client gave me a basic description of the weapon from a family diary that was kept by a distant ancestor. Using this basic description as a starting place, I researched the characteristics of the blades that were used during that period of history, and then made a proposal to the client. He approved it, and now I'm in the middle of the project."

"Who's the client?"

"Dr. James Martin. He's a neurosurgeon in Philadelphia. You're welcome to call him to confirm these facts, but you might want to wait for a couple of hours. It's 1:00 a.m. in Philly."

"Where do you do this work?" Andrea asked, her tone guarded, but no longer openly skeptical.

"I work in a converted barn at my ranch. I have a forge there."

"Do you have any employees?"

"No, it's just me. I . . . I try to re-create the conditions that existed when the weapons were made. So I do the work myself and use the same tools they used in that time period. This makes the end product as authentic as possible."

Andrea looked over at Caine and then looked back at the road. She could tell he was trying to allay her suspicions, but he didn't seem to be lying.

"That's . . . interesting. The last time we talked, you said something about having a run-in with these people. What was that about?"

Caine hesitated. Andrea noticed his hesitation and looked over at him, but his face was turned away. He was lowering the incline of the seat. When he finished, he turned back to her.

"I'm sorry. I didn't get much sleep last night."

Andrea looked at his face and could see the fatigue. The anger dissipated, and she felt a wave of reproach.

"I'm sorry, Mr. Caine. I don't mean to interrogate you. You . . . you probably saved my life back there and I haven't even said thank you. So let me say it. Thank you. Thank you very much. I . . . I'm just trying to find out how you fit into all of this."

"No apology necessary, and I'm okay with the interrogation," Caine said, a small smile on his face.

Andrea smiled in response.

"You were going to tell me about the other night," Andrea prompted.

"Yes. On Sunday, I was staying at my cabin in the San Bernardino Mountains. It's in a remote area. At about 2:00 in the morning, I was awakened by a low-flying chopper. I couldn't get back to sleep, so I walked into the kitchen to get something to eat. When I looked out the window, a group of armed men was circling the cabin. My—"

"You saw them?" Andrea interrupted. "How many were there?"

"At least four," Caine answered.

"Why didn't you call the police?" Andrea said.

"Andrea, my place is more than a mile from the road, and the town is another five miles to the west. There's no telephone service out there, either by a landline or cell phone. Calling the police and waiting around for help wasn't an option."

"What did you do?"

"I had to get out of there. I took off through the forest on my snowmobile. Whoever was after me fired a few shots in my direction when I was trying to get away, but luckily, they missed."

"And then?"

"Once I was clear of the area, I made my way into town and bought an old junker from a guy at a local garage, and drove off the mountain. End of story."

"Why didn't you go to the police when you reached the town?" Andrea said, an undercurrent of suspicion in her voice.

Caine hesitated and then answered, "What exactly was I going to tell the police? That a helicopter landed near my cabin and a group of men carrying automatic weapons tried to kill me?"

"Yes. That's what happened, right?"

"Yes, that is what happened, but it's more complicated than that. The police operate within certain parameters. Once a situation gets outside those lines, they assume that they're dealing with a crackpot or worse. This . . . this situation was way—"

"I'm not a criminal lawyer," Andrea said, "but the evidence was there to confirm your story. The forensic people would have found the bullets."

"Under two feet of snow?" Caine said, quiet skepticism in his voice.

"So what? With the proper equipment and resources, they could find them."

"Maybe they could, but it's unlikely they'd make the effort. This is not the FBI we're talking about. Snow Valley's a very small town. The local guys would be reluctant to commit the time and resources needed to find the bullets. It's far more likely they'd assume I was some kind of nut who should be locked up for a psych evaluation. I wasn't going to risk that. So I just got out of there." Caine could tell from the look that Andrea gave him that she wasn't buying it.

"Well, I'm certainly going to tell the Austin police about what happened tonight, and they damn well better believe me."

"Look, I think you should do whatever you think is right, I just—"

Andrea jumped on the doubt in his voice.

"Mr. Caine, there's a car back there that's off the road. That car will provide irrefutable proof for at least a part of my story, and once they trace the car, the police will find the driver, or at least the owner. It may take some time, but they will find out who is behind these criminal acts."

When she finished, Caine sat forward and turned to look directly at her.

"That...that car may not be there when the police arrive at the scene. In fact, I can almost guarantee it won't be there an hour from now."

"What are you talking about? Of course it will be there, or they'll have a record of it being moved."

"If my suspicions are correct, these people killed Richard Steinman, sent a chopper full of armed men to attack me in a remote cabin in the San Bernardino Mountains, bugged your apartment, and then arranged for a team to kidnap you at the Portman Lodge. They did all of that within seventy-two hours. That takes major resources. For these folks, making a car disappear from a country road would be small change."

Andrea stared at Caine and then looked out the front window.

"That's all pure supposition. None of those events may be connected, and I don't know you well enough to believe that they all happened in the first place. In fact, this may not be a very smart question to ask, since you're sitting next to me with a gun, but how is that you're such an expert in this business?"

Andrea regretted the sting in the question as soon as she finished, and looked quickly over at Caine. Caine was rubbing his eyes when he answered. His voice was calm, even regretful.

"Andrea, I sincerely hope all of these events are just a series of random happenstances because it improves our survival odds, and I'm all for that. As for being an expert, I'm not. But I was a soldier for fifteen years. I know weapons, tactics, and hand-to-hand combat. Most of all, I know something about staying alive when people are trying to kill me."

There was an awkward silence. Then Andrea looked over Caine.

"Look, I'm sorry, it's just . . . "

"I understand. We're both tired. In fact, I can barely keep my eyes open, so can I make a suggestion?"

"Sure, I guess I owe you at least that much slack," Andrea said, in an apologetic voice.

Caine surprised her with a small smile. "I think we need to find a safe place to get some rest. In the morning, we can try to get our bearings and put a plan together."

"I don't want to sound like a recording, but I think we have to go to the police, and we should do it tonight."

"If that's what you want to do, I'll do it, but I think you have to recognize what we're getting into. The sign back there said Williamson County. A minute ago, you mentioned the Austin police. Do the Austin police have jurisdiction over Williamson County?" Caine said.

Andrea hesitated, and then she realized what he was saying.

"No. We'd have to talk to the county police, and they would probably bring in the Texas Rangers."

"Like I said, I'll do whatever you want, but I have an idea that one way or another we're going to wait until morning to get any real help on this thing. We'll either be parked in a station somewhere, waiting until morning for a real detective to show up, or we'll meet this person in the morning, after a few hours of sleep in a comfortable hotel room. Nothing is going to get done tonight, and since I haven't slept in twenty-four hours, I have a real bias in favor of the second alternative."

Andrea looked over at Caine and then looked back at the road ahead. She knew he was right, and now that the adrenaline had subsided, she was having trouble keeping her eyes open. The idea of waiting four or five hours in a small-town police station, waiting for the morning shift to show up, seemed a waste of time. On the other hand, if they waited until the morning, they would have to explain the delay to the police. As she struggled with the problem, a solution came to mind. *Michael.* Michael was assistant district attorney for the City of Austin. He could introduce them to a senior detective in the Austin P.D. tomorrow morning. That would eliminate any credibility problem and give them the support of a top-drawer police force.

Andrea let out a breath and raised one hand off the wheel in a gesture of acceptance.

"Okay, John Caine, we'll do it your way tonight."

# CHAPTER
# TWENTY-SEVEN

*San Bernardino, California*
*December 6, 1999 / Monday / 2:15 a.m.*

Paquin and the rest of the team had relocated to the Sheraton Hotel in the City of San Bernardino after the chase. Paquin suspected they were all sleeping. Although he was tired, Paquin had stayed awake to field incoming calls about the status of the ongoing search effort. His operatives back in Austin were running Caine's name through the California Department of Motor Vehicle records, county real property records, national credit records, and phone records. As the information was collected, it was sifted for useful contacts and then handed off to a second group that was trying to find Caine through a discreet phone campaign. So far, all of their efforts to regain his trail had been unsuccessful.

As he reviewed another e-mail, his mobile phone rang.

"Paquin."

"Ray Insonna."

"Go ahead."

"We followed the woman to a lodge outside Austin. Chaney grabbed up the woman when she tried to run out the back door. Then someone else showed up and took her away from him."

"Did you see them?" Paquin interrupted.

"I only saw one attacker, a white male," Insonna answered.

"What happened?" Paquin said, restrained anger in his voice.

"Chaney was bringing the girl in the back door of the cabin. The guy followed him in and took Chaney out. Then—"

"How did he take him out? Is Mr. Chaney dead?"

"No, sir. He's alive. Chaney says the guy hit him with something, but I think he's lying. The guy used his hands."

"Where did they go?" Paquin asked.

"The two of them escaped in a pickup truck. We chased them and would've caught them, but this guy . . . the son of a bitch set up an ambush and took out the car. He blew the shit out of the windshield, and we went off the road. The car was totaled," Insonna said, his voice trailing off.

Paquin looked out the hotel room window at the dark mountains to the east. It had to be Caine. The coincidence was too great for any other explanation. Somehow he had made contact with the girl and taken her away from the team Paquin had assigned to interrogate and kill her.

Paquin looked over at the picture sitting on the small desk, which had been e-mailed to him an hour earlier. It showed a squad of Rangers in front of a building in Fort Bragg. The eight lean young men in the picture were all smiling. The man in the picture was a young soldier; probably enthusiastic, tough, maybe even smart. The man they were chasing was something more than that, a lot more.

"Were there any casualties?" Paquin said.

"No, all our players are okay."

"Is there any official involvement?"

"No. The site is way outside the city, and a tow truck will be here in minutes. Once it gets here, we'll head back to Center."

"Do you have any idea where the target is now?"

Insonna hesitated. "No, we're trying to track down the truck, but so far no luck."

"Very well, I'll be back tonight. Assemble as many assets as you can from our local resources and have Vargas call in anyone who's available in Mexico."

Insonna hesitated for a minute, remembering the figure on the hill in the fraction of a second before the windshield exploded. Without thinking, he said, "Sir, this guy . . . he's a serious player."

Paquin looked over at the picture again, remembering a similar comment made by Severino in his debrief.

"Paquin out."

Paquin called Severino and told him to wake everybody. They were flying back to Austin tonight.

# CHAPTER
# TWENTY-EIGHT

*Alsace, France*
*December 6, 1999 / Monday / 7:00 a.m.*

Etienne Ricard walked slowly down the cobblestone path that meandered along the perimeter of the seventy-acre vineyard. The light
frost covering the dormant vines woven through the rows of trellises
glistened in the early morning sun. When he reached the crest of the
small rise, Ricard could see his chateau below him.

The stone tower at the center of the rambling brick and mortar
building dated back over three hundred years. Three additions had
been added to this core structure over the years, leaving a six-room
home, surrounded by a low wall. The chateau was located in a small
valley surrounded by a series of rolling hills lined with row upon row
of wooden grape trellises.

Ricard was sixty years old, but he moved with the understated athletic
grace of a fencer. His spare muscular frame and erect bearing would have
been more at home on a man twenty-five years younger. Ricard's tanned
face was Romanesque in the classic sense, with a prominent nose, high
cheekbones, and a strong chin. His eyes, which were a striking blue-gray,
revealed more than a hint of the highly disciplined intellect within.

The chateau at the foot of the hill had been in Ricard's family for over a century. His father, grandfather, and great-grandfather had all been vintners, producing a well-respected red wine. Ricard had worked in the family business until he was nineteen years of age. Then, like his father, grandfather, and great-grandfather before him, he'd become a soldier, serving with the French army for thirty-five years.

During the last ten years of his service, Ricard had led a special operations unit attached to the French Foreign Legion. The unit's existence had been a carefully guarded secret, providing the French government with a lethal, but deniable, military option that could be deployed on a moment's notice. During its tenure, the unit had been quietly deployed throughout the world on missions ranging from rescue missions to assassinations. When it was disbanded, Ricard had quietly retired.

When he reached the low wall that separated the gardens surrounding the main house from the path and the fields beyond, a petite young brunette opened the back door of the chateau and waved to him with a smile. It was Marie, his twenty-two-year-old niece. She was visiting him from Paris for the week.

"Good morning, Marie."

"Good morning. You have a phone call from America. His name is Jacques."

An image of a tall, lean Haitian dressed in combat fatigues came to Ricard unbidden. He could almost see the smile on the rogue's handsome face, and the rakish cant of his beret. A small smile came to his face.

"Thank you, Marie, I'll be right there."

Ricard wiped his feet on the entrance rug and walked through the anteroom to his office. He draped his coat on the back of the chair in front a small desk and picked up the phone.

"Bonjour, mon ami," Ricard said, with a smile in his voice.

"Bonjour, Colonel, I was just calling to inquire about that fifty-year-old Bordeaux you've been saving for me."

"Poor man, the Texas sun must have addled your brains. I would never waste such a fine wine on a culinary Philistine," Ricard said, his smile widening.

It was a running joke between the two men. Jacques considered himself an aficionado of the world's finest wines, and after a near miss during the midst of a fire fight in Africa, Jaq had turned to Ricard and said, "Now, don't get yourself killed, sir. You owe me your best bottle of Bordeaux, after all."

"To what honor do I owe this call?"

"The honor is mine, old friend. However, I am concerned about our American friend."

Ricard knew Jacques was referring to John Caine, the only American who'd served in the Legion's black operations unit.

"Our friend believes that he is the subject of a professional inquiry. We are talking about a major player, with substantial resources."

"Does he know the player?"

"No."

"Does he know their objective?"

"Only that they want to retire him."

"Is there any question about this?"

"None. They . . . have been very persistent."

Jacques related everything Caine had told him, and Ricard considered the information in silence when Jaq finished.

"The resources . . . suggest a government outfit, but the tactics don't fit the profile," Ricard said, mentally working through what Jaq had told him. "I also can't imagine any government starting a fight like this on American soil. It would be too big a problem if the operation became public."

"We made a lot of people unhappy, sir." Jaq said.

"Yes, but very few of those people knew that *we* were the cause of their unhappiness. We need more information and we need our American friend to stay alive in the meantime."

Ricard's reference to "we" brought a knowing smile to Jaq's face. Jaq had been reluctant to disturb Ricard's well-deserved retirement, but he also knew that Ricard would never forgive him if he failed to tell him about Caine's problem. Although Ricard would never say so, Jaq knew the old soldier viewed the members of the unit as his family. When the unit had been disbanded two years after the end of the

Cold War, Ricard had elected to retire at fifty-five, rather than accept a different assignment.

"I will contact some friends here and find out what I can. I'll also let our Polish and Italian comrades know about this problem. How can I contact you?" Ricard said.

"Use the same number. It will forward to me wherever I am, and I'll call you back within five minutes, unless I am dead, or enjoying a fine wine," Jaq answered.

Ricard smiled when he answered, "Au revoir."

Ricard looked over at a picture on the wall behind the desk. It was one of the few pictures of the four men together—Jaq, MacBain, Vlasky, and Caine. The picture should never have been taken, because of the unit's covert nature, but Jaq had never been particularly interested in the Legion's regulations. Jaq had sent Ricard a framed copy of the picture several months after he retired. Caine was on the far left, Vlasky and Jacques were in the middle, and MacBain was on the far right.

Ricard reached over and picked up the picture and looked at it for a long moment. *MacBain*. He'd never thought about it before, but he realized that the picture must have been taken just before they were sent on the mission in the Republic of Congo.

The unit had been sent to Africa to deter an attack by a local warlord on a remote village along the Congo River. When the crisis arose, a French mining consortium was in the middle of negotiations with Kinshasa over the renewal of certain mineral rights. When the Congolese government politely asked for help with the warlord problem, the consortium pressured Paris to intervene. In order to provide an excuse for the intervention, Paris and Kinshasa put together a story about a group of French missionaries who were at risk. In fact, the missionaries were further down the river.

The operation should never have been assigned to the unit. It was too small to do the job without artillery and air support, which was unavailable. Although Ricard's superiors knew this, politics overrode the military reality.

Ricard had been assured that the mission was political, not military, and it would only last two days: the warlord would not risk an engagement with the French army. Ricard had also been told, in confidence, to evacuate the area in the unlikely event the enemy showed up in force, ready to fight.

When the warlord's company-size force had arrived unexpectedly, Caine, who was unaware of these facts, changed the game. As soon as the rebels threatened a group of local women, the American had provided defensive fire, sparking a general engagement. The warlord had initially pressed the fight, but after fifteen of his men were killed, he withdrew. MacBain had been fatally wounded in the fight, and died within minutes.

Ricard had never mentioned his orders to Caine, and his superiors had dropped the issue when the papers turned the incident into a heroic vignette: a small but unnamed Legionary force, facing impossible odds, had saved three hundred villagers from slaughter, which indeed they had. The French people loved it.

Unfortunately, Caine had discovered the truth on his own. Caine had been at a bar frequented by the Legion's soldiers in Paris one night, a month later. An indiscreet staff officer from Battalion HQ had described the incident, in generic terms, to a group of legionnaires. Caine was listening. The officer had explained to others at his table that the whole incident should never have happened: "some trigger-happy soldier" had started the fight. Caine had recognized the mission from the description, and he'd also recognized that he was the "trigger-happy" soldier in the story.

Ricard had belatedly learned of the incident in the bar after he had retired. He'd never had the opportunity to speak with Caine about it, and it was one of the few things in his life that he truly regretted. Now it seemed that fate was offering him a chance to make amends with the past. It was not an opportunity he intended to miss. For the first time in the past three years, he forgot the growing pain in his stomach.

# CHAPTER
# TWENTY-NINE

*Austin, Texas*
*December 6, 1999 / Monday / 6:00 a.m.*

Paquin looked out at the dark and semi-deserted streets of downtown Austin from the rear of the limousine and tried to ignore his irritation at Mason's insistence on a meeting. He should be working on finding the target, not listening to Mason's complaints and less-than-subtle threats. When they had spoken earlier, Paquin had considered refusing Mason's request, but decided to concede the issue. A delicate balance had to be maintained in his particular client relationships. If he tipped the scales beyond a certain point, Mason would quietly hire a replacement, and the new man's first assignment would almost certainly be to eliminate Nicholas Paquin. Paquin didn't think matters had reached that point yet, but then, he could be wrong.

Paquin remembered engaging in this same kind of analysis after he'd receive a call in the middle of the night from STASI headquarters, ordering him to attend an unscheduled "meeting." As he drove through the deserted gray streets of East Berlin each time, he would ask himself whether the Ministry or the KGB had decided he was a threat that needed to disappear.

The guard waiting in front of Helius for his arrival opened the rear door to the limousine.

"Good evening, sir."

Paquin nodded and followed the guard to the elevator bank inside the building. The guard inserted a key into the inside panel and pressed the button for the fifty-second floor, which held a secure conference facility.

The elevator opened to a spacious reception area. The twelve-foot ceiling was covered in a white marble striated with gray and gold. The walls were a jet-black marble, but the stark effect was offset by the series of golden sconces that were spaced at three-foot intervals throughout the room. A depiction of the Greek demigod Helius had been sculpted into each of the sconces and the light from within illuminated the outline.

Paquin ignored the room's elegance and walked down a broad hallway framed by two black Doric columns. The décor in the hallway transitioned from wall-to-wall marble to mahogany, and the floor to a black-lacquered wood. A plush red-and-green Oriental runner ran down the center. The walls were decorated with portraits of the Mason family patriarchs extending back 120 years. The only lights in the hallway other than the small lights along the ornate baseboard were those illuminating each portrait.

The double doors at the end of the hallway, which were also made of mahogany, extended from floor to ceiling. Paquin and Mason had met in the room on several other occasions. The room was Mason's personal conference room. A black keypad was located on the wall just outside the doors. As soon as Paquin touched the glass, the number pad lit up and he typed in the code provided to him on the way over.

Paquin slowly pushed open the door and saw Mason standing by the far wall looking out the window. When Paquin stepped into the room, Mason turned and looked at him as if he were a stranger, assessing him from head to toe. Mason was tall, tanned, and in excellent physical condition. He had a tennis player's body, and in fact was a skilled and avid player.

Mason's face was handsome in an aristocratic way, with a high forehead, a narrow, prominent nose, chiseled cheeks, and a strong, angular jawline. His iron-gray hair was trim but thick. Mason's eyes were his most distinguishing and unsettling feature. They protruded abnormally and had a striking greenish-blue cast, conveying the impression of a perpetual stare. When Mason's heavy gray-white eyebrows were added to the mix, the entire effect was cold and penetrating, even predatory.

Paquin knew the image was also the reality. Mason was a cold and utterly ruthless individual. In many ways, he was not so different from the top officers of the STASI and KGB that Paquin had reported to more than a decade ago in East Germany. The only real difference was Mason's social pedigree and national origin.

At a certain level, Paquin disliked people like Mason. He disliked their arrogance, the psychological games they played, and the natural contempt they felt for their fellow human beings, including those who did their bidding. On the other hand, Paquin was a realist. People like Mason paid well for his services. In return, he was willing to accept the burdens inherent in the relationship, at least up to a point.

Once Mason realized that Paquin was prepared to endure his stare for as long as necessary without saying anything, he changed tactics. A neat pile of financials was laid out at the head of the long mahogany table that dominated the center of the room. Mason walked over to the large leather chair in front of the stack and started to sit down. Then, almost as if it was an afterthought, he waved Paquin to a chair without looking in his direction.

"Please sit down, Mr. Paquin."

Paquin nodded and started across the room to the nearest chair. As he emerged from under the recessed lights that lit the entrance to the semi-darkened room, he realized that someone else was seated at the far end of the table. Although the figure was partially shrouded in darkness, Paquin recognized the outline as he approached a chair that was just past the one indicated by Mason.

A rich baritone reached across the room to him.

"Good morning, brother Paquin. It is, of course, a pleasure to see you again."

As he spoke, the figure at the end of the table leaned forward into the sphere of light shining on the table immediately above him, revealing an almost coal-black man with a bald head, broad, strong facial features, and a powerlifter's massive shoulders and arms. The smile on the man's face radiated absolute confidence and more than a hint of challenge.

"Good morning, Onwuallu. What an unexpected pleasure," Paquin said, keeping the surprise out of his voice. Although Mason acted as if he was too engrossed in the financials in front of him to notice the kinetic undercurrent of antagonism that flowed between the two men, Paquin knew otherwise. Mason had staged the confrontation. Now he knew why Mason had insisted on the meeting, at least in part.

Onwuallu served as Helius's liaison to the various African countries where Helius had economic interests, or was seeking to develop such interests. Unlike Paquin, Onwuallu's professional pedigree was not in the espionage trade. Onwuallu had been a top lieutenant in Charles Taylor's kleptocracy in Liberia, until Taylor's brutality and theft had spawned a rebellion, driving him from power. In his own words, Onwuallu was a "persuader of men," otherwise known as a torturer.

Mason undoubtedly knew that Onwuallu believed he, not Paquin, should be the head of Helius's security apparatus, which was why he'd arranged the meeting. What Mason didn't realize was that Onwuallu's ambitions had caused a fatal clash between the two men in the past, turning rivalry into deadly enmity. The incident had occurred six months after Paquin took control over Helius's security resources. Paquin had been advised by his predecessor that Onwuallu's primary function was to bribe African dictators when necessary to advance or protect Helius's interests. Onwuallu, however, viewed himself as being the unquestioned czar of all of Helius's security operations on the African continent. This difference in outlook had laid the foundation for the clash between the two men.

In 1995, Paquin had mounted a successful operation to extract one of Helius's corporate executives from the hands of a warlord in Somalia. Paquin, always suspicious of anyone he did not personally vet and hire, planned and implemented the operation without notifying Onwuallu, or more importantly, in Onwuallu's mind, seeking his consent. When Onwuallu learned of this perceived slight to his authority, he'd tried to compromise the operation by alerting one of the local drug lords about the extraction operation beforehand. Fortunately for Paquin, the betrayal had come too late to disrupt his plans. The extraction went off as planned.

The failed intervention had infuriated Onwuallu, making him that much more determined to punish Paquin for failing to respect his turf. A week later, the Somali who'd guided Paquin's team in and out of the sector of Mogadishu controlled by the drug lord was killed by one of Onwuallu's lieutenants.

After the killing, Onwuallu assumed that Paquin lacked the resources to discover who was behind the killing. The risk of retribution had never crossed his mind. This assumption had been in error. Within two weeks, Onwuallu's top operative was found dead, with a picture of the murdered Somali in his pocket.

Onwuallu had considered retaliating, but unlike Paquin, he lacked the necessary assets outside of Africa to exact retribution. He also realized that his own death was a near certainty, unless he succeeded in killing Paquin himself. Faced with this choice, Onwuallu had reluctantly stood down, but he'd never forgotten the incident, and neither had Paquin.

Paquin had come to the meeting prepared to deal with Mason's questions, complaints, and quiet threats. Onwuallu's presence made the situation more complicated and dangerous. Onwuallu would use any information disclosed in the meeting to obtain an advantage, with the end-game being Paquin's destruction. In the face of this threat, Paquin knew that he would have to be more circumspect, and this would impair his ability to respond to Mason's questions. Paquin also had to consider a far more ominous possibility. Onwuallu might be there to replace him. Although Mason might well contemplate that such a transition would be peaceful, Onwuallu would view the situation differently. He would have come to the meeting with a plan in place to kill Paquin as soon as he left the building.

After Paquin sat down, Mason closed the file that he was pretending to look at and sat back in his chair. Mason looked at his steepled hands for almost a minute, and then he spoke without looking up.

"Mr. Paquin, we seem to have a problem—a systemic problem. Helius sends out a team of your handpicked soldiers to eliminate a simple problem in California. Yet they fail miserably in this endeavor and lose a million-dollar helicopter in the process."

Mason stopped and looked over his steepled fingers at Paquin, awaiting a response. Paquin simply returned the stare, forcing Mason to continue.

"Very well, mistakes can happen. However, the very next morning your team made a *second* attempt to eliminate the problem and failed again."

Mason hesitated again, looking over at Paquin, who again made no effort to respond.

"Now I am advised that another team of *your* handpicked soldiers was sent out to deal with another problem. This time the target is the woman, Ms. Marenna. Once again your people failed in this effort, and worse, they allowed themselves to be ambushed by an unknown individual."

Mason's tone steadily climbed in intensity, ending with barely restrained scorn.

Mason stared over the top of his reading glasses at Paquin, all but demanding a response. Paquin remained quiet. He knew from experience that Mason's preferred manner was quiet intimidation. He would lay out what he considered to be the damning facts and then intentionally stare at whoever was the target of his dissatisfaction until the subordinate made the mistake of trying to provide an explanation, at which point in time Mason would hold up a restraining hand and advise the subordinate that he wasn't finished, forcing an apology from his mortified victim.

Paquin almost smiled as he recalled how the STASI interrogators used a similar technique. The difference was that in the STASI interrogations the subject received more than a restraining wave of the hand when the "interruption" occurred. He or she would be beaten to the floor. This treatment would induce the subject to hesitate too long before responding to future questions, which would then result in more beatings. The technique was designed to destabilize the subject physically and mentally to the point where complete subservience resulted. Paquin knew how to play this game better than Mason, so he simply waited, hiding all reactive emotions, in the face of Mason's stare and the arrogant smile that he could see on Onwuallu's face.

The silence continued. Then, with a quiet but audible sigh, Mason continued.

"Would you agree, Mr. Paquin, your organization seems to have a competency problem?"

Paquin didn't respond right away, playing Mason's own game. He looked out the window at the cityscape that was beginning to come alive. After what he considered a sufficiently long interval, Paquin turned, looked directly at Mason, and answered the question without emotion.

"Each team could have performed better. However, the core problem was a lack of intelligence."

Then Paquin hesitated until Mason responded to this comment, with the sought-after follow-up question.

"What are you talking about?"

"Two teams were sent out after what they understood to be soft targets. In fact, we're dealing with a hard target, a very hard target."

Onwuallu interrupted. "Or, Mr. Paquin, maybe you and your team have just grown too soft, no?"

Mason didn't allow Paquin to respond to Onwuallu's obvious provocation.

"What do you mean a hard target, and are you suggesting that the same target caused tonight's problem in Texas?"

Paquin leaned forward and looked directly at Mason when he answered.

"Yes, I am. Consider the facts. The first team was sent to take out what they understood to be a wayward accountant in the middle of the night. They approached this individual's cabin in the early hours of the morning. The target anticipated their attack and responded by creating a unique diversion. He fired a flare into the night sky: a flare that's specifically designed *to blind enemy soldiers.* That's not something you buy at the local hardware store. When that flare exploded, it temporarily blinded the assault team, and the target used this opportunity to escape on a snowmobile. The assault team then regrouped and pursued the target in the chopper. Once the target realized he was being hunted from the air, he planned and executed an ambush, taking out the chopper. Given these facts . . . only a fool would suggest that we're dealing with anything but a highly skilled and experienced professional."

Onwuallu started to interrupt with a growl, but Mason's raised hand stopped him. The quiet tension in the room was almost palpable.

"Tell me what you have learned about this hard target, as you say, Mr. Paquin."

Paquin nodded and continued. "My sources indicate the target is a former member of the U.S. Army Rangers."

Onwuallu scoffed, "So what. He's a soldier boy. I have listened to many soldiers scream and cry in Liberia when they were tested. This means nothing."

"Yes," Paquin said, looking at his hands, "I am sure you *tested*, as you say, many men, even a few soldiers. I'm also sure that every one of them was chained to a chair when you took their measure. The results might have been very different but for the restraints."

Rage sparked for a second in Onwuallu's eyes, but then he slowly smiled and spoke quietly, his baritone carrying an undercurrent of menace, "We shall see, brother Paquin, we shall see."

Mason watched the exchange, but his mind was elsewhere. "What else did your inquiries yield, Mr. Paquin?"

"The target left the army in 1980 and his file ends there, which makes sense, because it's a Pentagon file." Paquin hesitated a moment and then continued.

"However, the file included notations that suggested it had made the rounds to other agencies."

"What other agencies?" Mason interrupted.

"The CIA, NSA, and DIA," Paquin answered quietly.

Mason's face tightened and his steepled fingers lowered and interlocked in front of him, in a tight grip.

"What . . . does that mean?" Mason asked.

"It could mean a number of things. Caine could have been part of a covert operation while he was with the Rangers, or he could have just been reviewed for participation in such an operation and then passed over. Worst case, he could be CIA or DIA today. We don't know for sure. Our source doesn't have the clearance to get that kind of information."

"You need to acquire a more highly placed asset then," Mason responded with obvious irritation in his voice.

Paquin nodded for a moment, as if considering the idea, and then responded, "We could try, but that has its own risks. Top-drawer intelligence assets are very difficult to compromise, and a failed attempt could trigger an exhaustive investigation that could well have serious implications for Helius."

"Well, we don't want that, do we, Mr. Paquin?" Mason said, his face tightening. "Now tell me, why have you come to the somewhat fantastic conclusion that our California problem has found his way to Texas, identified the individual here that we are concurrently hunting, and then whisked her away from your supposedly competent and well-trained unit?"

Mason's voice was both skeptical and challenging, and Paquin could almost feel Onwuallu's responsive smile in the darkness. Had Mason asked this question an hour ago, Paquin's answer would have been simple: He didn't have one. At least not the kind of definitive explanation Mason was after. Fortunately, on the way in from the airport he'd received an update from the wire team monitoring the Marenna woman's condominium.

The update gave him the definitive factual support he needed to answer Mason's inquiry, but he decided not to disclose the information initially. Onwuallu's presence and his effort to suborn Paquin's position necessitated a more subtle game. He would guide Mason down a path that would intentionally heighten his fears and intensify his frustration at the lack of progress, then he would pull him up short with the release of the information. It was a dangerous game, but if it worked, Mason's sagging confidence in Paquin's abilities, and in his critical role in the chase, would be restored.

"I don't know for sure. I haven't had the time to analyze the facts in detail. But my preliminary read is that there are . . . just too many coincidences. In both situations the teams were confronted by a skilled opponent, and in both instances there was a common operational pattern. The target turned and fought only when required to accomplish his primary objective."

Paquin heard a quiet scoff from Onwuallu, but he ignored it. Mason's dissatisfaction with the lack of concrete information was what he needed, and it came right on cue.

"Mr. Paquin, that is all well and good, but you have not told me how this individual managed to identify and make common cause with our Texas problem so quickly."

"That's because I cannot without more information. My guess is that someone put the two of them together."

Mason's reaction was immediate.

"What? The only one who could have put them together would be someone within our network. Are you suggesting a leak? No one here knows. It would have to be someone—"

"In Mr. Paquin's organization," Onwuallu finished Mason's thought, his deep baritone quietly resounding across the table.

The room was deathly quiet. Paquin looked out the window, feeling the two men staring at him in the semidarkness. During his employment with Helius, Paquin had discovered that Mason's greatest fear was the possibility that a government informant would worm his way into his domain and bring down his empire from within. This fear was one of the reasons why Mason particularly appreciated Paquin's unique ability to design a series of blinds that kept an impenetrable wall between Helius and the black ops he ran around the world. Paquin's scheme played on this paranoia.

When Paquin answered, he continued to look out the window, avoiding Mason's gaze.

"That's possible, but unlikely. If such a source existed, he or she would already have access to sufficient information to bring the police to the door. No, I am inclined to believe that the recently deceased Mr. Steinman sent out a message to Mr. Caine before his demise. However, if you give me a moment, I may be able to obtain clarification."

Paquin took out his cell phone. He had five of them. Each phone used a different service, and each phone was registered to a different corporate entity. He used a different phone every day, and the numbers were switched every three months. Although it was possible that a determined government agency, with a roving wiretap authorization, might be able to intercept his signal, it would be very difficult.

Paquin dialed David Weill. Weill was in charge of Paquin's telecommunications espionage department. He was an expert in intercepting and monitoring information transmitted over any kind of telecommunications system. He was also expecting Paquin's call. Weill picked up on the second ring.

"Weill here."

"It's Paquin. I'm going to put you on a speaker. I need an update on Andrea Marenna's line."

"One minute. No calls were made from the subject's landline today. Six were made yesterday—three in, three out," Weill answered.

"I want to know about calls made to or received from a male caller with a California area code."

"One minute. There were four calls. One was a message left by a male calling from California. Marenna left a message for this same caller. Then there were two calls where they connected."

"Who was the male caller?" Paquin asked.

"He identified himself as John Caine."

"Was the name Richard Steinman mentioned in these exchanges?"

"Yes, sir. The transcript indicates that Steinman left a message for Caine and instructed him to call Marenna."

"Thank you," Paquin said, and terminated the call. "There's your answer."

"Steinman." Mason said the name as if it was something loathsome.

"That's right. Our information indicates that Mr. Steinman and Ms. Marenna met at law school. It would appear that Steinman made contact with Mr. Caine before his death, but it doesn't appear from this conversation that he had any contacts with Ms. Marenna about Helius. What those contacts were and what information was exchanged is not clear."

Mason hesitated. It was obvious that he didn't want to accept Paquin's conclusion, but felt compelled to do so by the facts.

"Very well, Mr. Paquin. That presents a real problem. You see, the information that Mr. Steinman—"

At this point, Paquin pointedly glanced over at Onwuallu and then glanced back at Mason. Mason's latent paranoia made the connection immediately. He stopped in midsentence and looked over at Onwuallu, who didn't understand what had just occurred.

"Mr. Onwuallu, your participation in this meeting has been very helpful. However, I know that you have a long flight back to Harare tonight, and I don't want to keep you from the pressing business you have there."

Then Mason stood up before Onwuallu could say anything. Onwuallu realized that he'd been outmaneuvered by Paquin, and he slowly stood up. He was looking down at the table as he stood up, but Paquin could see the rage in his eyes. By the time he looked over at Mason, the Liberian had regained control. He nodded politely to Mason, his face tight, but respectful.

"Thank you, Mr. Mason. It was a pleasure," Onwuallu said, his eyes on Paquin.

Mason just nodded and turned his attention back to the financials in front of him. Onwuallu continued to look at Paquin as he walked to the door. The restrained rage and almost kinetic threat in his eyes made it clear that Menard Onwuallu didn't consider the matter to be closed. At that instant, Paquin made a decision. Onwuallu would have a fatal accident once the current problem was solved. When Onwuallu closed the door on the way out, Mason continued as though he'd never been there.

"As I was saying, this development could be very problematic, indeed. If Mr. Caine communicated the information provided to him by Steinman to the press—"

Paquin quietly interrupted him, "We cannot be sure of anything based upon what we have, but we have to assume that Caine didn't obtain enough information to understand the whole picture. Otherwise he would have already gone to the authorities, or alternatively contacted us directly to negotiate a price. Either way, we have to proceed on that assumption."

Mason looked at Paquin for a moment before responding, "I agree with your assessment. Now tell me, where does that leave us? How do we find Mr. Caine and his new female friend, and eliminate them?"

Paquin stared as his hands for a moment, and then looked directly at Mason. "We have to pursue concurrent strategies. If we find the girl, we find Mr. Caine. This is her home turf, so it's likely that she selected their present refuge. As we speak, the resources necessary to find that location are working on the problem. We also know that Caine and the woman will be seeking more information. We have to focus on what they're after and get there first."

Mason nodded his head approvingly, and then raised an issue that Paquin had expected him to bring up earlier.

"Mr. Paquin, there is something in all of this that I don't understand. Why hasn't Mr. Caine contacted the police? It would seem an obvious course of action."

"There are a number of potential explanations. Mr. Caine could be a criminal himself, which means police support is not an option, or the explanation could be more complex. Now that Ms. Marenna's involved, I suspect the situation will change. She's a lawyer, so we can assume that she will try to gain help from law enforcement. When she makes that effort, we will intercept the communication, find her location, and eliminate the two of them," Paquin said, with quiet confidence.

"Very well, Mr. Paquin. I will leave the situation in your . . . capable hands, with the understanding that there will be no more problems."

Paquin just nodded, and Mason turned his attention back to the financials in front of him, signaling that the meeting was at an end.

*Austin, Texas*
*December 6, 1999 / Monday / 6:50 a.m.*

Onwuallu sat in a dark blue Lincoln Continental, staring at the front of the Helius Building. Rage was still pulsing through him. Paquin would pay dearly for his lack of respect. It was just a question of when and how. Based on what he had heard in the meeting, the "when" could be very close. Contrary to Mason's instructions, he intended to stay in Austin and make sure that possibility became a reality.

Onwuallu leaned back in the seat and reviewed what he'd learned. Mason had invited him to come to Austin to discuss Helius's efforts to secure drilling rights in Sudan from the Sudanese government. Negotiations had reached an impasse, and Mason wanted Onwuallu to find someone within the power structure in Khartoum who could be persuaded, for the right price, to intervene on behalf of the company.

After the meeting, Mason had unexpectedly asked him stay and to participate in a meeting with Paquin. According to Mason, he wanted Onwuallu's "insights" on a problem that Paquin was having difficulty resolving. Although Mason had described the problem as minor, Onwuallu could all but smell the anger, and more surprisingly, the fear, behind Mason's controlled facade. Onwuallu also sensed a potential opportunity to usurp Paquin's position.

As the meeting had progressed and the extent of Paquin's problems with this John Caine and Marenna woman had become clear, Onwuallu could barely restrain himself. The fool had all but opened the door for him. All he needed to do was to persuade Mason to allow him to take over the operation. Once he eliminated Mason's problem, he would have the political capital necessary to get away with killing Paquin. Then Paquin had turned the tables on him seconds before he'd weighed in with his proposal. Worse, Paquin had somehow managed to persuade Mason that Onwuallu should be excluded from the balance of the meeting. As he thought back on the final minutes, Onwuallu realized the phone call Paquin had made was staged. Unfortunately his little scheme had worked.

For now, Mason had decided that Paquin was indispensable. But that could change. If Paquin failed to eliminate John Caine and the woman quickly, Mason would be forced to look elsewhere for help. Onwuallu smiled to himself. Nicholas Paquin's life was about to get more complicated. He dialed a number on his cell.

"Porter."

"Mr. Porter, we will be staying in Austin for a day or two longer."

"Very good, sir."

"I have heard that Austin can be a dangerous city. Please acquire some protection for the two of us. Say two side arms, and something with a longer range."

"Very good, sir," Porter answered, a smile in his voice.

# CHAPTER
# THIRTY

*Austin, Texas*
*December 6, 1999 / Monday / 1:00 a.m.*

Andrea parked the truck on a narrow two-lane road just across the street from a collection of small wooden cottages that were clustered around a main building. The glowing oblong sign attached to the main building advertised the "Bluebonnet Motel." All of the cottages were dark, but a light was still on in the office in the main building. The parking lot was partially illuminated by a bug-encrusted light on top of the lamppost in the center of the lot. Three cars and a van were parked in the lot.

Andrea dropped her head back on the headrest and looked up at the roof of the pickup.

"I must be insane," Andrea said in exasperation.

Caine smiled. "It's not that bad, and you're the one who picked it out."

"You told me you wanted a hotel that accepted cash that wasn't an SRO nightmare in downtown Austin. This is the only place I know that . . . and by the way, I haven't been here in fifteen years. Now, please tell me why we can't simply check into the Hilton downtown?"

"Cash has no digital signature. Credit cards do. If these people have access to up-to-the-minute credit card information, the instant the Hilton runs your card or mine, which they will insist on doing, the bad guys will know exactly where we are. I don't know about you, but I've had enough excitement for one night."

"John, these people are not the police or the FBI. They don't have access to that kind of data," Andrea said.

"Sure about that? They found you and me quick enough."

Andrea turned and looked over at Caine. "If I was suspicious, which I totally am right now, I might be inclined to think that this whole thing—"

"—is a scheme to get you in a compromising position? Ye of little faith: I have that covered," Caine finished.

He stepped out of the truck, pulled out his cell phone, and punched in a speed-dial code.

"Hello, Tomas, it's John. Sorry to wake you. Listen . . . I know, but I have a problem. I'll tell you about it later. Right now, I need you to talk to someone. She needs to know that I'm a perfect gentleman. Answer any question that she asks, and this time don't lie," Caine said with a smile and handed the phone to Andrea.

"John, what's going on?" Andrea said, looking at the phone.

"His name is Tomas Moreno, *Father* Tomas Moreno. Ask him anything about me."

Andrea could hear the male voice on the phone demanding that Caine pick up, and she reluctantly accepted the phone. Caine closed the door of the truck, waved, and started across the street toward the motel.

Ten minutes later, Caine walked back across the street and climbed back in the truck. Andrea looked over at him without saying anything for a moment. Then she turned and started up the truck.

"Okay, we've established that you're a big supporter of a local Catholic school, you were an Army Ranger, and there's at least one person in the world who is confused enough to think you're a complete boy scout."

A smile played across Caine's face when he responded, "I couldn't pull anything over on Tomas, even if I wanted to. He's a former Marine drill instructor."

Caine pointed to the far end of the parking lot.

"Quail Cottage—the one over there on the right, and yes, there are two beds."

*Austin, Texas*
*December 6, 1999 / Monday / 7:30 a.m.*

Caine was already up and fully dressed when Andrea woke the next morning. He was sitting at the little table near the window, with a small pad of paper and a pencil. A large cup of coffee was in front of him. A second cup and a brown paper bag were on the far side of the table. When Caine realized that she was awake, he called, "Good morning" over his shoulder, but didn't turn around.

Andrea waved, but didn't say anything. She wanted to get in the bathroom and make sure she didn't look like too much of a nightmare before she sat across from another human being, particularly a male human being. Twenty minutes later, she came out of the bathroom feeling almost human. She walked over to the other chair at the small table and sat down. Caine pushed a paper coffee cup and a blueberry muffin across the table.

"Good morning. Breakfast is courtesy of your local Quick Stop gas station down the road," Caine said.

Andrea smiled. "Thank you. Why, it almost seems like I'm on vacation."

Caine returned the smile. "Not quite."

Andrea took a sip of the coffee and nodded at the pad of paper he was writing on. "What are you doing?"

"I've been jotting down some facts in an effort to try to bracket who's on the other side of this thing and why. Let me tell you what I have so far. Twenty-four hours ago, a group of men were airlifted to within striking distance of my cabin in Snow Valley. My guess is they were sent there to take me out. This tells me that the opposition has major resources and an organization in place capable of doing these things."

"They also seem to have found a way to get inside my townhouse and put a tap on my phone. Then they tracked me to the Portman Lodge and . . . tried to kidnap me," Andrea said.

165

When she mentioned the kidnapping attempt, the memory of the brutal experience came racing back, and a wave of involuntary fear swept over her. She glanced over at the curtained window.

Caine noticed the look. "It's okay. I've been watching."

Andrea looked over at him, but he was looking at the writing pad again.

"John, there's not too many people with those kinds of resources. It almost seems like a government thing, which doesn't make any sense. No law enforcement agency would pull something like this. It's too far outside the lines, and they would have no reason to. If the FBI, ATF, or some other agency wanted to take me into custody, they could have stopped by my office with a warrant," Andrea said.

Caine glanced up from the pad.

"You're right. If a government outfit is behind this, then it's foreign."

Andrea took another sip of her coffee and smiled.

"My life is just not interesting enough to attract that kind of attention," Andrea said, with a wry smile. "How about you?"

When Caine didn't react to the question, Andrea stopped smiling and leaned forward. "Is there a reason why you're not answering my question?"

Andrea's voice was polite, but Caine could hear the undertone of suspicion.

Caine hesitated and then said, "The answer to that question is a little complicated."

"Try me."

"Andrea, the military unit I was with for about a decade engaged in operations all over the world. Some of these operations would be of interest to any number of foreign governments. But that was a long time ago, and the feelers that I put out came back negative."

"Wait a minute. I thought you said you were with the Army Rangers? Anyone who wants to learn about United States Army operations can just look through past editions of the *New York Times* or *Washington Post*. They don't need to chase you around Texas to find out."

"Andrea, I'm not talking about the U.S. Army, and like I said, I think that road is a dead end. The key to—"

"What army are we talking about?"

"I can't answer that. There are secrecy laws, and there are people who could be put at risk by any disclosure."

Andrea looked at him, her face unreadable. Then she pushed her cup aside and laid both of her hands on the table in front of her.

"First, if people are trying to kill me because of something in your background, I think I have a right to know why. Second, I'm a lawyer. Keeping confidences is something I do for a living, and those confidences can be protected by the attorney-client privilege."

Caine looked at her for a moment.

"Explain to me how the privilege works and what I need to do to make sure it applies to what I tell you."

"The privilege protects confidential client communications. You hold the privilege. I cannot disclose any communications encompassed by the privilege without your permission, and except in extremely rare circumstances, I cannot be compelled under the laws of this state, or the laws of the United States, to break the privilege. As far as what you need to do to make sure it applies, if you hand me a piece of paper and that pen, I can take care of that."

Caine tore off a piece of paper from the pad and pushed the paper and the pen across the table.

Andrea picked up the pen and wrote a short paragraph on the paper and then handed the paper back to Caine.

"Please read the contract, Mr. Caine, and sign where indicated, if acceptable. We will work out the financial arrangements later," Andrea said with a smile.

Caine looked at the paper and then signed it at the bottom.

"Okay, what's next?" Caine said.

"Is the information that you are about to communicate confidential and are you providing this information to me in order to enable me to protect your legal rights? Say yes."

"Yes," Caine answered.

"Very well, the privilege applies. Now, where was I? Yes, you were about to tell me about this complicated situation."

Caine doodled on the pad a moment and then looked over at Andrea.

"After I left the Rangers, I served with La Légion Étrangère for ten years."

"I've never heard of it."

"I'm sorry. You would know it as the French Foreign Legion."

Andrea looked over at him, her face a mixture of confusion and disbelief.

"Are you serious?"

"Yes. It's not that big a deal. There are quite a few Americans in the ranks. The secrecy issue relates to the covert operations unit that I was assigned to during the latter part of my service. No one knew the unit existed, except the commander of the Legion, the head of the DGSE, and a few men at the very top of the French government."

"What did this unit do?" Andrea asked, her voice quiet.

"The operations covered a broad range from simple surveillance to high-intensity combat and everything in between. We were an off-balance-sheet resource that the French government used to quietly solve problems. None of our operations ever hit the newspapers."

"John, I don't mean to be rude, but it seems obvious to me that all of this must have something to do with you and that covert unit."

Caine shook his head.

"That was my initial read as well, but I think it's wrong for a lot of reasons. Very few people knew about the existence of this unit. To access the name and address of a former member of the unit, someone would need very high security clearance. It's possible someone pulled it off, but it's unlikely, and like I said, my inquiries in that direction have come up negative. From what I can see, your friend Steinman is the key to this. Otherwise, why would they have gone after you?"

"John, you called me, remember?" Andrea said.

"I did, but I made the call because Steinman told me to. But for his message, I never would have called. Second, your phone was tapped and a wire truck was sitting in your parking lot before I called you."

Andrea considered what he said for a long moment. When she spoke again, there was a reluctant acceptance in her voice.

"You're right. Richie's message seems to be the starting point. It's just hard to believe. Richie wrote about local legal developments, like petty crimes, small trials, investigations—that sort of thing. Something like this . . . he must have stumbled into it. What exactly did Richie say in that message?"

"I'll pull up the message and you can listen for yourself."

Caine's message service was through SBC, the local phone company. He dialed the message number and typed in his passcode. Instead of the typical greeting, he received a message advising him that the number was "no longer in service."

Caine tried the number of again and received the same message.

"Something's wrong here," Caine said and dialed information for the SBC help line. After spending five minutes working through a series of automated messages, he was told by the last message that operators were only available between 8:00 a.m. and 6:00 p.m. Pacific standard time. Caine glanced at his wristwatch. It was still only 6:00 a.m. in California.

Caine turned to Andrea and said, "I can't get through right now, but I have an idea that when I do, I won't like what I find out."

"What do you mean?"

"It would have been easy enough for someone to cancel my service and wipe out the messages. As long as you call from the phone the order came from, the phone company will usually accept the cancellation. That would be child's play for this outfit, but we can find out later on. I can summarize the message. Steinman said that I owned land here in Texas, or that I, let me see . . . should, that's what he said, 'should own the land.' The message was kind of cryptic, and there was a lot of noise in the background. He said the land was valuable. He suggested that I might be in danger because of this ownership interest."

Andrea listened, but the picture didn't make any sense to her. People stopped killing each other over title disputes a long time ago. There had to be more to it.

"Is it possible that you might be the beneficiary under a will or a trust that you're unaware of? Maybe the next beneficiary in line wants to make sure that you don't try to take back a property that was deeded to him or her on the assumption that you were dead."

Caine shook his head. "I'm an orphan. If I had a rich uncle out there, I think he would have surfaced a long time ago."

"This is too all too speculative. We need more information to figure this out," Andrea said.

"Agreed. So, how do we find out more about what Richard Steinman was doing before he died?" Caine asked.

Andrea didn't think about the question before she answered. "That's easier than you think. Richie kept an extra key in the planter just down the hall from his apartment. He was always losing his keys."

"I need to get into that apartment," Caine said, with quiet determination.

Andrea almost choked on the coffee going down her throat when she realized what he was suggesting.

"What? We shouldn't be going anywhere near that place. This is a police matter, or better still, an FBI matter. John, we were almost killed last night. Look, I mentioned this before. I know a prosecutor in Austin. This is someone I trust. We can't do this without help."

Caine could hear the frustration and fear in Andrea's voice. From her perspective, seeking help from the police or the FBI was the only option. From his perspective, it was just one option. Caine also suspected that Andrea was putting too much stock in her friend's ability to persuade either the Austin P.D. or the FBI to suspend the healthy skepticism they brought to cases where the facts were this far outside the box.

If he'd been on his own, Caine would have stayed away from the police until he had at least identified the enemy. If the opposition was a terrorist group or a foreign outfit seeking retribution, which he considered unlikely given Steinman's involvement, then he would contact his own resources in the intelligence community. They would bring him in as a friendly. If the threat came from some other source, then he would approach the authorities through a referral from one of his own intermediaries. Although the FBI or Austin P.D. wouldn't be too happy about his freelance efforts, they'd have a target other than John Caine to go after.

Caine looked up at Andrea. She was staring at him, her face a mixture of determination and anxiety.

"Okay. Let's see what your friend has to say. Things can't get much worse," Caine said.

Andrea felt a wave of relief.

"Why don't you call your friend and I'll check us out," Caine said and stood up.

After Caine closed the door, Andrea pulled out her cell phone. She started to press the first number when she realized that the phone screen was dark. *Damn! The battery is out.* She looked around the room and saw the phone by the nightstand. Then she pulled out her wallet to find her calling card.

# CHAPTER
# THIRTY-ONE

*Austin, Texas*
*December 6, 1999 / Sunday / 9:00 a.m.*

Jamie Wheeler was a professional, but not in the reputable sense of the word. Before being arrested by the Texas Rangers and spending five years in the Texas State Penitentiary, she'd been involved in hundreds of telephone scam operations. When Jamie Wheeler picked up the phone, she could become just about anybody, from simple, stupid, golly gee Jane, to Myra the demanding IRS agent. She could also mimic almost any accent and wear any emotion necessary to take down the mark. During her less-than-distinguished career, she'd fleeced hundreds of people out of hundreds of thousands of dollars.

Wheeler, who was a white supremacist by her own admission, had hated every day that she'd spent in prison. When she finally was released from that "sewer," she'd decided to find another line of work. Unfortunately, not many employers were willing to pay a forty-five-year-old woman with her criminal pedigree a decent wage. After six months of serving hash at a small diner on the outskirts of Houston for minimum wages and tips, manna had fallen from heaven. A gentleman with a European accent had stopped in for a cup of coffee and offered her a job.

Now Wheeler used her prodigious phone skills to obtain information, not money. The company that paid her check was called Severon Information Systems. Mr. Paquin had told her that Severon was an investigative firm that helped well-heeled clients to obtain information about their competitors. He'd also told her that secrecy was a critical part of Severon's business, and summary termination would result if she talked about her work outside the office. As far as Wheeler was concerned, that wasn't going to happen. Working for Severon was a killer job. The pay was good, the working conditions were the best she'd ever had, and she liked what she was doing.

Today Wheeler was looking for someone called Andrea Marenna, a thirty-four-year-old lawyer from Austin. Her phone persona was Megan Walsh, one of Andrea's old friends. Her story line was simple. Someone called Richard Steinman, a mutual friend, had unexpectedly passed away, and Megan knew that Andrea would feel terrible if she missed the funeral.

Wheeler's supervisor had provided her with a list of potential contacts to start the search effort. These initial contacts had led her to others "who might be able to help." Wheeler was authorized to advise the marks that Andrea had mentioned that she was going out to Granger Lake for the weekend, but for some reason she wasn't staying at the Portman Lodge, where she usually stayed.

Each time she was provided with a possible location, Wheeler would hand it off to another caller, who would then telephonically determine whether or not they had a hit. She was on mark number thirty-six, an elderly aunt. The woman remembered a small motel out in that direction where Andrea and her dad had stayed one summer. Aunt Kate seemed to recall that it was called the "Blue something Motel," but she was sure that the old place was closed by now. After hanging up, Wheeler took a pull on her coffee and ran a search on the computer in front of her. Sure enough, up came the Bluebonnet Motel. It was just outside Austin, about two miles from Granger Lake.

Wheeler dialed the number and put on her best "Southern belle" personality. She was an expert at pinning down the personality on the other side of the phone through voice attributes alone. In this case, she read the man who answered the phone as being over fifty and a smoker. His accent was East Texas, maybe even as far east as Arkansas. Once he started talking, she would nail down his social and educational pedigree and then modify her sales pitch to make him as comfortable and compliant as possible.

"Good morning. This is the Bluebonnet Motel."

"Well, good morning yourself. How is everything today at the Bluebonnet Motel?"

"The air is clean and the fish are plentiful. Why, there is just no place you'd rather be in the world."

"Well then, y'all reserve a room for me. I'll be comin' right over."

The voice on the other side of the line became even friendlier. "Why, ma'am, it just so happens that I've been keeping the best room open for someone just like yourself, so just let me know when."

"I wish I could just run right over there now, but I'm actually on an errand of sympathy. You see, a good friend just passed away . . . "

It took Wheeler less than five minutes to wrap Joe Carter, the sixty-five-year-old proprietor of the motel, around her tobacco-stained finger.

"I'd love to help, ma'am, but I just don't think I can. Last night only one party checked in, and he was a man."

Wheeler sensed a slight hesitation at the tail end of the man's answer, so she decided to coax a little more out of him.

"All right then, I guess I'll just have to keep looking."

The disappointment and the hesitation in her voice had its intended effect.

"I'm sorry I can't help, ma'am, although . . . I could say this, but I probably shouldn't."

Wheeler could tell from the man's voice that he was waiting for an excuse to continue. "Go on. I promise not to bite ya."

"Well . . . that guest I told you about . . . Let me see . . . Mr. Perry. Well, when he checked in, I went out back to have a smoke. Now, it's a good distance from the office to the end unit that he wanted, but I could have sworn I saw two folks get out of his pickup, and I was pretty sure that one of them was a young woman."

Carter lowered his voice when he said the last part, and Wheeler smiled to herself. *God, this good ole boy is a rube.*

"Is that right? Well, you know, I just wonder whether Andrea has found herself a new boyfriend. That's okay, mind you, but if she's keepin' him from the rest of us, that's just not fair. But don't worry, I won't tell her you told me. Not a word."

"Thank you, ma'am. We need every customer we can get this time of year, no matter what they're fishin' for."

He laughed at his own joke, and Jamie joined him. Although the old proprietor wanted to keep talking, Wheeler politely cut him off.

"I am so sorry, Joe, but my mom's calling on the other line, and I promised to talk with her this morning, so y'all have a great day out there. I'll be comin' to see ya for sure."

"You do that, ma'am."

Five minutes later, Paquin received a call from Wheeler's supervisor.

*Austin, Texas*
*December 6, 1999 / Sunday / 10:20 a.m.*

Severino parked the Ford Expedition on the dirt road that bordered the far end of the Bluebonnet Motel. The motel office was about thirty yards from the road. Paquin was sitting in the passenger seat.

"Are Juan and Miguel in position at the other end of the lot?" Paquin said.

"Yes," Severino said.

"I'll walk over to the office," Paquin said. "You stay here. If I see Caine or the woman, I'll call. Otherwise, no one moves until I give the order."

"Got it. What's the game plan?"

"If we find Caine and the girl here, we take them out."

"And the proprietor?" Severino asked.

"If we have to take out him out as well, so be it."

"Got it."

There were only two cars in the motel lot, an old red pickup truck and a blue minivan. Paquin knew that the pickup truck Caine was driving was a newer model and it was black. He suspected that Caine and the girl had already left the motel, but he kept his left hand on the Beretta in his left coat pocket.

Paquin had a new personality in place when he pulled open the old screen door and stepped into the worn office lobby. He intentionally thickened his slight German accent and smiled.

"Gutt morning. What a beautiful day!"

The old proprietor looked at Paquin's expensive suit and turned on the charm.

"Yes, it surely is, but we have pretty fair weather out here most of the winter. Folks seem to forget that, which is a crying shame. Why, I can tell you . . . I'm sorry, I don't want to run on here. How can I help you, sir?"

"My company is looking for a good spot for our annual retreat. A quiet, rustic place where our executives can rest, relax, and do some fishing."

The old proprietor's eyes widened and he broke into a description of the motel and the surrounding area that was rife with superlatives. Paquin interrupted him after a polite interval.

"Can I see the motel?"

"Of course. I'll give you the tour myself. Let me put this sign on the door to let folks know I'll be right back, and then we're off."

The proprietor walked with Paquin through the grounds, all the while promoting the unrealized charms of the Bluebonnet Motel, and the great fishing in nearby Granger Lake. Paquin quietly interrupted the other man's monologue.

"What kind of guests do you have this time of year?"

"Why . . . all sorts of people. Serious anglers who want to get in some quiet fishing, couples just looking for a quiet weekend. Why, just this morning, a young couple left. And today I expect—"

Paquin politely broke in.

"You said a young couple just left?"

"Yes."

"Did they say they had fun?"

"Well, most folks stop in for a chat before they leave, but these two were in a rush. Just stopped in for the night and scooted out about 9:00 a.m. They were in the Quail Cottage over there."

"Quail Cottage. How quaint. It seems to have a nice view. Can I have a look inside?"

"Sure. The beds were made up an hour ago, so it should be right presentable."

The proprietor continued his banter after they entered the bland interior of the worn but clean cottage. Paquin casually glanced at the phone on the nightstand between the beds and memorized the number. After they left the cottage, Paquin managed to extract himself from the proprietor's grasp, but he promised to return with the whole executive team for a final look-over.

As soon as the Expedition was back on the road, Paquin called for a trace on all calls made from the line at Quail Cottage within the last twenty-four hours, and he ordered a work-up on each of the receiving parties. Thirty minutes later, Paquin received a return call.

"Our contact at Southwestern Bell says that a call was made from that line just before 9:00 a.m. The call was made to a residence in Austin owned by a Michael Bosmasian. We searched that name, sir. Bosmasian's a lawyer. He's a prosecutor with the City of Austin."

# CHAPTER
# THIRTY-TWO

*Houston, Texas, FBI Field Office*
*December 6, 1999/ Monday / 7:00 a.m.*

William Spencer joined the FBI twenty-five years earlier, after graduating from Dartmouth College. He was Special Agent in Charge (SAC) of the Houston office. During his twenty-five years of service, he'd developed a reputation as a dedicated and effective special agent, and later, as an effective administrator and leader.

When he heard the quiet tones of the cell phone in his briefcase, Spencer glanced over at the small green clock, which looked like a small basketball, on his desk, Spencer, who was a lean six feet six inches tall, had received the clock from his teammates on the Dartmouth basketball team as a graduation present. It read 7:00 a.m. Spencer considered ignoring it, but the call was on his private cell phone. Not many people had that number, and those who did were important to him. He reached into the briefcase and pulled out the phone. The words "unknown" appeared on the screen.

"Spencer here."

"Good morning, Agent Spencer."

Spencer didn't recognize the male voice on the other side, but he detected a European accent, possibly French or Belgian.

"Good morning. Who is this?"

"We have a mutual friend, who shares an interest in M-1 rifles."

Spencer noted that the caller had ignored his question, but he didn't press the issue. The caller was referring to James O'Connor, a classmate and friend from Dartmouth, who'd joined the CIA right out of college. The two men were avid shooting enthusiasts. Each year they competed together in two or three "service rifle" competitions, where the contestants used refurbished but standard M-1 Garand rifles.

Although Spencer and O'Connor recognized there was a formal "wall of separation" between the two agencies, both legal and ideological, on occasion they informally ignored it. Whenever Spencer suspected that he was facing an international enemy on his home turf, he unofficially turned to O'Connor for help. O'Connor did the same when he needed assistance with a domestic player.

"Our mutual friend knows his rifles. How can I help you?"

"Actually, we might be able to help each other. We believe a helicopter went down about five miles outside a place called Big Bear, California. The crash would have happened on Saturday night, or very early Sunday morning. The GPS coordinates for the estimated location of the crash site will be sent to your private e-mail account."

"I see. Although I appreciate the tip, I'm sure the FAA and our Los Angeles office are already working the crash site. But I will check on it to make sure."

"I can assure you, Agent Spencer, no one is working on this crash site. In fact, all traces of the helicopter may well have been removed from the site by now. We believe the chopper was manned by a team bearing automatic weapons. They were hunting a man on the ground. There was a fight that led to this crash."

Spencer digested the information.

"Obviously, these circumstances would be of interest to the FBI. May I ask why they would be of interest to you?"

"The target is a retired member of our . . . community. We would like to know who is after him and why. Since this is a criminal matter, it would seem to fall within the jurisdiction of the FBI."

"We might be able to get to the bottom of this matter more quickly if the FBI knew the man being pursued."

"Indeed it might, but I cannot help you with that. I am sure the FBI will conduct a complete investigation."

"Is there anything else that you can tell me?" Spencer asked.

"No, not at this time. However, if any other information comes into my possession that could be of assistance to you, I will call. May I have your e-mail?" the caller asked.

"Yes," Spencer said, and gave the caller his personal e-mail address.

"Good day, Agent Spencer."

"Good day to you."

Spencer heard his e-mail notification chime a moment later. The address on the e-mail was jesmith@earthlink.net. Spencer suspected the account holder was nonexistent. He considered calling O'Connor, but rejected the idea. If O'Connor had been in a position to tell him about the situation directly, he would have done so. Spencer respected the message.

Spencer searched "Big Bear, California" on the Internet. He scanned the hits and pulled up the chamber of commerce site for the area. The city was up in the San Bernardino Mountains, in Southern California. Most of the area was a national forest. Spencer decided to call a contact in the FAA's Washington office.

"Sam Merriman."

"Hi, Sam, Bill Spencer."

"Bill, what a pleasant surprise. How can I help the FBI today?"

"Can you tell me if any aircraft went down in Southern California on Saturday night, or early Sunday morning? Actually, let me be more specific, near the town of Big Bear, California."

"That's easy enough. Let me pull the reports from that sector. Saturday, you say. I'll check a day on either side to make sure. No, nothing went down. I have other incidents during that time period down at Ontario Airport, hard landings, that sort of thing, but no crashes in that area. Why, is there something we should know about?"

"No. At least I don't think so. It was probably just an error on this end, but if it turns out to be something real, I'll let you know."

"Okay, stop in for lunch the next time you're in town."

"Count on it. Have a good day, Sam."

Spencer pulled up the name of the FBI's Los Angeles Bureau chief, Tobey Nelson, from his contacts list. The two men had worked together as part of the task force that investigated the Oklahoma City bombing and had become friends. Spencer suspected that Tobey would be sufficiently intrigued by the possibility that an aircraft had gone down in the nearby mountains, without a report being filed, to send one of his agents to investigate.

Spencer gave Tobey an abbreviated version of the tip that he'd received, intentionally omitting any suggestion that he might know the source of the information. Although his friend might have suspected there was more to it than that, he tactfully left the matter alone. Nelson promised to send an agent to check out the site, and to get back to Spencer as soon as he knew anything.

Eight hours later, Spencer got a call back from Nelson.

"Spencer."

"Hey, Bill, Tobey."

"Tobey. Look, like I said, it was no big deal—"

"Actually, it may be quite a big deal, or operation might be a better word for it."

"What did you find?"

"The agent I sent up there hikes those mountains all the time. She was thrilled to put on her boots and crisscross the sector bracketed by your GPS coordinates. After an hour of trekking, lo and behold, she found something that may well be a crash site."

"What kind of bird was it?" Spencer asked.

"Well, that's the interesting part. There was no bird."

"What?"

"According to Special Agent Yung, she would have missed the entire site, but for a set of truck tracks that she ran across when she was walking the grid. Someone had covered the tracks with snow, where they intersected with the road. She followed the tracks into the forest and found an area where there'd been a lot of activity. We're talking somewhere between eight and fifteen people marching around. She noticed an odd smell and decided to do some digging. Bingo. She found a big oil spill and took a few samples. She also took samples of other areas that smelled like fuel."

"Aviation fuel?" Spencer asked.

"The lab report will be here within the hour, but that's my bet."

"Where the hell did the chopper go?"

"Like I said, that's the interesting part. Agent Yung found the truck tracks, but no chopper."

"Tobey, they'd need a crane to get a chopper out of the forest. Someone would have seen it."

"Maybe, unless they cut it up with torches and hauled it off," Nelson said.

Spencer whistled to himself.

"That's right. Someone with real horsepower is involved, and I know my good buddy Bill Spencer is going to tell me all about it."

Spencer smiled. "I will, as soon as I find out."

"Okay, buddy, this is potentially a big deal, but as far as I'm concerned it's your show. Tell me how you want to run the investigation."

Spencer knew what Tobey was asking. He wanted to know if Spencer intended to run the investigation up the flag pole, or keep it local for a while.

"Since I don't know what we have here, I suggest that we both open local files and work the issue until we have something more substantial. You work the crash site and I'll try to trace the bird from this end."

"That works for me, Bill, but let's stay in touch on this," Nelson said.

"Done. I'll call you every couple of days."

"Great. All right, chief, I gotta get back to work. We don't work Texas hours here."

"Yeah, right. Thanks, Tobey."

# CHAPTER
# THIRTY-THREE

*Austin, Texas*
*December 6, 1999 / Monday / 1:00 a.m.*

Andrea flipped off the radio in the pickup truck, irritated by the incessant commercials. With the radio silent, the only sound was her fingers tapping on the steering wheel. She stared at the four-story apartment building in the middle of the next block. Richie's apartment was on the third floor in a corner. The older building overlooked the alley behind the building. Andrea looked at her watch. Caine had been in the building for nineteen minutes. *This is a mistake. We shouldn't be here.*

When she called Michael Bosmasian from the motel, he wasn't at home, and no one picked up at his office. It was too early. On the way into Austin, she'd reached his assistant. The woman was new and less than cooperative. She'd told Andrea that Mr. Bosmasian had just started a criminal trial and wouldn't be available until after 6:00 p.m. When Andrea asked for his cell number, the woman politely declined the request.

After dating Michael for a year, Andrea knew Michael's habits. He would call in for messages at the lunch break. She told his assistant to tell Michael to meet her at the Marian House Restaurant at 7:00 p.m. and she had left him a voice mail with the same message. The restaurant was within walking distance of the criminal court. If Michael received the message, she knew he'd get there.

The delay left seven hours to burn, and Caine had insisted that they use the time to try to find out who was after them and why. In Caine's mind, that meant a visit to Richie's apartment. Andrea had resisted the idea, but reluctantly agreed when Caine persisted, in part because she was worried that he would find a way to do it on his own, no matter what she said.

A part of the sidewalk across the street from the apartment building was cordoned off. A group of construction workers was excavating a part of the street. The main event was a man with a jackhammer in the middle of a shallow hole next to the curb. Periodically, the man would attack something at the bottom of the hole, generating a deafening roar. After several minutes of pounding, he would stop, and the entire group would gather around the hole to assess the progress. After a short consultation, the process would start all over again.

As she watched the workmen, an Austin Police car came around the corner and parked directly across from the apartment building. Andrea had no idea what the cop was doing, but she wasn't inclined to take any chances. She reached for her cell phone, which was plugged into the power outlet on the console, and dialed Caine's cell number. The jackhammer started up again, just as the phone started to ring. She pressed the phone against her ear in an effort to shut out the racket, but it was still difficult to hear anything even though all of the windows in the pickup were closed. Caine didn't pick up and the call rolled over to voice mail.

Andrea left a short message and decided to try again in five minutes. She changed her mind when another patrol car pulled in behind the first car. Andrea dialed Caine's cell number and once again it rang until the voice mail message started. *Why doesn't he pick up?* The jackhammer—Caine probably couldn't hear the phone over the noise, especially if he'd lowered the ringer volume on his cell before he entered the building.

Andrea gripped the wheel in frustration. The policeman in the second car seemed to be looking directly across the street at the front of the building. It was too much of a coincidence. They must be going into Richie's apartment, or worse, they were there to investigate a call about an intruder. She had to get in there and warn Caine.

Andrea reached over and pulled a Texas Rangers Jacket and a matching cap from the space behind the front seat. Her winter coat was still back at the Portman Lodge. When they'd stopped to buy a charger for her cell phone on the way into Austin, Caine had suggested that she buy a coat at the small sports outlet next door to the Radio Shack. When she passed on the idea, Caine had politely suggested that wearing something out-of-character was probably not such a bad idea. Andrea had taken the hint. The Texas Rangers coat and the matching cap were the least offensive things she found in the store, and they wouldn't seem out of place in Austin.

### Austin, Texas
### December 6, 1999 / Monday / 1:00 p.m.

Anders and Vargas were sitting in Vargas's Cadillac, halfway down the block from Steinman's apartment building. The car was four years old, black, and in perfect condition. Vargas had parked the Cadillac away from the building to avoid the dust from the construction. Anders looked around the spotless interior of the car, and grinned.

"So the beaner chicks you date like this ugly boat, do they? Makes sense. They got no sense of prospective, comin' from a dump like Mexico," Anders said, a scornful smile on this face.

"*Perspective*, Anders, that's the word. But that's still quite an effort for an illiterate like you. Have you been watching *Sesame Street* lately?" Vargas said, without looking away from the building.

"You know, Vargas, I am going to have to kick your brown ass one of these days. You're just not respectful enough of—"

Vargas raised his hand in a warning gesture, cutting Anders off. The two men watched an Austin PD patrol car cruise slowly around the corner and park across from the apartment building.

"No big deal," Anders said. "It's just a cop."

Vargas continued to watch the cop. He started to relax when the cop just sat there for several minutes, but his anxiety level climbed again when a second patrol car pulled in behind the first cop. This wasn't good.

Vargas thought the stakeout was a waste of time, but after listening to Insonna describe last night's ambush, he'd brought along his Heckler & Koch P7M13, with an attached suppressor. The gun was hidden in a compartment in the trunk. Anders's Glock 23 wasn't nearly as well hidden. He'd shoved it under his seat when he got in the car. If the police took an interest in the two of them and found a reason to search the car, the situation could get difficult.

When the cops made no move to get out of their cars, Vargas turned his attention back to Steinman's apartment building. About forty yards up the street, on the opposite side, a woman wearing a Texas Rangers jacket and matching hat was walking in their direction. Vargas couldn't see her face or her hair from that distance.

Vargas looked over at the picture taped to the Cadillac's dashboard. The woman in the picture was an attractive brunette with shoulder-length hair, attired in a stylish but conservative business suit. He looked back at the woman on the sidewalk and decided it wasn't the Marenna woman. Vargas looked over at the two cops, but his eyes wandered back to the woman as she approached Steinman's building. Something didn't add up. He picked up the binoculars on the seat and took a closer look at the woman. She was the right age, and he could just see the dark hair under the hat. When he added in the expensive watch, earrings, designer jeans, and perfectly manicured nails, the hat and coat didn't fit the picture.

Vargas turned to look at the picture and noticed that Anders had picked up on his interest. His eyes were fixed on the woman.

"She's the right age, and I would guess that she's a looker under the jacket. It could be her," Vargas said.

Anders grunted, opened the car door, and stepped out.

"I'll check her out. You let Paquin know we may have a hit," Anders said.

Vargas opened his mouth to object, but Anders had already closed the door. Vargas didn't want Anders to take the lead on the surveillance with the cops right there, but there was nothing he could do about it. He watched Anders stroll through the traffic to the other side of the street. *Good job, asshole, jaywalk in front of the cops.*

Vargas picked up the cell phone and dialed Paquin.

"Paquin."

"It's Vargas. We may have found one of the targets—the girl. Anders is checking it out."

"Is Caine in the area?" Paquin asked.

"We haven't seen him yet."

There was a short hesitation, and then Paquin continued. "If you can take them both out, do it. If you can take Caine out, do it. But I don't want the girl killed unless you can take Caine out at the same time. That will only make him more dangerous and harder to find. Are we clear?" Paquin said.

"Clear."

"I'm leaving now for your position, but don't wait for me to get there, if you have a kill within those parameters."

"Yes, sir."

"Good."

Vargas dialed Anders's cell.

"What do you want, Mex?"

"We have a go to put down Caine and the woman, or Caine by himself, but we can't kill the woman unless it's a twosome." Vargas hesitated, and then continued after glancing over at the cops.

"Anders, your Glock's here. So if you see them, don't start anything. Call and wait for me."

Anders didn't say anything.

"Are we clear on that, Anders?"

"Got it, Mex."

*Austin, Texas*
*December 6, 1999 / Monday / 1:00 p.m.*

Anders could see the girl on his right as he crossed the street. She didn't look in his direction, but he could tell she was aware of him. To allay her suspicions, Anders joined the line of patrons at the taco stand across the street from the Cadillac. Anders waited until the woman walked into the parking area underneath Steinman's building before stepping out of the line. When he was parallel to the police cars across the street from the apartment building, the first car pulled out into traffic and the second car followed. A smile played across Anders's face. He was looking forward to introducing this babe to a new kind of nightmare.

There were two large openings in the concrete foundation that formed the outside walls of the underground parking area. Anders climbed through one of these openings and dropped silently in front of an old van. He could see the woman. She was pulling open a gray steel door on the far side of the garage and entering the rear of the building.

When the door closed, Anders walked across the garage and stopped in front of the door. He listened briefly and then pulled it open. The door opened to a corridor that extended from the rear of the building to the front door. A wooden stairway that led to the floors above faced the front entrance. Anders heard the woman's steps on the front stairs as he eased the door closed behind him. He could tell from the sound that she was just approaching the first-floor landing. Vargas had told him that Steinman's apartment was on the third floor.

At the opposite end of the corridor, a window was open. Anders could see a steel fire escape landing through the opening. He jogged down the corridor and climbed through the window. There was a risk that the window on the third floor might be closed and locked, but Anders doubted it. During the winter, the tenants on the upper floors of these buildings used the window over the fire escape to blow out the excess heat rising from the lower floors.

Anders took the stairs up the fire escape two at time. His rubber-soled boots made no noise as he ascended. The window on the third floor was open, as he anticipated. He climbed through and glided down the corridor. The woman was just coming up the third flight of stairs. She was facing away from him. Anders positioned himself behind a large wooden post and waited. When he heard the woman's step on the far side of the post, he stepped out in front of her and jabbed the four fingers of his right hand into her solar plexus.

The force of the strike bent the woman over. As she desperately struggled to draw in a breath, Anders grabbed her and turned her back toward the stairs, lifting her bodily from the floor. He gripped her right arm with one hand and wrapped his other arm around her back.

# CHAPTER
# THIRTY-FOUR

The man stepped in front of her so quickly that Andrea had no time to react. Pain exploded in her solar plexus and suddenly she couldn't breathe. As she struggled to draw a breath, the man lifted her up and started to half carry, half drag her down the stairs. He had one arm around her back and his fist pressed up against the left side of her navel. His other hand gripped her right arm just above the elbow, in a crushing grip. When she tried to resist, he pressed his fist against her navel with brutal force. He was holding something hard in his fist, and he pressed it through her shirt, against her navel. It was a knife. The man lowered his head and put his unshaven cheek against her face. He smelled of chewing tobacco and sweat.

"That's right, babe, it's a real mean knife, and I will gut you like a fish if you make one goddamned sound. You and I are going to walk out of here like two lovebirds. You got it?"

There was a barely restrained brutality in the man's voice. The impression was magnified by the man's size and weight. He had to be over six and half feet tall, and she could feel the corded muscles in the arm wrapped around her back. Andrea sensed that the man was just waiting for an excuse to hurt her. She just nodded her head and continued to gasp for air.

As they walked down the stairs, the man's grip on her tightened to the point where he was almost carrying her down the stairs. When they started down the second flight of stairs, the man slowed and Andrea looked up from her hunched-over position. A middle-aged Latino man dressed in a pair of worn jeans was coming up the stairs. The big man guided her to the right side of the stairway, but the other man moved over to intercept them.

"Excuse me, I'm the—"

The man holding her didn't let him finish. He kicked the man savagely in the groin, pulling her forward with him as he struck. The impact of the kick lifted the smaller man off the floor. The man's face was a mask of agony and shock for second, and then he collapsed to the floor, without a sound.

"No," Andrea gasped.

"Shut up, bitch," the man growled, jamming the butt of the knife he was holding against her navel. Andrea felt as though her stomach was being driven into her throat. When she reacted to the blow by bending at the waist, she almost impaled herself on the blade of the knife.

As he yanked her forward down the steps, he whispered in her ear, "Hurts, dun it?"

A wave of terror washed over her, and Andrea felt her body starting to collapse. She forced herself to continue forward, knowing that if she fell, the knife would penetrate her stomach.

*Austin, Texas*
*December 6, 1999 / Monday / 1:20 p.m.*

Andrea replayed the plan in her mind, as they approached the door to the garage. She would only have seconds to attract attention. As soon as they stepped into the garage, she would scream for help and continue screaming as long as she remained conscious. The front of the garage was open to the busy street. Someone outside would come to help. They had to.

When the man pulled open the door, Andrea opened her mouth to scream, but froze in the middle of the effort. A deafening wave of noise came through the door. It was the jackhammer across the street. The sound was blasting into the parking garage and reverberating around the concrete chamber. She could scream at the top of her lungs and no one would hear a sound.

Anders looked around the garage and began to push her toward a corner that was shrouded in darkness. Andrea instinctively started to resist, but the iron grip around her chest tightened further, crushing the breath out of her. Anders bent over and pushed his face against hers. "I told you bitch, don't fu—"

"Excuse me, excuse me! You dropped something."

Anders froze. Then his head whipped around toward the sound.

"I have it right here. Just give me a minute."

Andrea couldn't see who was behind her, but she recognized the voice. It was John Caine. She thought about trying break free, but restrained herself. Caine would have a plan. She needed to let him make his move.

Anders turned back to her and leaned close again. "Any bullshit and I'll kill the shithead and cut your guts out."

Anders snapped the blade of the knife he was holding against her navel shut and slid the weapon into his jacket pocket. He switched the hand holding her arm from his right to his left, giving him more freedom of movement, but the grip on her arm was still painful. Then he slowly turned to face Caine, pulling her around with him.

Caine was down on one knee, about two yards away from them. He was searching through a worn brown leather briefcase. Andrea recognized the pair of glasses on the end of his nose. They were Richie's.

"It was a letter. I think. You dropped it on the way out the door. I was just coming out of my apartment. It's . . . it's in here somewhere. Just give me a minute," Caine said.

Caine didn't look up as he spoke, but continued to fumble with the briefcase. Anders couldn't resist the opportunity. He stepped forward, pulling Andrea with him, and swung his boot at Caine's head. Andrea tried to scream a warning, but couldn't get the sound past her lips. The boot was within a foot of Caine's head, when his hand shot out and shoved it away.

The move threw Anders off balance and created a gap between Anders and Andrea. Caine exploded off the floor, dropped the glasses, and stepped in between them. He brought his left elbow down on the crook of Anders's outstretched arm, dropping his body weight into the strike. Anders's hand was ripped off of Andrea's arm, drawing a grunt of pain and rage from the other man. Caine followed up the blow with a strike at the side of Anders's head. Anders twisted away from the attack, but the back of Caine's fist connected with the side of Anders's head, sending him reeling backward.

Anders regained his balance while Caine was guiding Andrea out of the way, and started back toward Caine, his face a picture of rage. Caine sprang out of Anders's path and snapped a side kick at his left knee. The kick was at the limit of Caine's reach, but it had enough power to knock Anders's knee out from underneath him. The big man fell forward, dropping heavily to one knee, his hands slamming into the concrete floor.

Caine moved in for another strike, not realizing that Anders was intentionally overreacting. Using his hands as a brace, Anders launched a back kick at Caine's groin. Caine tried to guide Anders's foot past him, but was only partially successful. The heel of Anders's boot caught Caine's left leg and spun him backward against a parked car.

Anders followed up on his advantage with stunning quickness for a man his size. He shoved himself off the floor and swung a crushing right at Caine's head. Caine dropped beneath the strike, guiding it over his head, and smashed the blade of his other hand into Anders's exposed ribcage, drawing a grunt of pain. Then he tried to step past Anders, positioning himself for a kidney strike, but the bigger man wheeled away, cutting off the attack.

Caine shifted his fighting stance from the left to the right and snapped a kick at Anders's left kneecap. Anders desperately lifted his leg off the floor to avoid a crippling blow. The ball of Caine's foot struck Anders's calf muscle, inflicting pain, but not a disabling injury.

The instant his striking leg touched the ground, Caine wheeled, using the leg as a post, and thrust a side kick at Anders's other knee. Anders was already off balance, but he turned away from the blow, and Caine's heel slammed into his lower thigh. The force of the blow drove Anders backward, and Caine followed, wheeling again with a third kick, but this time something went wrong. Caine seemed to slip as he wheeled and had to drop to one knee to regain his balance.

The mistake was the opening Anders needed. He exploded forward intending to do whatever was necessary to close with his smaller opponent and crush him with his greater strength. Caine heard Andrea's scream of warning behind him. For a fraction of a second, it seemed as if Caine was desperately trying to get away from Anders's charge. Then he took a quick step toward the onrushing giant and grabbed his outstretched arm and jacket. As Anders closed with the smaller man, Caine pivoted, dropped his center of gravity and threw Anders over his hip, in one explosive movement. Anders realized what was happening at the last instant and tried to slow his momentum, but it was too late. He flew forward and slammed into the side of an old Volvo with stunning force and dropped to the floor beside the car.

Caine started toward his dazed opponent, but then stopped abruptly. Another figure had entered the garage through the front entrance. Caine recognized the elongated barrel of the weapon the man was holding, and raced toward Andrea. She was standing just outside the steel door to the apartment building, her face frozen in shock.

"We have to get out of here, now."

The desperate edge in Caine's voice had its intended effect. Andrea wheeled and ran toward the door behind her. Caine caught up with her, yanked open the door, and shoved her into the hall. As he was pulling the door shut behind them, Andrea heard three sharp bangs against the outside of the steel door. Caine ignored the sound and grabbed her arm.

They raced down the corridor to the front door of the building. Caine threw open the door and they pounded down the concrete stairs to the sidewalk and into the street. He ran parallel to the traffic flow for a moment, pulling Andrea after him, and then dodged between the cars, drawing angry horns from the startled drivers. When they reached the far side of the street, Caine glanced over his shoulder and then raced around the next corner.

The next street was not as crowded as the first, and Caine increased the pace, forcing Andrea to run at a flat-out sprint to stay up with him. They pounded down the sidewalk, weaving between the people in front of them and running into the street when they couldn't find an opening. Andrea was gasping for breath when they reached the next block. Caine slowed and glanced behind them as they raced around the corner. Andrea followed his gaze. A muscular Hispanic man was just coming around the far corner at a full run. Caine pulled Andrea down the next street and increased his pace to a full sprint again.

When they raced around the corner at the end of the third block, a bus was just pulling out from the curb. Caine sprinted down the sidewalk, ran in front of bus and across both lanes of traffic, pulling Andrea with him. As the bus accelerated down the street, they raced beside it, using the vehicle as a blind. When the bus started to pull away from them, Caine struggled to stay within its visual protection, with another burst of speed. Andrea followed his lead, but she knew from the burning in her legs that she was reaching her limit. She was used to running long distances at a steady pace, not sprinting at the limits of her ability.

Just as they were about to lose the cover from the bus, Caine gasped out "There!" and they dodged through an open gate in a six-foot brick wall. As soon as they passed through the gate, Caine moved behind the cover of the wall. Andrea let go of Caine's hand and bent over at the waist, gasping for breath. Caine turned to her.

"We have to keep moving, Andrea."

Without waiting for her to reply, Caine grabbed her arm and guided her along the inside perimeter of the wall to the far side of the yard. The archway on the opposite side of the property opened onto the next block. Across the street was a small municipal park. The path through the park wound through a stand of cottonwoods.

They ran across the street and raced down the path, into the cover of the trees.

When they emerged on the far side of the park to the next street, Caine maintained a fast walk along the sidewalk until they came to the next intersection. They crossed the street with a group of people who were just getting out of work. On the other side of the street, a municipal bus with the word "Downtown" on the front was just about to close its doors. Caine ran toward the bus, pulling Andrea behind him. For a second, the driver continued to close the doors, but then he saw them coming and reopened the doors. When they reached the top of the stairs inside the bus, Caine pulled a five-dollar bill out of his wallet and said, "Will this get us downtown?"

"Sure will, and then some, but we don't make change. So you folks are gonna overpay by a dollar. Put your money in the slot," the driver said as he pulled away from the curb.

Caine dropped the bill into the plastic cylinder and they walked over and sat in the nearest empty seats. As soon as they sat down, Caine leaned over and whispered, "Tie your shoelace."

Then he bent over and started to work on his laces. When she hesitated, Caine nodded at the window. Andrea realized what he was doing and bent over to pull up her socks. Sweat was pouring down her face. As the bus pulled away from the intersection, Caine raised his head and glanced through the rear window of the bus. When he turned back to her, he shook his head, squeezing her hand softly. Andrea leaned against him. She was about to cry with relief.

"Andrea, do you know where this bus is going?" Caine said.

Caine's whisper brought Andrea back from the edge. She glanced ahead to get her bearings. As she read the street names, a map of Austin formed in her head. She knew the basic route the driver was taking.

"Yes."

"We need to find a place where we can get a cab."

"We'll be in the downtown area in about two miles. We should see signs for the Marriott or the Hyatt. We can get a cab out front," Andrea said.

Andrea glanced over at Caine when she spoke. He was looking through the window at the road ahead. Andrea looked down. He was still holding her hand. She suddenly realized that she didn't want him to let go.

# CHAPTER
# THIRTY-FIVE

Paquin walked through the wrought iron gates into the small park adjacent to the Helius Building. The security guard inside the gate nodded to him and said, "The park closes in forty-five minutes, sir."

Paquin nodded and walked down the cobblestone path toward the center of the park. The two-acre urban oasis was owned and maintained by Helius, but it was open to the public during daylight hours. Paquin followed the cobblestone walkway to a large fountain in the center of the park. A flower garden bordered the outside perimeter of the area. Four smaller paths meandered outward from this central point through a series of grass-covered mounds separated by a sprinkling of firs.

Paquin could see Mason standing on the far side of the fountain when he came around the last curve. Mason saw him coming, but didn't acknowledge him. He turned and began walking down one of the secondary paths. Paquin caught up with him and matched his pace. Paquin could see Mason's profile in his peripheral vision. A nervous tic played across the skin just above Mason's right eyebrow, and his jaw muscle flexed involuntarily. Paquin decided not to update Mason about the near miss outside Steinman's apartment building earlier in the day. Mason was already on the edge.

They walked together for a minute in silence and then Mason spoke without looking at him, controlled exasperation in his voice.

"Enlighten me, Mr. Paquin, about what you have done to solve our problem."

Paquin ignored the antagonism in Mason's voice. He didn't have time to get in an argument. He needed to get to the restaurant downtown to orchestrate the ambush.

"The girl has a relationship with one of Austin's senior prosecutors. His name is Michael Bosmasian. She's meeting him at 7:00 p.m., at a restaurant downtown."

Mason stopped beside a weeping willow tree and turned to look directly at Paquin.

"How did you find out about this meeting?"

"We searched the phone records at the motel where they stayed last night and found an outgoing call to the prosecutor's number. One of my operatives called Bosmasian's office and pretended to be a friend of the Marenna woman. His secretary told her about the meeting."

Mason nodded and started to walk down the path again.

"And what do you propose to do about this problematic meeting?" Mason asked.

"The woman and Bosmasian used to be lovers. A hysterical friend will contact the police just before Caine and the woman arrive at the restaurant. The caller will advise the police that Ms. Marenna intends to shoot Bosmasian and then kill herself. With luck, the police will do our work for us, but if they fail, our shooters will put them down."

"Very well, Mr. Paquin. Call me when it's done."

# CHAPTER
# THIRTY-SIX

*Austin, Texas*
*December 6, 1999 / Monday / 4:45 p.m.*

The Italian restaurant was located about half a mile south of where they left the bus. The concierge at the Marriott Hotel near the bus stop had recommended it. The interior was small, and the décor quaint and welcoming. There were about fifteen dark wooden tables covered in red-and-white-checked tablecloths. A small bar was located at one end of the room. A fire was burning in the fireplace at the other end.

It was still early for the dinner crowd. The restaurant was only about half full. Andrea and Caine were sitting at a table in the back of the restaurant, near the rear exit door. The glass of chardonnay sitting in front of Andrea was untouched. She was staring at the fire across the room. Caine tried to engage her in light conversation about the menu, but it didn't go anywhere.

"Andrea—"

"They were waiting for us, weren't they? They knew we were coming."

Caine swirled the beer around in the heavy glass mug in front of him, reluctant to talk about what happened.

"I don't think they knew we were coming. They knew it was a possibility, and they had the place staked out just in case. They must have recognized one of us when we entered the building and followed us in. I . . . I'm sorry I brought you there."

Caine's comment jogged her memory. Andrea remembered seeing the big man with the reddish hair outside the building. He must have recognized her and followed her in. As the memory replayed in her head, the fear and sense of helplessness that she'd felt when the monster dragged her down the stairs seized her all over again. She closed her eyes and struggled to slow her pounding heart rate. Then she felt a terrible rage. She wanted to kill him for what he did to her. She looked over at Caine.

"Why didn't you shoot him?"

Caine could hear the anger in her voice. He spread his hands out on the tablecloth in front of him.

"He was already pulling you down the stairs when I came out of the apartment. I looked for a shot, but he was all over you. At that range, the nine-millimeter shell would have punched through him and hit you as well. I couldn't take the chance. When I caught up with you in the garage, he was holding you right in front of him. That's why I had to get closer, but he attacked before I could pull the Browning."

Andrea looked away from him. Her right hand was gripping her left forearm so hard Caine could see the whites of her knuckles.

"Andrea, why don't we leave it alone for a while?" Caine said in a quiet voice.

"What happened when we were leaving the garage?" Andrea asked, ignoring his suggestion.

When Caine didn't answer right away, Andrea continued, her voice demanding an answer.

"You saw someone, didn't you? There was this sound, just as we ran out of the garage—what was it?"

"Someone else was coming in the front door of the garage. He was probably backup for the other Neanderthal, so I grabbed you and ran."

"But the noise, what was that noise against the door?"

"Bullets—three shots. We didn't hear much of a report, because the gun had a suppressor," Caine answered reluctantly.

"A suppressor? You mean like some kind of silencer?"

"Yes."

"But that means they were there to kill us."

Caine glanced at the front of the restaurant before answering. Andrea's eyes followed his glance. He could see the fear in her eyes.

"Andrea, I can't say one way or another whether they were there to capture us or kill us." Caine reached over and put his hand on her forearm. "Going over what happened won't—"

"I have to talk about it. I have to figure it out. I want my life back."

An elderly couple was sitting two tables away. The woman turned and looked over at Andrea, concern on her face. Andrea saw the woman's look and realized how loudly she was talking. She stood up and walked toward the door near the rear of the restaurant.

"Andrea," Caine said quietly and followed her out the door. "Wait, please."

Andrea stopped outside the door and placed her hands over her face. Her shoulders slumped and she started to cry quietly.

"What are we going to do? What are we going to—"

Caine put his hands on her shoulders.

"We're going to see your friend Michael. He's going to get us out of this thing."

Caine didn't believe that, but he knew that she needed something to hold on to.

"I'm sorry," Andrea said, gaining control of herself.

"There's no need to apologize. The last forty-eight hours have been crazy. Texas has become a lot more exciting since I left."

Andrea laughed in spite of her tears.

"Can we eat? I'm starving," Caine said.

"Me, too," Andrea said with a small, tired smile, and they walked back into the restaurant.

Caine kept the conversation away from the crisis during most of the dinner, but Andrea interrupted him in the middle of a question, after they ordered coffee.

"John, I'm sorry, I don't mean to interrupt."

"Please, go ahead."

"Yesterday, you told me that you were a native Texan. Where did you grow up?"

"I lived in Waco until I was eighteen."

"You also said you were an orphan. Did you live with another family member?"

"No. I did it the old fashioned way. I grew up in an orphanage."

"Are you serious?"

"Yes, they still exist. The orphanage where I lived was a converted ranch just outside of town. It was a run by the Jesuits."

Caine noticed Andrea's look of sympathy.

"St. Michael's wasn't a bad place. We worked and studied hard, but we played hard, too. The brothers were strict but fair. I really can't complain, but then I had nothing to compare it to. I don't remember any life before that. I was taken in when I was four."

"You don't remember anything?"

"Vague images at most, and I couldn't tell you whether those are real or just dreams."

"Is there someone at the orphanage that might remember you? Someone who might have some information about your family, or the property Richie mentioned?

"I don't think so, but I'm willing to give them a call in the morning."

"It can't . . . I'm sorry, my phone has been vibrating nonstop. Would you mind if I checked my messages?"

"No. Go right ahead," Caine said.

Andrea pulled out her cell phone and looked at the screen. She had five voice mails. She punched up the voice mail screen and looked at the numbers. All five were from Jill, her secretary, which reminded her, it was Monday. She'd missed a day of work and failed to check her calendar.

"What I am doing! I have to call in. I'm sorry. This will only take a minute."

Andrea punched in the speed dial number for her secretary.

"Andrea Marenna's desk."

"Jill, it's Andrea."

"Playing hooky, are we? Well, good for you, but you might have told me. Then I would have had something intelligent to say when people called."

"Sorry, it's been . . . a confusing day. Are there any crises that won't wait?"

"Not really. The stipulation in the Barredo matter was entered. So the status conference tomorrow is off calendar. That was the only court hearing you had this week, but you should check your voice-mails."

"Anything in the mail I should worry about?"

"No, nothing urgent that I can see. I thought you had a FedEx package, but apparently it was a mistake."

"What do you mean?"

"Megan logged in a package for you up front, but two minutes later the FedEx guy came back and took it away. He said it was for Anderson & Black upstairs."

Twenty-four hours ago, Andrea would have ignored the incident, but her world had changed.

"Jill, can you call up to Megan and see if she logged in who the package was from? I'll wait."

"Sure."

There was a minute of silence and Jill picked up again.

"Megan crossed out the name on the log, but it looks like R. Steinman."

Andrea's hand tightened on the phone. *They were watching her office as well as her house, and somehow they had known that she would be getting a package from Richie. How? How could they know that?*

"Andrea, is everything okay?" Jill asked.

"Yes . . . yes. Jill please send an e-mail around letting everyone know that I will be out on vacation for the next two days. If something critical comes up, call me on my cell."

"Done. Are you—"

"I'm okay, Jill. I'll call tomorrow. Thanks."

"Good night, Andrea."

Caine saw the look on Andrea's face when she hung up.

"What is it?" Caine asked.

"Richie sent me a package. After it was delivered, the FedEx man returned and took it back. He told the receptionist it was for another law firm upstairs. John, how could they have known it was coming, and how could they get to the delivery guy? We've had the same delivery guy for years."

"My guess is someone else picked up the package. He might have had the right uniform, but he wasn't FedEx. As for how they knew, they must have searched Steinman's apartment or car, and found a copy of the transmittal."

Andrea stared at the fire for a long moment and then looked back at Caine.

"I guess this tells us two things. Richie is definitely the focal point of whatever they're after. Second, we know they're still looking for whatever it is."

"You're . . . Hold on a minute, Andrea. I have a call on my cell."

Caine recognized the number. It was Jaq.

"I have to take this call. This is someone who's trying to help us."

"Jaq," Caine said.

"Of course it's Jaq. Where have you been? You're supposed to stay in contact."

"Sorry, buddy. It's been busy here. Did anything come up on the radar screen in France?"

"I spoke with the Colonel. He made a few calls to some of his friends at the Quay D'Orsay. They all came back negative. There are no known threats to the unit. Have you had any more problems?"

Jaq had switched to French when he asked the last question and Caine did as well.

"A few."

"Tell me."

"It's complicated, Jaq."

"Good. Educate your simple friend."

"From what we—"

"We?"

"Like I said, it's complicated. A reporter here in Austin left me a phone message last Friday. His name was Richard Steinman. The message was cryptic. Steinman said that I owned some land in Texas and that this ownership could put me in danger. He left me a call-back number, but told me to call a friend of his, Andrea Marenna, if I couldn't reach him. That's the 'we.' She's sitting right across from me."

"Is she good-looking?" Jaq said, a smile in his voice.

"Jaq . . . yes, as a matter of fact, she is," Caine answered, looking over at Andrea for a moment, who was staring at him.

"Okay. Now finish your complicated story," Jaq said.

"I didn't get Steinman's voice mail until the morning after the helo assault that I told you about. I called the paper where he works on Sunday and they told me that he was killed Friday night. So I called Andrea. She had no idea what I was talking about, but after talking with her, I decided to come down and do some investigating—"

"And you should have invited me along to look after you," Jaq interrupted.

"I got it, Jaq," Caine said and continued his story. "I tracked Andrea to a lodge outside of Austin last night. When I showed up, someone was trying to kidnap her. I took her away from the bad guys, but they wouldn't leave it there. They chased us. I took out their transport and we escaped."

"This is getting out of control. Go on," Jaq said, frustration in his voice.

"Today we went to check out Steinman's apartment to do some digging and bingo, we ran into the bad guys again."

"What happened?" Jaq said.

"They tried to take us out. We escaped. End of story," Caine said.

"End of story. This is not a story, man. It's a running battle! Is your mind broken? You cannot do this alone. You must go to ground until we can get there," Jaq's said. His voice was so loud that Caine held the phone away from his ear.

"Jaq, this is not your fight. It has something to do with whatever Steinman dredged up."

"I don't believe it. The enemy has too many resources. It has to be related to the unit. As soon as they've eliminated you, they'll come after the rest of us. We must fight this together," Jaq said.

A tired smile played across Caine's face.

"Thanks, Jaq. Thanks more than you can know. Look, we're going to try one more option. Then we'll find a hiding place. I'll call you from there."

Caine realized his mistake as soon as he finished.

"What option?" Jaq demanded.

"We're . . . we're meeting with a local prosecutor. He's a friend of Andrea's. She's convinced that he can help us, no questions asked. The meet is in one hour."

"A prosecutor? That's a mistake."

"Jaq, I have to do it. As soon as we're done with the meet, we'll go to ground and I'll contact you."

Jaq expelled a frustrated breath.

"I won't argue with you now. Stay safe, my friend. We're coming."

"Good night, buddy."

Caine smiled to himself. Jaq must be mellowing in his old age. Fifteen years ago, he would have raged at him in three different languages. When he looked up from the call, there was a questioning look on Andrea's face.

"Who was that and why did you speak in French?"

"That was a member of my old unit, Jaq. All Legionnaires speak French. It's the language we use in the field. It wasn't meant to keep you in the dark."

"It didn't. I speak French."

Caine colored slightly and gave her a small smile. "Touché."

### Austin, Texas
### December 6, 1999 / Monday / 5:00 p.m.

Paquin, Severino, Vargas, and Anders were in the operations center standing around a large table with a detailed street map of downtown Austin when Paquin's cell rang.

"Paquin."

"This is Wire 2. We have contact from the girl."

It took Paquin a second to place Wire 2. It was the team outside the offices of Kelly & White, the law firm where the Marenna woman worked. They had a tap on Marenna's direct extension.

"What do you have?" Paquin said.

"She just called in. I sent you the recording via e-mail."

"Good."

Paquin walked into the next room that served as his office in Austin and sat down in front of the laptop in the middle of the desk. He listened to the recording of the call several times. The woman was getting smarter, or she was learning from John Caine. The reference to voicemail in the call generated a red flag. What if Steinman had left her a voicemail? That could blow the disaster into the open. They had to wipe the system at her law firm.

Paquin picked up the phone on his desk. "Mehrdad, it's Paquin. I need you to get into a voicemail system and erase all communications received within the last three days."

Mehrdad ran a small phone and computer consulting firm in Austin. He was considered an expert's expert, and many of the big phone companies used him on their more complicated install jobs. If there was a way to get the system wiped, Merhdad would get it done.

After the call, Paquin returned to the table where the map was laid out. The team that he'd assembled for the ambush had been reviewing the plan for over an hour. It wasn't complicated, but it had to be executed in a downtown square, with a guaranteed police presence. There was no room for error.

"Okay, let's go over it again."

# CHAPTER
# THIRTY-SEVEN

*Austin, Texas*
*December 6, 1999 / Monday / 6:45 p.m.*

The cab that the maître'd called was waiting when Caine and Andrea came out of the restaurant.

"Where're you going?" the cabbie asked.

"Downtown, to the Marian House," Andrea said.

"I can do that," the cabbie said.

Andrea remembered Jill's reminder about her voicemails when the cab pulled away from the curb. She dialed into Kelly & White's voice mail system and began to work her way through the fifteen messages in her box. The cab was almost downtown when the fourteenth message started. It was from Richard Steinman.

Richie was on his cell phone. The noise in the background made it difficult to hear his voice. It sounded as if he was in a car race.

"Andrea, it's Richie. I need help . . . with a story. Look, I know this isn't fair, but I'm really in a bad spot. I need you to call a guy. His name is John Caine. He lives . . . he lives in Hesperia, California. Look, I know this sounds crazy, but I think this guy owns—"

Kelly & White's message software cut in and said, "Message continued."

Then Richie's frantic voice came back on.

"Andrea . . . shit . . . Please call this guy. Helius may want to kill him to prevent him from getting his . . . shit! Don't pull out, you frigging idiot! Andrea, he may be the last one. I don't know the guy, but I need him to call me. I'm going to try to send you a package . . . Amelia Teatro. She has the—"

The voicemail software voice cut in again. "Message ended."

Andrea held the phone in front of her and pressed the redial button. Caine had to hear the message. She heard Caine direct the cabbie to pull over in front of the park down the street from the Marian House. The cab pulled over just past a city bus stop, near the front entrance to the park.

When her voicemail came on again, Andrea turned to Caine and said, "John, I've got it. It's Richie! He's explaining—"

The screech of tires behind the cab cut her off. She turned around in the seat and looked out the back window. An Austin police car had just skidded to a stop twenty yards from the cab's rear bumper. Two officers jumped out. Their revolvers were drawn and pointed at the rear of the cab. The officer standing on the driver's side of the police car called out in a loud voice, emphasizing each word.

"This is the Austin police. Do not move! Put your hands on your head and step out of the car. All of you."

A fraction of a second later, the front windshield of the police car shattered, and the two officers dropped behind the car doors for cover. The strobe light on the roof of the car exploded a second later, and glass shards rained down on the crouching officers.

Caine shoved open the car door next to the sidewalk, grabbed Andrea's arm, and pulled her out of the car.

"Stay down! It's a setup. We have to get out of here."

Caine dropped to his knees and crab-walked the length of the cab, pulling Andrea behind him. He stopped at the front bumper and looked up and down the sidewalk. Cars were parked along the curb almost all the way to the restaurant. The cab was the last one in the line.

Caine pointed to the four-foot brick wall along the edge of the park. "They probably have a shooter in the park. If we stay below the top of the wall, he won't have a shot. When we get to the end of the wall, we can run down the alley beside the restaurant."

Andrea looked at him and nodded, her face a mask of fear and confusion.

"On three we go for the wall: one, two, three!"

When they reached the wall, they ran alongside it, staying in a crouch. Andrea looked down the street and saw a stocky figure just outside the entrance to the Marian House dressed in a suit. She recognized him right away. It was Michael. For a second he didn't recognize her, but then he called out.

"Andrea!" Then he began to run toward her.

"No!" Andrea yelled and tried to wave him off, but Michael kept coming.

### Austin, Texas
### December 6, 1999 / Monday / 7:00 p.m.


Onwuallu sat in the front seat of the Lincoln Town Car watching the black Chevy Suburban parked ten cars ahead, on the same side of the street. Porter was sitting in the passenger seat cradling an AR-15 equipped with a collapsible stock, a suppressor, and a 30mm scope. The Lincoln was parked in the southeast corner of the square.

Onwuallu and Porter had followed Severino and the two other men in the Suburban to the site, after waiting outside the building that Paquin referred to as "Center" for most of the day. The inside of the Lincoln reeked of smoke, fast food, and old coffee.

Onwuallu scanned the square through a small pair of binoculars. A large statue of a man on a horse dominated the center of the square. The statue was surrounded by a small grassy area. A three-foot wrought iron fence circled the grass. An upscale restaurant in a restored brownstone was located on the corner directly across the square from him. The sign above the entrance said "Marian House." A service alley ran along the right side of the restaurant.

To the right of the alley was a small wooded park that ran the remaining length of the square. The park was separated from the sidewalk by a four-foot wall. A tall archway in the middle of the wall provided access to the park.

As Onwuallu watched, a man wearing a backpack climbed out of the Suburban and walked across the sidewalk into an alley between the two buildings. The entrance to the alley looked directly across at the park on the other side of the square. Then the Suburban eased around the square and stopped at the corner diagonally across from the Lincoln. A second man stepped out and jogged into the park. The second man was also wearing a backpack. When the Suburban pulled out again, the light from the streetlamp illuminated the driver for a moment. Onwuallu recognized Tony Severino, Paquin's number-two man. Onwuallu was certain that Paquin himself was somewhere in the area, directing the operation.

Onwuallu could tell from the placement of the men that Paquin was setting up a kill zone. Apparently he expected the elusive John Caine and Andrea Marenna to make an appearance. Onwuallu smiled slowly to himself. Tonight he would play the part of John Caine's guardian angel. He intended to make sure that Paquin's carefully laid plan failed. Later, when Mason fired Paquin for his continued incompetence, Onwuallu would kill him. Then he and Porter would find and eliminate Caine and the woman.

As Onwuallu watched, a cab drove into the square and stopped in front of the park, about fifty yards down the street from the restaurant. Before anyone could get out of the cab, an Austin police car raced into the square, its strobe light flashing, and skidded to a stop behind the cab. Two officers jumped out of the car, guns drawn. The officer on the driver's side yelled something to the occupants of the cab. A moment later, the front windshield of the police car disintegrated, and the strobe light on the top of the car exploded.

Onwuallu suspected that the first shot came from the man in the park and the second from the shooter in the alley up the street from the Lincoln. Both shooters had to be using suppressors because the police didn't even look in the direction of the shooters after the shots were fired.

The two cops dropped to their knees behind the car doors, guns pointed toward the cab. Onwuallu smiled in admiration. The two officers assumed the people in the cab were the source of the incoming fire. Paquin's scheme was clever. Having the police eliminate Caine and the girl would be convenient.

"Very creative, Mr. Paquin," Onwuallu said.

Onwuallu opened the car door and turned to Porter.

"Mr. Porter, let's see what we can do to unravel Paquin's little soiree."

Porter stepped out the car and walked to the space in between the front of the Lincoln and the minivan parked in front of it. He dropped to one knee and pointed the AR-15 in the direction of muzzle flash he'd seen in the park. He rested his right elbow on the bumper of the minivan and braced his left elbow on his upraised knee. The sidewalk was empty and Porter's position was almost invisible from every direction but the street side.

Onwuallu stepped out of the car and leaned back against the driver's side door watching the scene unfold across from him. Caine was trying to use the wall along the sidewalk as shelter from the shooter he suspected was in the park.

Porter nodded toward the restaurant. "We have a new player."

Onwuallu turned his glasses toward the restaurant. A man in a dark business suit was standing in front of the restaurant. The man hesitated for a second, yelled something in the direction of Caine and the woman, and then began running toward them. Onwuallu immediately made the connection. The woman and Caine had set up a meeting with the man, which meant that he must be with the police or FBI. Paquin must have found out about the meet and set up the trap.

Onwuallu watched the man run toward Caine and the woman, expecting to see one of Paquin's shooters take him out, but nothing happened. *Paquin doesn't want the heat from this kill.* Onwuallu made a snap decision.

"Porter, take out the running man—one shot."

Porter's weapon coughed and the man in the suit stumbled and went down. The woman with Caine ran over and knelt beside the man on the ground. Caine had pulled out a gun and was scanning the park and the square trying to find the shooter. He backed over to the woman in a crouch and tried to pull her away from the man on the ground, but she resisted.

"I have movement in the park. The shooter is moving in for a shot, sir," Porter said without taking his eyes off the scope.

Onwuallu tried to locate the shooter in the park, but didn't see anything. He looked down the street to the alley, where the other shooter was located, but couldn't see anything from his position. He turned his attention back to the woman and Caine. The woman was still resisting Caine's effort to pull her away.

"Sir, the shooter in the park will have a shot any second," Porter said without inflection.

Onwuallu growled in frustration. "Get out of there, you fools!"

Onwuallu looked over at the two policemen. One of them had pulled out a shotgun and the second was talking frantically into the radio. He could hear police sirens approaching the square.

"Take out the shooter in the park," Onwuallu said, "then we leave. This place is getting too hot."

# CHAPTER
# THIRTY-EIGHT

*Austin, Texas*
*December 6, 1999 / Monday / 7:10 p.m.*

Michael Bosmasian was twenty yards away when he stumbled, a red spot blossoming on his white shirt as he fell to the ground. Andrea screamed, broke away from Caine, and ran toward him. Caine pulled the Browning from his jacket and scanned the square, but he couldn't spot the shooter. He ran over to where Andrea was kneeling beside Michael Bosmasian, staying in a crouch. She was holding Bosmasian's hand, crying. Caine moved beside her, trying to keep an eye on the park and on the street as well. Bosmasian saw the Browning in Caine's hand and tried to push himself up. Andrea put her hand on his chest and gently pushed him back down.

"It's okay, Michael. John is a friend."

Caine looked at Bosmasian's wound. Then he turned to Andrea.

"Andrea, we have to go," Caine said urgently.

"No! I won't leave him. He needs help!" Andrea screamed, without looking up.

Caine had received basic training in combat casualty care. He could see that the bullet had hit Bosmasian in the upper chest area, near the shoulder, missing all vital organs. His primary risk was from blood loss and shock. The emergency medical people would deal with those problems the instant they arrived, which, by the sound of the approaching sirens, would be any second.

Caine glanced over his shoulder again and reached for Andrea's arm, but she shook off his grip. Caine grabbed her arm, forcing her to look at him.

"The bullet passed through his shoulder area. No vitals were hit. The emergency med people will take care of him."

"No! I won't—"

"Andrea, *we* are putting him in more danger by staying here. They're shooting at us, not him, and as long as we stay here the cops won't let the medics treat him."

Andrea still refused to let him pull her away. Caine glanced over his shoulder again. He suspected they only had seconds before the sniper in the park moved to a position where he had a shot. He turned back to Andrea again, put his face within inches of hers, and said with desperate intensity, "Andrea, if we stay, we die *and Michael dies, too.* Do you want that? Would he want that for you?"

Michael Bosmasian was looking at Caine when he spoke, his face tight with pain. Bosmasian put his hand on Andrea's arm and rasped out, "Go. Get out of here, Andrea. Now!"

Andrea's resistance collapsed. She allowed Caine to pull her away from Bosmasian and willed herself to run alongside him toward the restaurant. The two ran at a crouch along the wall, until they came to a small service alley on the near side of the restaurant.

They followed the alley around the back of the restaurant, where it came to a dead-end against the building on the other side of the brownstone that housed the restaurant. Access to the next city block was barred by a nine-foot fence with razor wire at the top. There were no visible exits from the alley, other than a door that led back into the restaurant.

Caine looked around the alley a second time, trying to find another option. A large white delivery truck was parked in the corner, up against the fence. The top of the truck was flat, and it was about a foot higher than the fence. Caine ran over to rear of the truck and looked through the fence. There was another alley on the other side that led to the next block. A smaller delivery van was parked in the alley, on the other side of the fence. The roof of the smaller van was about a four-foot jump down from the truck on this side.

Caine turned back to Andrea and pointed to the top of the truck.

"We have to get over the top. We'll use the truck."

He climbed on the bumper of the truck and pulled himself onto the hood of the cab. From there, he reached down and helped Andrea up. Then he turned and climbed to the top of the cab of the truck and helped Andrea up again. He pointed to the smaller delivery van on the other side of the fence.

"Okay, three quick steps, then jump. Land with your knees bent."

The drop to the roof of the smaller van on the other side of the fence was three or four feet, but it looked ominous in the dark. Caine turned to Andrea and saw the hesitation on her face. He knew they had no time left. The police would be down the alley in force within seconds.

"You can do it," Caine said. "I'll go first."

He took two quick strides, cleared the fence, and landed on the top of the other truck, knees bent, with a loud bang. Caine turned to Andrea and backed up to give her room to land.

"Your turn," Caine said.

Andrea heard a car pull into the alley. Then a floodlight lit up the area behind her as bright as day. She jumped.

*Austin, Texas*
*December 6, 1999 / Monday / 7:10 p.m.*

Paquin's Lexus was parked near the southeast corner of the city square, diagonally across from the Marian House. When the cab entered the intersection, he spoke into the microphone on his headset.

"This is Control. The targets have arrived. Is everyone in position?"

Juan responded first. He was in the park.

"Position two, ready."

Miguel and Severino followed.

"Position one, ready."

"Position three, ready."

An Austin police car followed the cab into the square, its lights flashing, and skidded to a stop just behind the cab. The two policemen in the car came out with their guns drawn and yelled something to the occupants of the cab.

Paquin smiled to himself. *Right on time.*

"Position two, take out the windshield of the police car. Position one, as soon as Juan's round hits the target, take out the light on the top of the car. One shot only. Do not hit the cops. Are we clear?" Paquin said. The Nicaraguans confirmed his instructions.

The two men were armed with M-24 sniper rifles. The suppressors on the rifles were top of the line. The nervous cops wouldn't even hear the shots. They would just see the exploding glass and fire on the presumed source—John Caine and Andrea Marenna. If Caine and Marenna somehow survived, Miguel and Juan would take them out.

Paquin stared through a pair of night-vision binoculars at the police car. Juan's round punched a hole in the front windshield, and the strobe light on the top of the car exploded a second later, when Miguel's round found its target. Both cops dropped to their knees behind the car doors. Paquin suspected that they were looking for a target but couldn't find one.

"Position two, do you have a shot at the targets?"

"No, sir."

"Position one, what about you?"

"No, sir, he's using the cars as cover."

Paquin controlled his frustration. "Position three, are you in a position to take action?"

Severino was supposed to be an observer, but Paquin knew he was armed with a .45.

"I'm on it . . . Wait," Severino said, "we have a problem. The prosecutor has shown up."

Paquin looked across the square and saw a man in a white shirt and tie, carrying a suit jacket over his shoulder, outside the front of the restaurant. He was looking down the sidewalk in the direction of the cab.

"Position two, do you have a shot on the targets?"

"Negative, sir. They still have cover."

Paquin could see the problem through the binoculars. Juan was positioned to take out the targets in front of the restaurant. His shooting angle was from the park, across the top of the alley to the restaurant. Caine and the woman had parked fifty yards down the street from the restaurant. Caine was using the wall in front of the park for cover. Paquin scanned the area ahead of Caine. The wall stopped about ten yards short of the alley, leaving an opening for a clean shot.

"Position two, they'll lose their cover in about thirty yards. Take the shot as soon as you have it."

"Roger that."

Severino cut in, "This is position three. The prosecutor's running toward the woman."

Paquin turned the binoculars toward the restaurant and saw the short, stocky form of Michael Bosmasian running down the street toward the woman and Caine.

Paquin didn't want to take out the prosecutor, except as a last resort. That would focus every law enforcement resource in Texas on the case. He could do without that kind of attention.

"The prosecutor is not to be hit without my order. Are we clear on that?"

"Position one, clear."

"Position two, clear."

As Paquin watched, the prosecutor clutched his chest and fell to the ground.

"This is Control, who fired that shot?" Paquin said.

"Position two, no idea, sir."

"Position one, same here, sir."

Paquin looked over at the cops, but they were hunkered down waiting for backup, which, by the sound of the approaching sirens, was imminent. He had to get this done and get his team out of there.

"Position two, move to where you have a shot, now," Paquin said.

"Position two, roger that," Juan came back.

Paquin looked over at the prosecutor. The girl was kneeling beside him. The wall behind her still provided cover. Caine had run over and was trying to pull her away, but she refused to move.

"Position two, I have a shot.

"Take it," Paquin said.

"Roger that."

"Jesus!" Juan's voice blasted over the radio.

"Position two, what is your—"

"I'm under fire!" Juan yelled, fear in his voice.

"What?" Paquin said incredulously.

"*Si*, I'm under fire!"

Paquin looked around the square, but couldn't find the source of the fire. *What the hell is going on?* Paquin whipped the binoculars back to the prosecutor. Caine and the woman were gone. He looked further down the street and saw them disappearing down the alley next to the restaurant.

"Position three, can you intercept? Do you have a shot?"

Severino's muffled voice came back, "Two cop cars just drove past me into the square. I can't do anything."

Paquin watched in frustration as two police cars roared into the square, sirens whooping, followed by a larger black van. As soon as the van skidded to a halt, a SWAT team dressed in body armor and carrying M-16s jumped out of the back. The frantic chatter on the police band indicated that another wave of support was on the way. Within minutes, the entire area would be cordoned off and a massive search would start. They had to get out of there.

"Everyone evacuate now. Use the exit routes you were provided," Paquin said.

The three men confirmed his order and signed off.

Paquin did a U-turn on the street where he was parked and drove away from the square. Someone else had intervened to disrupt the operation; someone who wanted to stay anonymous and who had no problem trying to kill a member of Paquin's team. Paquin could only think of one person who fit that description—Onwuallu.

# CHAPTER
# THIRTY-NINE

*Orly Airport, France*
*December 6, 1999 / Monday / 10:00 a.m.*

Etienne Ricard and Joseph Vlasky boarded the Concorde at 10:00 a.m. Paris time. The two men were dressed in dark business suits, but the similarities ended there. Ricard was naturally slender and the dark blue suit he was wearing fit him perfectly. Anyone looking at his distinguished face, striking eyes, and full head of hair would assume he was a top executive with a large European or American corporation.

Vlasky, in contrast, was square and muscular to a fault. His facial features were blunt and his head was bald. When he walked through the airport, it seemed as though his bulging thighs and shoulders would burst free at any moment of the two-thousand-dollar Savile Row suit he was wearing. The Pole looked more like a wrestler than an executive, which, in fact, he'd been in his youth.

In 1981, Joseph Vlasky had been the proud captain of the wrestling team at the University of Gdansk. His dream had been to earn a spot on the Polish national team and wrestle in the Olympics. All of that changed when a drunk in a local bar had decided to beat up another college student when she rejected his unwanted attentions. Vlasky had intervened.

In the ensuing fight, the man who assaulted the girl had been badly injured. Although Vlasky had done nothing wrong, when the horrified bartender told him the unconscious man was a captain in the KGB, Vlasky knew his guilt or innocence wouldn't matter. If he stayed in Poland, he would end up either dead or in prison. The following day, a friend of his coach had secured him a berth on a freighter bound for France.

When the freighter docked at Marseille, Vlasky had swum ashore and tried to defect. Although the gendarme captain who listened to his story was personally sympathetic, he had his orders. The French government was not inclined to irritate both the Russians and the communist regime that ran Poland by granting asylum to a no-name Polish defector. The captain had advised Vlasky that he would be turned over to an official from the Polish embassy later that day.

Before leaving him alone in an unguarded office to await his handover, the sympathetic gendarme handed Vlasky a card and told him that the people listed on that card were less concerned about French government policy. They were also located less than one block away. The gendarme had been right. The Légion Étrangère had welcomed the services of the well-educated and physically fit Pole.

As the two men waited for takeoff, Vlasky smiled to himself. Ricard noticed the expression and lifted an eyebrow.

"It will be good to see everyone again. It's been too long," Vlasky said.

"Yes. It will be, and I'm sure that you won't mind a little excitement as well, non?"

Vlasky's smile widened further. Ricard remembered all too well that Vlasky was one of the few soldiers who enjoyed combat, and he smiled as well.

# CHAPTER
# FORTY

When they walked out of the alley to the street, Caine and Andrea merged into a flowing crowd of holiday shoppers. Christmas was only two and a half weeks away, and the boutiques, coffee shops, bookstores, and other retail outlets along the broad thoroughfare were full of shoppers. The loud holiday music playing on the outdoor speakers and the chatter from the crowd drowned out the noise from the police emergency taking place in the square one city block over.

Andrea and Caine walked down the sidewalk and joined the tail end of a crowd crossing the street. About halfway down the block, Caine looked behind him and saw an Austin Police car, with its lights flashing, trying to make its way down the crowded street. Two more police cars were parking at the other end of the block. They had to get out of there.

Thirty yards ahead of them, the street was bisected by a pedestrian mall with a wide, brick-covered walkway down the middle. Retail shops were located on both sides of the walkway. Caine steered Andrea around the corner, intending to escape the police cordon being formed by exiting at the far end of the walkway. As soon as he turned the corner, Caine saw two foot patrolmen standing in the middle of the walkway, about thirty yards away. The men were listening intently to their handheld radios.

Caine looked to his left and saw a small, festively decorated shop called "The Christmas Store." He guided Andrea into the store, without breaking stride, and spoke quietly, "We have to find a way past those two. In three minutes, this whole area is going to be swarming with angry men in blue."

As they entered the shop, Andrea noticed a display of large Santa Claus coats and hats in the rear of the store. She walked over to the display, and Caine followed.

"These might help," Andrea said.

She pulled one of the red coats off the rack and placed it against Caine's chest to check the sizing. A row of floppy red hats was arrayed on the shelf above the coats. Andrea picked out a hat and handed it to Caine.

"Try that on."

Then she turned to the woman's rack and selected a coat and hat for herself. To the left, she saw several large red baskets on another shelf. She pulled Caine after her and pointed to the baskets.

"We need two of them—the big ones."

As they approached the checkout counter, which thankfully was empty, Andrea grabbed four boxes of holiday cookies and turned back to Caine.

"We need three more. Make that four."

Caine followed her instructions, after glancing toward the store entrance. The elderly man behind the counter smiled at them.

"Going to have a party, are we?" the man asked.

Andrea forced herself to smile. Then she glanced at her watch in feigned apprehension and turned to Caine.

"John, we're late!"

The man at the checkout counter took the hint. He quickly rang up the purchases and started to pull out a large bag. Andrea smiled and waved away the bag.

"Oh, you can skip that. The office party is one block over. We were supposed to be there with the cookies ten minutes ago. So if you don't mind, we'll just dress up here and run right over."

"That'll be fine with me, ma'am. Cash or charge?"

"Charge," Andrea answered, handing the man her MasterCard. Andrea pulled on her coat and hat, while the man was ringing up the sale. Then she turned to Caine.

"Suit up, Santa Claus," she said with smile that Caine could tell was forced.

Caine pulled on the coat and hat, impressed with Andrea's quick thinking. Thirty seconds later, they walked back onto the mall wearing the Santa Claus outfits. As they walked down the walkway toward the exit at the far end of the mall, they offered the cookies to the people walking by with the greeting "Happy holidays from The Christmas Store."

Caine could see the two policemen ahead of them. They were standing in the open space between the two walkways in and out of the mall. He stiffened involuntarily as he heard the sound of steps rapidly approaching him from behind. Two more officers passed him on the left and joined the other two men. As they approached the four policemen, Andrea whispered, "I'll take the path closest to the police. You serve people on the other side."

When she approached the four officers, it took all of Andrea's willpower to put a smile on her face.

"Happy holidays from The Christmas Store, officers," Andrea said.

One of the officers, who was on the radio, smiled distractedly, but politely waved her off.

"No, thank you."

Andrea continued past them. She could hear the voice crackling through the radio.

"We're looking for a white male about six feet tall, with brown hair, and a woman about five eight."

The voice in the background was interrupted by a voice by her side.

"Can I try one?"

Andrea looked down. The speaker was a four- or five-year-old boy, whose mom was trying to pull him into a nearby store.

"Yes," Andrea said. "Go right ahead. Take your pick, and happy holidays from The Christmas Store."

Every muscle in Andrea's body was screaming *run*, but she ignored the feeling and knelt to offer the cookies to the boy. The incoming chatter from the police radio behind her was difficult to understand, but it was clearly describing the progress of the ever-expanding police dragnet.

"Now, don't be shy. Just go ahead take what you want," Andrea said, trying to politely rush the boy's decision.

From the corner of her eye, she could tell that she had a partial audience in the closest police officer. As the little boy looked over the cookies in the basket, she saw Caine working his way down the other side of the mall, toward the exit at the far end. When the little boy finally made his selection, Andrea stood and said, "Merry Christmas to y'all," coupled with a big smile for the benefit of the one officer who was still looking in her direction.

Ahead, Andrea could just see Caine walking down the broad steps that led to a landing and the doors to the next street. She walked in that direction, continuing to offer cookies to the shoppers. Most of the people near the exit were in a rush and politely declined. When she reached the bottom of the stairs, Caine was standing behind a column. On the other side of the column was a panel of glass doors leading out of the mall.

As she approached, Caine directed Andrea's attention to a traffic control officer, who was standing on the curb just outside the door. His motorcycle was parked on the street in front of him. The officer was watching the crowd coming out of the mall, while talking into a radio.

"We have to split up. They're looking for a couple. We can meet at another location," Caine said.

Andrea was instinctively against the idea, but she knew Caine was right.

"Where do you want to meet?" he asked.

Her mind raced for a second.

"Branion's Pub. It's on the corner of San Jacinto and Second. About ten blocks from here. Any cabbie can find it."

"Good," Caine said. "Dump the cookies and the basket in the trash over there. You can take one of the cabs in front of that Neiman Marcus down the street. Remember, you just got off work after playing Santa's elf and want to go home. Play the part and the police will ignore you."

Andrea hesitated. Her concern must have shown on her face.

"Relax, I'll be fine. See you in twenty. Now go," Caine said, glancing at the officer without turning his head.

Caine nodded to Andrea and walked toward the men's room at the far end of the landing. Andrea hesitated for a moment and then turned, dropped the basket of cookies in the trash receptacle, and walked to the doors. She could feel the officer's eyes on her. Halfway down the stairs outside the door, Andrea took off the red hat and rearranged her hair. When she finished, she walked down the rest of the stairs to the sidewalk. Andrea expected to hear the cop order her to stop with each step, but it didn't happen. When she reached the end of the block, she crossed with the crowd waiting for the light and walked over to the concierge in front of the Neiman Marcus. Two cabs were parked out front. She waved to the nearest cab.

"Where to, ma'am?"

"Branion's Pub."

# CHAPTER
# FORTY-ONE

*Austin, Texas*
*December 6, 1999 / Monday / 7:40 p.m.*

Caine left the Santa Claus outfit in the men's restroom near the exit to the mall. Without Andrea by his side and the basket of cookies, the disguise was a magnet for attention. He considered going back into the mall and trying to find a way out in the other direction, but one look convinced him otherwise. Three uniformed officers were standing at the front of the mall, and two plainclothes men were methodically working their way through each shop.

Caine looked around the landing. Someone had left a copy of the *Wall Street Journal* on the top of the trash receptacle against the wall. He grabbed the paper, placed it under his arm, and started toward the door. Behind him, he heard a tide of female giggles. He looked over his shoulder and saw a group of teenage girls coming out of the music store at the end of the mall. Caine slowed his walk to allow the girls to pass him. He held the door open for the entire group and followed them out, as though they were together. Caine looked over at the cop who was staring at him, cupped a hand over his mouth, as if hiding what he was saying from the oblivious teens in front of him, and said,

"We bought everything, as usual." The cop returned his wry grin and looked back at the door of the mall.

Caine walked past the group of girls once he was a safe distance from the mall entrance, but there was another problem further down the street. The police had set up another checkpoint. Caine slowed his pace. Two uniformed officers were standing on each side of the street watching every person that walked by. One of the officers was talking to a man fitting Caine's general description. The man was pulling out his wallet.

Caine looked around the area for another way out. In the middle of the block, he saw a men's shop with a brightly lit window display. Caine walked down the street and entered the shop. A well-tailored salesman in his sixties walked over to Caine and gave him a friendly nod.

"Can I help you, sir?"

"Yes, you can. I would like to look at a raincoat."

Caine was guided over to a three-way mirror, and the salesman brought over three trenchcoats. Caine was pulling on a dark blue coat when two figures appeared in the left panel of the mirror. It was the two detectives. The two men looked in the door of the shop and stared at Caine and the salesman for a moment. Caine shrugged into the coat and turned to the salesman with a smile and asked his opinion.

"What do you think?" Caine said.

"I think it fits you quite well, sir," the salesman answered, nodding his approval.

"I think so, too. I'll take it. Now, how about a scarf and a hat as well? Do you have any recommendations?"

Caine looked in the mirror at his reflection as he spoke. The two detectives were gone.

"As a matter of fact, I do," the salesman said.

Twenty minutes later, Caine left the store, twelve hundred dollars poorer, outfitted in a dark blue raincoat, a white scarf, and a stylish tweed hat. In his left hand, he carried a leather briefcase. The newspaper was in his right hand. As he passed the two policemen stationed at the end of the street, they didn't give him a second glance. One block over, he waved down a cab.

*Austin, Texas*
*December 6, 1999 / Monday / 8:00 p.m.*

Branion's Pub was a popular lunch spot and after-work bar. Since it was a weeknight, the crowd had started to thin out. Andrea sat down at an empty table in the rear of the bar area. She ordered a Chardonnay from the waitress and tried to read the paper someone had left on the next table, but found it impossible to focus. After twenty long minutes and a second glass of wine, the wait was becoming unendurable. The terrible image of Michael being shot minutes earlier, dueled with the fear that Caine had been captured, or worse, killed.

When the thirty-minute mark passed, Andrea's mind began to run through a series of options that ranged from waiting another five minutes to going back to the mall to calling the police and asking for help. Each time she went through the list, she would set a deadline for a final decision and then allow it to pass. Forty minutes after they'd separated, Caine walked through the door. She didn't recognize him in the new topcoat, hat, and scarf, until he took off the hat. Andrea was about to raise her hand to get his attention, when he looked over and started in her direction.

There was a tired but relieved smile on his face. Her pent-up frustration and fear were suddenly released and she stood up and gave him a hug without thinking. Caine returned the embrace, holding her for a long minute.

"I'm sorry. I had to change my look to get out of there. I also picked up two prepaid cell phones at a place down the street. Here's yours," Caine said apologetically.

"You're here. That's all that matters, although I think I almost lost my mind at least ten times in the past hour," Andrea answered.

Caine apologized again and said, "I need you to memorize this new cell number," handing her a piece of paper. Andrea looked at the number on the paper. It was an easy sequence to remember.

Caine took back the paper and tore it up. "Now tell me the number three times in a row."

Andrea complied. "Any more tests?"

"No. You passed," Caine said, a small smile coming to his face at the hint of irritation in Andrea's voice.

The waitress, whose clientele was ebbing away, interrupted them and asked Caine what he wanted to drink. Caine glanced at Andrea's drink and ordered a glass of the same.

As soon as the waitress left, Andrea leaned over the table slightly and said, "So?"

"So?" Caine repeated in confusion.

"So what happened!" Andrea said with exasperation.

Caine gave her an abbreviated version of what happened after they separated. Andrea was about to ask Caine another question, when she noticed he was watching a man who was approaching the table from the bar. Andrea looked over and saw a tall, portly man in his late thirties walking in their direction. She recognized the arrogant smile on the man's face and put her hand on Caine's arm.

"I know him," Andrea said. "He's a real jerk, but harmless. I'll try to get rid of him quickly."

Paul Yates was a partner in the Austin office of an elite New York law firm. Six months ago, Andrea had sat at the same table with him at a state bar function. Whenever there was a break in the program, Yates had a made a point of enlightening her about his athletic accomplishments on the Harvard gridiron, his intellectual and cultural acumen, and most importantly, his status as the most eligible bachelor in Austin. She remembered another lawyer at the table describing him as "the soul of arrogance" on the way out. The description fit Yates almost as well as the outrageously expensive made-to-order suit he was wearing. Andrea could tell from Yates's smile and manner that he expected her to be delighted to see him again.

"Andrea! How good to see you again. Are you taking advantage of the intermission to grab a quick drink as well?" Yates said, pointedly ignoring Caine.

"Hello, Paul, and no, *John* and I missed the show tonight," Andrea answered.

"What a pity. Sir Neville and the Academy of St. Martin were magnificent."

Caine was actually relieved that Yates had made a point of excluding him from the conversation, but Yates's reference to the orchestra brought back memories. Without thinking, he said quietly, "They always are."

Caine's comment, which was intended only for his own hearing, irritated Yates, who considered himself to be at the very pinnacle of the city's cultural elite. He turned to face Caine, as if suddenly realizing he was there.

"Really, you've heard them play before? That's interesting, since this is their first visit to Austin."

Caine was feeling the effects of two days without sleep and he wasn't particularly interested in what Yates was saying. He just nodded at Yates's comment.

Yates saw the response as an evasion and pressed the matter. "And where exactly did you see them?"

Andrea interrupted Yates's inquisition.

"Paul, don't you have anything—"

"Let me see," Caine said. "I attended three or four performances when I lived in Paris. That would have been at the Champs-Elysées Concert Hall. The new concert hall hadn't been built yet. I remember attending a concert at the Royal Albert in London, and I seem to remember attending one at the Musikverein, in Vienna, but that might have been the Chicago Symphony Orchestra. I'm sorry. It was so long ago I can't remember now," Caine said, speaking slowly as he worked his way through the memories.

Yates's superior smile had become fixed in stone. He glanced at his watch and said, "Well, good to see you Andrea and . . . John, did you say?"

"Yes. John," Caine answered.

Yates turned stiffly and walked back to the bar. In spite of the strain from the past forty-eight hours, Andrea had to cover her mouth to hold in the giggle about to burst forth.

"What's so funny?" Caine said.

"You'd have to know Yates. Even among his peers, who are not known for humility, he's known as an arrogant snob. Maybe he'll be a little more humble after discovering that someone else just might have one iota of cultural sophistication other than himself, but I doubt it."

When she looked back at Caine, the reality of their situation returned and with it the image of Michael Bosmasian being shot. Caine saw the look and reached over and took her hand.

"He's going to be okay, Andrea. And no, it wasn't your fault. I only spent thirty seconds with Mr. Bosmasian, but I have an idea that he would be the first one to get upset if you even suggested that."

Andrea looked at him and nodded. He was right. Michael would get angry at the suggestion. She forced herself to overcome the tide of emotion that threatened to overwhelm her. She needed to focus. Then she remembered Richie's voicemail.

"John—the voicemail from Richie, you have to hear it."

Andrea dialed the number that accessed her voicemail. Instead of the standard message requesting her private code, the message advised her that the voicemail system was not available at this time. Andrea remembered what Caine had said when he couldn't get into his own voicemail, but rejected the possibility of sabotage. Kelly & White's system had a top-of-the-line firewall, and the server was in a locked room in a secure commercial building. It had to be a routine maintenance issue.

"I can't get in right now. They must be doing work on the system. I should be able to get in tomorrow."

"Just tell me what you can remember," Caine said.

"The message was . . . frantic and it was hard to hear. Richie was in a car. I could hear the engine roaring like . . . like he was in some kind of race. He said you owned something and that Halus, no Helius, might be willing to do something. He could have been referring to Helius Energy here in Austin."

"The message that Steinman left me said the same thing," Caine said, "but he didn't mention Helius. That's a critical piece of information. What can you tell me about Helius?"

"Not all that much. I know it's a large energy conglomerate that has major oil and gas holdings in the United States and internationally. Their annual revenues are in the billions. I think their stock is listed on . . . no, actually they went private a while back, but I seem to remember seeing something in the *Wall Street Journal* about Helius coming out with a big bond issue on the NYSE. The company HQ is located about ten blocks from here."

"Who runs Helius?"

"A man named Carter Mason is the CEO and chairman. The Mason family started the company and they still own a controlling stock position. Mason has a reputation for being more than a little ruthless, but that description fits a lot of people that play in the oil patch."

"Andrea," Caine said, "Helius could fit the profile of who we're up against. Many of these outfits maintain private security forces—forces that hire a lot of ex-soldiers. They need this muscle to protect their people and assets in places like Africa, Russia, and Indonesia. Calling in one or more of these folks to hunt us down wouldn't be difficult."

"I guess it's possible, but I have a problem with the concept," Andrea said, shaking her head.

"Why?"

"Helius has plenty of high-priced lawyers. If they had a title problem on a property, they would either negotiate or litigate a resolution. If they ended up losing the fight, the title insurer that wrote the policy on the property would have to write a check for the purchase price. I just can't see Helius sending a goon squad after us because of some wild deed."

"This doesn't have to be a sanctioned operation, Andrea. One or more people in that corporate colossus could do something like this without the board's knowledge, particularly if they had Mason's support. If big money is involved, he just might be motivated enough to do things way outside the lines."

Caine could see that Andrea was still not buying it.

"Maybe. We need to find out what property Richie was talking about. That would tell us a lot," Andrea said.

Caine stood up. "I have to go to the restroom. Don't run away."

Andrea grabbed his arm.

"John, Richie gave me a name on the message."

"What do you mean, a name?"

"He said I have to talk to . . . Amelia Tater, no Teatro. Teatro was the name. Amelia Teatro."

"Did he say why?"

"No. He cut out before that."

"Do you know Amelia Teatro?"

"No, I never heard the name before, but she must be someone important. Richie was adamant."

"Okay. I'll be right back."

"Where are you going?"

"To the men's room."

"I'm sorry, you just said that."

*Austin, Texas*

*December 6, 1999 / Monday / 8:50 p.m.*

Yates tried to control his rage as he turned and walked back to the bar. He could just imagine the two of them chuckling at his expense. *London, Paris. Screw him!* That bozo had probably never been outside of Texas. As he stood near the bar staring at the television without interest, a line of text ran across the bottom of the screen. It was a news bulletin. It said that a local prosecutor had been shot in downtown Austin within the hour. Yates turned to leave the bar, but something in the message caught his attention. *The police were looking for a local attorney, Andrea Marenna, and an unknown male for questioning in connection with the incident.*

Yates was stunned. He looked over at Andrea Marenna and the man sitting beside her. A slow smile came to his face. He pulled the cell phone from the holder on his hip and walked out to the sidewalk in front of the bar. He didn't want to have any reception problems when he dialed 911. The recording of his call needed to sound just right. It might get played over the evening news.

# CHAPTER
# FORTY-TWO

*Austin, Texas*
*December 6, 1999 / Monday / 8:55 p.m.*

Severino and Paquin were searching the streets just outside the perimeter established by the police when Paquin received a call on his cell phone.

"Paquin."

"This is Center. Our source in the Austin PD just called. Less than a minute ago, they received a tip from a credible source indicating that Andrea Marenna is in a bar. The place is called Branion's. It's on the corner of San Jacinto and Second. SWAT is taking the lead on the call. You should have about a five-minute head start on them if you move now.

"Got it," Paquin said.

He called Severino. "We've found them. Meet me in front of a place called Branion's. It's on San Jacinto and Second. Tell Juan and Miguel to park behind the bar and come in the back door."

"Done," Severino answered.

Paquin parked the Lexus across the street and opened the glove compartment. He pulled out a flesh-colored facemask that covered the bottom half of his face, and drew a Glock 17 out from the holster under the seat. The Suburban pulled up alongside the Lexus as he was getting out of the car, and Severino stepped out. Juan and Miguel drove the SUV around the block to the rear of the building.

"We go in and take them both out, quick and clean. We exit through the back door. Clear?" Paquin said as they approached the entrance to the bar.

"Clear," Severino said, pulling a mini Uzi from under his coat.

When they opened the door to the bar, a tall, overweight man was waiting in the anteroom to the bar area. The man strode over to the two men, as if he were expecting them.

"I'm Paul Yates. I made the call."

Yates pulled up short when he saw the masks covering their faces. "What the—"

Severino stepped forward and smashed the Uzi into the side of the man's head before he could say another word. Yates dropped to his knees, wavered for a moment, and then fell forward onto his face.

Severino stepped past the body and eased open the door to the bar. Paquin scanned the bar area through the opening. He couldn't see either Andrea Marenna or Caine. He pushed the door open and moved into the larger room, followed by Severino. Paquin was holding the Glock in both hands, but he shielded the gun from the crowd sitting at the bar with his body.

The small crowd didn't notice the men initially, giving Paquin the opportunity to look over the rest of the room. He spotted Andrea Marenna sitting at a table in the rear of the room. She was looking at the screen of her cell phone and didn't see him. Caine was nowhere in sight.

"I have the girl," Paquin said, "but I can't see Caine. We can't take out the girl unless we get him at the same time."

Severino nodded and continued to watch the crowd in front of him.

One of the waitresses turned away from the bar with a tray of drinks and looked directly at Severino. The girl was in her early twenties. Her blond hair was tied back in a ponytail and she was smiling at a joke made by the bartender. She looked over at Severino and took in the mask and then the gun by his side. Her smile slowly disappeared and was replaced by a look of incomprehension, then fear.

Paquin noticed the girl and turned to Severino.

"Fire a burst into the ceiling. Get them on the floor and keep them there."

Then Paquin started across the room to the table where Andrea Marenna was sitting. Behind him, Paquin heard Severino fire a short burst from the Uzi into the ceiling. The blast drew screams of shock and fear from the people at the bar. Severino followed the burst with a series of shouted orders.

"Get on the floor! Did you fucking hear me? On the floor! Now! Get down!"

Severino fired a second burst into the ceiling and people began throwing themselves on the floor.

*Austin, Texas*
*December 6, 1999 / Monday / 9:05 p.m.*

Andrea's head snapped up at the sound of the gunfire. She stared at Severino in disbelief. By the time she saw the other man walking toward her holding a gun, he was only one table away. Andrea stood up, but the man cut off her move to escape.

"One step and I'll put a bullet through your knee," the man said.

The complete lack of inflection in his voice made the threat of violence seem that much more certain. When the man reached her, he spoke quietly, his eyes never leaving her own.

"Good evening, Ms. Marenna. Where is Mr. Caine tonight?"

Andrea surprised herself by answering the question without hesitation. "We had to separate to get past the police. We agreed to meet here. I'm waiting for him."

The answer was the truth, just not all of it. The man looked at her for a moment and she returned his stare.

"Very well, Ms. Marenna, walk to the rear door of the bar. I will be right behind you."

Andrea hesitated.

"You can walk, Ms. Marenna, or you can be dragged. It's your choice," the man said, never raising his voice.

Andrea turned and walked toward the rear door of the bar. The door to the restroom was partially open, and the inside was dark. Andrea knew Caine had the gun with him, and she also knew with absolute certainty that he would try to kill the man beside her before they reached the door. She started to ease to the right in order to give Caine a clear shot, but stopped when two Latino men burst in the rear door of the bar. Both men were armed.

The two men nodded to the man behind her and moved up against the restroom door to allow him to pass. Andrea felt as if a knife was twisting in her stomach. Caine was trapped in the restroom. There was nothing he could do to help her.

The sound of a heavy vehicle skidding to a stop outside the bar drew an instant reaction from the man beside her.

"Everyone out, now!"

### Austin, Texas
### December 6, 1999 / Monday / 9:05 p.m.

Caine was drying his hands in the men's room when he heard the burst of automatic weapons fire and the screams from the bar. He moved against the wall near the door, pulled out the Browning, and chambered a round. Then he turned off the lights in the room and eased open the door several inches. He could see Andrea's table from the opening, but couldn't see the bar area. A man of medium height with gray hair was standing beside her. He was wearing a face mask and a gray trench coat. He was also holding a gun. The man must have said something to Andrea, because she turned and started walking toward the rear of the bar. The man followed directly behind her.

Caine put the gun sight dead center on the chest of the man walking toward him, but then he hesitated. Killing one of the men would leave Andrea open to the other shooter, who had an automatic weapon. He needed to wait until both men were within sight. At this range, there was a good chance he could get both of them before they could return fire.

When the second gunman appeared in his view, Caine lifted his foot to shove the door open, but froze when something slammed into the outside of the wall he was leaning against. He backed up a step, and then another, expecting the door to the room to burst open. For a second, he was confused and then he realized that someone had shoved open the rear door to the bar, causing it to smash into the corridor wall.

There was no reaction from the two men in the bar, which meant they were together. Caine heard someone, possibly two men, up against the door to the restroom. He backed into one of the stalls for cover, the Browning pointed at the door. Outside the door, he heard someone order everyone out of the bar. There was movement, and then he heard the rear door of the bar close. Caine waited for a second, listening, and then eased into corridor, poised to shoot. It was empty. He glanced over his shoulder into the bar. The patrons were still lying on the floor with their hands behind their heads. He turned back to the rear doorway and eased it open. A black Suburban was just pulling around the corner into the street.

# CHAPTER
# FORTY-THREE

Austin, Texas
December 6, 1999 / Monday / 9:08 p.m.

Caine started to run down the alley toward the street, hoping to get a shot at the Suburban's tires, or at least to get a few numbers from the license plate. He pulled up short and dodged behind a dumpster when an Austin PD patrol car raced around the corner, heading toward the rear of the bar. The car slowed, turned on the floodlight attached to the driver's side, and eased into the alley. Caine looked back up the alley for a way out, but there was no exit. A six-foot wall was directly across the alley from him. He sprinted for the wall, caught the top ledge, and pulled himself over the top. He heard the car race up the alley on the other side of the wall.

Caine dropped into a second alley that ran alongside a large warehouse and ran toward the street at the far end. Thirty yards before he reached the street, a second police car pulled into the mouth of the alley, blocking his exit, and two officers burst out of the car. One of the men screamed "Freeze!" but Caine was already sprinting down a narrow walkway that ran behind the warehouse. Behind him, he could hear shoes pounding on the blacktop.

Caine knew he was at a severe disadvantage. The police had numbers, mobility, and centralized communications. They also knew the area. If they were able to box him in and bring in a chopper to help with the search, his chances of escape would be minimal. He had to stay ahead of the cordon they were trying to throw around the area by moving as fast and as far as possible.

Caine dodged in between two trucks that were parked behind the warehouse and sprinted for the wall at the far end of the walkway. He climbed over the wall and dropped into the darkness below, landing in a small yard behind an old dimly lit one-story house. As he crossed the yard, Caine picked up a scent that caused him to break into a sprint—dog shit. The last thing he needed was to have a run-in with a pit bull or a Rottweiler.

As he approached the nine-foot steel fence on the far side of the yard, Caine heard a rush of movement to his left—the dog. He ran parallel to the fence for one stride and then made a leap for the steel bar at the top. For a moment, he wasn't sure whether he was going to make it, but then he felt the cold metal under his sweaty hands. The dog threw itself against the fence below him, as he struggled to get one leg over the top of the bar.

Caine looked down and saw an enraged German shepherd backing up and gathering itself for a leap at his dangling leg. Caine struggled desperately to pull his legs out of reach, while maintaining his tenuous grip on the shaking fence. The dog was about to win the contest, when one of the cops dropped over the wall on far side of the yard. The dog instantly refocused its attention on the new intruder. The cop saw Caine on the fence, yelled "Freeze!" and started to reach for his gun, but stopped and threw up a defensive arm when he saw the dog racing toward him.

Caine dropped to the other side of the fence just as a second cop dropped into the yard behind him. He could hear one of the cops screaming at the other "Get it off me, goddamn it," as he ran across an enclosed parking lot behind a second warehouse.

Caine looked down the three-foot space that separated the two buildings. Two squad cars were cruising the street out in front. They had the entire street lit up with their floodlights. Caine sprinted across the rear lot behind the second building to a steel fence on the far side. There was a steep concrete slope on the other side of the fence and a series of concrete structures at the bottom. For a second, Caine didn't recognize what he was looking at, and then he realized it was a retention basin for storm runoff. The basin should run into a culvert at the other end. That might provide him a route past the police cordon.

Caine looked up at the top of the fence. Unlike the last fence, this one had barbwire at the top. He ran along the fence trying to find an opening. About twenty yards away, the steel mesh had separated from the pipe at the bottom. He dropped to his knees, pulled up the fence, and slid underneath. When he reached the other side, he scrambled down the steep concrete slope into the retention basin and then ran in between the concrete structures. As he was running by one of the blocks, his left knee clipped the edge of the concrete. The pain in his knee was agonizing, slowing his gait to a hobbling run.

The retention basin opened into a wide concrete culvert. Caine jogged along the bottom of the culvert until he found a narrow concrete stairway leading up the sloped wall. He jogged up the steps until he could see the street through the gated fence at the top. The street was clear, but he knew it wouldn't stay that way as he grabbed the fence and prepared for yet another climb. It wasn't necessary. The gate swung open.

"Thank God for small favors," Caine said aloud and jogged across the street, ignoring the pain in his knee. He continued his steady jog for another four blocks to the east, and then slowed as he approached a retail center and a busy city street. If he could grab a taxi or a bus, he would be out of the danger zone.

# CHAPTER
# FORTY-FOUR

*Austin, Texas*
*December 7, 1999 / Tuesday / 1:00 a.m.*

Andrea's wrists were handcuffed in front of her. That gave her some mobility, but escape was impossible. A three-foot chain connected the cuffs to a steel pipe, which passed from the wall behind her into the concrete floor.

There were no windows in the room. The only light came from a single phosphorescent lamp hanging from the ceiling. Only one of the four light tubes was working, and the weak yellow light barely illuminated the center of the room. A folding chair was pushed against the wall at the far end of the room, and the area around the chair was littered with fast-food wrappers. The corner of the room where she was confined was almost completely dark, and the concrete floor that she was sitting on was cold and hard.

Andrea stared at the dimly lit outline of the door at the other end of the room. *What were they waiting for?* The fear of the coming interrogation warred with her impatience. She rested the back of her head against the cold brick wall behind her and stared up at the corrugated steel ceiling fifty feet overhead. She had to get ready for this.

Andrea knew she had to give her captors a reason to keep her alive. She could only think of one story that would get her there: she had to convince them that John Caine remained a deadly threat despite her capture, and that he cared enough about her to trade his silence for her life. The question was how to do it?

Andrea finally settled on a simple stratagem. She would paint a picture using the facts that she knew, or could surmise, with almost absolute certainty—a picture that would scare the hell out of whoever was driving the bus at Helius. Andrea reviewed what she knew and prayed that it would be enough.

Richie's voicemail said that a property was at the core of the mystery—a property that had to be incredibly valuable. He also said that Caine was the rightful owner of the property, which meant there was some kind of title defect in the ownership chain. Although Andrea couldn't be certain, she was convinced the defect had to be in an old deed, a very old deed; otherwise, it would have been discovered years ago. If Andrea could persuade them that Caine knew these facts, and that he was continuing to pull together the remaining pieces necessary to complete the picture, they'd have to deal with him.

The next step in Andrea's strategy was more complicated. She had to convince her captors that she was a vital playing card in any negotiation with Caine. To get there, Andrea needed to persuade them that John Caine was in love with her.

An hour later, the lights in the room went off and the door opened. It was dark, but Andrea could tell that only one person had entered the room. She couldn't see his features in the darkness, but she could see he was wearing a suit and that he had a full head of hair.

The man picked up the folding chair from the opposite corner of the room, carefully brushed it off and then sat down about three yards away from her. For what seemed an eternity, he just sat watching her. Andrea desperately wanted to ask the man what he wanted and what they were going to do with her. She even thought about launching into her story, just in case he'd decided to kill her without an interrogation, but she didn't. She forced herself to wait.

Andrea knew from years of negotiations that patience was a powerful tool. If she spoke first, it would be a sign of weakness, desperation even. She had to wait for the man to begin the questioning process. Once it began, she had to limit her responses to the questions posed and give up nothing more.

After five minutes that seemed like five hours, the man spoke, quiet admiration in his voice.

"Very good, Ms. Marenna."

Andrea didn't respond.

"That is your name, correct?"

She detected a slight European accent: Austrian or German. It was the man from the bar.

"Yes," she answered, trying not to show fear.

"You and Mr. Caine have led us on quite a chase. Mr. Caine, in particular, has been quite an adversary."

Andrea waited.

"That is his name, correct? John Caine?"

"Yes."

Although Andrea could not see him smile in the dark at her restraint, she could almost feel it. This man had interrogated people before. She could sense it. The realization shook her. There were only two kinds of people who regularly interrogated people: Law enforcement people and professional torturers.

"Where is Mr. Caine now?"

"I don't know. As you may recall, I wasn't given a lot of time to say good-bye when we left the bar."

Her interrogator chuckled, an urbane, likable sound. "Indeed. Now, Ms. Marenna, I need to find out certain things. If you tell me what I need to know voluntarily, we will both be much happier. Do you understand that?"

The threat was quiet and polite, but it was crystal clear. Andrea hesitated, and then answered, "Yes."

Over the next hour and a half, the man asked Andrea a series of questions without a break. She stayed as close as possible to her predetermined script. Yes, they had figured out the basic parameters of Helius's problem. There was a title defect in a key Helius property. If the defect came to light, Helius would lose the property. They had figured out that Caine must have an interest in the property, directly or indirectly, and that Helius intended to prevent him from asserting that interest. No, Caine did not know which property it was, but he was working on that angle. She intimated that it wouldn't take him long, noting that Helius had recently filed a reporting document with the Securities and Exchange Commission listing every material asset the company owned. With that starting place, Caine could run down the major properties on the list and pull whatever reports were necessary to find the deed. It was only a matter of time.

Where did she fit into all of this? From what she could figure out, it had something to do with Richard Steinman. He apparently discovered the deed and was going to publish the whole story in the newspaper. No, she hadn't received anything from Steinman, but then she'd had very little time to check her mail lately. Then he hit her with it directly.

"Now, what about you, Ms. Marenna? Where do you fit in Mr. Caine's grand scheme?"

She knew this is where she had to step lightly. She couldn't over-play or underplay her hand. Success or failure would depend on how good her interrogator was. She framed her response based upon the assumption that he was the best.

"John . . . I mean Caine . . . He . . . We obviously don't know each other very well. There hasn't been time. John . . . Mr. Caine will do whatever is best for John Caine."

Her voice had started out haltingly, but then she'd rushed ahead as if she wanted to distance herself from the brief emotional window that she had unintentionally opened in the first part of her answer.

Although her interrogator continued to question her on other minor matters, after this exchange she detected a change. He was less interested in her answers. About ten minutes later, he ended the session.

"Is there anything you need, Ms. Marenna?"

"Yes. I need to go to the bathroom."

"Very well."

Then he left the room.

*Austin, Texas*
*December 7, 1999 / Tuesday / 2:15 a.m.*

Paquin closed the door to the darkened room and slowly walked across the dirty gray concrete floor of the warehouse toward the office on the far side. Caine and the woman had figured out the key facts. They knew there was a potential title defect in one of Helius's most valuable properties. They also knew that John Caine was somewhere in the chain of title. Armed with this knowledge, the two of them were a deadly threat to Helius. If Caine went public with the knowledge, a swarm of investigative reporters would scour the public records until they found the title defect.

Mason had told him that the disclosure of a potential title defect would derail Helius's upcoming bond issuance, costing the company $100 million in annual interest savings. Although Paquin could understand why Mason would be willing to kill Caine and the woman, and the reporter as well, over that amount of money, he suspected there was more to it than that. Whatever else was in play had something to do with Mason personally—something that could bury him.

Caine's knowledge left Mason with only two options. He could try to buy Caine and Marenna's silence, or he could have them both killed. Paquin knew that Mason would never accept the first option. The risk was too great. That meant he had to figure out a way to find and kill John Caine, and he had do it quickly. The question was whether Andrea Marenna could be used, willingly or unwillingly, to help them accomplish that objective.

During the interrogation, Paquin had tried to piece together the relationship between Caine and the woman, without revealing what he was after. The woman's answers to the more direct questions had been evasive but revealing. It was clear she had feelings for the man. She tried to convince him that Caine wouldn't put himself at risk to try to save her, despite the fact that this could result in her own death. Her answers could have been a clever effort at reverse psychology, but even if that was the case, there was something there. Paquin could hear it in her voice.

Paquin recognized that Caine might not have similar feelings for the woman, but the evidence suggested he did. Caine had probably learned everything he needed to know from the woman in their first day together. Yet he'd stayed with her. Even more telling, on two occasions Caine had put himself in harm's way to rescue her. His conduct could have been motivated by an old-fashioned sense of chivalry, instead of a romantic interest, but in either case it didn't matter. Paquin was all but certain that Caine would be looking for an opportunity to rescue the woman. He just needed to be sent the right invitation.

As he worked through the outline of a plan, Paquin realized that the rogue variable in the whole equation was Caine's background. His source in the Pentagon had been unable to provide him with any additional information, and the inquiries he'd made through other sources had all come back with nothing. At this point, all they knew was that Caine had the skills of a professional killer.

The knowledge gap bothered Paquin because it created a risk. Unfortunately, there was nothing he could do about it, except prepare an ironclad trap, which is exactly what he intended to do. Whatever John Caine's abilities, he would not escape this time.

Paquin walked by Julian Anders as he approached the office. The big man was sitting in an old chair just outside the office drinking a bottle of Coke.

"Why hide your face, Boss? You know the bitch is toast," Anders said, a grin playing across his face.

Paquin continued walking, but he knew where Anders was going with the question. He wanted to rape and brutalize the woman. Paquin was a killer, but he considered himself a gentleman. Anders needed to know that the girl was off limits until John Caine was dead.

"People who know they are 'toast,' Mr. Anders, are generally not inclined to cooperate, or alternatively, they are too cooperative. The captive who believes that he has a chance of survival is always a better source of information."

"Why, you don't have to worry about that. Y'all just leave it to me. I'll have that little honey singing like—"

Paquin stopped and cut off Anders's comment.

"No, Mr. Anders, you will not. *No one* will touch the prisoner, or cause the prisoner one moment of discomfort, without my say-so. We need her alive and well, both physically and psychologically, until Mr. Caine is a confirmed kill."

Paquin stopped, turned, and looked directly at Anders.

"I trust that we're clear on that," Paquin said, his voice quiet and without inflection.

Anders colored a little, but he continued to smile.

"For sure, Boss. For sure."

Paquin turned to the Nicaraguan, Juan, who was resting on a cot outside the office.

"Juan, bring the portable toilet to the woman. Put the longer chain on the cuffs so she can use it."

Then Paquin retrieved his valise from the office and left the warehouse.

Anders intercepted Juan when he was carrying the small portable toilet over to the room where Andrea was confined.

"I'll bring it to the woman, Juan, don't trouble yourself," Anders said and took the toilet away from Juan before he could answer. Juan shrugged and walked back to the office.

A smile played across Anders's face as he opened the door to the room where the woman was locked up. Anders liked hurting people. He liked the fear in their eyes when he came after them, especially when the victim was a woman.

In this case, Anders had a particular desire to humiliate and abuse Andrea Marenna. He was still enraged about the fight in the garage with Caine, and Vargas had made a point of not letting him forget it. Anders intended to make the woman pay for the slight, inch by painful inch. As for Caine, Anders would get to him later—after he'd told him about every single nightmare the woman had suffered before he killed her.

Anders turned the light off when he entered the room, but left the door open, allowing a path of weak light to cross the room. He strolled across the darkened room and placed the portable toilet in the middle of the strip of light, but stayed in the dark himself.

"Well, ma'am, it seems you have some business to do on this fine throne that I have so graciously delivered."

Then he stood there as if waiting for her to come over to the toilet and sit down.

Andrea could only see the outline of the man's big form in the dark, but the guttural drawl, now laced with a disgusting leer, was unforgettable. It was the monster who'd tried to kidnap her in the apartment building.

Where Andrea had sensed a calculated ruthlessness in the man who'd interrogated her earlier, this man was different. For him, cruelty was an end in itself. It was something he enjoyed. For the first time since the bar, she was terrified. Her terror mounted as he began to push the plastic toilet closer to her with his foot.

"Oh, that's right, you can't reach this, can you? Well, let me just give you a hand," the man said, a smile in his voice.

When he was within a step of her, another figure entered the room. The second man stepped through the light coming from the door and stood in the shadows at the far end of the room. The big man turned to look at the newcomer. Andrea could sense his anger at the interruption.

She couldn't see the other man's features in the dark, but his outline was visible. He was half a foot shorter than the man in front of her, but he was wider, with a weightlifter's physique. Andrea suspected it was the Hispanic man who'd chased them after they'd escaped from Richie's apartment building.

"You forgot the key and the longer chain," the man near the door said. The voice had an undercurrent of amused provocation.

"So drop the fucking thing right there. I'll deal with it."

"No can do. Juan asked me to take over his job, and you know me. I take my orders seriously, particularly when they come from the big boss," the Hispanic man said.

Andrea could sense the tension between the two men. They hated each other. For a second, she thought the big man was going to start toward the other man, even turn it into a fight, but he restrained himself. She had an idea that the only thing holding him back was the other man's reference to the "big boss." Somehow she knew that the Hispanic man was referring to the man with the European accent.

The big man kicked the portable toilet over on its side and walked toward the door.

"That's fine by me, Mex. This work fits you."

Andrea could almost feel the antagonism as the two men passed each other in the dark.

The Hispanic man made a point of staying in the shadow. He disconnected the chain from her manacles and dropped it on the floor. Then he reconnected a second chain that was almost twice as long as the first. It would allow her to stand and move around about three feet in either direction. When the Latino man finished, he reached over, righted the portable toilet, and pushed it within her reach. Although the man was respectful, Andrea didn't sense any willingness to help her.

He stopped at the door and spoke without turning to face her.

"I'll have Juan bring you a blanket, water, and a sandwich when he returns to remove the chair."

"Thank you," Andrea said and released the breath that she'd been holding.

# CHAPTER
# FORTY-FIVE

*Austin, Texas*
*December 7, 1999 / Tuesday / 12:00 a.m.*

The taxi driver looked over at Caine questioningly.
"You sure you want to stay at this place? This ain't no Holiday Inn."

Caine just nodded. "I know, but like I said, the magazine wants a story about single-room-occupancy hotels in Austin. So this is the ticket. And you did say this was the best of the lot, right?"

"Yeah, I did, but that's not saying much. Keep your hand on your wallet and your door locked."

"That I will do," Caine said as he handed the man a twenty and waved away the change.

Caine looked up at the façade of the five-story building from the sidewalk. The outside brickwork was old and worn, and the whole façade was more than a little dirty, particularly the windows. The blue neon sign above the door bore the improbable name "The Mariners Hotel."

Caine pushed open the scuffed Plexiglas door and walked into the small lobby. The man sitting behind the worn front desk was about fifty-five years old. He had a full, if unruly, head of salt-and-pepper hair and a matching mustache. His brown cardigan, white shirt, and black bowtie seemed almost as out of place as the hardcover book in front of him. The man looked more like an out-of-work history professor than the proprietor of a single-room-occupancy hotel located three blocks from the center of what could fairly be labeled Austin's "skid row" section.

For a moment, a look of apprehension crossed the man's face, but then it faded as he looked Caine over.

"Can I help your, sir?"

"Yes. A room for the night, if you have one, preferably not on the street side," Caine said as he scanned the lobby area. He noted that although the furniture was worn and the walls were a drab brown, the place was clean.

"We have a room on the third floor that's available. Cash or credit? If it's cash, you have to pay in advance, with a fifty-dollar holding charge, just in case there's any damage to the room."

"Cash."

"Very good. Please fill out the register."

Caine took the clipboard with a pen chained to the top, and filled in a fictitious name, address, and home phone number. He could sense that the man wanted to ask him a question, but was hesitant to do so. The man overcame his reluctance when Caine handed him back the form.

"Sir, you don't seem—"

"Like your typical customer? I guess I'm not," Caine said. "I'm writing a book, and I needed to get a mental picture of this kind of place to complete one of the chapters."

Caine could tell that this information piqued the man's interest, but Caine wanted to avoid any more questions.

"Can you direct me to the room?" Caine asked quickly.

"It's Room 303. That's three floors up, to the right, and about five doors down. Is there is anything else I can help you with?"

"No, but thank you," Caine said and walked over to the stairs.

Caine looked down each hallway as he crossed the two lower landings. They were all empty. When he came to the third floor, he walked down the empty corridor to the door of his room. He stood to the left of the doorway as he opened it. It was unlikely that anyone was waiting for him on the other side of the door, but the last few days had reawakened old habits.

When the door opened, he gave it a little push and waited until it hit the wall. The room was dark. He reached in and flipped on the light and entered the room. There was a small bathroom to the left, with a walk-in shower, a yellowed sink, and a toilet. Like the lobby area, everything in the room was worn, even threadbare, but it seemed to be clean.

Caine went back to the door and closed and locked it. The blinds on the windows were already pulled down. He left them that way.

Caine undressed and took a shower, running the water as hot as he could bear. He closed his eyes and let the water run down his chest and over his back. An image of Andrea's face flashed into his mind, and with it a wave of frustration and slow anger. After several minutes, Caine turned the water temperature to the coldest setting. The freezing blast pushed back the fatigue that was starting to catch up with him. He needed to stay awake.

The man in the bar could have killed Andrea at any time. He'd taken her alive for a reason. Helius needed both of them dead, which meant the other side would try to use Andrea as bait. If he wanted to get her back, he would need a plan and a lot more firepower than the Browning, which meant getting help from Jaq.

### Austin, Texas
### December 7, 1999 / Tuesday / 1:00 a.m.

The all-night "Electronic Café" was about six blocks south of the hotel, in a slightly better neighborhood. The inside of the place looked like a cross between a 1960s living room, with too many computers, and a coffee shop. Caine walked over to the twenty-something college kid behind the counter, who was playing a video game on his laptop.

"Coffee, time, or both?" The kid said without looking up from the game.

"Both. A large black Caribbean and one hour of Internet time."

"The coffee is a buck seventy-five. The hour will cost you ten."

Caine paid in cash and walked over to a computer against the far wall. He logged into the AOL account he used for business and typed in his passcode. There was the usual junk mail, three inquiries about possible new assignments, and an e-mail from Father Moreno asking Caine what the hell he was doing, and what he could do to help.

The most recent e-mail was an hour old. The sender was GenMassena@earthlink.com. The e-mail had to be from Jaq. Massena was Napoleon's most effective general. Like Caine, Jaq was a devoted military history buff, so he knew the name would be recognized.

Caine clicked on the message.

"Where the hell are you? If you cannot call me immediately, then e-mail me. Wherever I am, the message will find me."

Caine logged out of his account and opened a new AOL account as a new user under a false name and address. Then he e-mailed Jaq.

"Jaq, are you there? It's John."

He received an almost immediate response.

"Of course I'm here. What's your situation?"

"I think I've identified the opposition. They're affiliated with a company called Helius Energy. It's a large international energy company here in Austin."

"Are you sure? Why would they be after you?"

"I'm still not sure, but the information came from the reporter who started this thing, so I think it's real. The reporter said I own an interest in a property that has something to do with Helius, apparently an incredibly valuable property."

"Do you?"

"If I do, I don't know a thing about it."

"So they want to kill you over a property you know nothing about?" Jaq e-mailed back.

"There has to be something to it. No one would put together this big a hunt on bad information."

"Maybe they just don't like you. Where's the girl?"

Caine typed a reply.

"That's the bad news. They grabbed her. I'm going to try to get her back. I could use your help getting some heavy-duty hardware, and some comm support. I'll handle the rescue."

There was a hesitation, and then Jaq replied.

"We need to meet to put this together. I have a business associate in Austin. We can use his place. It's a warehouse. Is this connection safe?"

"Yes. I opened up a new user account a minute ago."

"Meet me at 122 Central Way, Building 16. Park in the back and come in the back door. I'll see you there tomorrow at 10:00 a.m. As for the rescue, we'll all do it. Stay well, friend."

Caine had expected Jaq to resist being kept out of the fight, but Caine intended to make sure the operation went down that way. This was his problem. Jaq's last comment confused him. *What was the reference to "all" about?*

Caine spent another twenty minutes looking up information on Helius. The data he pulled up confirmed what Andrea had said, but there were two pieces of information that were of particular interest. Apparently the massive bond offering Helius was bringing to market next week was critical. It would move the company from the "at risk" category into the black. Caine could see why Helius wouldn't want anyone raising a big title problem at this particular juncture. The timing of the offering might give him some leverage, but he suspected that he would need a lot more than that to get Andrea back alive.

The second piece of information came from two small human rights web sites. There were a series of messages about alleged brutalities committed by "Helius goon squads" in the third world. One allegation related to an incident in Venezuela. The second was in Cameroon. Caine glanced at his watch. It was 1:55 a.m. His hour was up and he was having trouble focusing.

Caine waved to the college kid behind the coffee bar as he headed out the door, and received a nod in return. The kid was talking to a girl at the bar. She was wearing a black T-shirt and jeans, and her hair was dyed almost the same color. She gave Caine a quick once-over as he walked out. Her face was cute, despite the stark white makeup and the dark lipstick. For a second, Caine saw Andrea sitting there looking back at him, drinking a latte with a friend on a Friday night. He blinked away the illusion, but not the anxiety and fear that came with it.

# CHAPTER
# FORTY-SIX

Austin, Texas
*December 7, 1999 / Tuesday / 2:00 a.m.*

The loft spanned the entire fifth floor of the Lancaster Building, an historically preserved jewel located in the center of Austin's most expensive urban enclave. The interior, which had been designed and decorated by an elite New York design firm, had been featured in *Architectural Digest*'s "Best of the West" section two years ago.

The loft was officially maintained at Helius's expense in order to provide Mason a place to stay when business demands forced him to stay in the city for the night. In fact, the loft existed to serve a different need: Mason's mistress lived there.

Mason stopped in front of the eight-foot window and looked down on the city street below for a moment. Then he walked back to the table, where he was trying, unsuccessfully, to focus on the latest analyst's report on the bond offering. A partially empty glass of Scotch was parked in the center of the report. Mason rarely ever drank more than two drinks at a sitting, but tonight he was working on his third.

He'd come to the loft intending to eat and get a few hours of sleep while awaiting the latest development from Paquin's team.

Unfortunately, his current mistress, a Brazilian girl he'd brought into the country a year ago, had denied him this respite. She'd badgered him with a series of inane questions, most of which he'd ignored until he belatedly figured out what she was after. Apparently the little genius had decided it was time to discuss their future. Her temerity had enraged him. *They* didn't have a future. As far as he was concerned, she had her role and was well compensated for it. Before Mason could set her straight, Paquin had called.

Mason had expected Paquin to tell him that Caine and the woman were finally dead, ending the nightmare, but that hadn't happened. Paquin's carefully planned operation outside the restaurant had turned into a disaster. Caine and the woman had escaped unharmed, and the local prosecutor, who was off limits, had been shot.

Mason gripped the edge of the table in front of him and closed his eyes. *The fools!* Now every law enforcement resource in Texas would be trying to find out who shot one of their golden boys. Paquin's insistence that his people hadn't put down the prosecutor was obviously ridiculous. Who else could have pulled the trigger? The situation was getting completely out of control.

Paquin had never failed to solve a company problem in the past. Sometimes the solutions had been messier than Mason would have liked, but the problem had always been solved, leaving Helius's reputation unscathed. This time it was different. It seemed that Paquin simply couldn't get the job done. Unfortunately, this was the one case where failure was not an option for the company.

The whiskey burned his throat as he emptied the glass. The surprise call that he'd received from Onwuallu an hour after the Marian House disaster came to mind. Onwuallu had called to tell him that he'd decided to stay an extra day in Austin to do some personal business. Apparently the Minister in Harare that Onwuallu had scheduled a meeting with had left for his hunting lodge, making further negotiations impossible until next week. The subject of the Caine problem had come up in the conversation and Mason had raged about the most recent disaster.

Onwuallu had quietly suggested that he might be able to provide some assistance, if only as a backup to Mr. Paquin. Making people disappear was a skill that he'd apparently perfected while working for the infamous Charles Taylor in Liberia. Two days ago, Mason wouldn't have considered the offer, but now that he had time to think about it, he decided Onwuallu might be right. Paquin could not be trusted.

The phone on the table interrupted his thoughts.

"Hello, Mason here."

"Paquin."

"Well, Mr. Paquin, have you *finally* solved our little problem?"

"No. But our position has improved. We found the woman and we now have her in a safe place."

"What do you mean, you have her? Why isn't she dead and buried? And where is Caine, goddamn it?"

Paquin could hear the alcohol in Mason's voice.

"They became separated. She was alone when we found her. That's also the reason why she's still alive. We need her."

"Explain."

"I interrogated the woman. I believe that she's important to Caine."

"What do you mean 'important,' and where exactly does that get us?"

"Important on an emotional level. I believe they have developed a romantic attachment. As to where that gets us, that's both simple and complicated."

"Mr. Paquin, I don't want any more complications. I want solutions. In this case, in particular, I want a permanent solution. Do you under—"

"Yes, I do understand," Paquin said, interrupting Mason's rant. "The situation is simple in this respect. I believe Mr. Caine will try to take the woman back from us. I also believe that he won't do anything with the information he's obtained about your precious deed problem, *which is substantial,* before he makes this attempt. The complicated issue is the how, when, and where Mr. Caine will make his move."

Mason hesitated and processed the information before responding.

"Very well, what do you intend to do?"

"We will use the girl as bait. We will lure Caine to a killing ground of our choosing, and we will put him down—permanently."

The uncharacteristic intensity in Paquin's voice surprised Mason. "Very well, Mr. Paquin, I will leave this problem and the solution in your capable hands. Is there anything more you need from me?"

Mason had not expected Paquin to ask for anything, but he did.

"Yes, there is," Paquin said. "To make sure that this matter is finally put to rest, we need to arrange a particularly lethal reception for Mr. Caine. That requires an isolated facility. A place that is remote yet defensible. The place that you refer to as the 'Old Ranch' fits the bill for a number of reasons."

The Old Ranch was a collection of old buildings located in a remote area well outside Austin. The property had originally been owned by a Mexican land baron before Texas became a republic. The structures on site were nothing to speak of. Just an old ranch house with three or four secondary buildings, enclosed by an old adobe wall. Mason had tried get rid of the property after his grandfather's death, but the old man had anticipated the move. He'd placed the ranch in a trust shortly before his death. The trust barred the sale of the property outside the family.

Faced with this restriction, Mason, who was the sole trustee of the trust, had taken the next best option. He'd transferred title to a charitable trust that was still within the control of the Mason family. The transfer had skirted the restriction in the trust, and it had generated a large charitable deduction. The charitable trust periodically rented the place out to schools, movie producers, and other users in order to keep up the front of a charitable use.

Mason had no problem allowing Paquin to use the Old Ranch, as long as whatever happened there remained secret, since title to the property was traceable to the Mason family.

"You understand, Mr. Paquin, that this asset is traceable to the Mason family?"

Paquin's response was careful, but direct. "Yes. Although there is a small element of risk, the location is so remote that it's highly unlikely anyone in the area will take an interest. You will have to decide whether our present exigency justifies the risk."

Mason had scrupulously maintained the wall that existed between Paquin's black projects and Helius, and the second wall maintained between Helius and the Mason family. Now Paquin was suggesting that he step outside that carefully crafted systemic protection. Mason was unhappy with the risk, but Helius and the Mason family were already on a precipice.

Mason suddenly hated Caine. He hated him for placing Helius at risk; for struggling to live when his death was necessary; and for forcing Mason to place his own position at risk, as a precondition to his own death. Mason suddenly wanted to kill Caine and the woman himself—to see them die before his eyes. Then the rage began to ebb and he reasserted control. He had to make a decision.

"You have the ranch. I will make sure that no one is near the place for the next month. That will give you time to repair any damage that may result from your meeting with Caine."

Mason hesitated a minute and then said, "One other thing. I will be out of the country on business for about three days. During two of those days, I will be difficult to reach. I assume you will have resolved our problem by the time I return?"

Paquin ignored Mason's question.

"Good night, Mr. Mason."

# CHAPTER
# FORTY-SEVEN

*Dallas, Texas*
*December 7, 1999 / Tuesday / 8:00 a.m.*

William Spencer waited impatiently for his computer to boot up. He was hoping Tobey Nelson had sent him an e-mail updating him on the investigation of the crash site in California. He would have called to check on the investigation, but it was two hours earlier in Los Angeles. Nelson wouldn't be in the office for at least another hour, maybe two, depending on traffic.

When the e-mail screen came up, he browsed through the list of messages. There was nothing from Nelson. Just in case Tobey had sent the message to his personal account, Spencer checked it. There was nothing from Nelson, but there was something from jsmith@aol.com, the anonymous source that alerted him about the crash. Spencer clicked on the message.

"Our latest information indicates that a company called Helius Energy is the hunter. We don't know the why."

Spencer recognized the corporation. Helius was a large energy conglomerate. Its headquarters were in Austin. Spencer found it hard to believe that Helius had anything to do with the attack in California. Why would Helius try to kill a retired intelligence operative?

Spencer ran a Google search on the company and scanned the material information. Then he ran the company through the "Edgar" database maintained by the Securities and Exchange Commission. He found two recent filings indicating that the company was in the process of registering a huge bond offering.

An hour later, Spencer received a call on his private line.

"Spencer."

"Hi, Bill, it's Tobey."

"Hey, buddy."

"I have an update on that matter we talked about yesterday. The agent I assigned to the matter went back out to our mysterious crash site. She conducted another circuit of the area and picked up a set of snowmobile tracks. She followed the tracks in one direction and they led back to a remote mountain cabin about three or four miles to the east."

"Was anyone home?"

"No, but the car was still in the driveway, which was odd, since the nearest paved road is about a mile away, and the town is about five miles from there. So either someone has a good set of feet, or they left on the snowmobile."

"Who's the owner?"

"The car and the cabin are registered to one John Caine, age forty-four He lives outside the City of Hesperia. It's on the east side of the San Bernardino Mountains, about sixty miles from the cabin. We called his house, but there was no answer."

"Did you run a check on him?"

"Yes, sir. Not even a parking ticket."

Spencer could tell by Tobey's voice that he had more.

"I also ran a wider search. I called our Pentagon liaison, and he checked to see if Mr. Caine was ever in the military."

"And?"

"Yes, sir. Our boy was a Ranger in the late seventies. But there's more. Although it took some heavy arm-twisting, the unofficial word that I got was Mr. John Caine worked black ops."

"For the army?"

"Not our army. Apparently Caine joined the French Foreign Legion after he left the Rangers, and was eventually assigned to a heavy duty special operations unit. That was all my contact's clearance could get him. He told me that if we wanted more, we would have to talk to our friends at Langley."

Spencer leaned back in his chair, trying to absorb the information.

"What the hell is going on here?" Spencer said.

"Good question. I was hoping you could tell me."

Spencer hesitated for a second. He wanted to bring Tobey up to date on the Helius information, but he didn't want to pull O'Connor into the open. Then he figured out a way to skirt the issue.

"I'm in the dark here, too, but there has been a development on this side that may help us. When I got in this morning, I received an anonymous tip."

"It seems you've been getting quite a few of those lately," Nelson said with both a smile and a question in his voice.

"We'll get to that. Anyway, the tip came by e-mail. The sender suggested that Helius Energy was behind the attack in California."

"Helius? Who's that?"

"It's a billion-dollar energy company. Their HQ is in Austin, but they have operations all over the world."

"Why would Helius try to kill a retired ex-special-ops soldier, and who, pray tell, is feeding you this information?"

Spencer expected the last question. Fortunately, Tobey's discovery of Caine's background with the French gave him a ready answer.

"The first contact I had about this matter came by phone. The caller had an accent—a French accent. I think French intelligence is quietly trying to look after one of their own."

Before Tobey could go further down that road, Spencer turned the conversation back to him.

"By the way, do we know whether the target was killed and cleaned up along with the chopper?"

"We can't say for sure, but we don't think so. Not if he was driving the snowmobile. We found a second set of tracks leading away from the crash site and we found the machine. It was parked in a stand of trees about a mile outside of town. Bill, give me a minute."

Spencer heard a voice in the background of Tobey's office. Tobey said thanks and came back on.

"Bill, I'm looking at two sets of phone records that were just faxed over."

"You've been busy."

"Yeah, I had Justice get a search warrant from the district court. Given what we have so far, it was easy enough. Of course the assistant A.G. has got wind of this matter and now wants in on it all the way."

"Oh boy," Spencer said.

"Bill, we have to bring Justice in on this. It's too big for us to keep in our back pocket any more, particularly with this French issue. Hell, State and CIA may want to know about this, too."

Spencer knew that Tobey was right. If Helius was the driving force behind this monster, then a whole lot of people would want to get involved in it. Spencer's problem related to one particular person in the Justice Department: someone in his own backyard.

"That's not my problem, Tobey. Helius is located in Austin. That's in the Western District of Texas. The United States Attorney for the Western District is Michaela Russo. I'm sure you recognize that name."

Nelson did recognize the name, and like Spencer he understood the politics that were an integral part of the U.S. Department of Justice.

The DOJ divided the country into regional offices, and each regional office was assigned a U.S. attorney. The individuals in these positions were political appointees, and more than a few of them had political ambitions. Marquee cases with a lot of press time were the proverbial coin of the realm. Any U.S. attorney who was cut out of a "hot" case in his or her region would be a very unhappy camper. In the case of Michaela Russo, who everyone knew had national political aspirations, her screams of rage would be heard all the way back to Washington.

"Russo, that's just great," Tobey said. "Okay, just tell me what you want to do."

Spencer considered his options. He wanted at least another day to get his arms around the case before he formally notified Russo of the investigation.

"How about this? I'll assemble as much data on the case as possible today. Tomorrow, I will e-mail Russo with a case summary. You tell the folks at Justice up there that you think Texas will be working the case, but you'll get back to them. If they push you, tell them to call Russo. By then she'll have the e-mail and they can fight it out between themselves."

There was a hesitation on the other side of the line.

"Works for me, buddy. This may be a joint effort, but as far as I'm concerned it's your show," Nelson said.

Spencer smiled to himself. What Nelson was really saying was *I'll follow your lead, but if there are any problems with Washington or Justice, I'll direct them to you.* Spencer was okay with that.

With the political issues solved, Spencer switched gears. "Do you see anything interesting in the list of calls?"

"Let me see. Nothing that jumps out at me on the home phone. Let me look at the list for the cell phone. No, no, and then a big yes! I got some good news. It appears as though John Caine has developed a big interest in the great state of Texas. Almost every call that I see here in the last forty-eight hours has a Texas area code. I'll have the list faxed to you right away. Your people can track down these numbers. I'll keep working this end."

"Thanks, Tobey. As soon as I get the results, I'll give you a call."

After hanging up, Spencer walked over to the window and looked out on the Dallas skyline. *What had they gotten into?*

### Dallas, Texas
### December 8, 1999 / Wednesday / 11:00 a.m.

The work-up on Caine's phone calls showed an early morning call on Saturday to the *Austin American-Statesman*, from a location in Riverside, California. Later that same morning, Caine had made two calls to one Andrea Marenna in Austin, Texas. One call was made from a location in Riverside, California. The second was made from Austin, Texas.

Caine had also called a cell phone number in Houston. The number was registered to a Bahamian corporation. One call was made from California. The second was made from Austin. Spencer circled the two names and handed the list back to the junior agent he'd recently assigned to the case, Ashley Morgan.

"I need everything you can get on Ms. Marenna and this corporation as soon as possible.

"Coming right up."

"Thanks."

Spencer watched the tall African American woman walk out the door. She was six months out of the academy. All of her reviews to date had been exceptional, particularly in the firearms field. She'd shot a perfect score three times in a row at the range, beating two old hands who were considered the best of the best.

The young agent's shooting skill made sense to Spencer, because he knew her background. Her father had been a sergeant in the U.S. Army Special Forces. After his knee had been permanently injured on a mission, the elder Morgan had spent twenty years as a firearms instructor at Fort Bragg. Agent Morgan had served as the master's avid apprentice. She was more than an expert marksman; she was a walking encyclopedia on firearms.

Spencer turned back to his computer and pulled up a form that every office was required to file with the bureau's central database in Washington. The report gave Washington a summary of each new investigation. The agent in charge of the investigation was required to assign a rating to the investigation that weighed the risk posed to the public by the alleged perpetrators, the geographic scope of the threat, and the resources that would be required to pursue the investigation. Spencer intended to give the new file a mid-level rating for now. This was defensible given the lack of clear data. It would also keep the matter from being swarmed over by his superiors, at least for a week or two. Once the picture became clearer, he would update the rating.

It took Spencer half an hour to complete his write-up. He labeled the matter a joint investigation with the Bureau's Los Angeles office. When he finished, he e-mailed the draft report to Tobey for approval and walked down to the duty desk, where an agent was reviewing incoming information about possible federal crimes within the Southwest region during the past twenty-four hours. The agent's task was to sift through the information and then prioritize the matters. Big issues such as bomb threats, major shooting incidents, and similar matters would be referred up the line for immediate attention.

Spencer stopped at the coffee station across from the agent and gave him a friendly wave.

"Anything exciting happening?"

The agent nodded affirmatively.

"Pretty big. There was a shootout in downtown Austin last night. It looks like a city prosecutor was shot."

Spencer just shook his head and started back to his office, but stopped before he reached the door and turned back to the agent.

"Can I see the write-up?"

"On the Austin shooting?"

"Yes."

"Here it is."

Spencer picked up the summary of the incident and the extracts from the police reports. The information was confusing. Apparently there had been a shootout, but it wasn't clear who was involved or why. As he started to hand back the report, a name at the tail end of the report flew off the page at him.

"Andrea Marenna, an Austin attorney, and a forty-year-old white male, about six feet tall, are considered persons of interest to this investigation."

Spencer turned to his administrative assistant.

"I need a flight to Austin. Actually get two tickets on that flight and inform Agent Morgan that she's going to Austin to investigate a new case."

# CHAPTER
# FORTY-EIGHT

*Austin, Texas*
*December 7, 1999 / Tuesday / 9:50 a.m.*

The address that Jaq had given him was in an older industrial area on the outskirts of Austin. Building 16 was a cinder-block-and-steel warehouse on a corner lot. The complex was protected by ten-foot barbed wire. The building across the street was of similar construction. A "For Lease" sign was hanging on the fence outside the building.

Caine drove around the block twice before pulling in the front gate, which was open. He followed the driveway to an alley in the rear and parked the pickup. Before getting out, he pulled out the Browning, checked the magazine, and turned off the safety. He put the gun back in his jacket, but kept his hand on it.

Caine walked past the loading dock to the steel door on the other side with the "Number 16" stenciled over it. The door opened and Jaq stepped out. The Haitian smiled and grabbed Caine's hand in an iron grip.

"You look like shit, Caine. It's lucky that Uncle Jaq is here to save your sorry ass. Of course, I brought along a little help, just in case."

"Thanks, Jaq, but all I—"

A deep baritone that Caine hadn't heard in ten years interrupted him. "A *little* help. What bullshit."

Caine turned and took in the sight of Sergeant Joe Vlasky walking toward him from the gap between the two smaller buildings on the other side of the alley. The Pole's face had a few more lines than it had a decade earlier, but he still had the physique of a powerlifter. If anything, the ex-legionnaire had added even more muscle to his square frame since the last time Caine had seen him. Vlasky grabbed Caine in a bear hug that crushed the breath out of him, and then gave him a slap on the shoulder when he released him.

"So where's the fight, corporal?" Vlasky said, a smile on his face.

A third voice called down from the flat roof of the warehouse above him.

"Giovanni! Up here."

Caine looked up and stared at the handsome face of Pietro Marchesano. The wiry five-foot-eight Italian was waving to him with both arms. His Mediterranean features didn't seem a day older.

"Buongiorno, my friend."

Caine waved back, too stunned by the appearance of the three men together to speak. Pietro had joined the team after MacBain had been killed in Africa. Any replacement joining the unit after that incident could have expected a long integration process, but it hadn't worked out that way. Pietro's quiet competence and skill, particularly as a sniper, had earned him the respect of every member of the unit after two missions. His irrepressible good humor, no matter what the circumstances, had done the rest.

As Caine looked at the three men, he was almost overwhelmed by emotion. The men had forged a bond of friendship, brotherhood even, despite their disparate backgrounds and personalities, during the decade they'd worked together. But there was something more— something that he'd never fully appreciated until the last three days. They'd been with him every time he'd faced the risk of death in the past. Knowing they were with him had made the challenge bearable. During the last three days, he'd been forced to stand on that precipice alone, knowing that any mistake would push him and Andrea into that abyss. The unrelenting psychological pressure and physical strain of that experience had brought him close to the breaking point. Seeing the three of them standing there lifted a massive weight from his shoulders.

Caine suddenly realized that one man from the team was missing: Colonel Etienne Ricard. Then he heard a voice from inside the door Jaq was holding open.

"Gentlemen, must I drink this fine burgundy all alone? Come!"

Caine walked to the doorway. Etienne Ricard was standing beside an old wooden table inside the warehouse. Five glasses circled a dark red bottle of wine.

"Corporal Caine, it has been far too long."

Caine unconsciously came to attention and saluted. Ricard casually returned the salute and waved him in.

"Too long indeed, Colonel," Caine said as he looked into the intense gray eyes of the man who'd been his commanding officer for ten years. Ricard was thinner than Caine remembered, and his hair had more salt than pepper in it, but his tanned and aristocratic bearing radiated the same quiet power and dignity that Caine remembered. Caine shook his head slowly. *They're all here.*

# CHAPTER
# FORTY-NINE

*Travis County, Texas*
*December 7, 1999 / Tuesday / 9:00 a.m.*

Andrea was awake when the wiry Latino in his late thirties opened the door to the room and turned on the overhead light. The man was of medium height. His hair was cropped short, and he had a hard, weathered face. His cheekbones and eyes looked more American Indian than Spanish. The sleeves on his sweatshirt were rolled up, revealing muscled forearms that were decorated by a patchwork of tattoos and small scars.

Andrea stared at the man as he crossed the room. He avoided making eye contact, but made no effort to hide his face. After disconnecting the chain, he led her out of the room to the back of a truck parked in the main warehouse. A second Latino man, wearing a worn flight jacket, was standing near the cab of the truck. He was younger and taller than the first man, but had similar hair and facial features. When Andrea glanced over at the man, he also made no effort to hide his face. In fact, he returned the look, grinned suggestively, and then made a comment to the man beside her in Spanish. Andrea understood the comment, but didn't react. She was thinking about their failure to cover their faces. Something had changed. They were no longer worried about her getting out of there alive. That should have terrified her, but it didn't. She was just too tired and numb to care.

The first man led Andrea to the back of the truck, which was open, and gestured for her to climb in the back using a small step stool. He followed her into the truck and reconnected the chain to a steel ring on the rear wall. Then he hopped back down to the floor of the warehouse. Four long steel boxes were stacked against one wall of the truck. The boxes were secured by two large black nylon straps. The rest of the truck was empty.

The two Latino men talked quietly in Spanish just outside the rear door. Andrea knew enough conversational Spanish to follow the exchange. The man with the tattoos on his forearms was named Juan. He was describing a confrontation that had occurred between a man they called Anders and a second man called Vargas. As she listened, Andrea realized that they were talking about the confrontation she'd witnessed the night before between the man who tried to capture her in the apartment building, Anders, and the man with the bodybuilder's physique, Vargas. The two men obviously didn't like Anders, because they both laughed when the first man described how angry he'd been when he left the room.

Ten minutes later, Andrea heard a man call over to the two men from somewhere in the warehouse outside her sight.

"Juan, close the truck. We're moving out."

Andrea recognized the voice. It was the muscular Latino man, Vargas.

The rear of the truck didn't have any windows, but Andrea could tell from the speed and relatively smooth ride that the driver was taking one the interstates out of the downtown area. Approximately an hour later, the truck slowed and transitioned to a secondary road that was slower. Half an hour later, the truck slowed again and turned off onto what must have been an unpaved road. The truck bounced and yawed back and forth, throwing Andrea up and down like a mannequin. When the truck finally came to a stop, sweat was pouring down her face and her arms were shaking from the strain of trying to hold herself in place.

The back door to the truck opened almost as soon it came to a stop. Juan hopped in, disconnected the chain, and helped her out the back. The man they called Vargas was waiting for her. When she saw him the night before, Vargas had been dressed in jeans and a sweater. Now he was dressed like a soldier. He was wearing desert camouflage pants, a tan sweatshirt, and sand-colored hiking boots. A holster with a large black pistol was attached to his belt. The sunglasses on his face hid his eyes, but not the features of his broad, handsome face.

Vargas looked at her briefly and said, "Follow me, please."

Andrea followed the man across a courtyard toward a small building to the right of the truck. The short walk gave her the opportunity to look over her surroundings. The collection of buildings looked like what at one time had been a working ranch, or even one of the original Mexican haciendas. The main building was a large adobe-and-stone mansion. The words "El Castillo" were carved into a log that was embedded in the adobe above the front doorway.

The architecture of the house fit its namesake. The doors and windows were arched, and a three-foot crenellated wall circled the edge of the flat roof. A cupola that was large enough to hold three or four people was located in the center of the roof, providing a 360-degree view of the surrounding ranch.

A second building to the left of the main house was smaller. The first two floors appeared to be of the same vintage as the main house, but at some point, possibly within the past twenty years, a third floor had been added. Andrea suspected that the structure was originally built to house the domestic staff.

The building that Vargas was approaching was to the right of the main house. From the outside it looked like an old bunkhouse that had been converted into a two-story house. To the right of this building was a smaller one-room structure.

The entire compound was surrounded by an eight-foot adobe wall that was patched in places with bricks and mortar. The area outside the wall was typical Texas Hill Country, with scattered trees and low rolling hills that went on for miles—long, empty miles.

Vargas held open the door to the old bunkhouse, and Andrea walked past him into the interior. From what she could see, the building was being used as a storehouse for excess furniture, equipment, and supplies. Vargas led her to a room in the rear of the building that was about six feet wide.

Steel storage racks were installed on the two longer sides of the rectangular room. The shelves were filled with cleaning supplies, cookware, an old television and VCR, and various other pieces of electronic equipment. As she followed Vargas into the room, Andrea noticed an old fax machine lying on its side in the middle of a shelf. The Latino man stopped about midway into the room and turned to face her.

"You have to stay here for about an hour. Then you will be moved to another building. There's a toilet over there that works."

Then he walked past her to the front of the room and closed the door behind him. Andrea heard him lock the door from the other side. As soon as she heard his footsteps recede and the door to the outside of the building open and close, Andrea checked the door. It was locked. She pushed against the door, but gave up after several tries. The lock was a dead bolt and the door was solid.

She walked around the room, looking over the old equipment and the boxes on the shelf. She stopped in front of the old fax machine and pulled it closer to the edge. Despite its age, the part of the technology that she might be able to use could still be operable: the internal phone line. If the machine still worked and the room had a phone jack, she might be able to dial Caine's cell phone. She wouldn't be able to talk with him, but if Caine brought the number to the police, they'd be able to trace the line and find her location.

Andrea found a phone jack and an electrical outlet behind the desk near the bathroom. Her hands were still in the handcuffs, but they were locked in front of her. Getting the fax machine off the shelf and over to the desk was difficult, but she managed to do it by pressing it into her stomach as she hobbled over to the desk.

Although Andrea lowered the machine to the steel desk as carefully as possible, the hard surfaces made an audible sound when they touched. She froze for a moment, listening, but there was no sign that anyone was coming to investigate. She turned back to the fax machine, checked the phone cable plugged into the back, and then plugged the opposite end into the jack in the wall. The plastic display on the front of machine remained dark. The machine didn't work.

"No way!" she said in a desperate whisper.

Then she noticed the on/off switch on the side of the machine and hit it. The display lit up and she heard a quiet whir. Andrea almost cried with relief. She typed Caine's cell number on the keypad. He answered on the second ring in a cautious voice.

"Caine here. Hello? Hello?"

# CHAPTER
# FIFTY

After a celebratory drink, the four men listened to Caine describe the events of the last three days. When he finished, Ricard questioned him about the details. In the middle of the questioning, Caine's cell phone rang. Only one person other than Jaq had his new cell phone number—Andrea. She'd memorized it in the bar minutes before she was seized. Caine looked at the number on the screen. It was an Austin area code.

"I have to take this."

Ricard nodded.

"Caine here. Hello? Hello?"

When no one answered, Caine hesitated.

"Andrea . . . is that you?"

There was no answer. The caller ended the call and called back three more times. Each time, no one responded to Caine's inquiries.

Caine typed the phone number into the address book in his phone and then stared at it. It had to be Andrea, or someone who'd forced her to give them the number. Caine closed his eyes for a moment. *I have to turn myself in to the Austin police or the FBI, tell them my story, and hope they'll immediately mount a rescue operation to save Andrea.* There was only one problem with that plan: it was pure fantasy.

The police considered him a suspect in the shooting of an Austin prosecutor. They would never accept his story without ironclad proof. That would take time, which was a death sentence for Andrea. At the end of the day, he had only one option—to take her back himself.

Caine felt a hand on his shoulder and opened his eyes. Ricard was in front him, staring at him with a look that he remembered, a look that commanded his attention.

"Sir, I need to find where that call originated. It has to be from Andrea."

Ricard held his hand out. "The phone, Corporal."

Caine handed Ricard the phone, and he walked out the door of the warehouse. Caine could hear him speaking in French. Three minutes later, he returned and gestured for Caine and the rest of men to sit.

"We will have the information in thirty minutes," Ricard said. "In the meantime, we need to know more about the enemy." He made Caine go over his story again.

Thirty minutes later, Caine's cell phone rang and Ricard answered it. The voice on the other side of the phone line spoke English, and Ricard made several notations on the pad in front of him. When the call ended, Ricard stood and spoke as he walked back and forth beside the table.

"I suspect you are right, Corporal. The call originated from a location about an hour and a half from here. It's in a remote area. The phone line and the property are listed under the name of El Castillo Ranch Preservation Society." Ricard hesitated a moment and then continued.

"The property was donated to this entity by a man named Carter T. Mason, the current chief executive officer and chairman of Helius Energy."

Caine slowly stood up, nodding. "That's it. That's where she is. I have to—"

"Corporal, it's a trap. They are inviting you to come to them. They are inviting you to die."

"I know, sir, but I have no—"

"Of course you do. We will *plan* an extraction rescue and then execute that operation as we have done so many times before."

Caine nodded his agreement, accepting Ricard's orders without thinking, but then he remembered that this was a different time and place. The memory of a death in a jungle far away returned.

"Sir, I cannot ask for your help with the rescue. I would be grateful for your help with the planning, communications—"

Ricard's quiet voice interrupted him.

"Corporal Caine, you *cannot* save her alone. It is impossible. You know that."

The words seared into Caine like a hot knife. Ricard was right. He might get close, with a combination of stealth and luck, but if they knew he was coming, there was almost no chance that he could take Andrea away from them without getting them both killed. He would need a lot more killing power. He would need more men; trained, skilled men.

Caine stood there in a place by himself, struggling with the terrible choice. Jaq's voice cut through his mental anguish.

"Stupid man. Did you really think that we'd let you keep this little soiree all to yourself? Such bad manners. That's what comes from living all by yourself in the desert. You must get out more, man."

Vlasky and Pietro chuckled. Vlasky walked over to the table and slapped Caine on the shoulder.

"Relax, buddy. This will be what you Americans call a 'walk in the park.'" Then Vlasky turned to Jacques with a challenging look. "So, island man, what kind of hardware do you folks have in Texas?"

A smile played across Jaq's face. "Why, whatever kind you need, Sergeant, whatever you need."

A small smile came to Ricard's face, as if he wasn't surprised by Jaq's comment. Then he turned to face the four men.

"Very well, gentlemen. Vlasky and Jaq will assemble the weapons and ammunition. Pietro, we will need transport: something that can carry six and the weapons, with off-road capability. Corporal Caine and I will put together whatever intel we can on the site."

Ricard looked down at his watch.

"It's twelve hundred hours now. Jaq, can you and Vlasky be back here by seventeen hundred?"

"Yes, sir."

"Good. And don't worry, Sergeant Vlasky, Corporal Caine and I will bring dinner."

Ricard's comment drew a smile from everyone, even Caine.

### Travis County, Texas
### December 7, 1999 / Tuesday/ 3:00 p.m.

Paquin looked out the window of the second floor office in the main house, at the rolling landscape outside the wall surrounding the compound. His trust in the woman's resourcefulness and determination had been vindicated. She'd found the old fax machine and managed to contact Caine. Now, all they had to do was wait for Caine to come to them.

Paquin knew that Caine had other options. He could go to the police or the FBI for help, or worse, he could write off the woman and go public. Paquin had the first option covered. His people were monitoring all police communications, and Helius's source within the Austin PD had been put on alert. Although he didn't have any contacts within the local FBI office, Paquin was almost certain they would bring Austin PD into the loop if they were contacted by Caine. When that happened, his contact would get word of the development.

Paquin had a backup plan in place, just in case Caine chose to go public and abandon the woman, but it was complicated and messy. Andrea Marenna's body would be left in a local hotel room. The crime scene would be carefully laid out so that all of the evidence pointed to Caine. Once he was in custody, other materials would be manufactured and carefully dribbled out to the press and the police in order to destroy Caine's credibility. As long as another Richard Steinman was not waiting in the wings to investigate Caine's incredible story, the plan might work, but Paquin didn't like the odds.

Paquin looked at the sky. It would be dark in about two hours. John Caine might have other choices, but Paquin instinctively knew

Caine wouldn't take them. He would come for the woman on his own, trusting in his own considerable skills. Although Paquin suspected that Caine's rescue effort would be formidable, he was also confident it would fail. No chances had been taken. This would be Mr. Caine's last operation.

Vargas knocked on the door and walked into the room.

Paquin turned.

"Mr. Vargas."

"The woman's in the small house. It's secure."

"Do you think she suspects anything?"

"No, sir."

Paquin gave Vargas a rare smile.

"I believe Mr. Caine will be paying us a visit later on tonight. Let's prepare for his arrival."

"Yes, sir."

# CHAPTER
# FIFTY-ONE

*Austin, Texas*
*December 7, 1999 / Tuesday / 7:00 p.m.*

Caine downloaded both ground-level and aerial pictures of the ranch from the Internet. There were five structures on-site: a main residence and four smaller structures. The compound was surrounded by a seven- or eight-foot wall. The area outside the ranch was rolling hills, with moderate cover. Only one dirt road provided direct access to the ranch, but there was another approach. Another dirt road came within five miles of the southern edge of the ranch. From there, they could close to within a mile by going off-road.

Pietro was back by the time Caine and Ricard returned with a black Suburban. Jaq and Vlasky returned at about seven thirty, driving a dusty white van. When Jaq opened the rear doors with a flourish, Caine was stunned at the firepower Jaq had managed to assemble. There were three HK MP-5A2 submachine guns, two mini Uzis, and five Glock-17s. Pietro slapped Jaq on the back when he saw the weapons and the boxes upon boxes of ammunition.

"*Magnifico!*"

"That's only the small stuff, buddy. Take a look at what Uncle Jaq has hidden in those two boxes over there," Vlasky said with a smile.

Pietro leaned into the van and lifted the top off a square wooden crate. Nobody said a word, but they all recognized the weapon. It was a C9A1 light machine gun. The C9A1 was a Belgian weapon that every member of the team had used before. It had a cyclic rate of fire of between seven hundred and one thousand rounds per minute and an effective range of six hundred meters.

Pietro slowly lowered the top, as if he was covering up a dangerous animal. Then he lifted the cover off the second box, which was longer and narrower. It was an M107 Barrett gun, the ultimate long-distance sniper rifle. It could shoot a fifty-caliber bullet over a mile with deadly accuracy.

When Caine moved forward to help with the unloading, Vlasky put a hand on his chest.

"Hold on there, Corporal. Let me just take this little jewel box out first. I don't want you dropping my C-4."

Caine slowly shook his head. After he'd left the Legion, Jaq had invited him to be a partner in his new business enterprise. As Jaq explained it, he was starting a consulting firm that would provide technical support to third-world customers buying arms from the international arms market. Since Caine had already started his own business, he'd passed on the offer. After looking at the firepower stacked in the van, Caine suspected that Jaq had graduated from a mere adviser to a heavy duty arms dealer. There was no other way he could have ready access to this kind of weaponry.

Jacques noticed Caine's look as he stared into the van and slapped his hands together.

"Snap to it, man. We don't have time for your gawkin'."

Caine smiled in spite of the growing anxiety in his gut. The balance of power had just shifted. If Andrea was still alive, they had the firepower to get her back and then some.

When Caine walked back into the warehouse after loading the last box of ammunition for the C9 into the Suburban, he noticed that Ricard was leaning over the table in the room pointing at the series of maps and pictures they'd obtained earlier, and Vlasky was standing beside him, listening. As he walked over to the sink to get a drink, Caine realized what had been bothering him about Ricard. The Colonel had always been on the lean side, but he looked almost emaciated in the glow of the overhead lights. Caine wondered whether he'd been sick. If that was the case, it didn't seem to be affecting his concentration or stamina. He was as sharp as ever.

As he looked around the room, Caine was surprised at how quickly each man had fallen into the old routine. Jaq and Caine were checking the weapons, Pietro was working on the communications gear, the optical equipment, and his new sniper rifle—the Barrett, and Ricard and Vlasky were putting together the rescue plan.

As Caine walked across the room to retrieve a bottle of water, a realization struck him: the other members of the unit had come to help him, but there was more to it. He could see it in their eyes. They wanted to recapture, for a short time—maybe the last time—the terrible intensity, adrenaline, and even the fear they'd left behind years ago. Caine suddenly realized that he did as well. He hoped they felt the same after it was all over.

Caine didn't realize that Ricard had quietly walked over to him, until he looked up. For a moment the two men looked at each other. It was as if Ricard knew exactly what Caine was thinking and wanted to set the record straight, before it was too late.

"Every man in this room chose to be here. You carry no responsibility for what will happen tonight, good or ill. You must accept that or you will put yourself and every man in this room at risk. More, you will dishonor their choice."

Ricard's admonition cut Caine to the quick. Ricard couldn't know about Caine's inner demon, but it was almost as if he could sense the fear. Caine looked at Ricard and nodded.

"Yes, sir."

# CHAPTER
# FIFTY-TWO

*Travis County, Texas*
*December 8, 1999 / Wednesday / 1:45 a.m.*

Andrea was bound to a wooden office chair in a dusty storage building at the far end of the compound. The old chair was made of oak, and the undercarriage, which rotated, was made of wood and iron. Her hands were handcuffed behind her. The chain that held the cuffs together was woven through the thick wooden slats that formed the back of the chair. The bottom half of the chair was chained to a nearby steel desk that easily weighed three hundred pounds.

Although she wasn't particularly uncomfortable, the wait was driving her crazy. She wanted to stand up, to walk, to do something. *Where is Caine? Why isn't he here with the police?* As she leaned over in the chair to try to get a better view through the hole, the door to the building opened. She couldn't see the man's face in the dark, but she recognized the outline. It was Anders. He closed the door and sauntered over to the steel desk beside her chair. When he reached the desk, he sat on the edge and stretched his legs out in front of him. Anders pulled out a pack of cigarettes, tapped one out of the pack, and flicked on his lighter. He put the flame inches from her face.

Andrea flinched away, but refused to look up at him. "So how's my little babe doin' all by her lonesome in heah? Gittin' a little anxious, are we? Yer probably missin' me."

Andrea stared straight ahead.

"Well, don't you fret, honey. I'll be back right quick. Me and the boys just have to *kill your little boyfriend*, and then there'll be plenty of time for us to cozy up."

Andrea froze and then looked over at Anders. There was a smile on his face. *What is he talking about? He couldn't know about Caine, or could . . .*

Anders smiled widened, as if he knew her every thought.

"Oh yeah, darlin', we know about your little phone call, or should I say fax call. Yes, sir. We're expecting Mr. Caine to make his appearance anytime now. 'Course, when he does, we're gonna have to burn his ass, but then that's jest too bad, ain't it."

Anders's voice became harsher as he continued.

"You see, Miss smart-ass lawyer, we're not as stupid as you assumed. We put that old fax machine in there for you to find. We knew you'd make the call and Mr. Dudley Do-Right would come a runnin' . . . right into this trap we got all set up for him."

Anders was leaning over Andrea now, and his face was inches from her own. His words were harsh and gloating.

"Smart thinking, bitch. You just bought your Mr. Caine an early grave."

Then the leer returned to his crude features.

"'Course, that means we'll have some quality time to get to know each other, at least until we put your ass into the same hole as Caine. But then, life's a *bitch* and then you die."

Anders stood up when he finished, and walked to the door. He paused at the door and spoke without turning around.

"And just for your information, Caine ain't bringing the boys in blue with him. He's ridin' solo on this run."

Then he walked out and slammed the door.

Andrea's throat was suddenly impossibly dry, and she had to struggle to swallow. Anders was right. She'd underestimated them.

The man with the European accent had played her for a fool and John was going to die for it. A wave of recrimination and powerlessness washed over her. For a moment, she almost began to cry hysterically, but squelched the feeling. She wasn't dead yet. There had to be a way out.

# CHAPTER
# FIFTY-THREE

*Travis County, Texas*
*December 8, 1999 / Wednesday / 3:30 a.m.*

The five men were lying prone behind the crest of a hill, about six hundred yards south of the compound. They'd been watching the site for two hours with two pairs of night-vision binoculars and a Swarovski spotting scope. There were three larger structures in the compound: a narrow three-story building at the western end, a large estate in the middle, and a smaller house at the eastern end. There were also two smaller structures. A one-room building on the eastern side of the smaller house, and a small barn in between the smaller house and the northern wall.

The unit had been able to identify three armed observation posts within the compound. The first post, designated Post One, was on the roof of the three-story structure at the western end. Two men were lying on the roof, one facing southwest and the other facing northeast. Each man was armed with an M-16. Post Two was in the cupola on the roof of the main house. Two men occupied that position as well, but it was impossible to identify their weapons in the darkness. Post Three was located in the second floor of the house near the eastern end of the compound. The interior of the house was completely dark, but three of the windows on the second floor were open. Since it was forty-five degrees outside, the windows were a dead giveaway.

Ricard's first objective had been to identify Andrea's location and confirm that she was still alive. Fortunately, one of men in the compound had solved the problem two hours earlier by lighting a cigarette inside the one-room building closest to the eastern wall. The flame from the lighter had illuminated the room for a fraction of a second, giving the unit a clear view of Andrea through a tear in a window shade.

The second objective was putting together a viable rescue plan. The bad news was they were attempting to gain access to a fortified position defended by occupants who were expecting an incursion. The good news was the three fire positions in the compound had been laid out to maximize the occupants' ability to kill Caine, not to protect Andrea. If they could reach Andrea and separate her from the enemy before a fight started, their prospects for success improved dramatically.

The third objective was a part of the second—finding an extraction point that would get them out of the compound safely. The only exit from the compound was at the western end, and Andrea was being held at the far eastern end. Using that gate as an extraction point would expose them to fire from all three gun positions if they were discovered. Infiltrating and extracting over the eastern wall would eliminate that risk, but it was also the most obvious route. They had to assume that entry point would be closely watched.

The terrain to the east also presented a challenge. The wall, which was eight feet tall, bordered a steep ravine. Getting over that wall and down the slope in the dark, without injury, wouldn't be easy under optimum conditions. Taking that route with a drugged or injured hostage, possibly under heavy fire, would be suicide.

As Caine scanned the compound for the hundredth time, memorizing every detail, his earlier confidence waned. Taking back a hostage by force was always high-risk. It only takes a second to put a bullet into the hostage's head. Negotiation was almost always the prudent course, but that wasn't an option here. These kidnappers weren't interested in ransom. Killing the hostage and the rescuer was the end game.

The plan Ricard developed was based upon a simple ruse that exploited the enemy's expectations and lack of intel regarding who they were facing on the other side of the wall. The men in the compound were expecting Caine to try to infiltrate the compound by stealth, and this is exactly what they would see. Vlasky would serve as the decoy, approaching the compound from the south using the long, straight ravine that passed by the eastern wall. Vlasky would give the men inside the compound enough visual sightings to keep their attention, but not enough to give them a target.

The men in the compound would expect Caine to follow the ravine to the point where it was closest to the eastern wall of the compound and make his insertion there. This wouldn't happen. About two hundred yards from the wall, the ravine passed behind a hill, making it invisible to the ranch for the next fifty yards. Once Vlasky reached this cover, he would race up the backside of the hill and set up the C9A1 behind the crest. This position would give Vlasky the ability to directly engage the three gun positions in the compound.

Pietro would be positioned on a second hill just to the west of Vlasky, about four hundred yards from the compound. He would use the Barrett rifle to provide surgical fire support, and his position would serve as the unit's communications base.

Once they were sure that Vlasky had been spotted approaching the compound from the southeast, Caine and Jaq would enter the compound over the north wall. Caine would make his way to the building where Andrea was located, while Jaq provided rear cover. Once Andrea was secured, Caine and Andrea would return to the north wall.

Since they couldn't find an acceptable extraction point, Ricard would create one. A section of the north wall was riven by a large crack that expanded into a fissure as it approached the top of the wall. At certain points, the opening was large enough to see through. Ricard would use the C-4 to blow a hole in the wall, allowing them to exit from the compound.

Once Andrea was secured, Pietro would leave his location and bring the Suburban around to the northern wall to pick up Andrea, Caine, Ricard, and Jaq. Vlasky would be picked up on the way out of the area. If everything went according to plan, the whole operation should take thirty minutes from start to finish.

# CHAPTER
# FIFTY-FOUR

Paquin had set up three fire positions within the compound. Severino, Anders, and Cochrane were located at the southern end of the ranch on the second floor of an old guest house. From that location, they could cover the approaches to the southern third of the compound.

Vargas and the two ex-Nicaraguan soldiers manned the fire position at the opposite end of the ranch. This position was located on top of what used to be the servants' quarters in the northwestern corner of the compound. The two Nicaraguan soldiers were lying on the flat roof of the structure. Each man was armed with an M-16. Vargas was inside the building, which was dark, armed with an Uzi.

The third position was located in the cupola on the roof of the main house. The two men in the cupola were former members of Mexico's national police force, the Policia Nacional Federales. They'd been sent to Paquin by a contact within the Mexican government. The contact described the men as corrupt but capable. Paquin disliked using unknown resources, but he had little choice in the matter. He needed mercenaries on short notice, who were willing to kill for money, without asking questions. The two ex-Federales fit those requirements.

Paquin's command center was in the large study on the second floor, directly below the cupola. He had expected Caine to try to infiltrate the perimeter of the compound at no later than four in the morning. Night vision equipment had been issued to all three fire positions in anticipation of this strategy. As the hours ticked by and each position gave the mandatory "all clear" sign every twenty minutes, Paquin had become increasingly apprehensive. When the digital clock on his desk turned over to 4:00 a.m., he stood up and walked over to the window facing the east side of the compound. He looked through a small break in the curtains at the distant horizon. Sunrise at this time of year was another three hours away, but the sky was already starting to gray. If Caine was coming, he needed the darkness.

For over ten years, Paquin had laid traps for defectors, spies, smugglers, and your average East German trying to escape to the West. The wait had always been the most difficult part of the process, particularly when the time window began to close and the quarry failed to show. He knew that it was a waste of time to obsess over what could have been done differently, but he found himself doing it anyway.

Caine had received the bait. He knew where the woman was being held and he knew that they would eventually kill her. If he wanted to save Andrea Marenna, he had only one choice. He had to take her back by force. The only unknown was whether Caine would risk everything for the woman. He had other options—safe, rational options. *Maybe I was wrong. Maybe—*

Cochrane's voice crackled over the microphone on his desk.

"Station One here, I think I have contact. Yes, sir, I definitely have contact."

Paquin walked backed to the desk and picked up the microphone. "Control here. What location? And how many?"

"I only see one, and he's coming up the ravine to the southeast, sir. It's got to be our boy. He's wearing cammos and his face is all blacked up . . . and from the size of the pack he's carrying, I'd say this hombre is loaded for bear."

"You're sure he's alone?" Paquin said, his voice insistent.

"Yes, sir," Cochrane answered.

"Control here. Station Three, do you have a visual?"

Vargas's voice came back.

"Not yet, sir. There's a rise blocking our view. We should pick him up in about thirty yards."

A wave of relief washed over Paquin. He'd planned every last detail of the operation. A hundred things could have gone wrong, but none of them had. Caine was here. Now they just had to put him down.

Paquin pressed the transmit button.

"Stay on him. Let me know when he gets to within fifty yards of the wall. *No one* is to take any action except on my order. Is that clear?"

"Station One, clear."

"Station Two, clear."

"Station Three, clear."

# CHAPTER
# FIFTY-FIVE

*Travis County, Texas*
*December 8, 1999 / Wednesday / 4:05 a.m.*

The base station for the two-way mobile radio system they were using for communications was located on the hill occupied by Pietro, about four hundred yards from the compound. Each man was outfitted with an earpiece, a throat mic, and a push-to-transmit actuator. The PTT was clipped to Caine's chest. Caine heard Pietro's voice over the mic.

"Tango here. They've taken the bait. All eyes are on Zulu." Caine nodded to himself. They'd spotted Vlasky's approach.

Caine heard Ricard's voice over the mic.

"Delta and Echo, you are go, repeat, you are go."

"This is Delta, roger that, Alpha," Caine answered.

Caine heard Jaq's voice a second later. "Echo here. We are go."

Caine looked forty yards down the wall, where he could just see Jaq's outline in the darkness. Caine turned to the wall and threw a grapple over the top, checked the hold, and went up the wall. Thirty seconds later, both men dropped into a crouch on the other side of the wall and scanned the compound.

## Travis County, Texas
### December 8, 1999 / Wednesday / 4:09 a.m.

Pietro watched Caine's approach from a second hill to the southwest of Vlasky's position, moving the scope alternately from Caine to the third observation post. Caine was using the limited cover available to him, but a disciplined observer looking out the rear window of the third observation point could have spotted him. They just had to hope that all the spotters in the compound were focusing on the point where they expected Vlasky to emerge from behind the hill. Pietro quickly scanned the men who were visible on top of observation points two and three; every pair of binoculars was focused on the ravine.

Pietro looked quickly to the hill to the east and saw Vlasky setting up the C91A. Then he turned the sight back to Caine. He breathed a sigh of relief once Caine reached the eastern side of the building where Andrea was located. Now he was no longer visible from the third observation post. Seconds later, Caine reappeared, glancing around the corner of the building.

Pietro quickly scanned Post Three. He couldn't see any movement and moved on to Post One at the other end of the compound. To enter the building, Caine would have to come through the side door on the south side of the building. He would be shielded from Post Three by the building, but Post One would have a direct line of sight on his position. Although it was dark, if someone in Post One looked across the compound with a good pair of binoculars, at the right moment, they could spot him.

"This is Tango. You're clear to move, Delta."

Caine's voice came back. "Roger, Tango. Moving now."

Caine slid along the wall of the building in a crouch and quickly glanced through one of the small glass panes in the wooden door.

His voice came over the mic, a barely audible whisper. "Delta here. Hostage identified. No hostiles visible. Attempting entry now."

Pietro watched Caine try the knob. It must have been locked. As Caine eased a pry bar out of the tool holster strapped to his thigh,

Pietro quickly scanned Post Three. The door on the first floor of the building was opening.

"Delta, this is Tango. Someone just came out of Post Three. He's just walked into the yard between the buildings. You're okay so far. Looks like he's taking a smoke. Hold for a minute."

Caine froze, crouched in front of the door, waiting for Pietro to give him the go-ahead.

"Tango here, continue to hold."

Vlasky's voice cut in. "This is Zulu, we have a problem. A spotter in Post One is looking in your—Delta, he's got you. Alpha, what's the call? This goes public in two seconds."

Vlasky voice hardened as he queried Ricard.

Ricard's' voice came over the mic, steel in his tone.

"This is Alpha. Get the hostage, now, Delta. Zulu and Tango, engage and destroy enemy."

# CHAPTER
# FIFTY-SIX

Andrea was familiar with the kind of chair she was chained to. The seat of the chair was connected to the base by a giant steel screw. If the seat was twisted in one direction, the chair lowered; if it was twisted in the other, it rose. Andrea started to rotate the chair around and around in circles, steadily increasing the height of the seat. She was hoping the seat would separate from the heavy base when she reached the end of the spiral. Although she would still be connected to the top half of the chair, she would be able to escape the building.

Progress had been slow, because the iron screw was old and rusted. Every turn required all her strength. Twice she'd reached a point where the chair would no longer turn. Each time she had been forced to rotate the chair a half turn backward and then whirl it back around, over and over again, smashing into the sticking point. When she finally broke through each jam, she'd almost cried with relief.

Sweat was pouring down her face. Every second she expected to hear the sounds of gunfire signaling John Caine's death. Suddenly the chair stopped turning. She rotated backward and tried again, but hit the same sticking point. She jammed her feet against the base of the chair to prevent it from moving, rotated backward and then whirled back in the opposite direction in a frustrated rage, pushing upward with her legs at the same time.

For an instant she didn't realize what was happening. She shot up and forward, free of the heavy base of the chair. Although she desperately tried to avoid falling, her legs wouldn't respond quickly enough. She twisted as she went down, trying to avoid landing on her face. The top half of the chair, which was still connected to the handcuffs, hit the wooden floor first. The right side of her body followed, slamming into the hard oak floor. The crash was deafening against the background of the utter silence outside. As she struggled to a sitting position, Andrea knew with terrible certainty that someone would come to investigate the noise. Anders would come. She had to get out of there.

Andrea struggled awkwardly to her feet and shuffled to the window beside the door, bent over at the waist by the chair. She looked out the crack between the shade and the window frame across the vacant yard to the building where Anders and the other men were located. The yard was empty. *Thank God.* Andrea shuffled over to the door, praying that it wasn't locked from the outside, and slowly turned the doorknob. She held her breath, as she pushed the door outward. It opened.

She looked through the open crack to the yard beyond. It wasn't empty any longer. Anders was standing in the middle of the yard, lighting a cigarette. Andrea's breath caught in her throat. After lighting the cigarette, Anders took a long drag and started to turn toward her. Then the night exploded.

A guttural roar bellowed outside the compound, followed by screams of pain at the other end of the compound. Anders spun around and looked over the wall, trying to find the source of the mechanical clamor. Then he turned in confusion, when he heard the screams of pain.

Andrea watched Anders's back. He seemed transfixed by whatever he was staring at. Then the windows in the second floor of the building to his right disintegrated and Anders threw himself to the ground. A hail of projectiles ripped into the side of the structure with impossible rapidity. Andrea stared at the nightmare, as if she were watching a terrifying movie. Somewhere in the back of her mind she realized that someone was shooting at the building from outside the compound: someone with an incredibly powerful machine gun.

She heard a man inside the house scream "Get down!"

The deadly rain of steel continued unabated, and then an explosion rocked the entire building, and night became day. The force of the blast slammed the door in front of her closed. Andrea scrambled backward in shock, toward the safety of the desk on the opposite side of the room. She hesitated when she reached the desk, trying to decide whether to hide behind it, or to go back to the door and try to escape. *What's going on?*

### Travis County, Texas
### December 8, 1999 / Wednesday / 4:13 a.m.

Anders was sitting on an old wooden chair in the darkened second-floor room of the guest house. The chair was uncomfortable and the cup of coffee he'd just poured from the thermos tasted burned, stale, and lukewarm. He was tired and cold, and he wanted a smoke, but Paquin had forbidden anyone to leave the room unless they received a direct order from him. Smoking had also been forbidden because it would reveal their position.

Anders looked over at Cochrane. He was sitting in a chair about two yards from one of the windows, staring into the dark through a pair of night-vision binoculars.

"Has he come out from behind the hill yet?"

"Not yet. Must be taking his pregame crap," Cochrane said with a chuckle.

"Fuck this. We should just go out there and kill the son of a bitch. I'm sick and tired of this goddamn waiting."

"Won't be long now, chief. This dude—"

The crash brought Anders to his feet so quickly that his coffee spilled on the floor. The noise came from the building where the woman was being held.

"I'll check it out," Anders said and walked to the door without waiting for an answer. He wanted to get out of the building before Severino came out of the bathroom. Severino wouldn't let Anders anywhere near the girl. Cochrane just grunted and continued to stare out the darkened window through the binoculars.

When he reached the dirt yard that separated the guest house from the storage building where the woman was located, Anders stopped to light a cigarette. *Screw Paquin and his rules.* He drew in a long drag and turned to walk over to the other building. The angry growl from outside the compound froze him in place. He stared over the wall of the compound trying to understand what was happening. Then he heard the sound of shattering glass and a scream of pain coming from the western end of the compound.

Anders whirled around. He could just see Vargas's position in the dim light. As he watched in stunned silence, someone dove off the roof of the three-story building and crashed to the ground below. The man lay on the ground unmoving, as the building behind him was scoured by a series of small explosions. For a moment, Anders didn't understand what he was seeing and then it slammed into him. *Someone's blowing the shit out of that place with some kind of goddamn machine gun!*

Suddenly the assault on the other end of the compound stopped. A fraction of a second later, hundreds of high-velocity projectiles ripped into the building next to him, dropping glass and pieces of wood on his head. Anders threw himself to the ground and struggled to press his body lower into the dirt as the hail of lead walked across the face of the building above his head. A second later, the white-hot missiles found the three propane tanks on the eastern side of the house. The resulting explosion hurled flaming steel shrapnel in every direction and illuminated the compound like the midday sun.

# CHAPTER
# FIFTY-SEVEN

*Travis County, Texas*
*December 8, 1999 / Wednesday / 4:15 a.m.*

The frontal onslaught against Station Three stunned Paquin. *What was Caine doing? A direct attack only made sense if he assumed the woman was already dead.* For a moment, Paquin feared that a special weapons unit from the FBI might be assaulting the compound, but then he rejected the idea. The police or FBI would announce themselves first and demand their surrender before they attacked. Paquin grabbed the radio to call Vargas, but an incoming call from Station One cut him off. It was Cochrane.

"Control . . . he's tearing the shit out of this place!"

Cochrane was screaming into the intercom, but Paquin had difficulty hearing him over the cacophony of background sound. He could hear the bullets slamming into the walls and furniture, and the sound of breaking glass. Severino was screaming something unintelligible over and over again. Cochrane started to yell something, when an explosion cut off the signal.

Paquin ran to the window and stared through the small gap in the curtains at the eastern end of the compound. A pillar of flame was reaching into the sky, illuminating the entire compound. As he watched, a piece of flaming steel crashed into the courtyard outside the window. Paquin stared at the burning piece of metal without comprehension for a moment and then it hit him. The shooter had hit the propane tanks on the south side of Station Three. *They had to take out that gun position.*

## Travis County, Texas
### *December 8, 1999 / Wednesday / 4:15 a.m.*

The two former Mexican Federales were resting against the three-foot adobe wall that ringed the flat roof of the main house when the shooting began. An M-16 was resting against the wall beside the smaller man, Arturo. The second man, Luis, was holding a Panther Long Range 308 rifle, with a Leupold scope. When the C9 opened up, the two men just watched the devastating attack unfold before them, in shock. Neither man made any effort to return fire.

When the propane tanks next to Station One exploded, the two men threw themselves flat against the roof and lay there unmoving. Arturo, who was closest to the radio, suddenly realized a voice was screaming at them over the radio.

"Station Two, this is Control. Respond now!"

Arturo crawled over to the receiver. "Arturo here."

Paquin's hard voice came through the speaker.

"Can you see the source of the fire?"

Arturo answered quickly and without thinking.

"No, sir."

"Use the glasses and find it, now!"

Arturo crawled across the roof and grabbed the binoculars that were lying beside his M-16. He eased his head over the wall and stared in the direction of the fire. He could see white flashes coming from a hill about two hundred yards outside the perimeter of the compound.

"It's coming from the hill. The hill to the southeast," Arturo said after lowering his head below the top of the wall.

"Engage that position. Do you understand me? Fire on that position!" Paquin yelled through the intercom.

"*Si, si!*"

Arturo belly-crawled over to Luis and grabbed him by the arm. Luis yanked his head around, his face a mask of fear.

"What the fuck you doin', man!"

"We gotta take out that shooter. You hear me? We gotta take out that fuckin' shooter!"

Luis tightened his grip on the Panther.

"I'll get that fucker. He doesn't know who he's dealing with."

Luis put the 308 against his shoulder and sighted in on the machine gun position. There was a distant crack outside the compound and Luis's body was thrown backward as if he'd been hit by a car. Arturo looked over at the body. There was a hole in the middle of Luis's chest about two inches wide. Arturo dove onto his stomach, just as he heard a second crack in the distance. The missile raced over his head and punched a hole through the wall on the opposite side of the roof.

Arturo grabbed the radio and started screaming hysterically.

"Fuck me, man! They killed Luis. They blew him totally away. They got some kind of cannon. Do you—"

A hail of bullets from the C9 began to scour the top of the wall in front of Arturo, throwing bits of adobe all over the roof. Arturo dropped the radio and crawled frantically over to the hole in the roof that led down to the second floor. He hesitated for a moment at the opening, struggling to get on the ladder, without raising his profile. The sound of a massive explosion eliminated his hesitation. He threw himself face-first through the opening.

### Travis County, Texas
### December 8, 1999 / Wednesday / 4:18 a.m.

Paquin was trying to raise Vargas on the radio when a second blast rocked the building. He instinctively dropped to his knees, grabbing the Berretta on the table as he went down. When Arturo plunged down the stairway into the room to his left, Paquin spun around, ready to take out the intruder. It took him a second to recognize the Mexican. His face was covered in sweat and dust, and there was a frantic, hunted look in his eyes.

Paquin ignored him and reached for the radio on the desk. "Vargas, this is Control. Come in."

When Paquin looked over at the Federale again, the man was pulling open one of the heavy velvet curtains on the south side of the room. Paquin reacted instantly.

"No! You'll draw their—"

The entire window suddenly exploded inward, high-velocity bullets hollowing out one window and then moving on to the next. The incoming missiles raced through the gaping holes and destroyed the array of computer equipment and camera monitors sitting on the command table in the center of the room. Now they were blind. Paquin glanced around the corner of the desk and saw Arturo's lifeless body on the floor in front of the shattered window.

One of the shooters outside the compound must have suspected that someone was hiding behind the large chair now visible through the shattered windows, because two heavy projectiles punched through the chair and blew fist-size holes in the wall just above Paquin's head.

"Scheiss," Paquin growled.

Caine had not come alone. There were at least two or three other men in the force assaulting the compound, if not a full squad. *Where had he found the support and military hardware?* Caine was no longer the quarry; he was the hunter.

Paquin knew that he had to reduce and centralize his defensive perimeter or his assets would be destroyed by the attacking force. Most of all, he had to retain control of the woman. That was the key to this fight, maybe even their survival. He tried Vargas on the radio again.

"Station Three, come in."

Vargas's voice came back. "Station Three here."

"Station Three, redeploy to the main house, now."

"Roger that, Control. Miguel is dead. Juan is wounded, but he can move. We'll come in the door on the east side. Station Three, out."

Paquin tried to contact Cochrane again.

"Station One, this is Control, come in."

Cochrane's voice came back in a whisper, followed by a series of coughs.

"Station One."

"Station One, get the woman and bring her to the main house. Use the rear door."

There was no response.

"Cochrane, did you hear me?"

Paquin could hear Cochrane hacking in the background. Then he answered in a hoarse voice.

"Yes, sir."

"What is your situation?"

"The . . . the house . . . Station One is on fire . . . from the blast. There's a lot of smoke. I'm . . . I'm just inside the back door."

"Where's Severino?"

"I don't know. I think the blast got him. I can't see shit in all this smoke."

"Where's Anders?"

"He left to check on the woman before the shooting started. He hasn't come back."

Paquin's face turned white with rage. He'd made it clear to Anders that he was to stay away from the woman. They needed her alive, especially now.

"Cochrane, get the woman back here, now. That is your only priority. Kill anyone that gets in your way, and that includes Anders. Are we clear?"

"Clear, sir."

# CHAPTER
# FIFTY-EIGHT

*Travis County, Texas*
*December 8, 1999 / Wednesday / 4:16 a.m.*

Caine could hear the C9 pouring rounds into the compound as he stood up, dropped the pry bar, and pulled the MP-5 into position. He stepped back and kicked the door just above the knob. The door exploded inward and he went through the opening in rush. He heard movement to his left and swung the MP-5 in the direction of the attacker. The room was dark, but Caine could see that something was wrong with the assailant rushing at him. The figure was bent over at the waist and moved awkwardly. This bought his attacker another second of life. Then Caine saw the hair and recognized the body shape. It was Andrea.

"Andrea, it's John, John Caine," Caine said in an urgent whisper as he pointed the gun at the ceiling and pressed his other hand against her oncoming shoulder to slow her down.

"Andrea, it's me!" Caine said, in a louder, more urgent whisper, when she started to struggle.

Andrea stumbled to a stop and looked up. Her face was tearstained, dusty, and, to Caine, beautiful.

"Where did you—"

Andrea's voice came out cracked and loud enough to carry outside the room.

"Shh. We have to get out of here, now," Caine said, stepping past her. He reached into the black nylon case strapped to his thigh and pulled out a pair of wire cutters. He cut the chain between the handcuffs and lowered the seat of the chair to the floor.

Andrea wheeled around and was in his arms. Caine held her tightly. He kept the MP-5 pointed at the still-open front door as he lowered his head and kissed her hair.

"We need to go. Stay right behind me."

Caine tapped the PTT and spoke into his throat mic.

"This is Delta. I'm coming out of the south side of the building with the package."

Vlasky responded.

"This is Zulu. I have your position. The area to the north that I can see is clear. When you move behind the buildings, you're outside my cover."

"Roger that, Zulu."

Caine tried Pietro.

"Tango, do you have a visual on the evac route?"

"Tango here. My line of sight is clear."

"Roger that, Tango. Coming out now."

Caine turned to Andrea.

"Let's go." Andrea just nodded.

Caine moved forward at a crouch toward the rear of the building. He could hear Andrea behind him. Caine stopped at the corner of the small house and glanced at the area behind the building. There was no sign of any hostiles. He moved forward, heading toward the north wall. Caine covered the black interior of the small barn to the left of their evacuation route with his MP-5, as they approached it on the right. He couldn't see anything in the interior. He slowed for a minute, debating whether to investigate the barn before moving past it, but decided to keep going. As he turned around to wave Andrea forward, Caine heard an explosion to his left, and a hammer smashed into his chest. As the darkness closed in, he heard Andrea's scream behind him.

# CHAPTER
# FIFTY-NINE

*Travis County, Texas*
*December 8, 1999 / Wednesday / 4:30 a.m.*

Anders jabbed the barrel of the shotgun into Andrea's stomach, doubling her over with pain.

"Move it, bitch. Get that piece of shit in there, or I'll kill him right here."

Andrea gasped in pain, but continued to drag Caine's unconscious body into the barn. She stopped when she backed into one of the wooden supports and looked over at Anders. His long unwashed hair was tied back in a ponytail. Dirt and sweat covered his face, and a streak of dried blood traced a line from his temple to his unshaven jaw.

Anders noticed her look, and his left hand whipped out, his face a mask of rage. Andrea tried to dodge his backhand, but it ripped across her ear and her chin, knocking her to the ground. She crabbed backward to the rear wall of the barn, looking past Anders, at John Caine's unmoving body.

Anders walked after her, unrushed. The rage and anticipation on his face was terrifying. He threw the shotgun that he was holding on top of a bale of hay and it dropped to the far side. He stopped about four feet away from her and reached behind him, drawing a knife from a sheath attached to his belt. The blade was a foot long and at least three inches wide at the base. It curved upward to a wicked point.

Anders admired the blade for a moment and then drew his thumb down the edge, drawing blood. He wiped the blood slowly on both sides of the blade, watching her as he performed the sadistic ritual. Then, with one stride, he closed the distance between them. She tried to stand and run to the right, but he grabbed her hair and yanked her backward, wrapping one giant arm across her throat and pressing her back against him. She could feel the leer on his face as he pushed his cheek against hers, holding the knife in front of her face with his other hand.

"Now, bitch," Anders said, "we're gonna play my game, my way. And you're gonna learn the rules real well."

A shadow stepped through the front door of the barn and eased to the left, out of the incoming gray light. Anders saw the movement and whirled around. The voice that spoke from the shadow seemed impossibly out of place. It was part upper-crust British, part Caribbean, and completely at ease.

"So what do we have here? A corn-fed country boy, who doesn't know how to mind his manners. Shameful, just plain shameful."

The figure strolled forward as he spoke, ignoring the deadly knife Anders was holding in front of him.

"Didn't your mama teach you any manners, man? Now, please take your ugly face away from that lady and let a gentleman escort her home."

The tall, lithe black man who stepped out of the shadows was dressed in the same desert fatigues that Caine was wearing. He ignored Anders and looked over at Andrea. A mischievous grin played across his handsome face, as he bent slightly at the waist and tipped his dark brown beret in her direction.

"Good morning, Ms. Andrea. Jacques Bertrand Maltier, at your service."

Anders was momentarily transfixed by the incongruous scene, but it only lasted a second. Rage flared in his eyes and he pressed his knife against Andrea's throat.

"Drop your gun, soldier boy, or I'll cut her head clean off before you can do jack shit," Anders growled.

The soldier moved forward slowly and turned slowly around, his hands extended. "Can't help you there. I left it outside. I didn't think I'd need much to take care of a piece of trash like you, except maybe an old broom. You wouldn't happen to have one of those handy, would you?"

Andrea felt Anders's jaw tighten against her cheek, just before he shoved her to the ground and walked forward in a crouch.

"Then you made a big mistake, shit head, 'cause I'm gonna carve up your black ass like a rotten goddamn pumpkin!"

Anders deepened his crouch as he moved forward. The black soldier responded by shifting into a side stance in a single fluid movement. The move placed his body perpendicular to Anders, and it moved him two feet closer to Andrea's position. Anders continued to move forward, circling to the other man's right. The black man reacted by gliding to the left into another side stance that eased him closer still to Andrea. A knife appeared in his hand, when he completed the transition. The knife was dull black from tip to haft, and unlike Anders's weapon, it had been made for only one purpose.

The grin on the soldier's face disappeared, as he settled deeper into his stance and began to work his way around Anders's right. The eyes that stared across the two yards that now separated the men were a study in deadly intensity. Anders slowed his approach as he began to realize the danger he was facing. He also realized, belatedly, that the other man had achieved a blocking position between him and Andrea. Anders reacted to this displacement by starting back to the right, but the black man anticipated the move. He slid into a new stance, cutting off Anders's effort and bringing the two men closer still.

Anders responded by slashing viciously at the black man's torso with the giant knife. The soldier stepped back and to the right, dodging the blow. Then he feinted toward Anders with blinding speed. The feint was followed by a blinding snap-kick that connected with the outside of Anders's knee. The blow shocked and enraged Anders. He responded by moving forward, with a series of vicious slashes that pressed the other man back toward the rear wall. Anders's last slashing blow connected with the black man's chest, bringing a gasp from Andrea.

The soldier allowed the blade to score the front of the vest covering his chest. Then he stepped inward, bringing him within striking range of Anders's body. His knife whipped upward in a slashing movement, cutting the back of Anders's striking arm. The wound drew a growl of rage from Anders and another flurry of attacks that drove the soldier back toward Andrea.

As Andrea watched the terrible battle, it seemed only a matter of time before the smaller man was gutted by one of Anders's savage strokes. Then he struck. The move was so quick that Andrea only remembered it after the fact, as she replayed the scene in her mind. The soldier twisted past Anders's incoming lunge, placing his body beside and perpendicular to Anders's body. His left hand guided Anders's blow past his head, and his right arm drove his own weapon into Anders's upper stomach.

As Anders's forward rush turned into a stumble, the black man did a 180-degree spin, placing him in the rear of the lunging giant. The soldier lifted his leg in an up-and-down piston-like movement, driving his heel into the rear of Anders's knee. The blow drove Anders to the ground. Anders tried to avoid landing on the knife embedded in his stomach as he fell, but only partially succeeded. When he rolled over onto his back, he was less than three feet from Andrea. An expanding black stain was covering his midsection and his eyes were already beginning to glaze over. The soldier walked over to Anders's body, kicked away Anders's knife, and then kicked him twice in the ribs. When there was no reaction, the soldier pulled his knife from the body, wiped it quickly on Anders's coat, and returned it to a sheath on his calf.

When he finished, the black soldier looked over at Andrea and saw her staring at the body. He quickly stepped into her line of sight, held out his hand, and said, "Come away, Ms. Andrea. This unpleasantness is over now."

Andrea took his hand and followed him, in a daze, to the barn door. She dropped beside Caine's body and started to reach for his face with her hands, but the soldier interrupted her.

"Wait just a moment," he said as he put two fingers against Caine's neck and looked at his chest. A slow smile came to his face. "Relax, Ms. Andrea. Johnny Boy will be okay. The slug hit the vest square. He may have a bruised rib or two, but he'll live."

Andrea looked at where the man was pointing and saw the ruined Kevlar plate through the torn vest. When she looked back at Caine's face, he was staring back at her.

"John, oh God, you're alive," Andrea said, holding his face in her hands, tears streaming down her cheeks. Caine stared at her, still in shock.

Caine gasped. "I'm . . . okay, Andrea . . . Vest stopped the slug, but . . . damn, it hurts."

The black soldier smiled and stood up.

"Nonsense, man, you're just out of shape. All that California sun, wine, and women, why, it's a wonder you can get out of bed in the morning."

As Andrea helped Caine to a sitting position, Anders's image sprang into his mind and he tried to stand up in a rush. A wave of pain lanced through his chest and it was all he could do not to scream.

"Jaq, there's a hostile," Caine gasped as he looked around frantically for his MP-5.

Andrea restrained him. "John, he's gone, he's . . . "

She looked back into the barn when she spoke, and Caine followed her glance. He saw Anders's body lying in the rear of the barn.

Jaq walked over with Caine's MP-5 and noticed Caine staring at the body.

"Don't worry about him," Jaq said. "He's just working on his manners."

"Jaq—"

Jaq waved him off and handed him the MP-5.

"Stop your lollygagging, soldier, and get to the extraction point. The colonel and I will meet you there in five."

Then he waved and jogged back toward the main house.

Caine and Andrea moved along the outside wall of the compound, staying clear of the main house, until they reached the gap in the north wall. Caine slowed and waved Andrea behind him when they closed to within twenty yards of the opening. Pietro's voice came over the radio, allaying his concern about a possible ambush.

"Delta, this is Tango. I'm right behind the wall you're approaching. You're clear all the way in."

Caine tapped the PTT. "Thanks, Tango. We're coming in."

Pietro was positioned behind one edge of the ten-foot hole blasted in the wall. He'd replaced the Barrett with an MP-5. The Suburban was about thirty yards beyond the opening. Caine turned to Andrea.

"Andrea, get in the truck. We may have to move out quickly."

"What about you? You can hardly move."

"I'm okay," Caine said.

He walked over and kissed her softly on the forehead, ignoring the pain in his chest. Andrea reluctantly turned and walked to the Suburban. Caine moved to the wall, to provide cover for Jaq and Ricard's retreat.

Ricard's voice came over the mic.

"This is Alpha. We're coming your way."

Pietro responded, "Roger that. We'll provide cover."

Caine watched Jaq's retreat. He fired a burst at the second floor of the house when Jaq moved from behind a well in the yard and started his withdrawal. Ricard was engaged in a parallel movement to the right, but something was wrong. He was moving too slowly and he was bent over at the waist. As Caine watched with growing trepidation, Ricard's pace slowed to an awkward shuffle.

Caine signaled to Pietro that he was moving out of his position and jogged over to Ricard, ignoring the pains lancing through his chest as each boot pounded into the hard dirt.

"Colonel, are you hit?"

"It's . . . nothing . . . Corporal. It's time . . . to leave this place."

Ricard's voice came out in short, painful gasps. Caine knew that Ricard was hit somewhere, but he knew that they couldn't stop. He started to reach for Ricard's arm, but restrained himself. He could tell from the look on Ricard's face that he was determined to leave under his own power.

Jaq ran through the hole in the wall and glanced back into the compound. Satisfied that there was no sign of any pursuit, he jogged over to where Caine was following Ricard to the rear of the Suburban. Caine made a gesture with his hand out of Ricard's sight, and Jaq nodded and moved ahead of him.

"Sir, you've been hit. We need to check the wound."

"When we're clear of the area, not now," Ricard said.

"Yes, sir," Jaq answered.

Caine helped Ricard into the rear of the Suburban and climbed in beside him. He glanced out the rear window of the Suburban at the receding compound, as they drove down the dirt road toward the interstate. There was no pursuit. Caine suspected that getting back into the fight was the last thing the men in that compound wanted.

Caine turned his attention to Ricard. He opened his Kevlar vest. There were no wounds in the chest area, but blood was visible just above his belt. The bullet had passed under the bottom of the vest. From the color of the blood, Caine suspected a major organ had been hit, possibly the liver or the pancreas.

Jaq was leaning over the rear seat looking at the wound. Their eyes met for a moment and Caine knew that Jaq had reached the same conclusion about the severity of the hit. Tears of frustration came to Caine's eyes. Ricard's hand grabbed his arm.

"Is there any pursuit?" Ricard said.

"No, sir," Caine said.

Ricard nodded.

"Vlasky?"

Jaq answered the question. "We'll pick him up in about a quarter of a mile and then get you to a hospital."

Ricard didn't say anything. Pietro pulled over a moment later, and Vlasky leaned the broken-down C9 against the seat and climbed in beside it. Jaq leaned over the seat and spoke to him in a quiet whisper. Vlasky's face tightened and he glanced back at Ricard and Caine.

Caine knew that the plan was to work their way back to Austin, using a series of secondary roads. The circuitous route was designed to make any pursuit more difficult, but he knew they had to change that plan. They had to get to a medical facility as fast as possible for Ricard to have a chance of survival.

Caine turned to Jaq as he applied a dressing to the wound from the first-aid kit.

"Jaq, tell Pietro to the take the interstate all the way in."

"No," Ricard said, slowly shaking his head.

"Sir, we can get to a hospital within an hour. There's a good chance—"

"It's too late. It's been too late for some time now," Ricard said in a quiet, but implacable voice. "Tell Pietro to pull over a mile off the main road. We need to talk."

Caine started to protest.

"Sir—"

Jaq's restraining hand cut him off.

"Let it alone," Jaq said. His voice was quiet, but the look on this face, like Ricard's, was resolute.

Caine looked over at Vlasky for support, but the Pole just nodded his head in solemn agreement. Caine was suddenly physically and mentally exhausted. He leaned back against the window and closed his eyes. The last thing he saw were the tears running silently down Andrea's face. He reached for her hand and found it.

# CHAPTER
# SIXTY

*Travis County, Texas*
*December 8, 1999 / Wednesday / 5:30 a.m.*

They parked the Suburban about a half mile off a secondary road in a vale surrounded by cottonwoods. The car was hidden from the road by a large rock formation. Caine and Jaq helped Ricard to a grassy spot facing east, where he sat down and leaned against a large boulder. The silent grimace on his gaunt face eased as he rested against the rock.

Caine glanced at his watch. The sun wouldn't come over the horizon for another hour, but the sky was beginning to lighten. Andrea knelt and handed Ricard a bottle of water. He took a small drink and squeezed her hand in thanks. Andrea began to cry quietly. Ricard touched her cheek lightly.

"Don't cry. This is a happy day. Gentlemen, sit and listen to an old soldier for a minute."

Ricard gathered himself and told them what Jaq and Vlasky already knew. He was dying from incurable stomach cancer. During the last six months, the pain had been increasing and his strength had begun to wane. When Jaq had told him about the threat facing John

Caine, he'd considered the opportunity a godsend: it was a chance to die in the field for a worthy cause, rather than in a hospice, inch by inch. For Ricard, the mission had been a success.

As he visibly faded, Ricard thanked each man for being his comrade in arms and friend. When Caine's turn came, Ricard looked at him for a moment. Then he stared at the distant horizon, where the rising sun was just beginning to illuminate the winter landscape, and began to speak quietly.

"In 1969, I was a newly minted first lieutenant in the Legion. My third mission was in Southern Guyana. A local warlord was threatening to attack a French mining facility unless he was paid a substantial bribe. My unit was ordered to defend the facility and the nearby village that provided the labor. Sergeant Daniel MacBain was a corporal in my squad. I was ordered to take two squads to the village and to establish a defensive perimeter. The rest of the company was ordered to defend the mining facility, which was about a mile away."

Ricard stopped for a minute, rested, and then continued.

"The incoming force was larger and better-armed than we anticipated. An hour before they arrived, we were ordered to fall back to the mining facility. The people in the village . . . they had stayed there, because we . . . because I told them we would defend them. I knew there would be slaughter if we left, and I protested the order. My commanding officer told me that I had my orders. I did . . . and I followed them."

Ricard paused again. He seemed to be struggling against an emotional wound that was even deeper than the injury that was killing him.

"MacBain was with me on the new perimeter. The screams . . . we could hear them. We were . . . we were that close, but we couldn't do anything. Nothing."

There was a long silence. Then he looked back at them.

"My honor . . . my soul was stained that day. Sergeant MacBain and I, we lived with that memory every day."

Then he looked directly at Caine and a small smile came to his face.

"Corporal Caine, you think, mistakenly, that Shabundo was a disaster of your making. Yes, I know what you learned in the bar that night. What you don't know is that we were advised that the warlord and his force were coming an hour earlier. Command ordered us to quietly abandon the village before the rebel force appeared. MacBain and I knew the nightmare was about to happen all over again. We could not bring ourselves to disobey the order, so we did something else. We delayed the evacuation. We knew that you would see the rebel force first because you had the high point. We also knew, Corporal, that you would start the fight if they attacked the women, orders or not. And, as we anticipated . . . as we prayed, you did."

Caine was stunned by the revelation.

"I didn't tell you because you would have been compromised in the inquiry that followed. As it was, you simply told the truth. You know the rest. The French public learned about the incident and made us out to be heroes, so the Legion buried the evacuation order. Unfortunately, you found out about it."

Ricard hesitated, then reached over and grabbed Caine's arm with surprising strength, his eyes demanding Caine's attention.

"So you see, Corporal, it was my responsibility that day, not yours. I was also with MacBain at the end. *He died thanking you for giving him the opportunity to regain his honor.*"

Ricard stopped, too exhausted to continue, and rested his head against the rock. He died ten minutes later. Although Caine mourned his loss, he knew Etienne Ricard had died the way he wanted to, just like Danny MacBain had all those years ago.

# CHAPTER
# SIXTY-ONE

*Travis County, Texas*
*December 8, 1999 / Wednesday / 6:30 a.m.*

Paquin stood in the courtyard in front of the main building and stared at the destruction around him. The stucco facade of the main building was pockmarked with innumerable holes and cracks, and the glass in the windows was gone. The jagged ten-yard breach in the north wall of the compound was still smoking, and chunks of concrete, brick, and stucco were scattered over a forty-yard perimeter.

Paquin turned and looked to the south. The fire started by the propane explosion had spread. The entire second floor of the guest house was now in flames. The ascending plume of black smoke would soon be visible for miles.

Vargas walked past the burning building with Juan and made his way over to Paquin. His face was covered in sweat and stained with dirt. Juan looked the same. Blood was showing through the bandage on his right arm.

"We completed a sweep of the compound. It's clear, sir. They took the woman with them," Vargas said.

Paquin nodded. "They accomplished their mission."

"Yes, sir."

"Did you find Severino and Anders?"

"Yes, sir. They're both dead. It looks like Severino was killed when the propane tanks blew. Anders . . . well, he picked a knife fight with the wrong guy."

"I see. Well, Mr. Vargas, we must leave this place and quickly. Apparently the police are on the way. Center estimates that we have about twenty minutes. Put the bodies in the back of the truck with the rest of the equipment. We'll evacuate using the road to the south."

"Yes, sir."

When Vargas and Juan were out of sight, Paquin pulled out his cell phone and dialed a number with a New York City area code.

"Sergei, it's Nicholas Paquin."

"Major Paquin. It's good to hear from you."

"And you too, General."

"How is Mr. Mason doing?"

"Not good," Paquin said. "In fact, the situation is terminal."

"That is unfortunate. Is there anything I can do for you?"

"Yes," Paquin said, "if you happen to hear about another assignment—"

"As a matter of fact, a gentleman in Peru would like protection for his family. Apparently those troublesome Shining Path people have decided he's impairing their profit margins."

"That would be of interest, Sergei."

"Where can I reach you?"

"Some place other than Austin, Texas. I'll contact you."

"Very good, my friend."

Five minutes later, Vargas drove up in the black Ford Expedition, followed by the truck.

Paquin climbed in the passenger seat and looked over at the Columbian.

"Would you have any interest in working in Peru, Mr. Vargas?"

# CHAPTER
# SIXTY-TWO

*Travis County, Texas*
*December 8, 1999 / Wednesday / 7:00 a.m.*

Caine sat in the back of the Suburban with Jaq and Andrea on the way back to the warehouse. The car was quiet. Each of them was dealing with the rescue and Ricard's death in their own way. When the Suburban pulled up outside the warehouse, Jaq pulled Caine aside.

"Don't go anywhere. We need to talk."

Caine nodded.

"What are we going to do with—"

"I will arrange for Ricard's body to be taken back to France. He would want to be buried in the family cemetery. Don't worry about it. I'll meet you inside."

Caine knew what Jaq wanted to talk about: how Andrea and he intended to stay alive. Helius's army of killers might have been temporarily thinned out, but the bench would be restocked and the hunt would continue. As far as Caine was concerned, they only had two options: staying under Helius's radar, which meant going underground for a long time, or persuading the police that they were the victims, not the bad guys.

Although Caine didn't want to play a game of hide-and-seek for the rest of his life, he was doubtful they could convince Austin's finest or the FBI that they were being pursued by one or more death squads secretly directed by the CEO of a large, respectable corporation. To pin the tail on that tiger, they'd need irrefutable evidence and a helping hand from a high-level law enforcement insider willing to listen. Unfortunately, they didn't have that kind of evidence, and the only law enforcement asset available, Michael Bosmasian, was lying in a hospital with a bullet in his chest.

Caine walked over to Andrea, who was waiting beside the car.

"Let's go inside and sit down for a minute."

Jaq joined them at the table that they had used to plan the mission ten hours earlier. Vlasky and Pietro sat down as well. Jaq didn't waste any time.

"You two have to disappear for a while."

Andrea's response was immediate. "Why? We haven't done anything wrong. We just need to set the record straight with the police."

Caine quietly interrupted her, knowing time was short.

"Andrea, I don't like it any more than you do, but we don't have any proof."

Vlasky nodded his head. "He's right, Ms. Marenna, you can't simply walk into—"

"I agree," Andrea said, "we can't just walk into the local police station and clear this matter up. But there *is* a way. You see, we do have proof, and I think we might be able to get some help from a powerful guardian angel."

"We're all ears, Ms. Marenna," Jaq said with a smile.

"Two months ago, Richard Steinman introduced me to Reed Franklin, the managing editor of the *Statesman*, after he made a speech to the bar association. Franklin is an incredibly powerful man in this city, and he's nationally recognized in the world of journalism. If I can persuade him that these people killed one of *his* reporters in order to bury a massive story, I think he will back us to the hilt. And once the story hits the front page, we'll be invulnerable."

"Andrea, that is all well and good, but we'll need—" Caine started, but Andrea finished his thought.

"Proof. I know. I have it. Do you remember when you first called me and suggested that my phone might be bugged?"

"Yes."

"I didn't really believe it, but I decided to throw the phone into my purse just in case, when I left for the Portman Lodge on Sunday afternoon. I was hoping to have someone check out the phone, but I never had the chance."

Caine shook his head.

"Andrea, they would have searched the cabin and taken whatever you left there. I'm sorry."

"I don't think so. The cabins at the Portman have a small alcove on the inside wall above the closet door. The alcove goes back about a foot into the wall. I know about it because I threw one of my dolls up there when . . . anyway, I know it sounds paranoid, but I always put my purse up there to keep it safe."

"Paranoid is good, Ms. Marenna," Jaq said.

Andrea returned his smile.

"There's a very good chance that my purse is still sitting in that little alcove. We just have to go there and get it. If that bug is in the phone, that's hard evidence. It will establish that someone is really after us, and the device may be traceable."

"Andrea, I think the bug is a good start, but I don't think it will be enough to turn Mr. Franklin into a believer," Caine said.

"There's more. Whenever I'm out of the office, Jill, my secretary, goes through my voicemails. If anything sounds important, she transcribes the message and puts the transcription into the case file. There's a chance, a good chance, that Jill transcribed Richie's last call. If that transcription exists, it's what we call a dying declaration. That's admissible in court. Even more important, the transcript will prove that Richie was killed in order to bury the story. That fact, gentlemen, will turn Reed Franklin into our personal crusader."

Caine looked over at Jaq, who leaned back in his chair and looked over at Andrea and Caine.

"It could work, but you folks will be taking a big risk," Jaq said.

Vlasky nodded. "He's right, but it's your call."

Caine reached over and put his hand on Andrea's shoulder and said, "Okay. Let's go see Mr. Franklin."

*Travis County, Texas*
*December 9, 1999 / Thursday / 11:00 a.m.*

Andrea had been right. Her purse was still hidden in the alcove at the Portman Lodge. Even more important, Jill had transcribed Richie's phone message and put a copy in the miscellaneous file she kept for Andrea. The transcription was critical because Kelly & White's phone system had gone down, unaccountably, on Sunday night. The crash had corrupted the memory on the voicemail server, wiping out the original recording.

Andrea had also been right about Reed Franklin. When Andrea told him that she wanted five minutes of his time to talk with him about the murder of one of his reporters, he'd agreed to meet with them that day.

They met with Franklin in a small conference room on the sixth floor of the downtown high-rise where the *Statesman* was located. Franklin was tall and spare, with a full head of white hair that framed a narrow face with a long, aquiline nose. The old patrician's face, which was not a forgiving visage in the first instance, could have been carved in stone when Andrea began her presentation. However, he didn't throw them out of the conference room when the five-minute mark passed, which Caine considered a small miracle.

At the end of Andrea's precise summation, Franklin looked over at the two of them, unimpressed, and said, "Where is your proof?"

Andrea reached into her briefcase and placed the phone on the table.

"That is my home phone. Inside it you will find a sophisticated listening transmitter, commonly known as a 'bug.'"

Franklin looked briefly at the phone. Then his eyes returned to Andrea.

"What else?"

Andrea returned his stare for a moment and then reached into her briefcase. She pulled out the transcription of Richie's phone call that Jill had made two days ago. An affidavit executed under penalty of perjury was attached to the transcription, confirming its veracity and accuracy.

Andrea slid the document across the table.

"Richie left a message on Kelly & White's voicemail on Friday night at approximately 9:00 p.m., shortly before his time of death."

"Why didn't you bring the actual recording, Ms. Marenna?"

"My firm's voicemail system was attacked by a sophisticated virus on Sunday night. The server was corrupted. The original was destroyed. That document is an exact transcription of the message that my secretary prepared before the server crashed."

"That seems rather convenient, don't you think?"

"No, I don't. That's been her practice for over five years, when I'm out of the office and the message seems important. She places the transcription on my desk in a miscellaneous correspondence file."

"I see."

Franklin made no move to look at the transcription.

"I would respectfully request that you read it, Mr. Franklin. It is the dying declaration of Richard Steinman, my friend, and one of *your* reporters."

There was the slightest hint of anger in Andrea's voice when she spoke.

Franklin looked at her without moving for a moment. Then he leaned over and read the transcription. He read the document at least three times before he looked up. When he did, the expression on his face had changed. There was the slightest hint of anger in his eyes. The editor slowly stood up and walked over to the only window in the room. He stared out at the skyline for several minutes in silence, before turning to look over at the two of them.

"Your story is fantastic—in some respects, even absurd. However, I had one of my people look into your background, Ms. Marenna, before you came here today. You are known as a competent and serious attorney among your peers. Concocting this story would seem inconsistent with your character, but then stranger things have happened. My people turned up very little about you, Mr. Caine, which does nothing for your credibility. As for Mr. Richard Steinman, I'm sad to say that I wouldn't have recognized him if he passed me in the hallway, despite the fact that he worked for this paper for more than a year. What I do know is that Mr. Steinman was a local legal events reporter. *He was not assigned to investigate Helius.* We also checked his files. There is nothing in there about Helius."

Franklin paused briefly and looked over at the transcription on the table.

"What tips the balance in your favor is not your proof, which is thin, but the possibility that one of my people may have been killed trying to bring this story to light. If that's the case, I have a responsibility to Mr. Steinman to publish his work. For that reason, I will help you."

Andrea let out a visible sigh of relief and Caine gave Franklin a small nod of thanks.

"Don't thank me for anything yet. Right now, you two are fugitives. This paper cannot aid and abet your evasion of the law. Therefore, the first step in this process, and it may well be the last, is to persuade the police or FBI to listen to your story."

Franklin decided to make his initial approach through a senior-level contact in the FBI with whom he'd worked in the past. There were more than enough violations of federal law for the agency to have a basis for jurisdiction.

Franklin's contact had been a special agent in the FBI's Houston office when the two men first met ten years ago. The FBI had discovered that one of Franklin's senior reporters was pursuing a corruption case that intersected with an ongoing FBI investigation. The agent in charge, William Spencer, had met with Franklin, and the two men had worked out a cooperative arrangement. The FBI was allowed to complete its investigation without a premature press disclosure, and Franklin's reporter was given the right to be on hand when the critical arrests were made. William Spencer was now Special Agent in Charge of the FBI's Dallas office.

When Franklin called Spencer's office, his administrative assistant told him that Agent Spencer was out of town. Franklin politely responded that he was the editor of the *Austin American-Statesman* and that Bill Spencer would definitely want to call him back within the next five minutes. Spencer returned the call three minutes later.

"Good morning, Agent Spencer. It's been a while."

"Good morning to you, Mr. Franklin, and yes it has."

"Your office told me that you're out of the office today. I hope I'm not interrupting a vacation."

"No. I'm actually in your neighborhood today."

Franklin hesitated for second and then decided to do a little fishing.

"Your presence in our fair city wouldn't happen to have anything to do with the shooting of Michael Bosmasian the other night?"

The hesitation on the other side of the line told him everything he needed to know.

"I will politely pass on that question, if you don't mind."

"Of course, but if you were working on that matter, I might be able to help you. In fact . . . assuming we can work out a few minor details, I might be able to bring the FBI up to speed on a criminal conspiracy, a very large criminal conspiracy, of which that shooting is just a very small part."

There was a long hesitation this time.

"Everything is off the record on this until we agree otherwise, right?"

Franklin smiled.

"Of course."

"Your assumption about why I'm here is on the mark. I don't have my arms around how big this thing is, but I can tell you that my office and another office are working on the matter jointly. I guess we have to figure out whether we're both circling the same bull."

"Well, if that other office is California and they're looking into a downed chopper, then there's no question it's the same bull."

"Okay, Reed, how do you want to do this?"

# CHAPTER
# SIXTY-THREE

*Travis County, Texas*
*December 9, 1999 / Thursday / 6:00 p.m.*

Agents William Spencer and Ashley Morgan were sitting in the waiting room outside the office of Michaela Russo, the U.S. Attorney for the Western District of Texas. Spencer was looking over his notes on the deal that he'd cut with Reed Franklin an hour earlier. The two men had agreed that Spencer and a representative from the U.S. Attorney's office would meet with Franklin, Andrea Marenna, and John Caine at 9:00 the next morning. The meeting would take place at the *Statesman.* Marenna and Caine would tell their story, the entire story, in Franklin's presence. Franklin would have the right to tape the entire meeting. After the meeting, the FBI and the U.S. Attorney's office would then decide how to proceed.

The deal gave Franklin a lot of power. He could spin the facts any way he wanted in the morning paper, and the tape recording would allow him to critique how the FBI and the U.S. Attorney reacted to the story. If Franklin decided that the FBI and the U.S. Attorney had failed to give the suspects a fair shake, he could work that angle into the initial article and in every follow-up. If it later turned out that he was right, Washington would be very unhappy about the bad press.

Spencer had called Russo about the deal an hour earlier. Initially, Russo had been congratulatory, even cooperative, but then the conversation had started to go downhill. Russo had wanted to schedule a press conference immediately after the meeting in order to announce the capture of two fugitives. Spencer had resisted, arguing that Andrea Marenna and John Caine were only "persons of interest" at this point. When Spencer tried to educate Russo about the growing body of evidence suggesting that Caine and Marenna were the victims of a criminal conspiracy, not the perpetrators, Russo had abruptly ended the conversation, citing a pressing meeting. Although unspoken, the message was clear: Michaela Russo had no intention of allowing William Spencer to deny her a victory speech. Spencer intended to change Russo's mind on the issue, one way or another.

"Sir, your body language suggests that we're about to get into a fight with Ms. Russo."

Spencer looked across the coffee table at Agent Morgan's strong but attractive features.

"Oh, we might have a polite disagreement or two."

"Yes, sir," Agent Morgan said, a smile touching her lips.

The door to the inner office opened ten minutes later and Michaela Russo strode into the room. The Assistant U.S. Attorney stood five-feet-four inches tall in heels. She was dressed in a dark blue designer suit that subtly accentuated her attractive physique. Although her cropped hairstyle was less than flattering, her large brown eyes, café-au-lait skin, and beautiful face were striking.

"Agent Spencer, good to see you again. And you are . . . ?"

"Agent Morgan, Ashley Morgan."

"A woman. Good. Come in. I don't have much time, but I'm sure this won't take long."

Then she turned around and walked back into her office.

Spencer stood and invited Agent Morgan to precede him into the office with a polite wave. Spencer noted that Agent Morgan, at six feet, topped Russo by a good six inches. The contrast surprised him. He remembered Russo as being taller, but he suspected that was more her personality than her height.

Russo walked behind her desk and looked down at her computer screen. Spencer and Agent Morgan waited patiently, continuing to stand. Russo looked up from the computer a minute later, as if remembering that the two FBI agents were there.

"Sit down, sit down. Now, as I understand it, we're going to arrest two suspects in connection with the Bosmasian shooting tomorrow morning. I'll have my staff set up a press conference for late morning. That will give us time to get our talking points in order."

"I'm sorry, Ms. Russo, I guess I wasn't clear on the phone. This is a meeting with two people who may have critical information regarding the shooting. At this point, they are persons of interest, not suspects. It's entirely possible that Ms. Marenna—"

"I've read the police reports and the witness statements, Agent Spencer. We have more than sufficient probable cause to arrest Mr. Caine and Ms. Marenna as suspects, if only on the basis of their fleeing the scene of the crime. Now, I know you have this arrangement—"

"Which I intend to honor."

"That's your choice, Agent Spencer, but I am not bound by it. If you're not inclined to participate in the arrest tomorrow morning, that's your choice. I will have the federal marshals accompany me."

Spencer had anticipated that Russo might try this approach. He was prepared for it. Poker was a game he played quite well.

"That is of course your choice, Ms. Russo. However, I would suggest you consider the fact that there is presently no evidence that any *federal* crimes have been committed, which means we have no jurisdiction. My arrangement with Mr. Franklin would have allowed us the opportunity to investigate the facts and potentially remedy that deficiency. However, since you are not inclined to allow that to happen, I feel bound to contact Marc Cohen, the City of Austin's chief prosecutor. The City of Austin clearly has jurisdiction."

Russo's eyes narrowed. Spencer was well aware of the fact that Russo considered Marc Cohen a future political rival. He stood up when he finished.

"Agent Morgan and I will refer Mr. Cohen to Mr. Franklin. He can make his own arrangements. I assume Mr. Cohen will bring you into the case at a later date, if he decides that the Justice Department has an interest in the investigation."

Actually Spencer knew that Cohen would do no such thing. In fact, Cohen would do everything in his power to make sure that Russo never came within a hundred yards of the case. For a second, Russo's anger at being outmaneuvered warred with her political instincts. The latter won out.

"Very well, Agent Spencer. We will do it your way. I will meet you at the *Statesman* offices tomorrow morning. Now, if you'll excuse me, I have other matters."

Agent Morgan started forward to shake Russo's hand, but she had already turned back to her computer screen. The two agents left without another word.

Spencer had no illusions about the victory he'd achieved. Russo would honor the letter of his deal with Franklin, but she would do everything possible to evade the spirit. Agent Morgan turned to Spencer as they walked across the parking lot to the car.

"Well played, sir. Of course, it will make for an interesting meeting tomorrow."

"It will indeed."

Spencer felt his cell phone vibrate in his pocket as he reached for the car keys. "Spencer, here."

"Agent Pohlson."

"Hi, Don. What do you have?"

"As you instructed, I've been keeping tabs on anything out of the ordinary having to do with Helius Energy. Well, I may have something."

"Go ahead."

"I just picked up a report from the Texas Rangers. Apparently a small war took place at a ranch about fifty miles outside the city two days ago. I did a quick search on that location. It's currently owned by an historical trust, but it used to be owned by the Mason family. Carter Mason—"

"—is the CEO and largest shareholder of Helius," Spencer finished.

## Travis County, Texas
## December 9, 1999 / Saturday / 9:15 p.m.

A detective from the Texas Rangers met Agents Morgan and Spencer at the El Castillo Ranch at about 9:00 p.m. The Ranger was about six feet, four inches tall, and despite his white hair, he looked like he had just walked off the college gridiron. The detective was polite during their inspection of the site, but he didn't volunteer much. Spencer suspected the Ranger wasn't particularly happy about giving the FBI a tour of "his" crime scene, when he could have been home with his family.

Although Spencer was uncomfortable with the imposition, he needed every piece of ammunition possible for tomorrow's meeting. To get that, he needed Ranger Corcoran's cooperation. When Spencer saw the Special Forces tattoo on the man's forearm, he smiled to himself and turned to Agent Morgan.

"Any thoughts about the weaponry that might have been used here, Agent Morgan?" Spencer said.

Corcoran was standing about four feet behind Agent Morgan, and Spencer could see the skeptical look on his face.

"The shells indicate that the people defending the ranch were armed with M-16s and Uzis. The assault force had HK MP-5As, but that's not what did most of the damage. There are too many holes in the buildings. My guess is someone on the other side of that wall worked this place over with a light, maybe even a medium, machine gun—something that could spit out between five and eight hundred rounds a minute, like an M-60 or the newer M-240B."

Agent Morgan walked over to the edge of the wall and pointed over the wall at the hills outside the compound and continued, "The incoming trajectory of the bullets indicates that the shooter or shooters were on those hills out there."

Spencer could see the expression on the Ranger's face change as the young agent went through her analysis.

"Anything else?"

"Well, this is somewhat speculative, sir, but some of the holes on the west side of the building are awfully big. My read is that a second shooter hit this place with a fifty cal. My guess would be a Barrett or a BMG."

Ranger Corcoran walked over to Agent Morgan, a look of respect on his face. "You know your hardware, ma'am."

Agent Morgan turned to the Ranger and smiled. "I should. My dad was a master sergeant in the U.S. Army for thirty years. He spent twenty of those years in charge of weapons training at Fort Bragg. I was his top student, even when I didn't want to be."

The Ranger's face lit up. "Is that right? Why, it might just be that your dad and I crossed paths a long time ago. I was a Green Beret for about ten years, and I spent quite a bit of that time at Fort Bragg."

"Well then, you would be the right man to tell us civvies what went down here."

The Ranger's reticence evaporated.

"Your so-called guess was pretty darn close. There were two gun positions on those hills out there. You're also right about the hardware, except the machine gun was a C9A. We still have a lot more forensic work to do here, but in my estimation, this was a well-planned and executed military assault. Yes, sir, the folks that hit this place knew their business."

It was almost 1:00 a.m. when Spencer returned to his hotel room in downtown Austin. At 1:30 he received a call from the assistant director of the FBI. Two additional people would be attending tomorrow's gathering. Agent Morgan was right. It was going to be a very interesting meeting.

# CHAPTER
# SIXTY-FOUR

*Travis County, Texas*
*December 10, 1999 / Friday / 8:50 a.m.*

The building where the *Statesman* was located had a small coffee shop in the lobby. Agent Morgan was sitting on one side of a table near the door with a laptop, typing up her notes from yesterday's walkthrough of the El Castillo Ranch. Spencer was sitting on the opposite side of the table looking over his handwritten notes and working on his third cup of coffee. He'd called Russo's cell phone twice that morning and left messages asking her to meet with them a half hour earlier so they could update her on what they'd learned, but they'd received no response. Spencer looked at his watch in frustration. It was 8:50 a.m.

At 8:55, Russo walked into the lobby holding a cup of Starbucks coffee and a small, brown briefcase. She saw Spencer and Agent Morgan, but made no move to stop as she walked toward the elevators.

"Shall we go, Agents?"

"Actually, I think we should take a few minutes to talk about some new developments that validate the allegations—"

Russo interrupted Spencer, but continued walking. "That's right, Agent Spencer—allegations. And, as far as I am concerned, bullshit allegations. So let's get your little meeting over with, so I can do my job, shall we?"

Spencer's face tightened, but he followed Russo toward the elevator bank. Agent Morgan was a step behind him.

"Very well, Ms. Russo, but I did try."

Russo's response was an exasperated snort.

When they walked out of the elevator, the receptionist conducted them to a formal conference room, with traditional dark wooden décor throughout. The conference table in the middle of the room could easily have seated twenty people. A tape recorder was sitting at the head of the table.

Russo entered the room first, intentionally preventing Spencer from opening the door for her. She had expected Franklin and the two "suspects" to be in the room waiting for her arrival, but they weren't there. The room was empty except for two men who were standing near the window at the far end of the room. One of the men was tall and lean, with a full head of gray hair. His prominent nose had been broken at least once, giving his strong features a rugged cast. The gray eyes he fixed on Russo when he looked over conveyed a sense of his formidable intellect and something else as well: a quiet sense of power.

The second man was shorter and almost bald. In contrast to the other man, his face was strikingly handsome. A friendly smile touched the corners of his mouth as he nodded politely to Russo, but the smile never reached his eyes. They stared intently at Russo, cataloguing every detail.

Russo looked at their expensive suits and assumed the two men were the *Statesman's* outside counsel. She started walking toward them, intending to make it clear that they were not to interfere with her interrogation of the suspects, but Spencer walked past her and reached the two men first. He extended his hand to the taller of the two men, a smile coming to his face.

"James O'Connor?"

"Yes."

"Bill Spencer, FBI. It's a pleasure."

O'Connor smiled and gripped Spencer's outstretched hand.

"The pleasure is all mine, Agent Spencer."

Then Spencer turned to the second man and extended his hand.

"Bill Spencer."

The smaller man gripped Spencer's hand, with both hands, as if they had been friends for years.

"Paul Henri Benoit at your service, Monsieur Spencer."

"And I am at yours, Superintendent Benoit. Welcome to the United States and the great State of Texas."

"Thank you. It is my privilege to be here."

Spencer then turned around to Russo.

"Gentlemen, this is Michaela Russo, U.S. Attorney for the Western District of Texas. Ms. Russo, let me introduce you to James O'Connor, Assistant Deputy Director of the Central Intelligence Agency, and Paul Henri Benoit, of the DGSE."

Russo tried to control the look of surprise on her face, but the effort was only partially successful.

"The DG—"

Benoit smiled apologetically.

"Directorate-General for External Security, Mademoiselle Russo. We are, shall we say, the French version of the FBI."

Spencer spoke as soon as Benoit had finished, forestalling the question that he knew was coming next.

"The attorney general has consented to Mr. Benoit's attendance at this meeting, and Mr. O'Connor is here because the CIA has expressed an interest in this case."

Russo was confused, but she understood the message Spencer was conveying. Her boss had authorized the two men to participate in the meeting. The issue was not subject to dispute.

Russo was about to invite Spencer to confer with her outside the room when Reed Franklin walked into the room. He stopped at the door and held it open. An attractive woman in her early thirties walked past him and smiled her thanks. Franklin spoke to her quietly as she walked by and gestured to a seat near the end of the table. The woman was dressed in a conservative business suit and a white blouse.

Her long brown hair accentuated her attractive face, beautiful brown eyes, and full mouth.

A man about six feet tall followed her into the room. He had light brown hair that was starting to gray at the temples and sideburns. His face was hard and chiseled, but handsome. Although the blue dress shirt and dark corduroy pants he was wearing were loose-fitting, they couldn't hide the muscularity in his neck, shoulders, and thighs. The man paused briefly at the door and his intense gray eyes scanned the occupants of the room. Then he walked over to the table and sat down beside the woman.

Franklin walked to the chair at the head of the table and made a welcoming gesture with his hands.

"Ladies and gentlemen, welcome. I am Reed Franklin, editor of the *Statesman*. My guests are Andrea Marenna and John Caine."

When he finished, Franklin turned to Spencer, who nodded politely.

"Agent Bill Spencer, FBI. This is Agent Ashley Morgan and Michaela Russo, Assistant United States Attorney."

Spencer turned to the two men at the end of the table.

"Let me also introduce James O'Connor and Paul Benoit. These gentlemen have been invited to participate in today's meeting by the attorney general."

O'Connor and Benoit nodded and then sat down. Spencer had expected Franklin to insist on knowing more about the two men, but to his surprise, the editor simply nodded.

Russo took the chair to Spencer's immediate left, placing her one chair away from Franklin and almost directly across the table from John Caine. When everyone was seated, Franklin took the lead.

"I want to thank everyone for coming today. As you are all aware, we're here to listen to Ms. Marenna and Mr. Caine tell us about a series of events that occurred this past week. In my humble assessment, Mr. Caine and Ms. Marenna have been the victims of a major criminal conspiracy that is newsworthy. As I told Mr. Spencer, I will be recording today's session and the *Statesman* will be going to press with that story tomorrow morning. Since I fully expect the perpetrators of this criminal conspiracy to scatter like mice once this story comes to light, I wanted to allow the law enforcement authorities every opportunity to position themselves accordingly. Now, why—"

Russo interrupted Franklin before he could finish.

"Mr. Franklin, I'm not interested in your story, no matter how inaccurate it may be. What I am interested in is the *interrogation* of these suspects, and since it is already 9:20, I suggest we get started."

Then Russo leaned across the table and placed a small tape recorder squarely in front of Andrea.

"We will start with you, Ms. Marenna."

Andrea's face tightened, but she didn't otherwise react to the provocation.

"Very well, let me start at the—"

"I will ask the questions, Ms. Marenna. You will answer them."

"No, Ms. Russo, you will not," Andrea said.

Russo was in the process of pulling a pad out of her briefcase when Andrea spoke and she froze in mid-movement. She turned and placed both hands on the table in front of her and looked directly across the table.

"Ms. Marenna, you don't seem to understand—"

Andrea leaned forward, interrupting her.

"Actually, I do understand, Ms. Russo. I understand that your department is supposed to be protecting honest citizens like Mr. Caine and me, not harassing us, I understand that—"

Russo started to stand, but Spencer intervened.

"Very well, Ms. Marenna, please go ahead."

Andrea looked over at Spencer and then slowly leaned back in her seat.

"Thank you, Agent Spencer," Andrea said.

Andrea's precise and detailed monologue lasted twenty minutes. A small yellow pad was positioned in front of her, but she only glanced down at it once during her presentation. Spencer and Agent Morgan made notes on the pads in front of them as she spoke. Russo just listened, unmoving.

When Andrea finished, Russo spoke first.

"Ms. Marenna, I am sure that Mr. Spencer has a host of questions about your . . . story, but I have just one right now. Do you have even one shred of evidence to back up your allegations against Helius Energy, or Mr. Mason?"

"Yes, I do," Andrea responded and reached into a briefcase beside her chair. She pulled out the phone from her townhouse and laid it on the table. She unsnapped the face plate and laid it back on the conference room table. Then she pointed to a small device attached to the interior of the phone.

"I believe that this is what is commonly known as a 'bug.'"

Russo glanced at the phone, but otherwise made no move to look at it. Spencer reached over with a pencil and carefully slid the phone across the table so that both he and Agent Morgan could see it.

"Come on, Ms. Marenna, you could have ordered that electronic device over the Internet. You'll have to do better than that." Russo stopped when she noticed that Spencer was shaking his head. He leaned over and whispered something in her ear. Russo made a dismissive motion and turned back to Andrea.

"What else do you have in the way of hard evidence?"

Andrea reached into her briefcase again and pulled out two copies of a typed document. She handed a copy of the document to both Russo and Spencer. She looked down at the men at the end of the table, but the taller man just held up his hand, signaling that the two men did not need a copy of the document.

"This is a transcription of a voicemail that was left for me at Kelly & White. The transcription was prepared by my secretary. I cannot give you the original of the recording from our phone system because the server was corrupted on Sunday night."

Spencer and Agent Morgan read the transcript together. Russo read the document, but her face remained unimpressed.

"Is that it?" Russo said.

"That is all the physical evidence currently in our possession, but I am sure that when Mr. Spencer sends his people out to the Portman Lodge, he will find bullet casings in the parking lot. There also may be a bullet lodged in Mr. Caine's truck."

"Ms. Marenna, even if your story were not so . . . fantastic, I would find it very difficult to believe it for one very simple reason."

Russo hesitated for a moment and stared across the table at both Andrea and Caine before continuing.

"*Honest* citizens generally go to the police when they discover that their phones are bugged and certainly when people start shooting at them. However, you and Mr. Caine made no effort to seek out law enforcement help of any kind, at any time, before this meeting. Forgive me if that leads me to doubt the bona fides of your story."

"That's not true, Ms. Russo. After I was attacked at the Portman Lodge, I . . . we did try to get the police involved. I called a friend of mine, Michael Bosmasian. He's a prosecutor with the—"

Russo cut her off. "I know who Mr. Bosmasian is, Ms. Marenna. I also know that he was shot last Monday night and that you and Mr. Caine fled the scene when the police arrived, leaving him bleeding on the sidewalk. Forgive me, Ms. Marenna, but the evidence that I have indicates that you arranged a meeting with Mr. Bosmasian with the intent of killing him, not to gain his assistance. In fact, isn't it true that all of this other nonsense is just a smoke screen? Isn't it true—"

Andrea slapped her hand down on the table, cutting off Russo's escalating tirade.

"No, no, no. Michael is one of my best friends. I would never—"

"Then why didn't you just call the police, or the FBI? Why a city prosecutor? And if Mr. Bosmasian was such a good friend, why did you flee the scene of his shooting? Why did you run from the police who came to the scene?"

Caine raised his hand from where it was resting on the table. The move was so unexpected that Russo's head snapped in his direction. Caine's eyes fixed on her and then he spoke in a calm, almost quiet voice.

"Because I insisted on it."

"Please go on, Mr. Caine," Spencer said.

Russo started to raise her hand to brush aside Spencer's intervention, but she noticed that the man from the CIA had leaned forward and rested his arms on the table. The message was subtle, but clear. He wanted to hear from Mr. Caine.

"Yes, Mr. Caine, please enlighten us," Russo said, as she eased reluctantly back into her chair.

"Andrea wanted to stay with Mr. Bosmasian."

"Then why, Mr. Caine, did you insist that she flee the scene?"

"We had no other choice. The site was a prepared kill zone. We were the targets, not Mr. Bosmasian. If we had stayed, we would be dead and in all likelihood Mr. Bosmasian would have died from his wound, if not from incoming fire."

"And why should we believe that someone other than you or Ms. Marenna shot Mr. Bosmasian?" Russo asked, almost before Caine finished his sentence.

Caine looked over at Spencer when he answered.

"Because you already know that. Mr. Bosmasian was put down by a high-powered rifle. I was carrying a Browning Mark III pistol. The ballistics, bullet velocity, and incoming trajectory take Andrea and me out of the equation. But again, you already know that."

Russo had no ready response and when Spencer just nodded slightly in confirmation, she let the issue go.

"Please continue, Mr. Caine. As I recall, you were describing the scene of the shooting," Spencer said.

"As I said, the site was a kill zone. There were at least two, possibly three shooters waiting there when we arrived. They weren't there to take out Bosmasian. They wanted us."

O'Connor looked over at Spencer and nodded quietly in response to Caine's analysis. The communication between the two men irritated Russo.

"So you admit that you *did* flee the scene?"

"Yes."

"And are we supposed to consider that an exonerating fact?"

"No."

Caine's frank responses and apparent lack of concern left Russo momentarily without a follow-up question, allowing Spencer to intervene again.

"Please continue," Spencer said.

Caine nodded.

"We ran down the alley beside the restaurant, jumped the wall, and made our way into the shopping area on the next street."

Russo interrupted. "Why, Mr. Caine, did you fail to turn yourself over to the police at that juncture?"

"The decision was based upon a combination of factors. To understand my perspective, we have to back up seventy-two hours," Caine said.

"Please do so, Mr. Caine," Spencer said.

Caine then described the helicopter assault on his cabin in Big Bear, the chase through the woods on the snowmobile, and the firefight that took out the helicopter. As Caine's narrative progressed, Russo's eyes narrowed and her mouth tightened. Finally, she exploded out of her seat, cutting him off.

"Mr. Caine, do you think I'm insane? Do you really expect anyone to believe this story? Let me see if I have this right. You were attacked in the middle of the night, in the mountains of Southern California, by a gang of killers in a helicopter? Then, you somehow shot down this helicopter and no one discovered any of this? Not police, not the FAA, not the FBI. Mr. Caine, what kind of fool—"

O'Connor interrupted Russo.

"Maybe, Ms. Russo, you should ask Agent Spencer whether he can confirm the helo crash?"

Russo stared at O'Connor for a moment and then turned to Spencer.

"*What* is he talking about?"

Spencer didn't look up from his yellow pad when he spoke.

"We recently obtained information indicating that a helicopter went down in the mountains in San Bernardino, California. The evidence from the site suggests that the aircraft was armed with a heavy machine gun that was fired before it went down."

"Where is this helicopter now?" Russo demanded.

"It's gone. The evidence at the site indicates that the entire bird was chopped up and moved shortly after the crash. We are still investigating the situation. I suggest that we defer this—"

"Why wasn't I told about this?"

Spencer's face tightened and he turned to look directly at Russo.

"Ms. Russo, let's allow the witness to continue, shall we?"

Russo looked at Spencer for another second and then glanced over at O'Connor and Benoit, who were looking at her. Russo reluctantly turned back to Caine.

"Very well," Russo said curtly, "Mr. Caine, please continue."

"After the attack on my cabin and what happened the next morning—"

Russo held up her hand.

"Stop. What happened the next morning, Mr. Caine?"

Caine then described the car chase, the shootout on Route 18, and his eventual escape. When he finished, Andrea was staring at him, along with the others.

Russo looked over at Spencer accusingly. He spread his hands out the table.

"Our Los Angeles office has confirmed that incidents of this nature occurred on the dates indicated."

Russo looked back at Caine for a moment, then leaned back in her chair and motioned for him to continue.

"To answer your original question, Ms. Russo, I decided not to go to the police at that time, because that would have made the two of us easy targets."

"In police custody?"

"Yes. We would have been placed in holding cells. Those cells are designed to keep people from getting out, not getting in. Unless we had special protection, we would have been killed within hours. That's why we contacted Mr. Bosmasian in the first place: to get that kind of protection. Unfortunately, they were one step ahead of us."

"Do you have any evidence to support that, Mr. Caine?" Russo said.

"None."

Russo nodded her head in satisfaction.

"Mr. Caine, if you and Ms. Marenna were the targets of the attack in the square, why did they shoot Mr. Bosmasian?" Spencer said.

"I can only guess. It may be that Bosmasian was getting too close, or it may have been a backup plan. Since the shooters were hidden, the police would assume that Andrea or I shot Mr. Bosmasian. Best case, the police would have killed us at the scene—worst case, the people after us could use the police as a resource to find us, which in fact they did."

"Are you suggesting that these people somehow bugged the Austin PD as well Ms. Marenna?" Russo said, her voice laced with sarcasm.

"No. I assume they just had a lower-level source in the department who was alerted to look out for incoming information," Caine answered.

"That's ridiculous," Russo said.

"Ms. Russo, this man Paquin and his goons got to the bar five minutes before the police arrived. Do you have another explanation for that striking coincidence?" Andrea said, the frustration evident in her voice.

"Why don't you go over your recollection of what happened in the bar, Ms. Marenna?" Spencer said, before Russo could respond.

"John and I split up after the shooting. We agreed to meet at Branion's Pub. I arrived first and waited for about forty-five minutes for John to show up. About twenty minutes after he arrived, two men entered the pub wearing masks and carrying guns. A few minutes later, two other men came in the back door. They were also armed. A man, who I later came to know as Paquin, came over to my table and forced me to come with him. They took me out the back door and pushed me into a black Suburban."

"Where were you when all of this occurred, Mr. Caine?" Russo said.

"I was in the men's room when they took control of the bar. I could see what was happening through a crack in the door."

"Given your past enthusiasm for a fight, Mr. Caine, why is it that you suddenly decided to adopt the role of a pacifist?"

Franklin responded to the question.

"Ms. Russo, the witness statements obtained by Austin PD indicate that the four men in the bar were armed with automatic weapons. Given those facts, I'm sure that *even you* would agree that it would have been imprudent for Mr. Caine to start a gun battle."

Russo's face reddened and she started to turn to Franklin, but thought better of it when Spencer straightened the angle of the tape recorder sitting in the middle of the table.

"I will ignore that comment, Mr. Franklin. Mr. Caine, would you please recount what occurred after Ms. Marenna was taken from Branion's Pub?"

"I followed them out the rear door of the bar, but they were already pulling into the street."

"And?"

"I left the area and spent the night at a hotel downtown."

"Again, you failed to go to the police?" Russo said.

"That's true."

"Continue."

"There's not much else. I received a call on my cell phone from Andrea. She'd managed to escape during the early morning hours, and I was able to pick her up outside the ranch where she was being held."

Russo turned her attention to Andrea.

"Please explain to me, Ms. Marenna, how you managed that."

"I worked on my restraints most of the night and managed to get loose."

"And you just walked past your captors?" Russo said.

"Yes. They had other problems at that point in time."

"Like what?"

"There was a gun battle going on. I was able to escape in the confusion."

"Are you serious?" The scorn in Russo's voice was palpable.

Spencer held up his hand apologetically to Andrea and then turned to Russo.

"Ms. Russo, the Texas Rangers received an anonymous call around 6:00 a.m. on Sunday morning. The caller reported gunfire and smoke at a ranch located about an hour outside Austin—the same location described by Ms. Marenna. When the Rangers arrived at the ranch, the site was deserted, but the evidence indicated that in fact an intense firefight occurred there.

"Agent Morgan and I visited the ranch late last night where this incident occurred. Based upon the evidence recovered by the Rangers, we estimate that as many as ten to fifteen combatants were engaged in the firefight. Preliminary ballistics indicates the combatants were armed with military-grade automatic weapons, including a light machine gun. There's also evidence that C-4 was used to blow a hole in one of the exterior walls."

Russo was staring at Spencer when he finished. "Thank you, Agent Spencer. That information is . . . useful."

Then she turned her attention back to Andrea.

"Ms. Marenna, I want to know exactly what you saw when you were leaving this ranch."

"I'm sorry, I don't recall very much, Ms. Russo."

"I find that hard to believe."

"I'm sorry, Ms. Russo. The next time I'm kidnapped and find myself in the midst of a raging gun battle, I promise to be more observant," Andrea snapped.

Benoit's cultured voice stayed Russo's rejoinder.

"Please forgive Madame Le Procureur, Ms. Marenna. I am sure she is just being thorough."

Before Russo could react to the subtle rebuke, Spencer used the interruption to move the questioning in a different direction.

"Mr. Caine, your record indicates that you were in the U.S. Army. Is that correct?"

"Yes."

"In fact, you were a Ranger."

"Yes."

"Have you been a member of any other military force, Mr. Caine?"

"Yes."

"And what would that be?"

"I was in the French Foreign Legion for ten years."

"What was your unit?

"The Second Parachute Regiment."

Caine actually had been a member of the Regiment before he'd been transferred to the Special Operations Unit commanded by Ricard.

Franklin stood up before Spencer could continue.

"Agent Spencer, may I suggest that we break for lunch?"

Spencer glanced at his watch. It was almost 12:00 p.m. O'Connor and Benoit stood up, making it difficult for Russo to refuse the suggestion.

"Very well, Mr. Franklin," she said. "However, Mr. Caine and Ms. Marenna will remain in this room. I assume you can have lunch brought in?"

Franklin seemed inclined to object, but Andrea answered, "That's fine."

# CHAPTER
# SIXTY-FIVE

*Travis County, Texas*
*December 10, 1999 / Friday / 12:10 p.m.*

Franklin stood up and walked to the window after everyone but Caine and Andrea had left the room.

"Well, that didn't go too badly. In fact, I really think you and Mr. Caine made some progress with Agent Spencer and maybe even with Ms. Russo."

Caine smiled at Franklin's attempt at optimism. Andrea didn't look up from the pad in front her when she spoke.

"Russo's not buying it. I don't particularly like her, but I understand her perspective. She can believe our story and initiate an investigation of a Fortune 500 company for sending a band of killers after two honest folks for unknown reasons. Or, she can assume that we're just two criminals spinning an elaborate yarn. For her, that's an easy choice."

Caine looked over at Andrea. Her face was drawn and tired. Caine reached over and turned her swivel chair so that she faced him.

"Have patience, Andrea. Spencer knows that the picture is more complicated than that, and don't disregard O'Connor and Benoit. My read is that O'Connor is CIA and Benoit is with the DGSE, the

French security service. They wouldn't be here if they thought that this was a simple criminal matter," Caine said.

Andrea nodded and then stood up.

"Mr. Franklin, do you have a computer here that I can use to access my e-mail? I need to check my calendar and messages, or I'm going to be out of a job."

"Of course, Andrea. There's a visitor office two doors down. The computer there will get you to the Internet."

After Andrea left the room, Caine looked across the room at Franklin.

"You didn't ask about Benoit and O'Connor when you opened the meeting," Caine said.

"No, I did not," Franklin said.

"You already knew who they were," Caine said.

"Yes."

"May I ask how?"

"Let's just say that an old friend of mine from Langley called me last night. He told me that two heavy hitters from the intelligence field would be willing to attend this meeting and lend a hand, if their names didn't appear in any of the articles published by this paper. I agreed."

Caine nodded. Franklin turned from the window and looked directly at Caine for a moment.

"I have an idea that you are a very interesting man, Mr. Caine. When this is all over, I surely would like to sit down with you over a bottle of fine scotch and hear your story."

# CHAPTER
# SIXTY-SIX

*Brandon, Arkansas*
*December 10, 1999 / Friday / 11:00 a.m.*

A melia Teatro lived in a small townhouse in Brandon, Arkansas.
She was seventy-two years old. When her husband passed away
ten years earlier, she had started dabbling in genealogy. Initially it was
just a hobby, but later she obtained a certificate from a local college
and launched a second career. Teatro's persistence, patience, and eye
for detail had enabled her to find unknown ancestors, heirs, and relatives for clients throughout the country.

When Richard Steinman's effort to find a living descendant of
Thomas O'Neill failed, a senior librarian at the University of Texas at
Austin had suggested he ask Amelia Teatro for help. Although Steinman had been skeptical that Teatro could succeed where he'd failed,
he'd had nowhere else to turn. Three minutes into the phone call,
Steinman knew that he'd found the right person, and Amelia Teatro
had found a challenge too enticing to pass up.

Her search effort encompassed federal, state, and local archives,
newspaper archives, church records, and finally the records maintained by local and national preservation societies throughout the

State of Texas. The exhausting search had taken three weeks, but Amelia had succeeded. She had found a surviving heir of Thomas O'Neill—just one.

On December 1, 1999, Teatro had sent Richard Steinman an e-mail with three compressed file folders. The folders contained all of the information supporting her findings. Also, in accordance with Steinman's instructions, she had sent a second e-mail with the same information to amarenna@hotmail.com. The next morning Amelia had left for a six-day cruise in the Caribbean.

The day after she returned from the cruise, Amelia sat down at her computer and pulled up her e-mails. When she worked her way through the list, Amelia came to a message informing her that the e-mail she'd sent to Ms. Marenna a week earlier had bounced back. Apparently Ms. Marenna's account was closed. Fortunately, Mr. Steinman had told Amelia that Ms. Marenna was a lawyer, which made finding her very easy for an expert like Amelia. She pulled up Andrea's name in the nationwide directory of attorneys maintained by Martindale-Hubbell and forwarded the e-mail to her new address.

# CHAPTER
# SIXTY-SEVEN

Russo, Spencer, and Agent Morgan were sitting at a booth in a small café a block away from the *Statesman* building. Spencer had waited until the three of them had finished their lunch before trying to persuade Russo that her "investigation" would be a lot easier if she changed her tactics.

"Ms. Russo, all I am suggesting is that we will obtain more information from Mr. Caine and Ms. Marenna if the exchange is less confrontational. I would also suggest that your theory that the two of them are somehow involved in the drug trade doesn't fit the facts. The operations were too well planned, equipped, and executed. I see this as ex-military, almost a private army."

Russo sighed with exasperation.

"Mr. Spencer, I assume we can agree that the plethora of Mexican and Columbian drug cartels are not prohibited from using ex-military personnel?"

"Yes, Ms. Russo, we can. However, in thirty years, I have never seen a drug cartel mount a airborne assault on a cabin located in the mountains in Southern California. It simply doesn't fit the profile."

"Well, maybe the profile has changed and you just don't know it. In any event, I find that theory a lot more credible than the idea that a respectable corporation sent out a paramilitary force to hunt down two nobodies, for no reason."

Russo stood up without waiting for a response, and Spencer and Agent Morgan stood up with her.

"One of the attorneys in my office has obtained a warrant for the arrest of Andrea Marenna and John Caine from District Judge Samuels. A federal marshal will be here to serve that warrant and take the two into custody within the hour. I intend to end this little drama as soon as he arrives."

Spencer's face was carved in stone. "I see."

*Austin, Texas*
*December 10, 1999 / Friday / 1:00 p.m.*

The office that Andrea was using was equipped with a desk, computer, printer, and phone. She used the computer to log into her firm's website and pull up her calendar; today and tomorrow were clear. Then she switched to her e-mail folder. Four of the seven e-mails were from the firm's administrator. The first e-mail advised all employees that a virus had corrupted Kelly & White's server and all messages before Saturday had been lost. The next three were updates on the resolution of the virus problem and the firm's ongoing effort to recover the lost e-mails.

One of the remaining three e-mails was from Jill. She asked Andrea to call as soon as possible. The second message was junk mail. The last message was from ateatro@aol.com. It had been sent to her two hours earlier. Initially, Andrea didn't recognize the name and started to move on, but then she made the connection. Richie had mentioned that name in his voicemail. Andrea clicked on the message. The sender was Amelia Teatro; Richard Steinman was the receiving party; Andrea was listed as an additional recipient. The message read:

"Dear Mr. Steinman, I am sorry for the delay. Attached are the documents. They confirm that John Caine is a descendant of Thomas O'Neill. As I said in our phone call last week, this was a difficult quest, but that's what made it fun. I even had to pull the records from the main archives maintained by the Catholic Diocese in Austin to put all the links in the chain together.

"I'll give you the short version. Thomas O'Neill's daughter, Mary, had a son named Michael. Michael had a son who was also named Michael. Mary, Michael, and Michael Jr. died in a fire. But the family line didn't end there. Two nights before he died, Michael Jr. married one Rosalie Viera, and she was pregnant with his son at the time of his death. Rosalie died in childbirth, but the child survived. The boy was named John, and he took the surname of Rosalie's parents—Viera. Since Michael and Rosalie's marriage and the birth of their son were recorded by the church, and these records are valid under state law for inheritance purposes, John Viera qualifies as an heir of Thomas O'Neill.

"John Viera later married Emilia Rios, and the couple had a son named John. In 1955, John Jr. married Ann Peters, and they had a son who was also named John. When John III was four years old, his parents were killed in a car crash. The boy grew up in Saint Michael's Orphanage in Waco, Texas. After he left St. Michael's, John III took the surname Caine. So, to finish the story, John Caine is a direct lineal descendant of Thomas O'Neill, the man who is the grantor on the deed that you gave me.

"All of the backup documents are attached. For convenience, I also attached a PDF of the deed you sent to me as well.

"One other thing: I may be getting old, but I think there's something wrong here. Between 1910 and 1918, there was a chain of accidental deaths in the O'Neill family. In fact, every single heir, other than John, Rosalie's son (who nobody knew about!), appears to have died within this twelve-year period. It's spooky. Good luck.

"You now owe me $2,800.

Sincerely,
Amelia"

When Andrea finished reading the e-mail, her heart was pounding so hard she had trouble breathing. She glanced up at the clock. Thirty minutes had already passed. She double-clicked the two compressed files attached to the e-mail and over thirty documents appeared on the screen. All the documents were in PDF format, except one, which was in Word format. Andrea suspected that the string of PDF files were copies of public records, such as birth and death certificates. The Word document entitled "Memo" was probably a summary of whatever Ms. Teatro had found.

Andrea saved the documents on the computer's hard drive and then began printing out copies. When the last page came out of the printer, she glanced at her watch. A full hour had passed since they had broken for lunch. The document entitled "Memo" was written on letterhead that identified Ms. Teatro as a certified genealogist. It seemed as if Richie had been trying to establish that John was the heir to someone who had died more than a hundred years ago. That didn't make sense to Andrea. If John was a distant heir who should have received a property distribution from a probate estate years ago, any claim would almost certainly be barred by the statute of limitations. Helius would know that.

The knock on the door wasn't loud, but Andrea felt as though she had been hit by electric shock. It took her moment to recover and answer.

"Yes, come in."

It was Franklin and John. The look on Franklin's face was grim.

"Andrea, I just received a call from one of our contacts at the federal court. Russo has obtained arrest warrants for you and John. I assume she will wait until the warrants get here, but not a minute longer. I'm sorry. I had a promise from Bill Spencer that they would listen to the whole story, but apparently Ms. Russo doesn't feel bound by that."

Although Andrea had feared that Russo would do something like this, the reality shocked her. She started to think about who would represent them in the criminal case, but suppressed the thought. She had to stay on task. Andrea looked at John for a moment and then turned to Franklin.

"Mr. Franklin, I think I just received everything we need. I believe these documents will not only explain, but document what has been going on. I need thirty minutes to go over them. Can you delay Russo for that long?"

Franklin looked at her for a minute and then smiled.

"Why, it would be a distinct pleasure."

# CHAPTER
# SIXTY-EIGHT

Russo walked into the conference room without knocking. Spencer and Agent Morgan followed her in. Franklin was the only one in the room.

"Mr. Franklin, I thought I made it clear that Ms. Marenna and Mr. Caine were not to leave this room."

Franklin had served in the Korean War as a young Marine, and he'd spent twenty years covering conflicts and crises all over the world as a foreign correspondent for three major newspapers. He knew how to deal with difficult people, particularly bullies. As far as he was concerned, Michaela Russo was simply another government lawyer with too much ego and too little sense by half. So he did the one thing that he knew she would find most irritating: he ignored her.

Spencer, who was standing behind Russo, couldn't hold back a grin. Russo's face turned scarlet and she raised her voice to just below a shout.

"Did you hear me, Mr. Franklin?"

Franklin still didn't look up from his paper, but after a pause, he did respond.

"I am old, Ms. Russo, not deaf."

"Well?"

After another pause, Franklin looked over the top of the newspaper at Russo, as if she were a quarrelsome child.

"Well, what, Ms. Russo? Is there a question pending that you would like me to answer? If so, I suggest you remember that you are a guest in *my* office."

For an instant Spencer thought Russo was going to explode, but she controlled herself.

"Where, Mr. Franklin, are Mr. Caine and Ms. Marenna?" Each syllable was enunciated with icy care.

"They are in the building. They will be here shortly."

"When, if you please?"

Franklin lowered the paper and glanced at his wristwatch.

"Approximately twenty minutes, Ms. Russo. I will have a pot of coffee brought in. I find that a good cup of coffee after lunch helps me get through the rest of the day."

A quiet knock at the door stayed Russo's verbal explosion. After a brief pause, James O'Connor and Paul Henri Benoit entered the room. O'Connor and Benoit nodded to the others, walked to the far end of the table and sat down. Franklin turned to the two men and said, "Gentlemen, Ms. Marenna and Mr. Caine will return shortly and we will continue. Would you like a cup of coffee while we wait?"

"Yes, thank you, Mr. Franklin. I'm sure that both Mr. Benoit and I would appreciate that very much," O'Connor said.

Benoit nodded and said, "Yes, thank you."

Although Russo did not want to leave the situation alone, in the face of O'Connor's and Benoit's gracious acceptance of the delay, she was reluctant to play the role of a petulant spoiler.

"Very well then," Franklin said as he stood and put down the paper, "I'll be right back."

When Franklin left the room, he made a point of closing the door. He waited outside the door for a moment just to make sure that Russo did not try to follow him. Then he walked down the hall and stepped into the room where Andrea and Caine had a series of documents laid out on the desk in two piles.

"You have twenty minutes. No more. After that Ms. Russo may well chew her way through the wall to find you," Franklin said, a grin on his face.

Andrea nodded her thanks and then turned back to the table. Caine smiled at Franklin and gave him the thumbs-up sign.

Twenty-two minutes later, Caine and Andrea walked into the conference room. Andrea was holding two large folders full of paper in her arms. Russo made as if to stand, but hesitated when Andrea placed one of the folders in front of Franklin and said, "It's all there."

Then she continued to the other side of the table to where Caine had just sat down.

Russo could restrain herself no longer.

"Where have you been, Ms. Marenna, and what is all this?"

Andrea remained standing, opened the remaining folder, and placed it on the table in front of her.

"This, Ms. Russo, is the evidence that documents exactly why Helius, or more likely the Mason family, has been trying to kill Mr. Caine and myself."

"It's a little late—" Russo started, but Franklin interrupted her.

"I'm sorry, Andrea. I neglected to start the tape again. There. Now, please go ahead. I know that the people who read the *Statesman* every day and the tens of millions of Americans who will read this story on the wire services tomorrow will want a full and complete account of this story."

The reference to millions of readers slowed Russo down. Her boss was a politician and his boss was the president of the United States, the most political of all politicians. Although she was skeptical, the stack of documents and Andrea Marenna's confidence were enough to persuade her to listen, at least until the marshal showed up with the warrants.

"Yes, please go ahead, Ms. Marenna," Spencer said politely, breaking the tie.

"Thank you, Agent Spencer. However, before I go through the documentary evidence, I need to summarize a complex, even arcane, area of real estate law that is at the very heart of the issue. Most people who buy or sell a piece of real property either buy or sell a fee interest or a leasehold interest."

Russo interrupted, "Ms. Marenna, I am sure that we appreciate this refresher on real property law, but this has nothing—"

"In fact, it has everything to do with this case. *It is this case.* Now, I need five minutes, Ms. Russo, no more."

Benoit was the first to respond to Andrea's plea for time.

"Please proceed, mademoiselle. The French government would welcome your explanation."

O'Connor nodded his head in agreement. Spencer took the issue out of Russo's hands.

"Please continue."

"Thank you. In most instances, when a buyer purchases, say, a home, the buyer receives what's called a fee estate. In essence, the buyer acquires all of the owner's rights, title, and interest in the property, leaving the seller with nothing. However, the owner of a piece of land does not have to sell the buyer *all* of his or her rights in the land. The seller can retain certain rights. The variations on what he can retain are quite numerous.

"The variation that is relevant here can be illustrated by the following example. If I deed the City of Austin a property for use as a park, I can provide in the deed that if the land is ever used for any other purpose, then it reverts to me. What is important to remember for our purposes here today, is that this right of reentry, or power of termination, can potentially be triggered and exercised many years in the future."

Andrea paused for a moment and then continued.

"Now, deeds that include these kinds of restrictions can create major land use problems, as a result many states restrict their use or have statutes of limitation that cut off these rights if they are not exercised within a certain time frame. In Texas, the statute of limitations is ninety years after the triggering event. However, when that statute was enacted, it only applied to deeds executed after 1900. This still left open the problem of termination rights included in deeds recorded before the turn of the century. To deal with this problem, Texas passed a "Sunset Law" law ten years ago. This law states that all powers of termination included in deeds recorded prior to 1900 must be exercised by December 31 *of this year* to be valid. Now, with that background, I would like to hand you a copy of a grant deed relating to a very large property in West Texas."

Andrea reached into the manila folder, pulled out a stack of papers, and passed them around the table, retaining one copy for herself and Caine.

"What you have in front of you is a deed. The deed reflects an ownership transfer that occurred in 1885. The grantor in the deed is Thomas O'Neill, and the grantee is a Jackson Mason. Please put your finger on the first WHEREAS clause. Now count down ten lines from that and read the clause that states: 'Provided, however, that if Grantee, or any party taking from him ever extracts any mineral substance of any kind from the Property for profit or gain, then title to the Property shall, as of the date of the first extraction, revert to Grantor or to his surviving heirs and descendants, free and clear of all rights, including any liens or encumbrances that did not exist as of the date of this deed.'"

Andrea looked up from deed and looked around the table. She had everyone's interest.

"What does this have to do with you and Mr. Caine?" Russo said.

Andrea turned her attention to Russo.

"Everything. I did some research on this property while you were patiently waiting for me after lunch. In the past ninety years, millions of barrels of oil have been extracted from this property. In the late seventies, the owner thought the field's reserves were finally played out, but a smart petro-engineer convinced the owner to drill another hole—a very deep hole. This strategy worked. The deeper well struck another reservoir of oil—a massive reservoir. The property described in this deed is called BlackJack. It is the fifth most productive oil field in the United States today."

Andrea hesitated for a moment and then leaned across the table. She stared directly at Russo.

"Pursuant to the reversion clause in this deed, which is still valid and enforceable in the State of Texas for another three weeks, title to BlackJack reverted to Thomas O'Neill's heirs the day the first oil well started pumping oil in 1910. That means every dollar taken out of that land was properly payable to his heirs, not to the oil company working the fields on that property. We are talking about *billions* of dollars when interest is considered."

Spencer sat straighter in his seat and Franklin leaned forward in his chair, waiting for Andrea to continue.

"The man who bought the property in this deed was Jackson Mason. His son William started a company called Mason Oil. In 1981, Mason Oil was renamed Helius Energy," Andrea said.

"What are you saying?" Russo demanded. "Do you claim to be an heiress of this Thomas O'Neill?"

"No, Ms. Russo. Not me. Mr. Caine is an heir."

"What! But why . . . why did they go after *you*? Why were you being hunted by these . . . so-called killers?"

Franklin responded before Andrea.

"I think I can answer that question."

Franklin hesitated as he gathered his thoughts.

"One of the *Statesman*'s reporters, Richard Steinman, was preparing a story on Helius. He was doing it on his own time, without our help and without our knowledge. Apparently he discovered the deed that you have in front of you and confirmed that the original Thomas O'Neill in fact had a living heir. Unfortunately, it appears that Helius, or someone behind Helius, found out about Richard's discovery before he could bring it to light. About five days ago, he was killed in what we all thought was a tragic automobile accident. But now, I have confidence that it was a murder."

Franklin stopped for a minute. Everyone in the room was silent. Then he continued.

"Richard Steinman and Ms. Marenna were close friends. He tried to tell Andrea about his discovery the night of his death, but only partially succeeded. This communication made Andrea a target."

Andrea nodded and picked up where Franklin left off.

"The communication from Richard is the voicemail transcription you have. He also tried to send me a package, but it was intercepted by the Helius people. Fortunately, he did one more thing. He told the genealogist who researched John's background to copy me on the e-mail when the research project was complete. I only just received that message today. That's why I was late from lunch, Ms. Russo."

Andrea looked over at Caine. He was shaking his head.

"Andrea, how do you know that I'm an heir? I told you I was an orphan."

Andrea sat down and placed her hand on Caine's arm.

"Richie hired Amelia Teatro, a genealogist. She pieced together the lineage from the original Thomas O'Neill, record by record. The chain is clear, John. I have it right here."

Andrea looked into John Caine's eyes and smiled for the first time that day.

"It's an amazing story. Thomas O'Neill's daughter, Mary, married and had a son—Michael. Michael married Rosalie Viera in the summer of 1918. The marriage was recorded in a bona fide church record on July 31, 1918. Michael died, along with his mother and father, two days later, but Rosalie was already pregnant with Michael's child. Rosalie died in childbirth nine months later. The genealogist found a letter that Rosalie wrote to her unborn child. Michael's family had been against the relationship, so the couple married secretly. Michael died the day before the couple was going to announce the marriage."

"And the child?" Franklin said.

"Rosalie's parents raised the child. He was named John Viera. John married Emilia Rios, and the couple had a son, who they named John. John Jr. married Ann Peters and they had a child, who was also named John. Four years later, John Jr. and Ann died in a car crash. Apparently there were no relatives to the take John III, so he was brought to the Saint Michael's Orphanage. When John III left the orphanage at the age of eighteen, he changed his last name to Caine."

Andrea stopped for a moment and looked at Caine.

"Why did you...?"

"Change my name to Caine?" Caine answered, a bemused look on this face. "The orphanage had a policy. They wouldn't answer questions from the kids about their parents, at least not before the age of eighteen. In retrospect, I can understand why. Some of the kids were true orphans, but some had been abandoned. Disclosing the information would have caused . . . problems. They told us . . . we could be whoever we wanted to be when we left, so I became John Caine."

"Why Caine? Was there..." Andrea asked quietly.

"It . . . it doesn't matter," Caine said, a distant look in his eyes.

The room was quiet for a moment, and then Caine turned to Andrea.

"By the way, who are the other heirs? There must be others?"

"John, the genealogist searched for other heirs. It's in her memo. She couldn't find any. Every one she could track down died before you were born. The odd thing is, all the obituaries she collected described homicides or accidents. Her search covered four separate families over a period of almost twenty years."

Agent Morgan spoke for the first time.

"If everything that Ms. Marenna has said is accurate, there may be a very simple but terrible explanation."

Spencer turned and looked at the young agent, his face grim.

"Mr. Caine's ancestor was outside the chain of . . . "

Russo, irritated at the cryptic exchange, interrupted Spencer's thought.

"Exactly what are you talking about, Agent Morgan?"

Agent Morgan leaned forward so she could look down the table at Russo directly.

"Killing some of the heirs would accomplish nothing. Killing *all of them* would bury the problem forever."

Caine slowly eased back into his chair, his face a mask of stone.

Russo stood up very slowly. Her face was difficult to read, but it was clear she had reached a decision. She looked over at Caine and Andrea. Caine was lost in contemplation. Andrea was holding his right hand, her face ashen. Russo cleared her throat, gaining their attention.

"When confronted with a . . . confusing factual chronology like this, the Justice Department must maintain a careful neutrality until its investigation is complete. That is particularly true in a case like this, where the allegations are somewhat . . . out of the ordinary. This may take some time. While the investigation is ongoing, we would want both of you to relinquish your passports, and my inclination is to place you in protective custody for a short time, until we get our arms around this. That will give us convenient access for interviews and questions, and provide you a safe refuge. I will work with Agent Spencer to arrange that."

Andrea turned to Caine and spoke to him quietly. He listened and then nodded. Then she turned to Russo.

"Ms. Russo, are we in agreement that this arrangement is both temporary and voluntary?"

Russo's face tightened, but she nodded her head. "Yes, that is our expectation at this time. However, we would like you both to come to the Federal Building immediately, so we can make arrangements. Again, for your protection."

Andrea looked over at Caine, who gave her a quiet nod.

Franklin stood up and looked at Russo when he spoke.

"Given what we have heard today and the evidence that we have seen, I cannot imagine it would be for anything else."

# CHAPTER
# SIXTY-NINE

*Austin, Texas*
*December 10, 1999 / Friday / 3:00 p.m.*

Onwuallu parked the Lincoln on the second floor of the parking structure. Caine's pickup truck was parked on the same floor. He could see the entrance to the building where the *Statesman* was located through a gap in the concrete wall in front of him. Onwuallu smiled to himself. The federal prosecutor had unknowingly disclosed Caine's location when she filed a detailed application for an arrest warrant with the federal court two hours earlier. One of the intake clerks at the court was married to a detective in the Austin PD, who was working on the case. When the clerk saw the application for the warrant, she called her husband, and this information was picked up by Helius's source within the department.

The hit that Onwuallu planned was simple. Caine and the woman would be killed as soon as they walked into the garage. After the kill, Onwuallu and Porter would walk out the back of the garage and drive away in a car that was parked on the street. The Lincoln would be picked up two days later, after all of the noise had died down.

Onwuallu turned to Porter when John Caine and Andrea Marenna walked out of the building.

"It's time for us to finish Mr. Paquin's work."

"Exceptional, sir."

### Austin, Texas
### December 10, 1999 / Friday / 4:30 p.m.

Andrea and Caine followed Spencer and Russo through the lobby of the building onto the street. Agent Morgan had stopped off at the restroom upstairs. Russo turned to Caine just outside the front entrance.

"Since you're not familiar with the city, Mr. Caine, I want you to follow Agent Spencer's car back to the Federal Building."

The statement wasn't a question, and it ignored the fact that Andrea was very familiar with the city. Caine nodded. The two of them had made their deal. They could only hope that the Justice Department's investigation uncovered whatever else was necessary to make Russo a believer.

The concrete parking structure across the street from the *Statesman* building spanned the entire block. The pedestrian entrance that was closest to where Caine parked his truck was at the far end of the block. When the signal changed, Russo and Spencer stepped into the crosswalk. Caine and Andrea followed a short distance after them.

Caine scanned the sidewalk in front of the parking structure, as he walked across the street. It was empty. Two African American men were just starting down the stairs at the end of the parking garage where his truck was parked. They disappeared behind the wall as they started down the next flight of stairs. One of the men looked like an NFL lineman. The second man was shorter and leaner. Both men were wearing long, dark raincoats and business suits.

Caine would have considered the men unremarkable, but then they did something that drew his attention. They stopped at the next landing and waited there. When Caine and the rest of the group were about sixty yards away, the two men started down the last flight of stairs. They disappeared from sight at the bottom of the stairs.

Caine turned his attention to the archway at the bottom of the stairs that led out onto the sidewalk. He had come down that same flight of stairs earlier in the day. They had to come out that way. There was no other exit.

Caine slowed his pace, expecting the men to come out of the entrance any second, but they didn't. He could feel the adrenaline pouring into his system. *Where were they?*

When they were within forty yards of the entrance, Caine made a decision. He grabbed Andrea's arm and guided her over to the rear of a van parked by the curb.

"Something's not right. Stay behind the van. If you hear gunfire, crawl along the outside of the cars back the way we came. I'll be right back," Caine said. The urgency in his voice stayed any argument.

Caine then jogged ahead and closed with Spencer, who was a yard behind Russo.

"Agent Spencer." Caine's clipped tone brought Spencer to a full stop. When he turned, Caine held up two fingers and pointed at the entrance to the parking structure ahead of them with hard emphasis. Russo turned and only caught the last of Caine's hand movements. A look of irritation crossed her face, but it disappeared when Spencer pulled a Glock 22 out of the holster on his hip.

Caine was in motion the moment the larger of the two men stepped onto the sidewalk. The man was carrying a pistol equipped with a long suppressor. Caine grabbed Russo and dove onto the trunk of a white sedan parked in the street. He caught a glimpse of the second African American man coming around the corner of the entryway as he rolled off the car onto the street, bringing the struggling Russo with him. The second man was carrying an AR-15, also equipped with a suppressor.

Caine heard the distinctive rhythm of automatic weapons fire as he hit the ground. The windows of the car above his head exploded, throwing glass all over the street. Russo suddenly stopped struggling against his grip. Caine heard Spencer yell, "Freeze, FBI!" Caine looked over the trunk of the car at the sidewalk. Spencer had taken cover behind a stanchion on the side of the parking structure. The two men on the sidewalk were unimpressed. The man with the AR-15 raked the outside of the stanchion with fire, forcing the agent back into the corner.

Caine turned to Russo, who was squatting on the street beside the car clutching her briefcase to her chest. She opened her mouth to scream when the man with the AR-15 fired another burst, but Caine cut her off.

"Quiet. Go that way. Stay down and move fast. Get across the street as soon as you can. Use the traffic as cover. Clear?"

Russo nodded.

"Go."

Russo dropped the briefcase and started crawling back down the street.

Caine heard two shots from Spencer's Glock and a responsive burst from the AR-15. Caine suspected that the shooter had a thirty-round magazine, which meant that he still had plenty of ammunition to keep Spencer pinned down while the other shooter came after him. Caine turned and started to move rapidly down the street after Russo. *Damn!* She was only one car ahead of him. Caine glanced back up the street and saw a massive figure come around the front of the car and point the muzzle of a long black suppressor at him. The giant man smiled as he pulled the trigger. Time seemed to slow down.

Caine heard two gunshots, but didn't feel the burning pain of the bullets slamming into his body. A stunned look appeared on the shooter's face and he slowly dropped to his knees, staring at Caine as he went down. For a moment he held himself there, wavering. Then he fell forward. Caine looked across the street in confusion. Agent Morgan was standing in between two cars in a classic shooter's stance, her weapon pointed at the man on the ground.

Caine suddenly realized the other shooter had stopped firing. He glanced through the shattered window of the car and saw the other shooter in a crouch, sighting in on Agent Morgan. Caine turned his head and yelled.

"Get—"

There were two explosions. Caine looked at Agent Morgan expecting her to fall, but then he realized that the shots came from Spencer's

Glock. He turned back to the sidewalk. The other shooter was down, and he wasn't moving. Spencer was down on one knee beside the stanchion, his pistol pointed at the man on the ground.

Caine let out the breath that he had been holding and looked down the street. He could see Andrea coming out from behind a car near the crosswalk. Russo was kneeling beside a minivan, crying. Caine suspected that her assessment of the merits of their case might well have changed for the better.

# CHAPTER
# SEVENTY

The G3 landed with only the slightest bump, causing a ripple in Mason's second martini. He turned and looked at the rear of the luxurious cabin, where Bianca, his new mistress, was still sleeping in one of the seats. He could just see the golden brown of her young legs through the blanket that partially covered her. Mason decided he wouldn't wake her just yet. The limo would be waiting on the tarmac. He could make his calls from there and wake her later. His first call would be to Paquin.

The woman's visa was still in process. Mason knew that he was taking a risk bringing her into the country illegally on his private jet, but the risk was nominal. Helius's airstrip was a private facility, and it was located within a small township about forty miles outside of Austin. The local authorities were more than respectful of Helius's expressed desire for privacy.

Mason finished the last of his drink and stood up, irritation playing across his face. The copilot had lowered the stairway to the tarmac minutes ago. His driver should have come in to pick up his bags.

Mason waited another minute and then walked to the doorway. His staff was well aware of his insistence on exact compliance with his personal demands.

Mason's irritation level ratcheted up another notch when he looked down the stairs leading to the tarmac. No one was in sight. He walked down the stairs, keeping his eyes on the steel steps. When he reached the tarmac and looked up, he could see the limousine was parked in the usual spot, but something was wrong. Six people were standing beside the car. He didn't recognize any of them. Mason's initial reaction was confusion and then anger.

As he walked toward the group, Mason saw his pilot and driver standing further away, near the building that bordered the airstrip. A man in dark glasses was standing beside them. Neither man would meet his eyes. Mason's stare came to rest on the woman in the middle of the six people standing by the limousine. There was no respect whatsoever for his position in the woman's face. If anything, there was a hint of scorn in her eyes. She was holding a rolled-up paper in her hands like a royal sceptre.

Before Mason could say anything, she walked over to him. Three men wearing dark suits followed her. Two of the men were younger and wore sunglasses. The third man was older. There was a small bandage on the side of his face. The woman stopped about three yards from Mason and opened the paper.

Mason spoke first.

"What, may I ask, is the meaning—"

"No, you may not ask, but you *will* listen. My name is Michaela Russo, United States Attorney for the Western District of Texas. These men are with the FBI."

Then the woman returned her attention to the paper in front of her and began reading it aloud.

"Carter T. Mason, you are hereby placed under arrest by the United States government. You have the right to remain silent . . . "

The woman's strident voice continued through a litany that Mason had heard on television and in the movies innumerable times, but could not conceive of anyone having the temerity to read to him.

A terrifying thought struck him like a blow in the stomach. *What if Paquin had . . . no, that isn't a possibility.* Then Mason regained control. This woman had one thing right. He was Carter T. Mason, and she had made a colossal mistake in presuming to invade his airport and place him under arrest. He would destroy her.

As soon as the woman finished reading, the two men in sunglasses came forward with a pair of handcuffs. They placed them on Mason's wrists and walked him over to the small building just behind the limousine. The woman waved to the door and a crowd of people flowed out. The microphones and cameras told the whole story. Mason looked over at the woman, a cold rage on his face. She'd planned this. She intended to parade him through these press-hounds like some kind of criminal.

Mason started forward, but then he realized that the woman had turned and was looking back at the jet. Mason twisted uncomfortably in the grip of the men on either side of him. He could just see Bianca's revealing dress and the stunned look on her face as she came down the stairs of the G3. His rage and frustration at the embarrassment almost induced him to struggle against the two men holding him, but he controlled himself, knowing it would be futile.

"And who, Mr. Mason, is this?" Russo said, with open scorn, as she moved toward Bianca. The young woman covered her mouth and ran back into the jet.

A hard smile played across Michaela Russo's face and she turned to one of the FBI men holding his arm.

"Check to see if she has a passport. If she doesn't, place her under arrest as well." Then she turned on her heel and headed over to the press. Mason's face was ashen as he was pulled forward by the remaining FBI agent.

# CHAPTER
# SEVENTY-ONE

*Alsace-Lorraine, France*
*December 18, 1999 / Saturday / 1:30 p.m.*

The ancestral home of the Ricard family was located outside a small picturesque village in Alsace-Lorraine. Ricard's funeral, which had been a quiet affair in the local church, had been held the day before. After the service, Caine and Andrea had decided to stay in the village another day before returning to the maelstrom in Texas.

True to his word, Franklin had featured the "Helius Affair" on the front page of the *Statesman*. Every major newspaper in America had picked up the story the next day, and quite a few around the world as well. Mason had resigned as the head of Helius after the story broke, and he remained incommunicado despite the score of reporters camped outside his mansion. The phalanx of lawyers defending him had made it clear that he denied any wrongdoing.

The new chairman of Helius, a nationally recognized business leader, had instructed all Helius personnel to fully cooperate with the Justice Department's investigation. He had also made a settlement offer to John Caine—a very large settlement offer.

As the couple walked down the worn cobblestone path that meandered through the old village, Andrea realized she was falling in love with John Caine. She glanced over at him for a moment, and tried to reach some conclusion about his feelings toward her, but failed. She knew he liked her, but was there more than that? There were hints, but she didn't want to misconstrue them. John Caine was difficult to read in the best of circumstances, and the past week had been anything but.

Andrea was so deep in thought that she didn't realize that Caine had stopped, until she had walked past him. He was staring at a gray headstone in a small cemetery bordered by a worn stone wall. Caine turned and looked over at her for a moment and then looked back at the cemetery.

"Do you remember when you asked me why I chose the surname Caine after I left the orphanage?"

"Yes. You didn't answer."

Caine nodded and continued, "I used to help out at a ranch back in Texas, doing yard work, painting, that sort of thing. The woman who owned it, Sarah, was in her eighties. She died the month before I left. There was a cemetery plot on the property that I used to look after—just a single tombstone. I could tell it was important to her, but she never spoke about it.

"The priest who spoke at her funereal said the grave was empty. Her . . . Sarah Caine's husband had been killed on the beach at Normandy during the war. The body . . . it was unrecoverable. She'd had the stone laid so she could bring him flowers every day, which she did, for almost thirty years. I never forgot the words on the tombstone. 'Jonathan Caine, beloved and remembered.' That's where the name came from."

Caine paused for a minute and looked into the distance, his eyes glazing over.

Then he turned and faced her. "The flowers . . . every single day . . . Until I met you, I didn't understand it."

Then she was in his arms, and the nightmare was finally over.